Love in Full Bloom

OTHER BOOKS EDITED BY MARGARET FOWLER
AND PRISCILLA McCUTCHEON

*Songs of Experience*

# Love in Full Bloom

Edited by Margaret Fowler
and Priscilla McCutcheon

BALLANTINE BOOKS • NEW YORK

Grateful acknowledgment is made to the following for permission to reprint previously published material:

*Curtis Brown, Ltd.*: "Of Love and Friendship" by Arturo Vivante. Copyright © 1973 by Arturo Vivante. First published in *The New Yorker*. Reprinted from *The Tales of Arturo Vivante*. Used by permission of The Sheep Meadow Press and Curtis Brown, Ltd.

*Delacorte Press/Seymour Lawrence*: "Tell Me a Riddle" by Tillie Olsen. Copyright © 1956, 1957, 1960, 1961 by Tillie Olsen. Used by permission of Delacorte Press/Seymour Lawrence, a division of Bantam Doubleday Dell Publishing Group, Inc.

*Farrar, Straus & Giroux, Inc. and Wylie Aitken & Stone*: "Christmas Roses" from *A Fanatic Heart* by Edna O'Brien. Copyright © 1984 by Edna O'Brien. Reprinted by permission of Farrar, Straus & Giroux, Inc. and Wylie Aitken & Stone.

*William Heinemann Ltd.*: "Indian Summer of a Forsyte" from *The Forsyte Saga* by John Galsworthy. Reprinted by permission of William Heinemann Ltd.

*Houghton Mifflin Company*: "We Are Nighttime Travelers" from *Emperor of the Air* by Ethan Canin. Copyright © 1988 by Ethan Canin. Reprinted by permission of Houghton Mifflin Company. All rights reserved. "September Song" from *September Song* by William Humphrey. Copyright © 1990 by William Humphrey. Reprinted by permission of Houghton Mifflin Company/Seymour Lawrence. All rights reserved.

*International Creative Management Inc.*: "The Girl Across the Room" by Alice Adams. Copyright © 1976 by Alice Adams. First appeared in *The New Yorker*. Reprinted by permission of International Creative Management, Inc.

*Milkweed Editions*: "The Courtship of Widow Sobcek" was published in *The Importance of High Places* by Joanna Higgins (Milkweed Editions, 1993). Copyright © 1993 by Joanna Higgins. Reprinted by permission of Milkweed Editions.

*Ontario Review Press*: "The King Is Threatened" from *Death's Midwives* by Margareta Ekstrom (translated by Eva Claeson). Copyright © 1985 by Margareta Ekstrom. English translation copyright © 1985 by Eva Claeson. Reprinted by permission of Ontario Review Press.

*Random House, Inc.*: "My Man Bovanne" from *Gorilla, My Love* by Toni Cade Bambara. Copyright © 1960, 1963, 1964, 1965, 1968, 1970, 1971, 1972 by Toni Cade Bambara. Reprinted by permission of Random House, Inc.

*Simon & Schuster, Inc.*: "Letter to the Lady of the House" from *The Fireman's Wife* by Richard Bausch. Copyright © 1990 by Richard Bausch. Appeared originally in *The New Yorker*, October 23, 1989. Reprinted by permission of Simon & Schuster, Inc.

*University of Illinois Press*: "Mrs. Moonlight" from *Water into Wine* by Helen Norris. Copyright © 1988 by Helen Norris Bell. Reprinted by permission of the publisher, University of Illinois Press.

*Harriet Wasserman Literary Agency, Inc.*: "The Man with the Dog" from *Stronger Climate* by Ruth Prawer Jhabvala. Copyright © 1966 by Ruth Prawer Jhabvala. Reprinted by permission of Harriet Wasserman Literary Agency, Inc., agent for the author.

*Watkins/Loomis Agency, Inc.*: "Bar Bar Bar" from *The Year of the Hot Jock and Other Stories* by Irvin Faust. Reprinted by permission of the author and the Watkins/Loomis Agency.

Library of Congress Catalog Card Number: 93-90479

ISBN: 0-345-38221-8

Cover design by Kathleen Lynch
Cover illustration by Mitzura Salgian

Manufactured in the United States of America
First Edition: January 1994
10 9 8 7 6 5 4 3 2 1

# $\mathcal{C}$ontents

# Introduction

"Yes, I, an old woman, a grandmother many times over—I hunger and burn! And for whom? For an old man."
> —from "The Man with the Dog"
> by Ruth Prawer Jhabvala

"He led her inside and they lay together side by side, hands touching, eyes closed against the dark. 'I love you, Mrs. Moonlight.' "
> —from "Mrs. Moonlight" by Helen Norris

"I am an old woman. But I am still a woman. A woman in love. I am not afraid of making a fool of myself."
> —from "September Song" by William Humphrey

"Love has no age, no limit, and no death."
> —from "Indian Summer of a Forsyte"
> by John Galsworthy

"Their eyes continued to look at each other with a timeless and mutual thirst."
> —from "The King Is Threatened"
> by Margareta Ekstrom

The realization that love in old age is as varied, deep, and passionate as at any other time of life surprised us. Like most people, we had associated romantic love with youth, and not with age. We had assumed that love in old age was more often companionate rather than sensual, that the business of living a long time had exhausted passion, and that the aging face and body deflected romance. We knew, of course, that old people have deep feelings, but we were not aware of the intense, private, and emotional love relationships that we found in many stories as we pursued the research for our anthologies. In fact, when we arranged the collected fiction by subject matter, the largest single group was love stories. Nothing had prepared us for the compelling impact these narratives had or for their depth of fervor and vitality. Surely, the stories reveal a new and enlightening truth about old age today.

Historically and traditionally, love has been the province of youth, and literature, in reflecting life, has mirrored this reality. Young lovers—such as Romeo and Juliet, Eloise and Abelard, Cupid and Psyche— have danced their way across the centuries in myths, fairy tales, ballads, and novels. Old people, like Dickens' crazy Miss Havisham, for instance, or Shakespeare's Malvolio, have been relegated to the sidelines, viewed as beyond romance, or as asexual, obscene, or ridiculous when involved in affairs of the heart. Modern epithets like "old roué," "old goat," and "dirty old man" perpetuate this general disparagement of old lovers. Being in love has long been considered inappropriate behavior for people of mature years.

Today, increased longevity, greater mobility, and changing mores have altered the way people live in their late years. Elderly people are freer to live as they choose, and attitudes about appropriate behavior are beginning to change. Alerted by our reading of contemporary short stories about love in old age, we began to notice essays in periodicals, films, and newspaper accounts commenting on the new phenomenon of dating, courtship, and marriage among elderly people. Love is at last beginning to be seen as an integral part of human nature that does not turn off like an electric light when a person reaches the age of fifty, or seventy-five, or even ninety. Current literature echoes this new consciousness. Images of all kinds of romantic relationships in *Love in Full Bloom* confirm this modern dimension in the experience of aging.

Love in old age, however, has different dynamics than in youth. Outward appearance and beauty no longer set the stage for romance as they once did; older lovers, although still strongly affected by chemistry, are more attracted by the kind of person their partner has become. The experience of living over a long lifetime develops a diversity and a richness of character that is more important than an attractive face. Failures of the body are more acceptable than failures of the soul.

Social, financial, and racial differences are not as influential as they were at younger ages. Older people are less affected by societal pressures and often don't invest conformity with much importance. Some of the stories describe new liaisons that would have been shunned in youth. For instance, Howard Fu and Carrie Greenbaum in "Bar Bar Bar," coming from totally different backgrounds, meet on a bus, enjoy each other's company, and fall in love.

Yearning, however, is just as real in older people as it is in younger, and as likely to result in impossible fantasy. The elderly Miss Hawkins, in "Christmas Roses," "had a very definite and foolish longing to be going into the lounge bar with a young escort." Most of the encounters, as at any age, start with flirtation—a compliment, a mannerly gesture—and sometimes lead to romance.

Time, more of it, on a day-to-day basis, less of it in terms of years left to live, plays a crucial role in the stories of older lovers. Free from the frantic daily responsibilities of jobs and child raising, on the one hand, older people have time to nurture and savor intimacy. There is time to initiate new connections. John Jielewicz in "The Courtship of Widow Sobcek" finds time to take his curtains every week for the widow to wash so that he can be with her. And there is time to revive a marriage: In "We Are Nighttime Travelers," Frank and Francine, who have lived almost separate lives side by side for many years, find time for new communication that leads to a fervent reunion.

On the other hand, older people are acutely aware of

the brevity of life and the urgency of living for the moment. The feeling that there is just one last opportunity to have a fling or to declare one's love can precipitate a romance. With relatively little time left and therefore less to lose, they can afford to take a chance. And the lovers have no use now for coy pretense or indecision. "Can you come right away? I need you," says Mrs. Gideon in "Mrs. Moonlight" in a phone call to her friend, Robert, who she hasn't seen or talked to for sixty years.

An unexpected element found in some of the stories is the intensity of the passion portrayed. Desire does not subside with age, but is as strong as always. Even in a nursing home, the protagonists in "The King Is Threatened" find ways to carry on a passionate relationship. In the majority of the stories, the main characters feel and react strongly, whether to heartache or to romance. Virginia is enraptured by a phone call from an old lover in "September Song," Miss Hazel, in "My Man Bovanne," is wounded by her childrens' criticisms, and John, in "Letter to the Lady of the House," is heartsick over the petty bickering that has become the essence of his marriage.

The stories of older lovers are complex; few are simple "boy meets girl and they live happily ever after" tales. Each protagonist has past experiences and relationships that raise difficult questions for new liaisons. Should an elderly woman leave her infirm but dull husband for a last chance with a dashing lover? How can people regain control of their lives from well-meaning

but meddlesome children? What about annexing someone else's frail husband, whose wife happens to be
bored with him? Can a woman expect to live finally as
she chooses in old age, or must she still be subject to
her husband's wishes and his concept of the way to
live? These issues are intrinsic to old age, and there are
no easy answers.

Other barriers to the fulfillment of love do exist. The
breakdown of the body can be a deterrent to romance.
In "Bar Bar Bar," Howard's sudden stroke puts him in
the hospital and prevents his marriage from taking
place. When John Jielewicz, in "The Courtship of the
Widow Sobcek," slips on the ice, he too lands in the
hospital and is therefore temporarily unable to visit
the Widow. Interfering and disapproving children may
try to thwart a courtship. But the stories show that ul-
timately love can be so strong that the characters rise
above these roadblocks to their happiness. In spite of
suffering because her children disapproved of her love
affair and cut her out of their lives, the protagonist in
"The Man with the Dog" continues her association
with her amour.

The stories definitely dispel the fairy-tale notion that
romance always leads to a "happily ever after" ending.
Sometimes changing circumstances brought about by
age create a new tension in a relationship. Retirement
can afford fresh options and chances to develop in different ways, to turn outward to new contacts and
communications or inward to discover one's own inner
being. New facets of the relationship can be explored

but the former mutuality between a husband and wife working toward the common middle-aged goals of work, family, and community may now disappear. Each spouse may have totally different views of a desirable future. In "Tell Me a Riddle," Pa wants to sell the house and move to the Haven to enjoy the rest of life in leisure and sociability, but Ma wants to stay home in peace and quiet. "She would not exchange her solitude for anything. Never again to be forced to move to the rhythms of others. . . . Being able at last to live within." Such disparate needs can sorely test a marriage.

With the seasoning of age, however, many of the characters have developed the forgiveness, forbearance, and thoughtfulness that continue to nourish the spirit of the relationship and keep it alive. Yvonne, in "The Girl Across the Room," meditates about her husband's need for her as they dine in a quiet restaurant, and understands the depth of her commitment. The more fortunate long-term lovers overcome the schism of their relationship by finding ways to reach out for a second chance. They realize that renewal is worth working for, and that their love may be deepened with effort.

*Love in Full Bloom* focuses on an area of late life that has been largely ignored, and emphasizes a positive, hopeful aspect of old age. The love stories help to right the balance between youth and age by putting aging persons on a par in one arena of their lives with younger people; love is not dependent on youth or on the power and endowments of youth, but centers on the basic relationship between two people. The stories affirm that this very human emotion, for so many years denied open expression in old people, is beginning to be claimed again by those fortunate enough to find and nurture romance. Hopefully, as time goes on, love will be accepted as an appropriate and joyful component of age.

We chose our title, *Love in Full Bloom*, to express the book's central theme: Beyond the mere budding of romance in youth, love in old age is in full flower—passionate, seasoned, and mellow. Far from diminishing as time goes by, the capacity for love seems to deepen and strengthen. The stories resoundingly attest to the endurance of love throughout life. In the midst of the losses and deterioration of old age, in the face, even, of death, they speak of the lasting mystery, magic, and vitality of the human heart.

MWF

PBM

# Part 1

# FANTASY, FLIRTATION, AND ROMANCE

# Christmas Roses

### BY EDNA O'BRIEN

*M*iss Hawkins had seen it all. At least she told people that she had seen it all. She told her few friends about her cabaret life, when she had toured all Europe and was the toast of the richest man in Baghdad. According to her she had had lovers of all nationalities, endless proposals of marriage, champagne in every known vessel, not forgetting the slipper. Yet Miss Hawkins had always had a soft spot for gardening and in Beirut she had planted roses, hers becoming the first English rose garden in that far-off spicy land. She told how she watered them at dawn as she returned accompanied, or unaccompanied, from one of her sallies.

But time passes, and when Miss Hawkins was fifty-five she was no longer in gold-meshed suits dashing from one capital to the next. She taught private dancing to supplement her income and eventually she worked in a municipal garden. As time went by, the gardening was more dear to her than ever her cabaret had been. How she fretted over it, over the health of the soil, over the flowers and the plants, over the overall design and what the residents thought of it. Her success with it became more and more engrossing. She introduced things that had not been there before, and her greatest pride was that the silly old black railing was now smothered with sweet-smelling honeysuckle and other climbing things. She kept busy in all the four seasons, busy and bright. In the autumn she not only raked all the leaves but got down on her knees and picked every stray fallen leaf out of the flower beds, where they tended to lodge under rosebushes. She burned them then. Indeed, there was not a day throughout all of autumn when there was not a bonfire in Miss Hawkins's municipal garden. And not a month without some blooms. At Christmas was she not proud of her Christmas roses and the Mexican firebush with berries as bright as the decoration on a woman's hat?

In her spare time she visited other municipal gardens and found to her satisfaction that hers was far better, far brighter, more daring, while also well-kempt and cheerful. Her pruning was better, her beds were tidier, her peat was darker, her shrubs sturdier, and the very branches of her rosebushes were red with a sort of inner energy. Of course, the short winter days drove Miss Hawkins into her flat and there she became churlish. She did have her little dog, Clara, but understandably Clara, too, preferred the outdoors. How they barked at each other and squabbled, one blaming the other for being bad-tempered, for baring teeth. The dog was white, with a little crown of orange at the top of her head, and Miss Hawkins favored orange, too, when she tinted her hair. Her hair was long and she dried it by laying it along the length of an ironing board and pressing it with a warm iron.

The flat was a nest of souvenirs, souvenirs from her dancing days—a gauze fan, several pairs of ballet shoes, gloves, photographs, a magnifying glass, programs. All these items were arranged carefully along the bureau and were reflected in the long mirror which Miss Hawkins had acquired so that she could continue to do her exercising. Miss Hawkins danced every night for thirty minutes. That was before she had her Ovaltine. Her figure was still trim, and on the odd occasion when Miss Hawkins got into her black costume and her stiff-necked white blouse, rouged her cheeks, pointed her insteps, and donned her black patent court shoes, she knew that she could pass for forty.

She dressed up when going to see the town councillor about the budget and plans for the garden, and she dressed in her lamé when one of her ex-dancing pupils invited her to a cocktail party. She dressed up no more than three times a year. But Miss Hawkins herself said that she did not need outings. She was quite content to go into her room at nightfall, heat up the previous day's dinner, or else poach eggs, get into bed, cuddle her little dog, look at television, and drop off to sleep. She retired early so that she could be in her garden while the rest of London was surfacing. Her boast was that she was often up starting her day while the stars were still in the heavens and that she moved about like a spirit so as not to disturb neighbors.

———

It was on such a morning and at such an unearthly hour that Miss Hawkins got a terrible shock concerning her garden. She looked through her window and saw a blue tent, a triangle of utter impertinence, in her terrain. She stormed out, vowing to her little dog and to herself that within minutes it would be a thing of the past. In fact, she found herself closing and reclosing her right fist as if squashing an egg. She was livid.

As she came up to it Miss Hawkins was expecting to find a truant schoolchild. But not at all. There was a grown boy of twenty or perhaps twenty-one on a mattress, asleep. Miss Hawkins was fuming. She noticed at once that he had soft brown hair, white angelic skin, and thick sensual lips. To make matters worse, he was asleep, and as she wakened him, he threw his hands up and remonstrated like a child. Then he blinked, and as soon as he got his bearings, he smiled at her. Miss Hawkins had to tell him that he was breaking the law. He was the soul of obligingness. He said, "Oh, sorry," and explained how he had come from Kenya, how he had arrived late at night, had not been able to find a hostel, had walked around London, and eventually had climbed in over her railing. Miss Hawkins was unable to say the furious things that she had intended to say; indeed, his good manners had made her almost speechless. He asked her what time it was. She could see that he wanted a conversation, but she realized that it was out of keeping with her original mission, and so she turned away.

Miss Hawkins was beneath a tree putting some crocus bulbs in when the young visitor left. She knew it by the clang of the gate. She had left the gate on its latch so that he could go out without having to be conducted by her. As she patted the earth around the little crocuses she thought, What a pity that there couldn't be laws for some and not for others! His smile, his enthusiasm, and his good manners had stirred her. And after all, what harm was he doing? Yet, thought Miss Hawkins, bylaws are bylaws, and she hit the ground with her little trowel.

As with most winter days there were scarcely any visitors to the square and the time dragged. There were the few residents who brought their dogs in, there was the lady who knitted, and there were the lunchtime stragglers who had keys, although Miss Hawkins knew that they were not residents in the square. Interlopers. All in all, she was dispirited. She even reverted to a bit of debating. What harm had he been doing? Why had she sent him away? Why had she not discussed Africa and the game preserves and the wilds? Oh, how Miss Hawkins wished she had known those legendary spaces.

That evening, as she crossed the road to her house, she stood under the lamplight and looked up the street to where there was the red neon glow from the public house. She had a very definite and foolish longing to be going into the lounge bar with a young escort and demurring as to whether to have a gin-and-tonic or a gin-and-pink. Presently she found that she had slapped herself. The rule was never to go into public houses, since it was vulgar, and never to drink, since it was the road that led to ruin. She ran on home. Her little dog, Clara, and she had an argument, bared their teeth at each other, turned away from each other, and flounced off. The upshot was that Miss Hawkins nicked her thumb with the jagged metal of a tin she was opening, and in a moment of uncustomary self-pity rang one of her dancing pupils and launched into a tirade about hawkers, circulars, and the appalling state of the country. This was unusual for Miss Hawkins, as she had vowed never to submit to self-pity and as she had pinned to her very wall a philosophy that she had meant to adhere to. She read it, but it seemed pretty irrelevant:

> *I will know who I am*
> *I will keep my mouth shut*
> *I will learn from everything*
> *I will train every day.*

She would have ripped it off, except that the effort was too much. Yet as she was able to say the next day, the darkest hours are before the dawn.

As she stepped out of her house in her warm trouser suit, with the brown muffler around her neck, she found herself raising her hand in an airy, almost co-

quettish hello. There he was. He was actually waiting
for her by the garden gate, and he was as solemn as a
fledgling altar boy. He said that he had come to apol-
ogize, that after twenty-four hours in England he was
a little more cognizant of rules and regulations, and
that he had come to ask her to forgive him. She said
certainly. She said he could come in if he wished, and
when she walked toward the toolshed, he followed and
helped her out with the implements. Miss Hawkins instructed him what to do: he was to dig a patch into
which she would put her summer blooms. She told him
the Latin names of all these flowers, their appearance,
and their characteristics. He was amazed at the way
she could rattle off all these items while digging or
pruning or even overseeing what he was doing. And so
it went on. He would work for an hour or so and too-
tle off, and once when it was very cold and they had to
fetch watering cans of warm water to thaw out a certain flower bed, she weakened and offered him a coffee. The result was that he arrived the next day with
biscuits. He said that he had been given a present of
two tickets for the theater and was she by the merest
tiniest chance free and would she be so kind as to come
with him. Miss Hawkins hesitated, but of course her
heart had yielded. She frowned and said could he not
ask someone younger, someone in his own age group,
to which he said no. Dash it, she thought, theater was
theater and her very first calling, and without doubt
she would go. The play was *Othello*. Oh, how she
loved it, understood it, and was above it all! The jeal-

ous Moor, the telltale handkerchief, confessions, counterconfessions, the poor sweet wretched Desdemona. Miss Hawkins raised her hands, sighed for a moment, and said, "The poor dear girl caught in a jealous paradox."

As an escort he was utter perfection. When she arrived breathlessly in the foyer, he was there, beaming. He admired how she looked, he helped remove her shawl, he had already bought a box of chocolate truffles and was discreetly steering her to the bar to have a drink. It was while she was in the bar savoring the glass of gin-and-it that Miss Hawkins conceded what a beauty he was. She called his name and said what a pretty name it was, what an awfully pretty name. His hands caught her attention. Hands, lovely shining nails, a gleam of health on them, and his face framed by the stiff white old fashioned collar, held in place with a gold stud. His hair was like a girl's. He radiated happiness. Miss Hawkins pinched herself three times in order not to give in to any sentiment. Yet all through the play—riveted though she was—she would glance from the side of her eye at his lovely, untroubled, and perfect profile. In fact, the socket of that eye hurt, so frequently and so lengthily did Miss Hawkins gaze. Miss Hawkins took issue with the costumes and said it should be period and who wanted to see those drab everyday brown things. She also thought poorly of Iago's enunciation. She almost made a scene, so positive was she in her criticism. But of course the play itself was divine, simply divine. At the supper afterward they discussed jealousy, and Miss Hawkins was able to assure him that she no longer suffered from that ghastly complaint. He did. He was a positive pickle of jealousy. "Teach me not to be," he said. He almost touched her when she drew back alarmed, and offended, apparently, by the indiscretion. He retrieved things by offering to pick up her plastic lighter and light her cigarette. Miss Hawkins was enjoying herself. She ate a lot, smoked a lot, drank a lot, but at no time did she lose her composure. In fact, she was mirth personified, and after he had dropped her at her front door, she sauntered down the steps to her basement, then waved her beaded purse at him and said, as English workmen say, "Mind how you go."

But indoors Miss Hawkins dropped her mask. She waltzed about her room, using her shawl as partner, did ooh-la-las and oh-lay-lays such as she had not done since she hit the boards at twenty.

"Sweet boy, utterly sweet, utterly well bred," Miss Hawkins assured herself and Clara, who was peeved from neglect but eventually had to succumb to this carnival and had to dance and lap in accordance with Miss Hawkins's ribald humor. God knows what time they retired.

Naturally things took a turn for the better. She and he now had a topic to discuss and it was theater. It, too, was his ambition; he had come to England to study theater. So, in between pruning or digging or manuring, Miss Hawkins was giving her sage opinion of things, or endeavoring to improve his projection by making him say certain key sentences. She even made him sing. She begged him to concentrate on his alto notes and to do it comfortably and in utter freedom. Miss Hawkins made "no no no" sounds when he slipped into tenor or, as she put it, sank totally into his chest. He was told to pull his voice up again. "Up up up, from the chest," Miss Hawkins would say, conducting him with her thin wrist and dangling hand, and it is true that the lunchtime strollers in the garden came to the conclusion that Miss Hawkins had lost her head. "No, thank you very much" was her unvoiced reply to those snooping people, these spinsters, these divorcées, et cetera. She had not lost her head or any other part of her anatomy, either, and what is more, she was not going to. The only concession she made to him was that she rouged her cheeks, since she herself admitted that her skin was a trifle yellow. All that sunshine in Baghdad long ago and the hepatitis that she had had. As time went by, she did a bit of mending for him, put leather patches on his sleeves, and tried unsuccessfully to interest him in a macrobiotic diet. About this he teased her, and as he dug up a worm or came across a snail in its slow dewy mysterious course, he would ask Miss Hawkins if that was a yin or a yang item, and she would do one of her little involuntary shrugs, toss her gray hair, and say, "D'you mind!" He seemed to like that and would provoke her into situations where she would have to do these little haughty tosses and ask, "D'you mind!"

It was on St. Valentine's Day that he told Miss Hawkins he had to quit the flat he was lodging in.

"I'm not surprised," she said, evincing great relief, and then she went a step further and muttered something about those sort of people. He was staying with some young people in Notting Hill Gate, and from what Miss Hawkins could gather, they hadn't got a clue! They slept all hours, they ate at all hours, they drew national assistance and spent their time—the country's time—strumming music on their various hideous tom-toms and broken guitars. Miss Hawkins had been against his staying there from the start and indeed had fretted about their influence over him. He defended them as best he could, said they were idealists and that one did the crossword puzzles and the other worked in a health-juice bar, but Miss Hawkins just tipped something off the end of the shovel the very same as if she were tipping them off her consciousness. She deliberated, then said he must move in with her. He was aghast with relief. He asked did she mean it. He stressed what a quiet lodger he would be, and how it would only be a matter of weeks until he found another place.

"Stay as long as you like," Miss Hawkins said, and all through this encounter she was brusque in order not to let things slide into a bath of sentiment. But inside, Miss Hawkins was rippling.

That evening she went to a supermarket so as to stock up with things. She now took her rightful place alongside other housewives, alongside women who shopped and cared for their men. She would pick up a tin, muse over it, look at the price, and then drop it with a certain disdain. He would have yin and yang, he would have brown rice, and he would have curry dishes. She did, however, choose a mild curry. The color was so pretty, being ocher, that she thought it would be very becoming on the eyelids, that is if it did not sting. Miss Hawkins was becoming more beauty conscious and plucked her eyebrows again. At the cash register she asked for free recipes and made a somewhat idiotic to-do when they said they were out of them. In fact, she flounced off murmuring about people's bad manners, bad tempers, and abominable breeding.

That night Miss Hawkins got tipsy. She danced as she might dance for him one night. It was all being exquisitely planned. He was arriving on the morrow at five. It would not be quite dark, but it would be dusk, and therefore dim, so that he need not be daunted by her little room. His new nest. Before he arrived she would have switched on the lamps, put a scarf over one; she would have a nice display of forsythia in the tall china jug, she would have the table laid for supper, and she would announce that since it was his first night they would have a bit of a celebration. She ferreted through her six cookery books (those from her married days) before deciding on the recipe she wanted. Naturally she could not afford anything too extravagant, and yet she would not want it to be miserly. It must, it simply must, have "bouquet." She had definitely decided on baked eggs with a sprinkling of cheese, and kidneys cooked in red wine, and button mushrooms. In fact, the wine had been bought for the recipe and Miss Hawkins was busily chiding herself for having drunk too much of it. It was a Spanish wine and rather heady. Then after dinner, as she envisaged it, she would toss a salad. There and then Miss Hawkins picked up her wooden spoon and fork and began to wave them in the air and thought how nice it was to feel jolly and thought ahead to the attention that awaited him. He would be in a comfortable room, he would be the recipient of intelligent theatrical conversation, he could loll in an armchair and think, rather than be subjected to the strumming of some stupid guitar. He had suggested that he would bring some wine, and she had already got out the cut glasses, washed them, and shone them so that their little wedges were a sea of instant and changeable rainbows. He had not been told the sleeping arrangements, but the plan was that he would sleep on a divan and that the Victorian folding screen would be placed the length of the room when either of them wished to retire. Unfortunately, Miss Hawkins would have to pass through his half of the room to get to the bathroom, but as she said, a woman who has danced naked in Baghdad has no hesitation passing through a gentleman's room in her robe. She realized that there would be little debacles, perhaps misunderstandings, but the difficulties could be worked out. She had no doubt that they would achieve a harmony. She sat at the little round supper table and passed things politely. She was practicing. Miss Hawkins had not passed an entrée dish for years. She decided to use the linen napkins and got out two of her mother's bone napkin holders. They smelled of vanilla. "Nice man coming," she would tell her little dog, as she tripped about tidying her drawers, dusting her dressing table, and debating the most subtle position for a photograph of her, from her cabaret days.

At length and without fully undressing, Miss Hawkins flopped onto her bed with her little dog beside her. Miss Hawkins had such dratted nightmares, stupid rigmaroles in which she was incarcerated, or ones in which she had to carry furniture or cater on nothing for a host of people. Indeed, an unsavory one, in which a cowpat became confused with a fried egg. Oh, was she vexed! She blamed the wine and she thanked the gods that she had not touched the little plum pudding which she had bought as a surprise for the Sunday meal. Her hands trembled and she was definitely on edge.


In the garden Miss Hawkins kept looking toward her own door lest he arrive early, lest she miss him. Her heart was in a dither. She thought, Supposing he changes his mind, or supposing he brings his horrid friends, or supposing he stays out all night; each new crop of supposing made Miss Hawkins more bad-tempered. Supposing he did not arrive. Unfortunately, it brought to mind those earlier occasions in Miss Hawkins's life when she had been disappointed, nay jilted. The day when she had packed to go abroad with her diamond-smuggling lover, who never came, and when somehow, out of shock, she had remained fully dressed, even with her lace gloves on, in her rocking chair for two days until her cleaning woman came. She also remembered that a man proposed to her, gave her an engagement ring, and was in fact already married. A bigamist. But, as he had the gall to tell her, he did not feel emotionally married, and then, to make matters worse, took photos of his children, twins, out of his wallet. Other losses came back to her, and she remembered bitterly her last tour in the provinces, when people laughed and guffawed at her and even threw eggs.

By lunchtime Miss Hawkins was quite distraught, and she wished that she had a best friend. She even wished that there was some telephone service by which she could ring up an intelligent person, preferably a woman, and tell her the whole saga and have her fears dismissed.

By three o'clock Miss Hawkins was pacing her floor. The real trouble had been admitted. She was afraid. Afraid of the obvious. She might become attached, she might fall a fraction in love, she might cross the room,

or shyly, he might cross the room and a wonderful surprise embrace might ensue, and Then. It was that Then
that horrified her. She shuddered, she let out an involuntary "No." She could not bear to see him leave, even
leave amicably. She dreaded suitcases, packing, good-
byes, stoicism, chin-up, her empty hand, the whole unbearable lodestone of it. She could not have him there.
Quickly she penned the note; then she got her coat, her
handbag, and her little dog in its basket and flounced
out.

The note was on the top step under a milk bottle. It
was addressed to him. The message said:

YOU MUST NEVER EVER UNDER ANY CIRCUMSTANCES COME
HERE AGAIN.

Miss Hawkins took a taxi to Victoria and thence a
train to Brighton. She had an invalid friend there to
whom she owed a visit. In the train, as she looked out
at the sooty suburbs, Miss Hawkins was willing to
concede that she had done a very stupid thing indeed,
but that it had to be admitted that it was not the most
stupid thing she could have done. The most stupid
thing would have been to welcome him in.

# September Song

## BY WILLIAM HUMPHREY

Who has never daydreamed that the phone will ring and the caller be an old lover?

Virginia Tyler was now seventy-six, and that fantasy, foolish to start with, had become embarrassing. Yet though it was twenty years since she had heard from John Warner, sometimes, sitting by the fire at night and studying the flames, it returned to her. She would have to shake her silly old head to clear it of its nonsense.

And then it happened! As she would say in her letter to the children announcing her intention to divorce their father and remarry, her heart leapt. She had thought it had withered and died, and been half glad it had—unruly thing! She did not know until then that it had lain dormant, like those seeds from the tombs of the pharaohs that, when planted, blossom and bear.

Toby was in the next room, doing his daily crossword puzzle.

"Is it for me?" he called.

Outwardly calm, she said, "No, it's for me." Inwardly, both ecstatic and furious, she said, "It's for *me!*

*Me!*" His smug assumption that every call was for him!

Into the receiver she said, "Hold on. I'll check it out upstairs."

The phone had to be left off the hook so as not to break the connection. But she had no fear that Toby might listen in on the conversation. He was incurious about her private affairs. As far as he was concerned, she had no private affairs, no life of her own apart from his. And he was right: she didn't have, though she had once had, and a wild one it was.

It is said that as we die our lives pass in review before our eyes. It was as she was brought back to life that Virginia Tyler's did.


Listening to that voice on the phone, she was lifted into the clouds. She saw herself in flight, alone, at the controls of her plane.

To join her lover she had taken flying lessons. Her friends all thought she had gone out of her mind. At her age! Then already a grandmother!

"This grandmother has sprouted wings! I'm as free as a bird!" she said as she touched down on her solo flight.

Toby, who had a fear of flying, was proud of her. He gave a party in her honor to celebrate the event. Actually, though she pooh-poohed it in others, she too was afraid of flying. Her fear was a part of her excitement, and a source of pride. For her love's sake she risked life and limb. Winging her way to him, earth-free, added zest to the affair, and youth and glamor to her image of herself. Outward bound, leaving home, she was a homing pigeon. Her path was so direct the plane might have been set on automatic pilot, guided by the needle of her heart.

John too was a licensed pilot. It was he who first interested her in flying. They were winged; they were mating birds. They nested in many far-away places. She did not share Toby's interest in cathedrals, art museums, yet though she resented his pleasure in traveling by himself, his lone European pilgrimages gave her the opportunity to be with John. He would tell his wife that he was off to a conference in Cleveland, Birmingham, Trenton. She would wonder why they always chose such dreary places, and decide to stay at home. The lovers would alight for a week on Nantucket, in New York City. Registering at a hotel as husband and wife, answering to the name "Mrs. Warner," never lost its thrill for her.

Planes were for rent at the local airport. Her visits to Boston to see her mother became more frequent. Toby was pleased that she and her mother now got along so much better than always before. She said that now that her mother was old she felt she must make up to her for the bad feeling between them over the years. Her mother said, "I'm just your excuse to fly that fool airplane. At your age!"

On her forty-eighth birthday Toby gave her a Piper Cub. That brought her a twinge of remorse.

"Now that you own your own plane you're flying not more but less—hardly at all," he said. "Don't you like it? Did I buy the wrong kind?"

"Oh, I'll get back to it in time," she said.

She wondered at his lack of suspicion, and his misplaced trust in her shamed her. It also rather irritated her. Was it that she was too old, too long settled, too domesticated to be suspected of any wrongdoing? She was so conscious of her guilty happiness she felt it must show in telltale ways of which she herself was unaware. She had read *Madame Bovary* and remembered Emma's saying to herself in awe, "I am an adulteress!" She felt transfigured, hardly knew herself. This alteration in her *must* show, if not to Toby then to others. She half-hoped it did! Her dread of disclosure had to contend with a wild wish to have the whole world know. They took her for a middle-aged matron, conventional, unadventurous, yoked to a dull, inattentive husband. They should only know! As for Toby, he took her for granted. Wouldn't it give him a shaking up if she were to tell him!

They never considered getting divorced and marrying each other. As she could see, his deception troubled John, but the guilt he felt was as much toward his son for what he was doing to his mother as toward her. Bruce adored his mother. At twenty-three he showed no inclination toward any other woman. It was doubtful that he would ever marry. He adored his father, too. Adored him as the consort of his queen. Marcia was a fiercely proud woman—perhaps even proud of enduring a marriage that went against her grain. To be divorced would humiliate her.

She too balked at the step. Toby was a one-woman man and without her would be helpless in a hundred little ways. She pitied him—another reason for not loving him—but while it often grated her, she took a certain satisfaction in his dependence upon her. She was fond of Toby, in her way. Some of his habits irritated her: his reading at meals, his smoking in the car, etc., but she was fond of him—or so she kept telling herself. She did not love him, but she shrank from hurting him—or from the guilt she would feel if she did. She told herself that given the choice between her deceiving him and her leaving him, he would choose to have her stay. She had her children, too, whom she hesitated to shock, whose censure she dreaded. And she feared her mother, a Boston puritan, one of a long line, with strict views on sex, marriage, duty, self-denial. A formidable woman. Once when somebody said to her offhandedly, "Well, nobody's perfect," she took it as a personal affront. Drawing herself up stiffly, she said, without a trace of self-irony, "*I* am. If I weren't I'd change."

And both were daunted by the prospect of such upheaval, the loss of disapproving friends, the sheer undertaking of creating a new life in a new place. Bad though they might be, old habits were hard to break, and fresh frontiers, while beckoning, were also scary when you reached a certain age. It made you feel old, cowardly and lazy to admit it, but it was easier to rock along with things as they were.

Still, despite all these deterrents, she would have made the break if he had urged it. But, as when they danced, he led, she followed.

"If only both of *them* would find others," he said, which would not only have freed them but salved their consciences. "But Marcia doesn't like men. Except Bruce."

"And Toby has got me," she said. "Old Faithful. Or so he thinks."

To receive letters from each other in secret both rented boxes in post offices where they were unknown. Yet it all ended when Marcia found one of her letters to him. She was almost ready to excuse his carelessness. He had been unable to destroy it! Any one of her letters to him was a giveaway. They were not the gushings of a girl with a crush on, say, a professor. They were her pillow talk, the uninhibited outpourings of a long-somnolent woman to the Prince Charming who had awakened her with his kiss. Asbestos sheets rather than writing paper would have better suited their contents.

In his last letter he wrote that he had promised Marcia never to see her again. But his love was undying.

The Piper Cub was sold.

Her wings had been clipped.

———

Over the succeeding years:

The children all left home.

Married.

Had children.

Toby retired.

He grew increasingly hard of hearing and that made him less talkative than ever. One mate's deafness made the other one dumb. She pitied him for his infirmity, yet his refusal to get a hearing aid exasperated her. She had to repeat everything she said to him. It was so frustrating! She knew that his resistance to a hearing aid was not because he was vain of his appearance. Of that he was all too careless. It was that to wear one would be a constant reminder, like eyeglasses, false teeth, of decay. She was ashamed of her irritation with him, but that did not keep her from feeling it.

She knew that people long together grew impatient with one another's ways and weaknesses and magnified them out of all proportion. His chronic sinusitis was an affliction he had not sought, yet his honking into his handkerchief so annoyed her that sometimes she had to leave the room. It was he who should leave the room.

He had always been bookish; his hardness of hearing made him burrow still deeper into books, leaving her more than ever to herself. One winter evening, snow flying, wind moaning, the two of them sat in silence before the fire, he reading, unconscious of, indifferent to whatever she might or might not be doing. To see just how long this could go on she sat there for hours.

At last she rose, took his book from him and tossed it into the fire.

"Now what did you do that for?" he wondered aloud as she made her way upstairs.


Now had come the call she had waited twenty years for, never expecting it. It was as though some dear one had come back from the dead. And as though she had too.

"That was John Warner on the phone," she said. The care with which she enunciated the name conveyed the need she had felt to place the person.

"John Warner?"

"Mmh. Remember him?"

"John Warner ... Oh, yes. Yes. Long time no see. What's with him?"

"His wife has died."

That would make it sound as though his wife had *just* died. That he was newly in need of sympathy, condolence. But she had died three years ago. Three years! Oh, why had he waited so long to call her? Three precious years! All that time lost when there was so little time to lose, to live! Yet she could explain his hesitancy to herself. She could imagine him longing to call her but thinking, "After all these years? She has forgotten you, you sentimental old fool. No doubt she replaced you with another lover. You're too old for this nonsense—and so is she. What right have you to disturb her settled life? There is not an ember left of what was once a fire—not on her side. With three children she's a grandmother many times over—a great-grandmother by now."

But he had called! He had overcome his fear of looking ridiculous, of being laughed at, rejected. He had trusted in her faithfulness, had trusted that she would respond. He alone of all the world believed she still had a heart that did not just pump but palpitated.

"Oh, dear! Poor man. Yes. His wife was a very beautiful woman."

"Mmh. You have no trouble remembering her, I see."

She was doubly jealous.

"He says he would like to meet me. In the old days he used to be rather . . . fond of me." This last she said in a musing tone, as though after all these years just now recalling it. "If you can believe that." Her little jab was lost on him.

"Where is he?"

"In Boston."

"Then of course you must go. Poor man! To lose his wife."

A meeting between an elderly widower, recently bereaved, still in mourning, and a onetime friend who just happened to be of the opposite sex, a seventy-six-year-old great-grandmother, contentedly married for half a century: what could be more innocent?

She resented the assumption that her capacity for love, for adventure—even for mischief—had been worn away by the abrasion of time. It had just been rekindled. What the world would ridicule as her silliness aroused her defiance. No fool like an old fool, all would say; act your age. That was just what she was doing. Who better than she knew her age? The stopwatch was running, and her countdown to zero was for a launch.

"But you're a woman of seventy-six!" Those were his first words to her when, on her return home from Boston, she asked him for a divorce so that she might marry John Warner. The trip had been like a weekend pass from prison. Now she was demanding her parole. She felt she owed no apology. She had earned her freedom by her years of good behavior.

John showed his age and she was glad he did. She had feared that he would find her too old. He did not try to tell her that she had not changed, and she was glad of that too. He accepted her as she was. He said, "You look wonderful!" And his eyes shone with a light that she had not seen in a man's since last looking into his.

They drove down to the Cape, to his saltbox on the shore. They strolled on the beach. Arm in arm. Together they prepared the meal and dined at home. He was still all that he had been, and he made her feel that she was too. A few wrinkles—what were they? The intervening years vanished as though at the wave of his wand. It was she—*she!*—across the table from him, in the candlelight's flattering glow. No book lay

on the surface separating them. She did not mind his
self-assurance; she liked his certainty that she was
his.

He had let her know over the phone something of
what she might expect if she agreed to meet him. He
held her hand, and it was the splicing of a long-severed
electric connection, the current restored; but he did
not want just to hold hands. He paid her court, turning upon her all his charm, his wit, but briefly—
telegraphing his intentions. She appreciated his
gallantry, but she must not prolong it. There was not
time for coyness. He had a lot to accomplish in a
short while—more, indeed, than she guessed. For just
picking up where they had broken off all those years
ago and carrying on as before was not what he had in
mind. He had in mind much more than that.

After dinner they danced. He had mapped out his
flattering but needless campaign of conquest down to
orchestrating on tape the background music. They
swayed to:

> *You were meant for me.*
> *I was meant for you.*

To:

> *Although you belong to somebody else,*
> *Tonight you belong to me.*

To—in the sultry voice of Marlene Dietrich:

> *Falling in love again—*
> *Oh, what am I to do?*
> *Long as I'm near you*
> *I can't help it.*

Being the music of their youth, it made them feel young. Until the finale, in the cracked old voice of Walter Huston—his proposal to her in song:

> *For it's a long long time from May to December*
> *But the days grow short when you reach September*

She needed no persuading to spend those remaining days with him.

"But you're a great-grandmother!" said Toby.

"I do not need to be told my age. Nor that I am not acting it. I see it in the mirror. I feel it in my joints. I am an old woman. But I am still a woman. A woman in love. I am not afraid of making a fool of myself. What you are afraid of is my making you look foolish. You won't miss me. You will still have your books, your slippers and your pipe.

"Your first words to me ought to have been, 'I love you. Don't leave me. Give me a chance to prove my love to you and to win back yours.' It would have done you no good. It's too late in the day for that. But it is what you ought to have said."

"Well! This has certainly been a whirlwind romance."

"I liked him when I knew him before. Now, as you have so chivalrously pointed out, I have got no time to lose."

In truth, she both did and did not feel her age. Her years with Toby after the loss of John had dragged by, they had piled up. And yet in their very sameness they ran together, uncountable, all one. They were easily shed. They were like a sleep. A sleep from which she had now awakened.

"So," she said. Discussion was at an end, it was time now for decision. "Are you going to give me what I want, or do you mean to contest it?"

"Well . . . If that is what you want . . ."

So that was how much she meant to him! Not worth putting up the least fight for. Her heart sped on wings to her old, her new lover.

Then her conscience told her that she was being unfair. If he was so readily acquiescent it was because he had been stunned, crushed. In just one minute, the duration of an earthquake, his familiar world had crumbled.

"This is a pretty big step," he said. "Are you sure of your own mind? Don't you want to think it over?" Then with a feeble attempt at humor, "Lots of auld lang syne riding on this, old friend."

She was moved, but moved to pity, not to a change of heart. That was no longer hers to change.

She wrote the children, braving their condemnation for her faithlessness to their father, their embarrassment over her geriatric folly. That she not seem still more ridiculous than she did, she had to reveal to them her affair of long ago with the same man. This was not someone new to her. To confess herself a one-time adulteress to her children was preferable to having them think she was so depraved as to fall illicitly in love for the first time at her age. All three approved, her daughter applauded, even reveled in the revelation of her former affair. Poor Toby! What treacherous little beasts children were! It made her wonder about the example she was setting her daughter. She had had misgivings about that marriage, and about what its breakup would mean to her grandchildren. Their encouragement brought with it a pang. It showed how pitifully apparent to them over the years had been her need for warmth, her lack of love. It was an acknowledgment of how little time she had left in which to find a crumb of the true staff of life.

She announced her intention to her brother Thornton. As she had expected, he was scandalized. If she persisted he might well disown her. Thornton had never married; that was how awesome a step he considered holy matrimony to be. He inveighed against divorce. Those of his friends who got one were scratched from his address book. He needed only sandals and a robe to seem like Moses down from the mountaintop bearing the tablets of the law, a list of Thou Shalt Nots inscribed in stone by the fiery forefinger of God. She was not fond of Thornton—he had been a prig from his youth; but she was afraid of him. On matters of devotion and duty he spoke with the voices of both their dead parents, all their ancestors. Yet even the scorching she got from him did not deter her. Thornton was like a firefighter setting a fire around a fire to contain it and let it burn itself out. But her heart's fire blazed on unchecked. Opposition only fanned its flames.

Thornton's opposite was the lady lawyer recommended to her, a specialist in divorce. Separating people was not only her profession, it was her passion.

"Go for it!" she urged. "Never too late to make the break. I know men. Totally inconsiderate. I say being born male is a birth defect."

"It is my intention," she said, "to remarry immediately."

She was not only a fool, said the other woman's look; she was an old fool, of which there was none like.

Toby might have made things extremely unpleasant for her if he had been so inclined. The law, had he invoked it, was on his side. He was the injured party. He might have charged her with desertion, adultery, and have turned her out without a dime. Might have advertised in the town paper, "My wife having left my bed and board, I will no longer be responsible for debts in-curred, etc."

He never threatened her with such actions. Instead there would be an equal division of their common property. The house and its furnishings would either be sold or else he would buy it from the estate at the as-sessed value. She would be financially independent.

"You must be provided for in case this marriage of yours should break up. I owe that to the mother of my children," he said. It was as if he were *her* father, doing his duty by her but washing his hands of an errant child by settling a competence upon her.

"It won't break up," she said.

"One never knows. Ours did. After fifty years."

"Forty-nine," she corrected him. "It only seems longer."

He made one condition, to which she agreed: that she will everything of hers that had once been his in part to their children.

He was being fair. What was unfair was his fairness. His irreproachable uprightness was inhuman. It dis-armed her. If he had threatened her, railed at her, she could have defended herself.

Nothing so tried the patience as a saint.


"I'll go by way of—" And he mapped his route. Since growing old they always did this whenever either of them set off alone for someplace. Thus if he or she was not back when expected the state police could be told where to look. He was off now to see his lawyer to draw up the settlement.

She watched him struggle into his coat. Painful arthritis in his left elbow made this difficult for him. But he would refuse her help now. She had forfeited her right to help him. Neither did she straighten his hat, as she had done all their married life. He always got it on slightly crooked. It made him look as if he were headed one way while the rest of him was going off at a tangent. Oh, dear, what would become of him without her to look after him?

She watched him make his way to the garage. He was the picture of rejection. He looked like one of those homeless old men who, bent beneath the weight of their overcoats summer and winter, tramped the highways aimlessly, endlessly. He not only looked like one: his pride, or rather his humiliation—his tattered pride—would never permit him to ask one of the children for a home in his solitary old age.

What would become of him? He could not look after himself. He had never been able to. A more helpless, more dependent man could not be found. Perhaps he would sell the house and go into one of those senior citizens' retirement complexes where the elderlies' wants were all attended to. That thought gave her a wrench. It also held up to her, as in a mirror, an image of herself. In the hunch of his shoulders, in the hang of his head, in his slow gait she saw her own age reflected. Two-thirds of their years they had spent together. She could be sure that in all that time he had never had a thought unfaithful to her. She wished she could think he had. Then she wished she could unwish the wish. It was unworthy of her.

If only John had called her those three years ago! Then the burden of her guilt toward Toby would have been worth it. The saddest of all expressions: if only . . .

He hesitated, stopped, turned around and looked up at the house. "Poor man! To lose his wife," she then recalled his saying of John. For the sake of her belated and sure to be short-lived happiness she was making of him the same lonely object that he had generously pitied in the other man, her lover. Was he hoping that at the last minute she would call him back? Was he thinking of returning, asking her to reconsider? If he did, what would her answer be? A moment ago she would have known, now she was unsure. Oh, let him turn again, get on with it, she prayed. Let him decide for me. But when he did just that she was frightened— frightened of herself.

She felt her purpose falter as the weight of her years settled upon her. It forced from her a sigh of resignation. It sounded to her like her last breath.

From the door she called him back.

Now what? his carriage seemed to say as he plodded up the walk.

"Please, Toby, forgive me, if you can," she said. "I'm sorry. It won't happen again. I'll stay. If you want me."

He nodded wearily.

Well, she asked herself, what warmer welcome back was she entitled to?

Her brother would say, "I'm glad you came to your senses." Her daughter would be disappointed in her, would think she was a fool to throw away her last chance for a little happiness. Her sons would think she had nobly sacrificed herself. There was nothing noble in it. Her heart longed for what it was too old for.

"I'll try harder," he said.

Then it was her turn to nod wearily.

Around her neck she felt a collar tighten. He and she were teamed together to the end by the yoke of years.

But whereas before she had told herself that she might still have quite a long time left to live, she told herself now that at least it would not be for long.

# My Man Bovanne

## BY TONI CADE BAMBARA

Blind people got a hummin jones[1] if you notice. Which is understandable completely once you been around one and notice what no eyes will force you into to see people, and you get past the first time, which seems to come out of nowhere, and it's like you in church again with fat-chest ladies and old gents gruntin a hum low in the throat to whatever the preacher be saying. Shakey Bee bottom lip all swole up with Sweet Peach[2] and me explainin how come the sweet-potato bread was a dollar-quarter this time stead of dollar regular and he say uh hunh he understand, then he break into this *thizzin* kind of hum which is quiet, but fiercesome just the same, if you ain't ready for it. Which I wasn't. But I got used to it and the onliest time I had to say somethin bout it was when he was playin checkers on the stoop one time and he commenst to hummin quite churchy seem to me. So I says, "Look here Shakey Bee, I can't beat you and Jesus too." He stop.

1. A compelling need.
2. A brand of dipping snuff.

So that's how come I asked My Man Bovanne to dance. He ain't my man mind you, just a nice ole gent from the block that we all know cause he fixes things and the kids like him. Or used to fore Black Power got hold their minds and mess em around till they can't be civil to ole folks. So we at this benefit for my niece's cousin who's runnin for somethin with this Black party somethin or other behind her. And I press up close to dance with Bovanne who blind and I'm hummin and he hummin, chest to chest like talkin. Not jammin my breasts into the man. Wasn't bout tits. Was bout vibrations. And he dug it and asked me what color dress I had on and how my hair was fixed and how I was doin without a man, not nosy but nice-like, and who was at this affair and was the canapés dainty-stingy or healthy enough to get hold of proper. Comfy and cheery is what I'm tryin to get across. Touch talkin like the heel of the hand on the tambourine or on a drum.

But right away Joe Lee come up on us and frown for dancin so close to the man. My own son who knows what kind of warm I am about; and don't grown men all call me long distance and in the middle of the night for a little Mama comfort? But he frown. Which ain't right since Bovanne can't see and defend himself. Just a nice old man who fixes toasters and busted irons and bicycles and things and changes the lock on my door when my men friends get messy. Nice man. Which is not why they invited him. Grass roots you see. Me and Sister Taylor and the woman who does heads at

Mamies and the man from the barber shop, we all
there on account of we grass roots. And I ain't never
been souther than Brooklyn Battery and no more country than the window box on my fire escape. And just
yesterday my kids tellin me to take them countrified
rags off my head and be cool. And now can't get Black
enough to suit 'em. So everybody passin sayin My Man
Bovanne. Big deal, keep steppin and don't even stop a
minute to get the man a drink or one of them cute
sandwiches or tell him what's goin on. And him
standin there with a smile ready case someone do
speak he want to be ready. So that's how come I pull
him on the dance floor and we dance squeezin past the
tables and chairs and all them coats and people standin
round up in each other face talkin bout this and that
but got no use for this blind man who mostly fixed
skates and skooters for all these folks when they were
just kids. So I'm pressed up close and we touch talkin
with the hum. And here come my daughter cuttin her
eye[3] at me like she do when she tell me about my
"apolitical" self like I got hoof and mouf disease and
there ain't no hope at all. And I don't pay her no mind
and just look up in Bovanne shadow face and tell him
his stomach like a drum and he laugh. Laugh real loud.
And here come my youngest, Task, with a tap on my
elbow like he the third grade monitor and I'm cuttin
up on the line to assembly.

"I was just talkin on the drums," I explained when

3. Giving a sharp look.

they hauled me into the kitchen. I figured drums was my best defense. They can get ready for drums what with all this heritage business. And Bovanne stomach just like that drum Task give me when he come back from Africa. You just touch it and it hum thizzm, thizzm. So I stuck to the drum story. "Just drummin that's all."

"Mama, what are you talkin about?"

"She had too much to drink," say Elo to Task cause she don't hardly say nuthin to me direct no more since that ugly argument about my wigs.

"Look here Mama," say Task, the gentle one. "We just trying to pull your coat. You were makin a spectacle of yourself out there dancing like that."

"Dancin like what?"

Task run a hand over his left ear like his father for the world and his father before that.

"Like a bitch in heat," say Elo.

"Well, uhh, I was goin to say like one of them sexstarved ladies gettin on in years and not too discriminating. Know what I mean?"

I don't answer cause I'll cry. Terrible thing when your own children talk to you like that. Pullin me out the party and hustlin me into some stranger's kitchen in the back of a bar just like the damn police. And ain't like I'm old old. I can still wear me some sleeveless dresses without the meat hangin off my arm. And I keep up with some thangs through my kids. Who ain't kids no more. To hear them tell it. So I don't say nuthin.

"Dancin with that Tom," say Elo to Joe Lee, who leanin on the folks' freezer. "His feet can smell a cracker a mile away and go into their shuffle number post haste. And them eyes. He could be a little considerate and put on some shades. Who wants to look into them blown-out fuses that—"

"Is this what they call the generation gap?" I say.

"Generation gap," spits Elo, like I suggested castor oil and fricassee possum in the milk-shakes or somethin. "That's a white concept for a white phenomenon. There's no generation gap among Black people. We are a col—"

"Yeh, well never mind," says Joe Lee. "The point is Mama . . . well, it's pride. You embarrass yourself and us too dancin like that."

"I wasn't shame." Then nobody say nuthin. Them standin there in they pretty clothes with drinks in they hands and gangin up on me, and me in the third-degree chair and nary a olive to my name. Felt just like the police got hold to me.

"First of all," Task say, holdin up his hand and tickin off the offenses, "the dress. Now that dress is too short, Mama, and too low-cut for a woman your age. And Tamu's going to make a speech tonight to kick off the campaign and will be introducin you and expecting you to organize the council of elders—"

"Me? Didn nobody ask me nuthin. You mean Nisi? She change her name?"

"Well, Norton was supposed to tell you about it. Nisi wants to introduce you and then encourage the older folks to form a Council of the Elders to act as an advisory—"

"And you going to be standing there with your boobs out and that wig on your head and that hem up to your ass. And people'll say, 'Ain't that the horny bitch that was grindin with the blind dude?' "

"Elo, be cool a minute," say Task, gettin to the next finger. "And then there's the drinkin. Mama, you know you can't drink cause next thing you know you be laughin loud and carryin on," and he grab another finger for the loudness. "And then there's the dancin. You been tattooed on the man for four records straight and slow draggin even on the fast numbers. How you think that look for a woman your age?"

"What's my age?"

"What?"

"I'm axin you all a simple question. You keep talkin bout what's proper for a woman my age. How old am I anyhow?" And Joe Lee slams his eyes shut and squinches up his face to figure. And Task run a hand over his ear and stare into his glass like the ice cubes goin calculate for him. And Elo just starin at the top of my head like she goin rip the wig off any minute now.

"Is your hair braided up under that thing? If so, why don't you take it off? You always did do a neat cornroll."[4]

"Uh huh," cause I'm thinkin how she couldn't undo

4. Cornrow, a hairstyle in which all the hair is interwoven from the scalp into small braids.

her hair fast enough talking bout cornroll so countrified. None of which was the subject. "How old, I
say?"

"Sixtee-one or—"

"You a damn lie Joe Lee Peoples."

"And that's another thing," say Task on the fingers.

"You know what you all can kiss," I say, gettin up
and brushin the wrinkles out my lap.

"Oh, Mama," Elo say, puttin a hand on my shoulder
like she hasn't done since she left home and the hand
landin light and not sure it supposed to be there.
Which hurt me to my heart. Cause this was the child in
our happiness fore Mr. Peoples die. And I carried that
child strapped to my chest till she was nearly two. We
was close is what I'm tryin to tell you. Cause it was
more me in the child than the others. And even after
Task it was the girlchild I covered in the night and
wept over for no reason at all less it was she was a
chub-chub like me and not very pretty, but a warm
child. And how did things get to this, that she can't put
a sure hand on me and say Mama we love you and
care about you and you entitled to enjoy yourself cause
you a good woman?

"And then there's Reverend Trent," say Task,
glancin from left to right like they hatchin a plot and
just now lettin me in on it. "You were suppose to be
talking with him tonight, Mama, about giving us his
basement for campaign headquarters and—"

"Didn nobody tell me nuthin. If grass roots mean
you kept in the dark I can't use it. I really can't. And

Reven Trent a fool anyway the way he tore into the widow man up there on Edgecomb cause he wouldn't take in three of them foster children and the woman not even comfy in the ground yet and the man's mind messed up and—"

"Look here," say Task. "What we need is a family conference so we can get all this stuff cleared up and laid out on the table. In the meantime I think we better get back into the other room and tend to business. And in the meantime, Mama, see if you can't get to Reverend Trent and—"

"You want me to belly rub with the Reven, that it?"

"Oh damn," Elo say and go through the swingin door.

"We'll talk about all this at dinner. How's tomorrow night, Joe Lee?" While Joe Lee being self-important I'm wonderin who's doin the cookin and how come no body ax me if I'm free and do I get a corsage and things like that. Then Joe nod that it's O.K. and he go through the swingin door and just a little hubbub come through from the other room. Then Task smile his smile, lookin just like his daddy, and he leave. And it just me and this stranger's kitchen, which was a mess I wouldn't never let my kitchen look like. Poison you just to look at the pots. Then the door swing the other way and it's My Man Bovanne standin there sayin Miss Hazel but lookin at the deep fry and then at the steam table, and most surprised when I come up on him from the other direction and take him on out of there. Pass the folks pushin up towards the stage where

Nisi and some other people settin and ready to talk, and folks gettin to the last of the sandwiches and the booze fore they settle down in one spot and listen serious. And I'm thinkin bout tellin Bovanne what a lovely long dress Nisi got on and the earrings and her hair piled up in a cone and the people bout to hear how we all gettin screwed and gotta form our own party and everybody there listenin and lookin. But instead I just haul the man on out of there, and Joe Lee and his wife look at me like I'm terrible, but they ain't said boo to the man yet. Cause he blind and old and don't nobody there need him since they grown up and don't need they skates fixed no more.

"Where we goin, Miss Hazel?" Him knowin all the time.

"First we gonna buy you some dark sunglasses. Then you comin with me to the supermarket so I can pick up tomorrow's dinner, which is goin to be a grand thing proper and you invited. Then we goin to my house."

"That be fine. I surely would like to rest my feet." Bein cute, but you got to let men play out they little show, blind or not. So he chat on bout how tired he is and how he appreciate me takin him in hand this way. And I'm thinkin I'll have him change the lock on my door first thing. Then I'll give the man a nice warm bath with jasmine leaves in the water and a little Epsom salt on the sponge to do his back. And then a good rubdown with rose water and olive oil. Then a cup of lemon tea with a taste in it. And a little talcum, some of that fancy stuff Nisi mother sent over last Christmas. And then a massage, a good face massage round the forehead which is the worryin part. Cause you gots to take care of the older folks. And let them know they still needed to run the mimeo machine and keep the spark plugs clean and fix the mailboxes for folks who might help us get the breakfast program goin, and the school for the little kids and the campaign and all. Cause old folks in the nation. That what Nisi was sayin and I mean to do my part.

"I imagine you are a very pretty woman, Miss Hazel."

"I surely am," I say just like the hussy my daughter always say I was.

# The Courtship of Widow Sobcek

BY JOANNA HIGGINS

Warmed by his feather-tick, John Jielewicz lay in bed and studied the ceiling. What day was it? Then he knew, and time began once more. Saturday; overcast and dull. It looked like snow. He got up quickly, made coffee, and set to work. After washing his cup and saucer, he mopped the linoleum in the kitchen and bathroom, dusted the spools of his furniture, and vacuumed the rose-patterned rugs of his living room. Then he rinsed out his opalescent glass spittoon in the basement. His housecleaning finished for the week, he filled the bathtub, threw in his long underwear and shirt, and lowered himself into the hot water. The day was half gone.

Steam clouded the mirror, and late afternoon light illumined pale swans and lily pads floating on turquoise wallpaper. He considered the week. On Monday he'd spaded the garden, and on Tuesday he'd chopped wood. He'd worked at Chet's on Wednesday and Thursday, making Polish sausage and pickled bologna. Then on Friday, but what had he done on Friday? The stoker? No. The garage? No. The car? The yard? No.

What then? How could he forget in just one day? The stoker? No. The basement, the stoker, the coal? Yes, the coal! He'd taken the Plymouth to Townsend's and ordered a ton of coal. Then he'd come home, checked the coal bin, and swept the basement.

It was good to think of the work ahead. Soon Chet would be getting big Christmas orders for smoked hams and sausages, and he would be busy. Years of working with casings in icy water and handling cold meats had twisted his hands, and they ached with changes in the weather. He held them beneath the hot water. Next to his thin legs, as white and veined as church marble, his hands looked like gnarled stumps. But they were good hands, he thought, hard-working hands. And he'd done his share of work in his time—the lumber camps, the farm, the store. What else was there besides work? People sometimes said: "That John Jielewicz. He sure knows how to work!" That made him pull back his narrow shoulders and walk proudly.

"Pa," his daughter had said on one of her Sunday night visits, "move in with us." Casting her eyes around the big rooms, she'd said, "Why all this work, Pa? You don't need so much work at your age. And for what? Who sees it?"

Removing his pipe, he'd said, "I see it." Then he'd leaned over his chair to spit into the spittoon, defying all the ranch houses on the south side of town.

The bath water was getting tepid and uncomfortable; he added more hot water, soaped himself with a bar of Fels Naptha, and ducked his head twice under the water. Then he soaped the underwear and the shirt, rinsed them, and pulled the plug.

Later, dressed in clean clothes, his hair parted in the center and combed flat down like feathers, he cleaned the tub and hung his washing on a line running between plum trees in back. Then it was time for confession.

Driving to church in his Plymouth, he took stock. Anger? Yes. Cursing? Yes. Lying? No, never. Any of the others? For years he'd confessed his sins to Monsignor Gapzinski, and the old priest knew him by name. "John," he'd said once, before giving the absolution, "you're a strong, good man, but think about Our Lord's words, 'Everyone who exalts himself shall be humbled.'" Later, in a dim pew, he'd made his penance of one rosary but hadn't bothered about the words. When he'd finished the last decade of the rosary and blessed himself, he rose and walked proudly past lines of people still waiting to confess.

That night, the lines seemed much slower. After a long wait, he finally entered the coffin-like box, and when the panel slid open before his eyes, began his confession in Polish. But an unfamiliar voice interrupted and asked if he could speak English.

Startled, he asked, "Where is Monsignor?"

"He's ill," the unfamiliar voice whispered. "Please pray for him. I'm Father Jim, and I'll be filling in for a while."

How could it be? he wondered. Monsignor sick? Such a good man, too. The unfamiliar voice again interrupted, asking him to begin his confession in English, if he could.

"I was angry this week," he said. "I cursed." He stopped and waited for the priest's response. His eyes adjusting to the darkness, he could just make out a black crucifix and a hearing aid device on the wall before him.

After some time, the priest said, "And is that all?"

When he didn't speak, the priest went into a lengthy sermon. His voice rising above a whisper, he talked of flames of love and flames of anger; he talked of charity and God's love. The words ran together, and, unable to keep up with their flow, he lost interest and thought instead of what he would do after Mass the next day. The Lord's Day was not for work, he knew, but a little raking couldn't be called work. He'd raked his own leaves several times, but leaves from neighbors' yards were always blowing into his. He would do a little raking; then maybe he would put another coat of varnish on the woodwork in the archway. He liked wood to be shiny.

The priest broke into his reverie. "And do you understand the nature of your penance, then?"

"Excuse me?" he said in Polish.

"English, please," the priest said loudly.

"I'm sorry. I don't hear you."

The priest raised his voice even more. "Instead of regular penance, which implies punishment," he said, "I would like you to try thinking—all this coming week—of God's love for you. Whenever you can, think of His goodness and of the goodness of life. Do this when you feel anger or when you wish to curse. Do you understand?"

Astonished and confused, he couldn't speak.

"Good," said the priest, after a moment. He gave the absolution, the Latin rushing like water.

Then the small wooden panel slid shut, and he was finished. Outside the confessional, he thought people stared at him; he lowered his eyes. Lights burned only near the confessional, and farther up the nave he could kneel in half-light. He took his usual pew and out of habit began his rosary. But blessing himself with the metallic cross, he suddenly remembered that it wasn't his penance. What was it, then? Something about love when he felt like cursing. No, that wasn't it. It was something about God and love, flames and cursing. He couldn't get it right. Now how do you like that? he said to himself, feeling anger grow. To make matters worse, his stomach started acting up, burning and heaving. He turned around to survey the waiting lines. People were standing as if frozen in the aisles. He looked to the front of the church; the statues, in shadow, seemed miles away. The sanctuary lamp burned red. He was angry now and unsettled; he didn't feel like a new man. It was the priest's fault. The priest had ruined it, and he wouldn't be able to receive Communion tomorrow. I'm not about to stand in line all over again, he told himself. I might as well work tomorrow, then, and be hanged for it.

After a supper of lard on bread, cold sausage, and

coffee diluted with milk, he rocked in his dimly lit living room. Smoking his pipe and spitting into the clean spittoon, he mulled over the priest's words—the few he remembered. They seemed like clues or pieces of a puzzle, and he wished he'd listened better. Flames he said to himself. Flames and love, whatever that meant. Well, he knew about flames, that's for sure. As if it happened the day before, he saw his white-eyed team of horses rearing up against a sky black as hell with smoke. Half-mad himself, he'd fought the crazed beasts to a standstill while Masha got things into the wagon. He knew about flames. But flames and love and how it tied together with cursing, he couldn't figure out.

Cursing, he thought. Now there was his failing. He'd never forgotten the time a storm caught him plowing. The steel-blue sky cracked apart in a dozen places, and the horses lunged, toppling the plow. Straddling a furrow of stony earth, he'd cursed the lightning and the horses, the plow and the field. He'd called on a hundred demons. It seemed he could touch one of the bolts, so close they came, snaking into the earth. The air stank with sulfur. He got the plow unhitched and ran with the horses while rain made rivers of the furrows. In the house Masha, pale as death, was running from room to room, dipping her fingers in a jar of holy water and sprinkling the walls, the floors, the babies. Still cursing, he'd stood dripping wet in the kitchen, while rain blew in the open windows and glasses rattled in the cupboards. Masha had run into the kitchen and sprinkled water on him. Just then a stream of light poured in one window and out the other, burning the very air. It had snaked across the entire kitchen, missing them by inches. Masha, her hand held out as if paralyzed, water still dripping from her fingers, had only said, "See, John? See what your cursing brings?" For a long time after that, he hadn't dared to curse.

How could anything like that be connected with love? he wondered. The new priest must be a little touched. Masha had been a little touched, too. She'd been a good woman, a good worker, but too holy. Once, she came back from the village and went straight into the parlor without saying a word. There, she lit a candle before the statue of the Virgin and then sat, still as a stone, before that little flame. He'd called her and had even asked if she was sick. But there she sat, pale as death. She wouldn't answer him; she wouldn't even look at him. She held a rosary in her lap, but her fingers didn't move over the beads. The parlor grew darker and colder as the day lost it light, and the candle burned more brightly in that dimness. It cast shadows over the Virgin's mantle, and it seemed the figure was moving. Frightened, he left her alone in the room. Finally, long after the candle had guttered out, Masha appeared in the kitchen. He was making pancakes, and flour dusted the planks under the table.

"John," she said, scared as a child. "I seen her."

"Who?"

"The Virgin."

"No."

"Oh yes. On the timber cut going to the church."

He was quiet, afraid of what more she might say.

"She was so bright, I fell down and covered my face. I cried because she was so beautiful, so beautiful."

He hadn't liked it one bit. People would say she was touched, and it wouldn't look good. But he'd been surprised when just the opposite happened. People started saying she was a saint. That made him proud of her even though he didn't think she was a saint. She was just a woman. Couldn't they see that?

As he smoked and waited for bedtime, he looked around the room. His oval wedding picture, his plant in the alcove, his clock, all were sunk in shadow. Shadows blurred the shape of his wife's rocker at the end of the double living room. Sometimes, depending on the play of shadows, it seemed the rocker moved, as if brushed by a wind. "Sleep, Masha, sleep," he would say then. When the clock on the closed gramophone struck ten times, he rapped his pipe against the spittoon and abandoned the living room to darkness. His back resting on a pad of sheepskin, his thin body covered by a heavy feather-tick, he too slept. Outside, the underwear stiffened and moved on the line like a ghost in a frost-blasted garden.

That night he slept badly, and all the next day unfinished business plagued him. At Mass he'd sat in the pew, like a bump on a log, he thought, while everybody else went to Communion. By the time his daughter came for her visit, his stomach was good and sour.

"So, Pa," she said. "What did you do today?" She wore a Sunday dress too tight about the waist.

"Do?" he said irritably. One leg made a sharp angle over the hassock. "There's always something to do around here." The smell of fresh varnish still hung in the air.

"Pa, come live with us. We'd like you to." She motioned at the lofty ceilings, the corners. "There's just too much work here."

She's lying, he thought. How could they want him? His stomach turned, and a sour liquid rose in his throat.

"Son of a bitch!" he said in Polish. "I need my powders." He left her alone in the living room.

When he returned from the bathroom, she said, "Pa, go see a doctor with that stomach of yours. 'Powders'! What are these 'powders' you get at Wiesneski's? Go see a real doctor."

In one sharp Polish sentence he cast all doctors into the flames of hell. Then he took his pipe and calmly rocked while his daughter struggled into her coat.

"At least," she said, standing, "why not sell and get something smaller, maybe closer to us?"

"Bah," he said, and spat into the spittoon.

Then she was gone, and he heard her old Hudson start up in the driveway. In the quiet he smoked and rocked and studied his plant. Masha was the one who could grow plants, he thought. She could make sticks grow, while he had to fight the damned soil for each and every potato. He'd been waiting for a long time now for those bright blue and orange flowers promised in the catalogue. It'll be a cold day in hell, he thought. Behind the plant, the radiators hissed. It's too damned dry in here, he decided, and went to the kitchen for water.

After watering the plant and filling the cake pans on the radiators for humidity, he had time for another smoke. Letting his thoughts go where they would, he remembered old Mr. Smigelski. Once Mrs. Raniszewski had said after church, "Merry Christmas, Mr. Smigelski!" Bowing, the crazy fool shouted, "Ass to me, ass to you!" How she'd looked when he said that! Every time he saw Smigelski after church, he was tempted to say, "Ass to me, ass to you, you crazy fool!" He said the words as they were intended: *As to me, as to you.* Now what did that mean? Whatever happens to me, let it happen to you? Or, what you say to me, let me say to you? That must be it. The crazy fool! He laughed just thinking about it.

When the clock chimed ten times, he rapped his pipe on the spittoon and rose from the rocker. Before turning off the floor lamp, he saw that his lace curtains were getting yellow. It was time to take them to the Widow Sobcek.

But he forgot about the curtains during the week; there was too much other work to think about. The stoker clogged somehow, and he had to crawl around in the dust, fixing it. Then four shingles blew off the roof, and he dragged out his wooden ladder from the garage. Extended its full thirty-five feet, it was just long enough to reach the north gable. Up he went, hand over hand, with shingles, hammer, and nails in cloth bag at his side. The ladder was springy; wind puffed his jacket and blew in his face. If it should slip, he thought, imagining the old ladder sliding sideways across the clapboard, sending him and his damned shingles all to hell. But it didn't slip, and he finished the job. Only when he was back down on the frozen ground did he feel his legs trembling. Dragging the ladder back into the garage, he was proud of himself. It'd been a job worth doing.

On Saturday, he remembered the curtains. After his housecleaning and his bath, he pulled a straight-back chair to the radiators. Standing on the chair, he freed the curtain rods, pulled off the stiff panels, and let them fall into a wicker basket. "Damn it to hell," he said at the dust. "Pfoo!" He got down and surveyed the bare windows. They looked empty, like Mrs. Kranak's windows during Lent. She took down her curtains on Ash Wednesday and didn't put them back up until Holy Saturday. Her empty, dark windows reminded him of something; he wasn't sure just what, but it wasn't good. How could she stand it all those weeks? On Easter Sunday he was relieved to see her white curtains against the wavering panes of glass. Looking at his own windows, he saw he would have to wash them on Monday. The stained-glass pieces at the top were dusty and dull; the windowpanes were streaked and murky. Before leaving for the Widow's, he had to wash dust from his hands.

Turning his green Plymouth off First Avenue, he drove into a neighborhood of plain houses, fenced gardens, and small yards. No stained glass in the windows; no fancy fretwork on the gables. All was simple and neat and stark in the later afternoon light. The bare yards had a wintry look, and children in winter jackets and caps played in old piles of leaves.

He drove slowly over broken concrete, conscious of his sour stomach. It was churning and heaving. That morning he'd put a spoonful of butter into his coffee and taken an extra measure of the powders, but nothing did the trick. He had a sudden thought, as jarring as a glimpse of a snake disappearing in a rockpile. *What if this is some great sickness?* The thought shook him, but gripping the steering wheel he told himself; *No, by God. Not yet. Not John Jielewicz!*

Scowling, he parked his Plymouth on gravel in front of the Widow's house. The streets had no curbs in her neighborhood. His scowl deepened when he recognized, parked just ahead, the shiny beast of a car that always reminded him of a hearse. It belonged to Mrs. Stanley, a divorced woman with black hair and red fingernails. "Czarownica!" he said, lifting his basket from the back seat. She was a proud, mean witch, and it bothered him to think the Widow washed the woman's curtains. He would never do that.

There was room for only one at a time on the narrow sidewalk, and he had to wait for Mrs. Stanley to pass. She carried white curtains over one arm, a white veil over the black fur of her coat. As she passed, hairs on the coat rose, like a dog's, and caught the light. He scowled, but she ignored him. His stomach heaved and fluttered.

Waiting on the porch, he looked over the Widow's yard. Bare maple limbs interlocked above raked grass, and mounds of leaves were heaped over the garden. Low gray clouds in the west reflected pale colors. Earlier every day now, he said to himself, thinking of the sunset.

A small woman wearing a bib apron over a flower-print dress opened the door. "Mr. Jielewicz," she said, "good to see you." She held the door for him, then closed it. Inside, she wiped steam from her glasses. "How are you?"

He set his basket near a drying frame holding a stretched curtain and thought of the black coat and of his stomach. "I'm no good," he said. "No damned good." He looked around the small kitchen. As always, the Widow's linoleum was polished, and the windows were steamed by washing and cooking. In one window she had hung three glass shelves of African violets, and he could see, behind the purple flowers, a gloomy December sky. "I will sit awhile and rest," he told her.

"That's good," she said. "Sit. I will rest, too." But holding the back of a kitchen chair for support, she made her way to the stove. There, a bowl and plate had been warming, and she poured *kvass* and cut two pieces of bread from a loaf cooling on the cupboard.

Slowly, she moved between stove and table, carrying

the bowl before her like an offering. She made a second trip for the plate of bread and a spoon. "Eat, Mr. Jielewicz," she said. "Eat and feel better."

He stirred the rich brown soup, with its raisins and prunes and *kloski* like small clouds. When did he last have *kvass* like that? he wondered. Steam rose from the bowl. Masha, he thought. Masha had made *kvass* like that. Ten years in March, then. Taking a blue handkerchief from his pocket, he wiped his brow and very quickly his eyes. When he finished the soup, he looked up. The Widow was watching him.

"It's good," he said. "It settled my stomach."

"Have more," she said. Both hands on the arms of her chair, she slowly lifted herself up. Her legs were wrapped in layers of support stockings, as thick as children's winter leggings.

"Sit," he said, getting up. "I can wait on myself."

While he finished the second bowl of *kvass*, the Widow began attaching a curtain to a drying frame, carefully inserting small pins through the lace to preserve its design.

"Do you get tired doing that every day?" he asked.

"Oh," she said, "yes and no. Some days, when my legs hurt, yes. Today, no." Then she gathered a curtain from the basket and, holding up one end, let it fall between them. "Each so different, so beautiful," she said, "that I don't get so tired."

Through the white lace he saw a young girl. Like . . . but he blocked the thought. Startled, he felt blood rush to his face. Then she let the curtain fall into the basket, and the Widow Sobcek appeared again, gray hair and glasses, the housedress and thick stockings.

Behind the African violets, the sky was growing darker; it was time to leave. He sighed as he put four dollar bills on the oilcloth. She took two of the bills, tucked them into her apron pocket, then pushed the remaining bills toward him. "Take," she said, as she always did when he overpaid. "Take. I don't need."

Driving from the Widow's in the December dusk, he saw that it would snow. All was still and cold and gray. In time for evening confession, he drove down side streets and took stock. Anger? Yes. When? He remembered: that fool of a priest, the penance left undone. Now what? The Plymouth slowed and came to a stop in the middle of a block. He would get worked up, he thought, going back to that priest. He waited for his stomach to start acting up, but it was strangely quiet. Should he go home or should he try it again? On the windshield flakes of snow appeared, hanging there like the Widow's white lace. *So beautiful,* she'd said. He thought of the priest's words—the clues he'd tried to figure out. The Plymouth began to roll forward. He turned on the windshield wipers, and the stone-gray road appeared under the headlights. At the intersection of First and Maple, he turned right, toward the church.

It was nearly a year later when his daughter said, on a Sunday evening, "Oh, Pa, everyone's talking about you. It's awful."

He heard sleet at the windowpanes, a low whispering sound. He leaned over his chair and spat into the spittoon. He drew on his pipe before speaking. Then he said, *"Plotka!"*

"No," she said. "Not gossip. They're right to talk. It's crazy, that's what it is. Here you are running over there every week with curtains! Everyone's laughing, but I don't think it's so funny. I think it's . . ."

"Not every week."

"No, but you know what I mean. Every month, then. Just as bad. Don't look at me like that. I'm not the one to blame. People are saying a lot of things. They're saying that . . . that you don't know what you're doing. Oh, Pa!"

He thought over the words. Well, maybe it was crazy. What would she think if he told her about the lace? Ever since the Widow held the lace curtain in the air between them, he'd been seeing lace everywhere. When he cleaned out the stoker, the clinkers looked like lace. So did the ice when he chopped it off the sidewalks. Everywhere lace! At first it'd bothered him and he worried, but then he got used to the idea and began to look at things to see how close they came to the Widow's lace. He was surprised. Sugar in the sugarbowl, the stars at night, even the thorny hedge at his property line. One day while cutting the grass, he saw light coming through little openings in the hedge, and right away he thought: *Lace!* Shadows of tree limbs on grass, car tracks on snow, birds flying through the air—all reminded him of lace. So did the feathery tops

of new carrots and even the rougher edges of cabbage
and potato plants. It *was* crazy! One day he made a list
of all the things that reminded him of the lace curtain,
and he was astounded to find over fifty items. He put
the list away in his safe, but added to it every week.
Crazy? Well, what of it? He wanted to laugh. Lace everywhere! He would make a joke, and she would
laugh, too. "Ass to me, ass to you," he said, thinking
of Mr. Smigelski. He laughed, showing brown stubs of
teeth.

But she was alarmed, and her eyes flew from him to
the oval wedding picture to the alcove. "Oh, Pa," she
said, "cut out this silliness! Act your age."

The problem was, he thought, he didn't feel his age;
he wanted to be foolish. "If I acted my age," he said,
"I'd be dead!" He laughed. At the rate he was going, he would probably find lace in the grave as well!

"Pa," she said thoughtfully, "what did you do with
your plant?" She was looking at the empty space in the
alcove where his plant on its pedestal had been for
years.

The alcove looked larger, he thought, without the
plant, and the curtains showed better. Should he tell
her? It was last Holy Thursday, he remembered, when
he'd taken the plant to the Widow's. How she'd
laughed when she opened the door. "There's a plant
growing out of your head, Mr. Jielewicz," she'd said.
He must have looked foolish, with those big gray-green
leaves, like rabbit ears, hiding his face.

"Now what are you smiling about?" his daughter

was saying. "You won't tell me where you took the plant, but I know! I thought I saw it at the Widow's when I took my curtains there, and I was right. Only I didn't know it could have such nice flowers. Think what you're doing Pa. Think of Mama, for heaven's sake." She blew her nose in a Kleenex. "Oh dear," she said, putting the wad of tissue in her purse. "I have to get home. John has a cold, and I'm getting it. One thing after another. If you moved in with us, like we wanted you to, none of this would be happening." She got her arms into heavy coatsleeves.

How old was she now? he wondered, studying his daughter. She didn't look like the little girl who'd tangled rolls of string at the store and drew pictures on pink butcher paper. He looked to the wedding picture on the shadowy wall. They'd stood so still, so straight, facing the big camera: Masha, young, thin, unsmiling; himself solemn as a minister and thin as a rail in his new suit.

Standing and buttoning her coat, she said, "For heaven's sake, Pa, at your age, you don't want to be marrying again."

So, he thought. *So.* He saw the Widow in her house-dress and felt slippers. A poor woman. He thought of his old safe in his bedroom closet, hidden behind his black suits. His name was printed in gold letters over the combination, but the light in the closet was too dim for it to show. When he opened his safe to get money or to add to his list, he had to use a flashlight. Then he thought: John. Who is John? That is my name. He remembered. John was his grandson, a boy he seldom saw, a little boy—small and pale and weak. He wondered why his daughter always left the boy at home when she visited. Not seeing the husband didn't bother him, but he would like to see the boy now and then. He looked at Masha's rocker, but it was still. I should marry again, he thought, and leave them nothing. His stomach began a faint stir. The *plotki*! He drew in on the pipe and exhaled a great cloud of smoke. That's what they're worried about. She's speaking for the others. He thought of his two sons and daughter who lived in other states and only visited at Christmas. Then they talked about the bad roads and how the town was going to the dogs. He should marry! The idea was pleasing; how they would worry then! But something intervened. He saw the Widow's rough hand pushing the dollar bills toward him. *Take,* she'd said. *Take. I don't need.*

His daughter tied a wool kerchief under her chin and slipped on gloves. "Well, I'm going, Pa," she said. "Don't forget about dinner at our house next week. You said you would come."

She's tired, he thought. He saw her small house on its barren lot—all clutter and light. No comfortable shadows or large rooms. He didn't like going there. But there was something he wanted to do. What was it? The oilcloth. Yes, what else? The dollar bills. Yes. "Wait," he told his daughter. "Wait just a minute."

He left her in the living room as the clock was striking nine-thirty, and returned several minutes later. Dangling car keys from a gloved hand, she stood near Masha's rocker. "You know, Pa, we still have to talk over this other thing."

"Never mind that," he said. "Give this to the boy. Give this to John."

Startled, she took the unsealed envelope and with gloved hands opened it. "Pa!" she said, as she lifted out a thick packet of bills. "What is this craziness? What's the matter with you!" She tried to push the envelope and bills into his hands, but he stepped back.

"Take," he said. "It's for the boy. For school. For anything."

"Oh, Pa!"

In a moment he was encircling her heavy bulk with his bony arms.

"Never mind," he said. "Never mind."

Only when she moved back, wiping her eyes, did he notice the bunch of lace at her neck. Gathered with a black velvet ribbon, it fanned out like the top of a carrot.


Holding a bag of salt in one hand, he let go of the ice-coated porch rail, and his feet took to the sky. That's how he explained it to his daughter at the hospital.

"I saw every kind of star," he told her.

"Never mind stars," she said. "You could have broken your back. Then what?"

But he was too tired to answer; his eyelids shut of their own accord, and he saw stars whirling about his head. He dozed. When he opened his eyes, she was still there.

"I'm going home," he said.

"You can't! What do you want to do, Pa? Fall again?"

He wanted to tell her they had no right keeping him in the hospital when he wanted to go home, but the words wouldn't come. Instead, he dozed and saw a big black hearse slowly backing up to an open door. He was on a cart, rolling toward the car's dark cave. Terrified, he opened his eyes.

"I'm going home," he said, struggling to rise. "I have . . . things to do."

She was beside the bed, holding him back. "Pa! You're not supposed to move. Your ribs are all cracked. Look, here's your lunch. And the nurse!"

"Well, Mr. Jielewicz," the nurse said. "Full of pep, are you? The doctor was right. They don't make 'em like you anymore!"

"I hope not," Eleanor said to herself, but he heard.

It seemed his hair was standing up like a shock of hay, so he brushed at it with a stiff, bandaged hand. Shame, shame, he thought, to be lying here like a baby while strangers walked around the bed looking at him. A young girl wearing a dress of pink stripes swung a narrow table over the bed and set a tray of food on it. He looked at the colors: green, yellow, brown, something red on the side. It looked like his workbench in the basement, where he cleaned his paintbrushes.

"I'm not eating," he said. "I'm going home." He closed his eyes.

"Pa!"

"Don't worry, Mrs. Kirchner," he heard the nurse say. "If he won't eat now, he'll be good and hungry later."

His eyes still closed, he saw himself getting up, putting on his underwear, pants, and shirt, starting the Plymouth and driving home. Then he would . . . But what day was it? Was it still Wednesday?

"What day is it?" he asked his daughter, as if from a great distance.

"What did you say, Pa? I can't hear you."

"Day," he said. "What day?"

"Day? Oh! It's Saturday."

Saturday! He struggled to put the week back together. On Monday he had . . . but he couldn't remember that far back. Tuesday, then. On Tuesday he . . . he worked at Chet's. That's right. It was raining when he drove home. Then it got cold. The next day everything was ice. The trees, the bushes, and the utility wires. The steps and the side of the house. Sunlight was everywhere. Icy tree limbs shone like glass against the blue sky. So bright. So, so bright. He dozed again.

When he awoke, the Widow was there, placing a bowl of *kvass* on the table where the tray of food had been.

"I see in the paper about your fall, so I come," she said. "Eat, Mr. Jielewicz. Eat and feel better."

Was he dreaming? But no, steam rose like incense from the bowl, and he could smell the rich soup. His eyes burned. Suddenly he remembered what he'd seen just before the dark. Sunlight on polished steps. And near the edge, where icicles dripped from the roof, designs as fine as flowers. *Lace.* Then his legs flew from under him and pellets of salt rose in the air like confetti.

One week later, he awoke from a nap and knew it was long after lunchtime. A tray of cold food sat on the bedtable. The Widow hadn't come; something was wrong. All that week she'd come, bringing him good food: *kvass* and ham, chicken and dumplings, *pierogi* and apple pie. He watched the doorway and imagined her walking in, wearing the *baboushka* and long gray coat, the galoshes. The doorway remained empty.

That Monday the doctor had checked him and said he could go home if he promised to be careful. He'd thought a bit and asked the doctor if he could perhaps stay a day or two longer. "Why?" the doctor wanted to know. Then he'd lied. "A little pain yet," he'd said, avoiding the doctor's eyes.

"What time is it?" he asked the girl in pink stripes who brought him a glass of juice.

She looked at her wristwatch. "Three-thirty," she said. "Why? Expecting company?" She laughed, straightened the blankets, then took away the untouched food.

He waited, every minute expecting the Widow to appear in her *baboushka*, coat, and galoshes. The curtain soon made a long shadow on his bed, and then he knew she wouldn't come. It was too late. He was wide awake now; something nagged him. What was it? The Widow shuffling into the room. Yes. What else? Her long gray coat and the heavy boots. Yes. And? Then he knew. Dear God, he said to himself, let me burn forever in hell if I have done a bad thing!

He swung his legs out from under the sheet and blanket; when his bare feet touched the cold tile, he was chilled. He stood, feeling sore all over, but he walked to the closet and found his clothing. He recognized the shirt; he'd been wearing it when he fell. It was so long ago, he thought. He undid the white hospital gown and let it fall to the floor. Then he pulled his underwear up over the bandages. He dressed quickly. Hurry, hurry, hurry, he said to himself, tangling his shoelaces. He looked at the other bed, prepared to lie, but his roommate slept, tubes feeding his arms.

At the doorway he waited for the corridor to clear. He saw nurses talking together at the desk near the elevator; pretending he was just a visitor, he walked to the elevator and turned his back to them. Doors mysteriously opened, and he stepped into the bright cubicle. Free, he thought, pressing buttons. Down, down he went, his heart pounding and his stomach fluttering.

In the mild air outside, he saw a taxi waiting, as if for him. A taxi! He'd never hired a taxi. Did he have any money? Dear God! He rifled his pockets and found two dollar bills in his pants. Waving the bills in the air, he pounded on the window, startling the driver. He shouted the Widow's address.

The driver got out and walked around the car to open the back door. "Well, hop in, then," he said.

Holding his side, he climbed into the back seat. Hurry, hurry, hurry, he said to himself.

"Nice day," the driver said, starting up a loud clock on the dashboard. "Looks like spring will get here yet."

They were off. He looked out the window and saw puddles of water in the gutters and black-crusted snowbanks in yards. Already the grass seemed green where snow had melted. Hurry, hurry, hurry, he said to himself.

When the driver came to open the door for him, the clock on the dashboard had stopped ticking. "That'll be one dollar and fifty cents."

"Take," he said, thrusting the bills at the man. He rushed up the narrow walk.

At the Widow's door he knocked, but there was no answer. He tried the door, and it opened. Stepping inside, he heard her voice coming from the living room. She was lying like a fallen bird, her legs covered with a thick woolen blanket. What had he done! Dear God in heaven, he said to himself, strike me dead. Bury me in ashes!

"Mr. Jielewicz!" she said. "What are you doing here?"

His side ached, and he couldn't find breath to speak. Finally, he was able to say, "What is the matter, little lady?"

"Oh," she said, "my legs got tired. Not so bad, but everyone wants clean curtains for Easter, and I can't walk so good now." She sat up and turned on a table light. "Mrs. Stanley came today and says she needs her curtains no later than tomorrow. Now, no curtains."

That witch, he thought, seeing the woman in her black coat. What does she need with clean curtains! Under his bandages everything hurt and burned.

"Tomorrow, I will be better," the Widow said, as if she believed it.

He looked at the thick stockings and the felt slippers and knew what he'd done. Dear God in heaven! She'd walked to the hospital all those days.

"Where are the curtains?"

"Oh no, Mr. Jielewicz. You can't do them!"

"Tell me how."

In a room off the kitchen he knelt, ignoring a great pain in his side, and plunged his bandaged hands into a washtub of hot water. Steam rose when he lifted a curtain into the air. Water poured off the material and light from the setting sun made rainbows all over the soapy lace. "Dear God!" he cried, seeing once again the Widow's face behind the veil. In his joy, he nearly upset the tub.

# Bar Bar Bar

## I

*F*ight, that's all they did lately and they had another one, a humdinger, and Howard Fu got on the bus absolutely determined to prove to Thomas that he wasn't sick in the head, that he knew *exactly* what he was doing, when it was time to stop he always stopped, and at this stage of the game why the hell did he have to explain anything to anybody, and that definitely included his son. That's when he saw her, with all the smoke coming out of his ears.

She was smiling out the window like the world was a gorgeous oyster, and she continued to smile (he would almost call it a grin, but a grin was something pasted on Mongolian idiots, and she was sure as shooting neither one), yes, to *smile* all the way through Queens, across the crazy quilt of Manhattan and even through the Lincoln Tunnel, about the dullest stretch of ground in America, unless in smiling you could hold back the mountain of water just waiting to pounce on frowners. When she continued like that through the turnpike, he really had to say something, polite, impolite, she had to know something he didn't know.

"Excuse me, but you certainly must like this trip."

She turned the Our-Gang comedy face to him (except it wasn't nasty, nor from that moment, whenever he saw it, even in his mind, could you ever call it nasty).

"Actually, it's my first time. That is, in forty years. I went to Atlantic City with my husband during the war." The smile slid far back, then returned. "I understand it's changed."

"It's changed all right." He felt his neck (that's where he always got it, just like the expression, right in the neck), he felt it loosen up for the first time since he got up and knew he was in for it with Thomas. "Excuse me for saying so, but sometimes a person needs a little help if they don't know the ropes, don't be too bashful to ask."

"Oh," she said, "that's very nice, but I'm no gambler. I just like to look at other people and at things in general. Perhaps I'll walk out on the Steel Pier for old time's sake."

He didn't want to say it, but with Howard it was up front or nothing; besides, he didn't want to think of that smile disappearing in the morning fog.

"There's no Steel Pier no more." Say it and get it over with.

She did cut down a fraction of an inch, but she was game; it reminded him of Ruffian, and in his reminding, he begged her pardon for the comparison; also, of course, Ruffian was a filly; yet there was this thing about her, like a filly . . . "I should have known," she said gamely, "that's how it goes."

"That's how it goes, all right."

"Oh well, I'll settle for the boardwalk; there *must* be a boardwalk."

"Oh sure, there's a boardwalk," and he felt so good about letting her have her boardwalk that he repeated his offer.

"I'll send up a smoke signal if I need any help," she said with the game smile.

"You never know. I'll ride up to the rescue. With my white hat on. It'll say, 'Play at Claridge.' "

Not only did she smile, she giggled; Harriet never giggled in her entire life; to be more exact, when he cracked wise, she stared.

"Thank you," she said. "I'll keep my eyes peeled."

And that was that. Howard turned to his copy of *Winning Blackjack* and she looked out the window at the fascinating Jersey scenery and that's how they rode the rest of the way. The one time he looked up she was still doing it; anybody who could love Jersey must have had a permanent wave on her mouth. But it made him smile a little, too, and when they turned off onto the expressway, he began to feel the old surge of excitement.


It was some bomb. If they dropped it on Hong Kong it would wipe out the whole damn city.

He got this young black girl at Resorts who was glued to cards that topped him by one; she was scooping in his chips so monotonously that he was tempted to push them toward her as soon as she dealt him his nine, ten or picture. For that made it even worse: he was getting good cards; twice he hit twenty, twice she hit blackjack. By the time he slammed out to change his luck, he was down by seventy-five.

The salt air, plus the knowledge that win, lose or draw, the ocean would continue to do its number, calmed him down. He strolled into Bally's bound and determined to just worry about his own hand, the hell with the dealer.

She was in Bally's. Standing behind a red-faced lady with Popeye forearms who was working two bandits with so much alternate intensity that his shoulder practically ached. He cleared his throat, excused himself, and when the smiling face turned, asked her how she was doing.

"Hello there. Oh, I'm just watching. How about you?"

"Fair." (Never knock your luck; it could punish you even more.)

She turned to the red-faced lady, watched her snap down the arm, stare in disbelief.

"She's not breakin' the bank," Howard said.

Gazing once more, but not believing, the woman said over a chunky shoulder, "The bank hates me, I pumped both of these dry yesterday." She gave the arm a shot and it was no love tap and she said to the watching, smiling face, "They're all yours, the little rats," and stalked indignantly away.

"Wanna give it a try?" Howard said. "Sometimes, they give one person a hard time, then turn right around."

"Why should that be?"

"Search me, they got funny moods, I had a dog like that once. How about it, you got any quarters?" He copied her smile. "I don't wanna corrupt you."

"Oh it's too late for that," she said, not batting an eye. He noticed how smooth her blue-white hair was, not that it was plaster, but it stayed where it was supposed to stay. "I've never been lucky," she said while he was careful not to look at her hair. "I bought a sweepstakes ticket every year for thirty years and never won a dime."

Probably phonies, he thought, but never tell them. "Here, try a quarter," he said.

"Oh no, I have my own from the bus. Is this where you put it?"

"Correct. Right there."

She slipped in a quarter like it was made out of silk, pulled the arm very gently toward her and eased it back up; you would think it was sprained.

They gazed at two cherries, and five quarters tinkled out.

"Hey," Howard said, "I told you. Beginner's luck."

"It seemed so easy," she said, shaking her head and smiling at the cherries.

"Winning is so easy it can make you think you invented it," he said solemnly.

She nodded, she was a listener. "Well," she said, "as long as I'm Thomas Edison I'll put it all back."

"Well, it's your money, but why not keep three quarters and play two?"

"How about playing three?"

"Okay, that's a decent compromise."

She slid in the silk coins and caressed the arm down and then up. One bar revolved into the window and held, then another, then very promptly the third.

"Holy catfish," Howard said.

Even while she was asking, Are three bars good? the quarters jingled out; they were acting like they couldn't *wait* to be nice to her; quarters could do that with certain people . . .

"Three bars *must* be good," she said; he looked her over; yeah, she was sincere.

"They're excellent," he said. "You wanna pick up your loot or just leave it there and let it pile up?"

"Oh I'll leave it there, I'm not even playing on my money."

Pittsburgh Phil couldn't have said it better. She inserted three quarters with hands as soft as a great shortstop and did the nice easy pull. A 7 spun into place, then another; the third 7 didn't even hesitate. The quarters were Niagara Falls. Watching them with the smile, although she wasn't fainting dead away, she said, "I always did like that number."

"Lady," he said, "the main thing is the number likes *you*."

She turned full face while the last of the quarters tumbled out. "Well, at least for the moment, and you've been very helpful. I forgot my manners. I'm Carrie Greenbaum."

He shook the soft hand. "I know. I'm Howard Fu. You used to bring your husband's shirts to my place."

"Oh I'm sorry, sometimes I have a terrible memory." The smile flashed away, but then returned. "Of course. Your wife was . . . Oh dear . . ."

"Harriet. Practically the same name." And about the only thing that *was* the same . . . "Yeah," he said, "Mr. Greenbaum was a very nice man."

"Yes, he was." She smiled down at the pile of quarters. "He'd be so happy to see me winning . . ."

They had lunch in an indoor mall, which, he explained to her only when they were finished, used to be the site of the Steel Pier. She handled it fine. While she listened carefully, he explained that he was retired now, but between Atlantic City and Belmont he was busier than ever. He had always done a nice job of listening, so he nodded and said uh-huh as she told him she was also pretty busy, with Schools for Israel and fund-raisers like International Cheese Week and different Caribbean festivals at the temple. Still, there comes a time when you just want to be by yourself. He said, Pardon me, but that's the understatement of the week. Over ice cream she said, "There's a French laundry in your old place, isn't there?"

"Yeah," he said with a shrug. "But it's still mine. Up to a point. The rest of it belongs to my son."

"It must be gratifying to have your son follow you in your business . . ."

He looked into the clear eyes. "Not if he changes it to a French laundry."

She nodded very slowly as if memories were making her head pretty heavy. "That's what they call progress, isn't it?"

He nodded back, hard. "That's just what he told me. 'Progress, Pop'"

After paying the check—she insisted on at least leaving the tip—he asked her if going into Playboy would bother her. She said, No, why should it? Well, my daughter-in-law gave me holy heck when she found out I went in there, so I never tell her anymore, but if *you* don't mind, I got very lucky there last week . . . She said, Sure, let's go.

He didn't get lucky. But Carrie did. She scooped out forty more dollars in quarters and her fingers got so grimy that he got her a couple of towelettes. What a nice touch, she said. With a smile that he had to work on he said, "I'm glad one of us could use them."

"Well, what's the verdict on Atlantic City?" he said as they sped through Jersey.

"I had a delightful day, Mr. Fu. I really did. And I

appreciate your showing me what to do. I'm only sorry you didn't have a good day."

The funny thing was he didn't feel like bashing the window; his neck wasn't even stiff. "I got a philosophy. There's always *mañana* . . . How about it, Mrs. Greenbaum?" He didn't translate, it wouldn't be necessary . . .

"Well why not?" No song and dance about plans or checking the calendar; just why not? And instead of beaming out at the miserable Jersey moonscape, she listened with complete attention as he explained the maddening intricacies of blackjack and the absolute treachery of roulette.

## II

Howard left the house quickly the next morning without giving Thomas and Barbara time to do anything except exchange one of their fast glances. Carrie was right on the dot, waiting in front of the stationery store where they had bought the bus tickets the night before. Central America Night would just have to limp along without her.

"Did you tell them you weren't feeling so hot?"

"Oh no." The smile shut down a little. "I never do that. I told Jenny something else had come up." She brightened and so did he. He had goofed, but it was buried. Harriet would ride a goof like it was a six-day bike race.

When they got to Atlantic City they took the jitney to Harrah's, because, Howard explained, they had the same first initial. All right, she said.

As they walked into the clatter and bustle he asked her if she'd like to try a little blackjack. She could play it small because they kept the minimum down till later, but there was nothing like your own personal money to get in the swing. She didn't think so, she would just wander around until, and she smiled wide, she found a machine that had been absolutely miserable; they could meet right here for lunch. Okay, he said, don't forget to ask for towelettes. She liked that, he could tell. And she didn't wish him luck, she wished him *oceans* of luck.

He sat down at a table that was sending out letters of invitation, and decided to play it super-safe for a while to get a jump on recouping yesterday's disaster. He worked through two packs of cigarettes and managed to stay even, although a Puerto Rican dealer who kept rotating his shoulders like he was working out for the football season thought that tossing him an ace, a picture or a ten as a first card was a federal offense.

"How is it going?" the quiet voice asked.

He turned. A smile, but a concerned smile. "Hello, Bar Bar Bar. Hanging in, keepin' my nose above water. How about you?"

"Not so terrific today. I only won ten dollars."

"There's this thing about only winning ten dollars. It beats losing. Like that." He pointed at his stand-pat hand of fifteen and the PR dealer's twenty. "Okay." He picked up his remaining chips and stood. "Let's move to another table."

"Why?"

"Change my luck."

She turned as serious as he had seen her these two days. "I don't know anything about it, except what you told me, but if I may, why not just change your strategy? That way you don't give in to superstition."

He said gently. "People who play cards are superstitious."

"Maybe they shouldn't be."

He looked at the now-serious face and sat down and the dealer said, Are you in, sir? and he answered, Yeah, I'm in.

When his three cards added up to sixteen he turned to her. And she nodded, just like that. He scratched the top of the table softly and for a moment closed his eyes. He opened them to a four.

"Twenty should do it," she whispered.

He whispered back, "Don't hold your breath. This guy is from the FALN. He gets twenty-one. Watch."

He got nineteen.

"See?" she said, as he picked up two chips and fondled them, gazed at them. "Another thing . . ."

"I hear you."

"You should think more positively, if you don't mind the advice."

"I don't mind."

The dealer rotated his shoulders and began to shuffle. Howard said to her, forgetting the whisper, "Okay, from now on, I think positive."

"How will you do that?"

"How? Just think in this whole wide world *I* am the guy that has to win."

"I suppose that's all right . . ."

He swiveled around on his chair. "Hey, don't stop now."

"Well . . . I just think it's more productive if you take the personal aspect out of things . . ."

"How are you gonna take the personal aspect out of cards?"

"Well, *every*thing is personal when it comes to that."

The dealer rolled his neck and asked him to cut. "I never cut," he said and handed the yellow cards to the man beside him who shrugged and cut. He said to her as the dealer packed the cards in the tray, "How would *you* think positive?"

"Oh . . . I don't know . . ."

"How, Carrie?"

The amazingly smooth forehead crinkled. "Let's see. All right, you asked for it." Crinkly smile. "When I was having my first child, Franklin, I was frightened to death. So I thought about Magellan."

"Magellan?"

"That's right. I decided if he could overcome a tremendous challenge, so could I."

The dealer cleared his throat. Howard swung back and pushed in two chips for ten dollars. Along came a four. He sighed, scratched, kept scratching and built up to eighteen. A sweep of the hand cut the dealer off. Over his shoulder he whispered, "What did he do?"

She bent close to his ear. "He sailed around the world for the first time. The *first* time. He was my greatest hero in high school."

"Was he a blackjack player?"

"Oh no. Well I don't think so." Without even looking he knew the smile was a honey. "Franklin," she whispered, "was beautiful and completely normal."

He looked down like he was studying his knees and closed his eyes. One thing he had was an imagination; Barbara had often said that, the last time when he told her Thomas would make a terrific Red Guard. Lonely, tough Magellan sailed through the casino on his way around the world: sharks, whales, cannibals, blowguns, headhunters, Amazons, Harriet's crazy family, seaweed, tidal waves, Jap savages, goof-off crew . . . He opened his eyes. The PR dealer's shoulders were quiet as a rock. His cards were so far over that Magellan was yelling with laughter all the way from Borneo.

They went to Atlantic City five times the next week. The third time she thought she would like to try a little roulette. He said you might as well see what a miserable game is all about. "I don't wanna tell you what to do, but you might want to take it easy and start out playing colors." She placed five chips on the black, but then at the last second murmured, "Oh heck," snatched them up and plunked them down on 13. He gazed in absolute agony but zipped up his twitching lip. The ball raced around the wheel like the nutty hamster he had bought Thomas at seven. It nestled in 13.

"Holy Moses," he croaked.

The croupier, a tall Irish girl, shoved stacks of chips at Carrie who smiled at them. She continued to look and smile while he kept his big mouth shut, but then she pushed one of the stacks back on the 13. There was a limit.

"Look," he said, "you're the Monte Carlo kid, but the odds against a number coming right back are out of sight."

"You think so?"

"It's my opinion, but ask anybody."

"What should I do?"

"Well . . . why not spread it around, you can even lap over two numbers, even four numbers . . ."

"But doesn't that reduce what I win?"

He had to look and nod at the Irish girl who grinned right back. "Yeah," he said, "but it covers you pretty good."

"But I have a hunch about the thirteen."

"Then take a piece of it."

The Irish girl got serious and hovered over her wheel. Carrie neatly placed her chips around the board, including a piece of the 13. The hamster started racing, the girl rasped out, "No more bets." He lit a cigarette.

The ball couldn't wait, it made a beeline for the 13 like Mom and Pop were waiting and he was late for dinner. Miss Dublin placed her glass tube on the magic number, swept the table clean, pushed a small stack at Carrie and a young girl in shorts up to there.

"From now on," he said, "if I open the biggest mouth in America, don't listen."

"Oh I'll listen, all right." She patted his shoulder. "But I'll still play my hunch."


And that's what she did. The following week at Belmont. They were leaning on the rail at the paddock. She explained.

"You mean," Howard said, "if the horse *looks* at you while he's walkin' around?"

"That's right."

"If that's your hunch, that's your hunch . . ." He glanced at her sideways. "But isn't that very *personal*?"

"Well yes and no. Most of them ignore me. That's fine, that's their privilege. But if one *looks*, then it's between the two of us. It's a connection. He's telling me, let's trust each other, that's a *partner*ship."

"Suppose a few look?"

"I have a theory. One will always look harder."

"Okay." He leaned on the rail and looked hard; one horse glanced casually at him, but he was acting so rank it must have been a warning glance. He turned. "How about this? Take the second-hardest look and fill out an exacta?"

"What's that?"

"You pick one horse to win and one to come in second. Exactly."

"Howard, are you saying, pick one horse to lose?"

"Well, I'm saying come in *second* . . ."

"Second is losing," she said quietly.

"Forget it," he said. "Exactas drive you nuts."

That afternoon her system produced two winners. He hit no winners, but he did pick a forty-two-dollar exacta in the seventh. He didn't tell her.

When he walked into the house that night Thomas was waiting near the fireplace with his arms folded. Barbara was sitting near the TV with her legs crossed in that double-jointed way and she was holding on to one knee. He walked past them into the kitchen, pulled out a Budweiser, popped the ring and walked back. He sat down in his chair, drank and set the can down in an ashtray. Nobody asked him if he wanted a glass; they knew better.

"How'd you make out, Pop?" Thomas said.

"Not too bad." He took another drink.

"What's not too bad?"

"So-so."

"Did you break even?"

"Close."

"How close?"

He drank again. "Win some, lose some. Are you the district attorney?"

Barbara switched legs like greased lightning and grasped the other knee.

"No, Pop," Thomas said.

"So what's the third degree?"

Thomas leaned against the mantel, straightened out one of the smiling photos. "No third degree, Pop. We just don't want you to go overboard."

"I'm a big boy." He smiled at Barbara who shifted very slightly but didn't go into the crossover express.

"How did Mrs. Greenbaum make out, Pop?"

"Not too bad." He drank and set the can down with a clank.

"Want another one, Pop?"

"No thanks, I'll sit tight."

"Okay, Pop. Pop, can I ask you a question without you getting defensive?"

He looked them both over. "I don't know. Try. I don't promise a thing."

They finally did it, one of their speedball specials; they exchanged glances so fast a man with bad eyes would have missed it. Now that he had the signal, Thomas said, "Aren't you two getting very friendly?"

"What's it *to* you?"

"You said you wouldn't get defensive, Pop."

"I didn't say peanuts."

"Wait a minute, Thomas," Barbara said, still hanging on to her knee. "Dad, all we're trying to get at is the question of a possible relationship between you and Mrs. Greenbaum. That's all."

"That's a lot."

"Pop—"

"Please hold it, Thomas." She had a nice low voice when she was leaning on Thomas. "Dad, look at it this way. This neighborhood is very important to us. You and Tommy worked like dogs to get where we are. Dad, the neighborhood is an open book."

"Yeah?"

"You told me that yourself, remember?"

"I remember."

"Sure you do. Dad, a lot of people are very aware that you and Mrs. Greenbaum have been seen together."

"Is it in the paper?"

The speed-glance. "Dad, they are very aware of it."

"So what?"

"Simply the fact that you are *vul*nerable." She leaned forward an inch and over the clenched legs looked at him with big, serious eyes.

"I'm doing okay," he said.

She sat back that inch. "Of course you are. And we want you to *continue* doing okay—"

"That's all we want, Pop. We don't—"

Her firm, slender hand was stopping traffic. "Hold it, please, Thomas." Thomas held it. "Dad, being vulnerable, you could get involved before you know it."

"We're not eloping tomorrow."

"Pop, why do you have to—"

"All right, Tom, all right. Thank you. Dad, we know you're not. That's not the point. The point is A leads to B, B leads to C. Before you know it . . ." Barbara always cocked her head to one side as she shrugged, like she was covering two bets. He flashed to Carrie and the calm, inner smile.

"She happens to be a very nice person," he said.

"Dad, I would not argue that statement for one second."

"Her husband was also a very nice person. Paid cash. On *time*." He looked at Thomas. He looked at her.

"Of course, Dad. More than nice. Excellent. Both of them."

"He never gave me a hard time."

"I'm sure of that, Dad." Thomas let out a little sigh which she jumped right on top of. "Dad, they are and were excellent. No argument. But you are a very *special* man. You are *our* concern. We don't want to see that special man get hurt." She actually sat back, with her legs crossed. The room was quiet; if you have nothing to say, you have nothing to say. He and Barbara understood that. Not Thomas.

"Pop, do you bet for her?"

She stared at Thomas. Howard said, "What does that mean?"

"What I said. Do you bet for her with your money?"

"I cash in every T bill and give it to her. I also bet for Frank Sinatra."

"If that's supposed to be an answer, it's nowhere, Pop."

"Oh Tommy, Tommy—"

"Just take it easy. Whose father is he?" She folded

into herself so hard she might never be able to get up. That was perfectly okay with Thomas. He nodded. "All right, Pop, you said you were a big boy so I'll give it to you straight. From one big boy to another—"

"Go on, big boy."

"All right. You know what they call them in Miami?"

"Dolphins?"

"Ha ha. Anthony Wang's kid goes to school down there, he'll tell you. *Barracudas.*"

"Is that a fact?"

"Call him up right now and ask him."

"Anthony's a jerk and his kid takes after his father."

"Did you ever?" But she was holding onto herself and Thomas had to keep charging on his own. He let go of the mantel. "All right, Pop. Ask somebody impartial. Ask Max. The druggist. You know what he'll tell you? *She* always wore the pants. *Always.*"

He swung casually to Barbara, the poor kid had made a very game effort. "Hey, impartial? Max made a play for her. She told me herself. And the woman is a hundred percent honest."

He kept looking at Barbara, which was driving Thomas up the wall, the way it used to with Harriet. "Yeah, Pop? Yeah? Well, I got news for you. Hot off the press. They *always* wear the pants."

She came suddenly out of her trance. "Oh Tom, must you always fall back on stereotypes? The next thing you'll—"

"I asked you once, whose father is he? It is time to

call a spade a spade for crissake. I only want the man to put a zipper on his wallet as well as his pants."

"God, how gross. You are making this unbelievably gross."

"You think so? You think a man curls up and goes to sleep at his age? He's a strong man. He's a healthy man. You think *she's* packed it in? Max says she goes to Elizabeth Arden once a month. She knows—"

"Never mind what she knows. Will you come out of the gutter and discuss this rationally?"

"Are *you* naive? Do you realize how naive you are?"

But Howard was outside, walking fast and hard to Cuddahy's and thinking how quiet and peaceful and smiling she always was.

She wasn't smiling. She was sitting in the kitchen, listening to Franklin. Franklin across the table, softly, firmly: "It happens to be a fact, I couldn't possibly make it up. They'd rather gamble than eat."

"Maybe it's exaggerated a bit," she said gravely.

"Mama, they'll bet on the number of hairs on your head. Which floor the elevator will stop on. It's just a way of life. Did you ever hear of fan-tan?"

"No."

"It's a card game. It's practically baseball to them. The national pastime."

"He didn't make me do anything I didn't want to do, Franklin."

His mouth drooped for an instant but then straightened out. "I'm not trying to upset you," he said. "If it sounds that way, I'm sorry."

"I know, Franklin."

"I *want* you to enjoy yourself."

"I know."

"But in appropriate parameters."

She sat quietly and then reached over and touched his hand. "Don't aggravate so."

He patted her hand and said, "I'm Papa's son, I can't help it."

"He could have helped it and so can you. Franklin, you have no idea how beautiful the horses are."

He looked around the room before answering. "He never went to the track in his *entire* life."

"Neither of us did."

"May I ask a question?"

"Of course."

"What would he say?"

"I really don't know."

"Do you think he would say throw your money away on fan-tan?"

"I doubt it, Franklin."

"I'm going to tell you something. I never mentioned this because I never like to bring my work home. Last year we had to let a top man go after just six months. Number three in his class. Law Review. He just couldn't stop. It got into his blood. Like hepatitis."

"I promise I'll be careful."

He got up and walked to the refrigerator and came back and sat down. When he did that . . . "Mama, I'm going to do something I really don't want to do. It has never been my style, but I couldn't look at myself in the morning if I didn't do this. Mama, I do not want you to go to Atlantic City with that man again. If you enjoy it that much and feel it's important to you, it's *that* important to you, then *I'll* take you. I'll call in sick. That includes Belmont."

She covered his hand and said gently, "Thank you, that's very sweet. But it will have to be the week after next. Next week we're going to Las Vegas."

They spent four days at Caesar's Palace and she broke even while Howard lost a hundred, which he said was breaking even for him. The day after they flew back, since the horses had left Belmont, they drove up to Saratoga. They stayed in a motel outside of Glens Falls because it was so spur-of-the-moment, but they caught all nine races every day for six days, including the Sanford, where, he told her, Man o' War had been upset by Upset. And when they drove home, no one said anything to anyone. The next day, however, Howard called and asked if she could come over, it was fairly important, but take your time.

He met her at the door and they walked inside and there was Franklin, standing in the center of the living room having one of his earnest conversations with two people. They could only be Thomas and Barbara, no need even for an introduction. Although she got one, quickly from Howard, earnestly from Franklin. Along with, "Here, sit down, Mama."

He pointed to a lovely recliner and she took it, although she didn't recline. Howard pulled a hard chair alongside the recliner and sat down rather hard. Crossed his arms. Thomas and Barbara remained seated on a convertible sofa. Franklin slouched in the middle of everybody with his hands in his pockets. That meant he was chairman.

"Mama," he began, "and Mr. Fu," and he smiled at Howard who didn't smile back, "the three of us have taken the liberty of chatting together and we all agree that the time has come to openly discuss this situation." Thomas opened his mouth, but Barbara squeezed his arm and he shut it. "We," Franklin said, "that is, we three, really think the whole thing should be ventilated."

"All right," she said.

Scrunching his eyes together, which showed he was thinking hard, Franklin said, "Mama—and Mr. Fu—we could be wrong, although we don't think we are, but we believe a situation like this can only grow more complicated. Do you see our point?"

"I see it."

"Going to Atlantic City, or even to the track on a single-day basis is one thing. Going on extended trips is another. It puts the whole thing on a different plane. You see my point?"

"Yes, I do see it."

With his arms still folded, Howard said, "We stayed in separate rooms."

"That rates a medal, Pop," Thomas said before Barbara's hand could shoot out. Howard shrugged.

"Thomas," Franklin said, "we *did* agree?" Thomas sat back, Barbara nodded. Franklin scrunched his eyes some more (he'd had terrible crow's feet at seventeen) and said, "Mama—and Mr. Fu . . . Howard . . . it's quite obvious we cannot stop two adults from seeing each other. Even if we wanted to. The question is, where do we go from here?"

She looked at Howard and he gave her a quick nod. "We *had* thought of going to Reno," she said.

Thomas rolled his eyes around the room while Barbara clutched tightly. Franklin unscrunched his eyes. He even smiled. "In the old days, Mama," and he looked at everybody, "folks . . . in the old days they said so-and-so went to Reno to get Reno-vated. Meaning divorced."

"They had casinos before Vegas," Howard said.

"Really? I guess that took the sting out of Reno-vating." He walked to Carrie and peered down. "Mama, how involved are you?"

She felt Howard's eyes. "We enjoy going out," she said.

He took his hands out of his pockets. "Quite frankly, Mama, are you talking marriage?"

She turned toward Howard's eyes and Franklin's voice followed: "Mother, you have always been the most honest person I have ever known. . . . Are you?"

"No."

She looked up at Franklin who gazed at her for a moment, then stepped back and nodded at Thomas and Barbara. So fast that it could easily have been missed, they nodded back.

Howard was out of his chair like he had just hit a 50-1 shot, and everyone jumped, and he was pumping Franklin's hand and saying, "Mr. Greenbaum, you're okay, you're terrific," and he practically yanked Carrie to her feet and he said, "Holy smokes, Carrie, how about it, you wanna get married?"

Into the deathly silence she said, "Why yes, Howard."

### III

Stephen Greenbaum flew in from Fort Worth. He and Franklin had a meeting with Rabbi Weiss which was not too productive because the Rabbi kept saying why not look at the bright side, but never described the bright side. Meanwhile, Thomas and Barbara talked to Father Villensky, but Father Villensky hadn't seen Howard in twelve years and strongly suspected he'd gone back to Confucianism, in which case he wouldn't touch it with a ten-foot pole, this wasn't the old days, you know.

After a week of on-and-off discussions with her sons, Carrie told them, "We've decided to get married in Reno."

Franklin, who was looking very tired, said, "I don't know what's happening around here."

"It will be the best thing," she said, patting his hand.

"Do they have a temple in Reno?" he said, holding the bridge of his nose.

"How about going on TV in a casino?" Stephen said. Franklin stared at him.

"We'll go to a justice of the peace," she said.

"How about a little girl playing the wedding march on a baby grand?" Stephen said, and as Franklin stared, he murmured, "Jesus Christ."

"That's enough, Milton Berle," she said.

"You know me, Ma," Stephen said. "I'm harmless."

"I know you."

Franklin let go of his nose. "What about afterwards, Mama?"

"Afterwards we'll come back and set up housekeeping."

"Where?"

"Howard's cousin is in a new building near Mulberry Street. He can get us in."

"You're going to live in Chinatown?"

"It's a lovely building. It has balconies."

"Balconies? In Chinatown? Jesus Christ."

"Just keep calm, Franklin."

"Did you hear that, Steve?"

"I heard." He glanced at Carrie. "Ma's right, take it easy, Frankie. Ma, let me talk to him."

She got up. "All right, I'll have some Sanka, then I'm

going to take a bath and go to bed. It's enough for one night. I'm getting very tired of this, Steve."

"I know, Ma. You go inside and make your Sanka. I'll talk to him."

"No comedy, Steve."

"No, Ma, I promise."

She walked into the kitchen without another word. After a long time, with his head nodding, as if he were back in temple as a little boy, Franklin said, "My one wish, which has obviously been granted, is that there's no heaven."

Stephen nodded too, but hard, twice. "So he can't look down and see, right?"

"You got it," Franklin said. "He wasn't the world's greatest father, but he didn't deserve this."

"Frankie, maybe it's not so terrible."

Franklin looked at his brother; he was too tired to scrunch his eyes. "You sound like Weiss."

"Don't be a goddam idiot, Frankie."

"Thanks very much for your support. I knew I could count on you. Steve, I realize you're the original free-thinker and Tommy Manville was your role model, but I'll tell you what I think: I think it is *obscene*."

"She won't get pregnant, Frankie."

"Will you please cut that out? With my luck, there *is* a heaven, and he *is* looking down."

"All right, Frankie, you know what he would say? I'll tell you *exactly* what he would say. You want them to live in Jamaica Estates?"

———

Stephen flew back to Fort Worth the next day, but left a note saying please call when you hit Reno, I'll jump up and buy you a wedding brunch and cheer for you at the wheel of fortune. She called him that night and said she just might take him up on it.

They were to leave on a Wednesday. On Tuesday afternoon the phone rang in Franklin's office. Since Martha was on her coffee break, he picked it up and barked, "Yeah, Greenbaum."

"This is Thomas Fu."

"Oh. Yes. Look, Thomas, if you don't mind a little advice, let's leave it alone. Once the troops go in on D day, you can't pull them back."

"I don't know about D day, but you can relax."

He looked into the phone, shifted it to the other ear. "Your priest got to him?"

"No way. He's in the hospital."

". . . Hospital?"

"He got up during the night to go to the bathroom and keeled over. We heard this noise, it sounded like the ceiling came down. We found him on the floor."

". . . Yes?"

"We called 911, they're really on the ball, the ambulance got here in nothing flat."

"Yes?"

"The medics were right on the ball, I told them I'd write a letter for their file. It gives you some hope the city's coming back."

"What happened at the hospital, Thomas?"

"They admitted him immediately. One look, he was in, no red tape."

"Yes? And?"

"They think it's a stroke."

"Christ."

"They're not a hundred percent sure yet, but they're pretty sure. His right side is paralyzed and he can't talk."

". . . What's the prognosis?"

"They don't know yet, but it doesn't look too good. He's a tough old bird, but like they said, at his age you never know. Your mother is with him. It's funny, you never know, do you?"

"My mother?"

"She came right over as soon as I called. We figured it was the right thing to do."

"Of course. Where is he?"

"Saint Catherine. They've been great, they run a real tight ship."

"Yes, I've heard . . ."

"I don't want to jump the gun, but I think I better start looking around for a home."

"That's an arm and a leg, Thomas."

"You're telling me? That's why I better start looking."

"Do you have power of attorney?"

"Thank goodness. My cousin straightened me out on that when I took over the business."

"If you need any help . . . ?"

"Thanks, but Wallace is excellent. Well, it's crazy, but you can relax now."

"So can you, Thomas."

"Not exactly. I got the home to worry about."

"Of course. Can I visit?"

"You better call the hospital. And be prepared, I don't think he'll know you."

"Well . . . I'll give it a try."

"Okay, but be prepared. I'm not even sure he knows *me*."

"Thank you, Thomas. I appreciate your calling."

"Sure. Isn't this a kick in the pants?"

He rang off and immediately called Forth Worth. Then the hospital.


The lady at the desk asked his name and then walked to a phone and dialed and said, "He's here." She asked him to please wait. A tiny doctor from somewhere in East Asia came striding down the corridor, shook his hand and said he was very pleased he had come, please, let's talk over here. He took Franklin's arm and steered him to a leather sofa in the patient-lounge area. He briskly gave Franklin his name: it came out like Vanloppis or Tanlappis; Franklin called him sir. Sitting down, he looked like a high school boy.

"I'm the attending physician for Mr. Fu and I understand you are very interested in him, therefore I felt I should talk to you."

"That's very decent of you, sir. How . . . bad is it?"

"We are not sure yet. I have directed more tests. I prefer not to say too much until the results come back."

"Of course. Perhaps I should come back when you have a handle on things."

He shook his head briskly; he did everything like a brisk little brown bird. "Makes little difference. As long as you do not have a cold or other infection, it's all right. Infections are terrible."

"I understand, sir. I don't have a cold."

"Good. I really want to talk to you about your mother. Mrs. Carrie Greenbaum. She *is* your mother?"

"Yes, sir . . . Did she take it very hard?"

He nodded briskly. "I would say yes."

". . . I was afraid of that . . . Is she still here?"

Brisk nod. "She is in a room on his floor."

"Sir?"

He leaned forward and his white coat drooped on the floor. He said, "Your mother came to visit. The nurse on duty, a very competent person, came in to check on Mr. Fu as directed. She found your mother sitting very stiffly beside him and as a competent nurse she became alarmed. She spoke in quite a loud tone to your mother but received no response . . ."

"I don't quite follow you, sir."

"Please bear with me and all will become clear. The nurse immediately called me and I immediately came and examined your mother." Three brisk nods. "There was no response. She was unable to move at that point. We took the liberty of examining her purse, for this appeared to be an emergency. We discovered your name and number and I directed the nurse to call you." Nod, nod. "But of course you were on your way here. Fortunately, we had a bed. I took it on myself to place your mother in this hospital. You may wish to move her. Frankly, the professional care of this institution is the equal of those in Manhattan or even London. But that is up to you."

"I . . . this place is fine . . . I'm sure . . ."

"You can believe me. You will have to fill out some forms at the desk. You can do it later."

"I appreciate that . . . Sir, did she . . . have a . . . stroke?"

"Frankly, I am not sure. My own opinion is this: It is not an organic condition. As far as I can now see."

". . . What does that mean, sir?"

"I would say it is an hysterical reaction."

"Sir. I don't want to sound as though I'm questioning anything you've said, but I should tell you that my mother is an *amazingly* calm person . . ."

Sure enough, a brisk smile. "It is a question of semantics. We say hysterical in the sense of a *functional* response. Let me see . . . a state of mind?"

"You mean a shock?"

Brisk shrug. "Good enough. A shock."

"Can I see her?"

"No reason why you cannot. 303. Mr. Fu is in 307. Perhaps seeing you will help. Notify the nurse instantly if something extraordinary occurs. You can fill out the forms later." He held out his hand and Frank-

lin took it and they shook briskly. "Good luck, Mr.
Greenbaum, we try with equal force, no matter the
age, I have seen this condition a number of times."
And he was striding briskly down the hall with his coat
flapping around his ankles.

She was staring at the ceiling when he walked in, but
as he approached the bed her eyes shifted and fixed on
his face. The pupils were very dilated. He didn't sit
down.

"Mama, do you know who I am?"

She looked up at him.

"It's Franklin." He wanted to touch her hand but he
didn't. "You can fight this," he said.

She looked up at him.

"I feel terrible about . . . the whole . . . thing. Everybody feels terrible . . . But you can't let it lick
you . . ."

She looked up at him.

He wanted to touch her forehead, check for fever.
"We're with you all the way . . . I called Steve, he's flying back . . ."

She looked up at him.

"Mama, that doctor looks like a very good man.
They work extra hard . . . You have terrific willpower,
next to you we were all cream puffs . . . Why don't you
try, Mama?"

She looked up at him.

"Mama, I have a client whose brother-in-law is a top

man at Rusk. I'll talk to him. This will work out, you'll see. But you have to cooperate."

She continued to look at him and he wanted to bend down and kiss her, but he turned and walked out and downstairs he filled out the forms. Then he went back to the office.

It was close to midnight when Carrie opened her eyes. She waited for a bit, then very carefully reached over and bent the gooseneck lamp close to the table and turned it on. She drew her legs up and out of the covers. Slowly, she lowered the guard rail. She swung around and located her slippers, then turned off the lamp. She sat there for a moment. Now she eased into the slippers, walked toward the crack of light under the door. She reached the door, opened it, looked out. The nurse at the end of the corridor was sipping from a cup and looking at a magazine.

She stepped out, closed her door, walked swiftly the few yards, keeping close to the wall. She opened the door to 307 and slipped inside. She closed the door, waited until she could see and then walked to his table and turned on the gooseneck and bent it far down. She lowered the guard rail and sat on his bed beside him.

His eyes fluttered open. He stared up at her. She leaned close to him and whispered, "It's all right, it's me, Howard, don't be afraid . . . Howard? Blink once if you can hear me. Go on."

He blinked once.

"Very good. Now, I want you to pay careful attention. Listen carefully now. You have a blackjack hand
of fifteen. You have decided to play it very bold. Howard, either you want a card or you don't. Remember,
*bold*. All right now, blink once if you want a card for
bold, blink twice if you just want to stand pat."

He stared up at her.

"Come on now. Once for bold, twice to stand pat."

He blinked once.

"*That's* a good boy. And you got a six for twenty-
one! Very good. Now Howard, listen to this. If you get
one bar when you play the bandit, how many more do
you need to win? Come on, Howard, how many? Blink
the number."

He blinked once. Again.

"That's *excellent*. You're doing beautifully. You see
how we'll work together? No matter what? Blink once
if you understand that."

He blinked once.

"Beautiful." She bent closer. "Don't worry and don't
be afraid; they'll never trick me into leaving you. All
right? Blink once if it's all right."

He blinked once.

"That's my Howard. All right, let's try another.
You're at the roulette wheel. You have all your chips
on thirteen. The wheel is spinning. Now Howard, you
can be very personal and just think about yourself, or
you can think about Magellan the way I showed you.
Now concentrate. Blink once if you're going to worry
about yourself. Blink *twice* if you're going to reach out

and go for Magellan. I'm right here, Howard, I'll *always* be here. Come on, is it going to be Magellan, Howard?"

He stared at her. A small round tear began to blossom at the inner corner of each eye.

# Of Love and Friendship

BY ARTURO VIVANTE

My father was a philosopher, who, right to the end of his life, thought he would make a living from his books. My grandfather, a law professor in Rome, soon saw this wasn't likely to happen and, in the hope that his son could become self-supporting, bought him a country estate in Tuscany, a few miles outside of Siena.

The place was rather remote, and Siena, though a pretty town, wasn't the lively center it once had been. It was, in fact, dormant. Tourism, which before the First World War had livened the town up and which was to liven it up again after the Second, was—with Fascism and the Depression—down in the thirties. The university, though one of the world's oldest, had only the faculties of medicine and law. The hospital, also ancient, was the single busy place except for the market on market days. The schools, most of them converted from monasteries and convents, retained their original bare, ascetic look. On winter evenings the town was positively grim. Stark, too, with its narrow, windy streets. As if the cold and frozen Middle Ages

weren't enough, the walls were pasted with death no-
tices, and you were quite likely to meet men in black
hoods—members of the medieval confraternity of the
Misericordia—leading a funeral procession. The mor-
bidity rate in Siena was among the highest in the nation. Owners of the nearby villas—stodgy, titled
people—for the most part passed their time in a club,
playing bridge or billiards. My mother would have preferred Florence. Much. But she wasn't used to having
her own way, and raised no objections to the choice of
Siena.

To make up for its lacks, she and my father—both of
whom had grown up in Rome and liked company—
invited friends, old and new, to come and stay. There
was an eccentric English painter of moonlight scenes.
Once, she arrived from Rome sometime during the
night, set up her easel in the middle of the drive, and at
dawn, her painting finished, rang our doorbell. There
was a lanky, clever, spectacled French poet and illustra-
tor in plus fours with the energy of an electric eel. And
there was a young woman writer from Florence with
long bleached-blond hair and plenty of makeup, a hy-
pochondriac, insanely in love, often in tears. She was
supersensitive, had mediumistic powers, and sometimes
in her bedroom late at night she, my parents, and another friend would have séances, from which my two
brothers, my little sister, and I were always excluded.

My mother was apt to change her mind about company and claim she wanted to be alone. The guests, she
said, were fine—very dear, congenial, and all that—but

everyone had the right to a bit of solitude. "Soon they'll go and we'll be alone, *cocchino*," she would tell me, and pat my knee. But when they finally did go— and sometimes they stayed for months—she would often fall into a silent, sombre mood. And we looked forward to a visitor, for then—at least at the front door—she would be forced to smile. We depended on her smile. Guests brought it on, and a hundred other things, of course—a brood of newborn chicks, fluffy and golden in a basket, looking up at her in unison, or the sun shining on a newborn leaf, or perhaps a letter. Not my father's jokes, I'm afraid, or his attentions. But a newborn leaf! An urge to draw it, or paint it, or embroider it (she said threads came in a greater variety of colors than did pigments) would assail her, and for a happy day it was a love affair between her and the leaf. She was a painter born. She never had an exhibition, though. She didn't care. She was too modest and at the same time too proud. Beyond worldly contest. A woman busy with the children and the house, and with her husband, who kept calling her—to read a paragraph he had written, to accompany him somewhere, to ask her for advice. She was never too busy to listen, never resentful of being interrupted, always ready to put away her work, though with a sigh. Most of her canvases were hidden in closets when they should have been hung not just in the house but in a gallery, a museum.

The relationship between her and my father: the hardest to imagine, the hardest to describe. Affectionate, loving even, but not passionate, not voluptuous—at least not on her part. Guests sometimes told me what a wonderful marriage my parents' was, that they'd never seen one that fared so well. Oh, they had the highest praise for it, and all the time I knew they were way off. She admired him for his being uninterested in a career, for his taste, for his liberal political opinions, for his tremendous dedication to his work. She believed in his philosophy. He was an extreme idealist, and most of the time she saw him as unassailably right. But she strained to understand his concepts. She was ready to agree with them, but they usually were beyond her grasp, just beyond her grasp; or, if she understood them, she wasn't able to argue with him about them, discuss them with him—only question them, ask questions, which he would answer affably but never in her language. An elusive element ran through his words, which in vain she tried to seize. She admired him, surely, but his thinking was beyond her. He encouraged her; he told her she had a very philosophical mind indeed, for there was no understanding a concept fully—everything needed to be deepened. She said he told her he'd married her because she didn't go by conventional values. Now, she asked, what kind of a reason was that for marrying you?

Did she love him? Or, rather, how did she love him? Almost like a son, like someone who had to be helped, comforted, humored, and consoled. But not quite like a son, either. He was more exacting than a son—irritable, willful, and so determined. At times, if she didn't take notice of something he was saying or misinterpreted something he had said or interrupted him, he would turn against her in a rage. I remember his sharp, hateful, self-righteous tone of voice—no swearing, insults, threats, or even shouts; just the tone. His lips taut. The words that seemed to be uttered by clenched teeth—by nothing soft, like lips or tongue, but only by the teeth. Words that came out rattling like small shot, propelled against her. I remember the silence with which she bore his anger. And rarely, perhaps stretching her arms down and back disconsolately, her replies, in a small voice: "Oh, but listen. . . . What can I say? I'm sorry." She didn't like people to make scenes, and for this reason, I think, she never left the room. I remember the stony silence that would follow, and her gloom.

Sometimes she couldn't stand it anymore. She seemed exhausted, at her wit's end. She wanted to be far away, alone. Once, wistfully, she told me that in her young days a workman had paid her some attention. "He talked to me as I walked along the Tiber. A bricklayer. I wonder what life would have been like with him. Simpler, perhaps. But then I wouldn't have had my little boys, my *ragazzini*," she said, and brushed her palm down my face lightly. And sometimes she would say, "I'll pack a small bag and leave; I feel like leaving; I'm going to leave; oh, yes, I am leaving." But she always stayed. She and he slept in separate rooms, as far apart as the big house would allow. But often he would be calling her, calling her, calling her . . .

And then about 1936, to save the situation, there came a guest who, especially in my mother's view, wasn't like any other guest we'd had—a complete original, and one for whose departure she never hoped. He would stay with us for a week or two, and come perhaps three or four times a year. No, he wasn't like anybody we had ever seen. Millo, that's what my mother called him. In Siena, he didn't go to the museums or the cathedral but, with a big old leather briefcase and a penknife, he went to the public park. His business was with the trees. He would be seen chipping away at the bark as if he had really come on something. A policeman or other public-spirited citizen would amble over to see just what he was up to. Everyone was curious about him. "Are you after mushrooms? Snails?" Smiling, and in a Genoese accent that sounded strange and worldly-wise to Tuscan ears, he would explain that he was collecting lichens, that this little thing he was cutting off the bark was, in fact, a lichen, and tell them its Latin name. Immediately they would start calling him *"Professore."* If they failed to be impressed, he would go on to say that some lichens had medicinal properties; this was almost certain to rouse their appreciation. Lichens, he told them, weren't parasites. The way he talked about them, they seemed to be possessed of all qualities. The little cut he made on the bark was insignificant, almost invisible, and he would be allowed to continue his pursuit. He had a scalpel and a hammer, too, and sometimes he chipped at a rock—for lichens, like moss, and perhaps more than moss, grew on practically anything and in just about any part of the world, even in the polar regions and the desert. This extraordinary interest, he explained, took him not just to parks and gardens but to deep woods and remote mountains. Ah, he was a cunning one for sure, or mad, and in either case they let him chip away.

Why such a passion? Well, for their beauty, mainly. Pale green and yellow, orange and gray, tenuous blue, silver, and almost white, spread by the wind or growing by contiguity, they improved the looks of almost anything they stuck to. Nor did they interfere with the host, except to give it cover. They made the tile roofs golden. They grew on ugly walls and monuments until their ugliness quite faded. They contributed to the ruins part of their weathered look. They were the hand of time, its patina, its gift, or an instrument it wielded. And if you looked at them closely you saw the marvel of their structure: lacework, filigree, touch-me-not golden curls. Always an adornment on the bare. How did nature manage to be so unerringly tasteful? Was it, as with the clouds, the magic hand of chance?

Soon Millo had most of us enthusiastic about lichens. My younger brother even started a collection of them.

My parents bought him a small microscope. With it, one could get lost in the leafy and branchlike maze. Another world, it seemed. Not flat, as in a slide, but three-dimensional, with shadows of its own, a place where hanging gardens mixed with orange goblets and gossamer strands. Millo himself had discovered several new species of lichens. Some bore his name. He had sold collections to Harvard, Columbia, and a number of other universities. We were most impressed.

"I've given them the discards," he would say. He was only joking; according to my mother, he sent excellent specimens, beautifully packed. "You should see those boxes," she said after she and my father had driven to Genoa to call on him. His own collection was in a state of flux—he was continuously exchanging samples with lichenologists in Sweden and other countries. In Italy he had the field to himself.

"Is this rare?" my younger brother and I would ask him, running in from the woods to the house, and always he would look at the samples with joy and encouraging exclamations. "Oh, oh, look what they've found!"

My mother seemed rejuvenated. It was as if he had borne into the house a gift that brought new life. My father, too, looked through the microscope and marvelled, going as far as to say—I have it from a letter—that the *Cladonia verticillata* had the pureness and beauty of a Donatello. And the cook, who also looked through the microscope, went into praises of nature that sounded something like those of the chorus in

Greek tragedy. We went for drives, and now there was more purpose in our outings,. "Oh, we've found some rare ones," he would say, and, putting a hand on my younger brother's shoulder once, he added, "And Sandro found one that may be quite new—a new species altogether. Of this I am sure: I've never seen it before; I just don't know it."

Was he serious?

Millo was friendly with my father, listened to him and read his work, agreed with it and praised it, but no more than my mother could he discuss it at length. And with my elder brother, who was very studious and not as fond of lichens as the rest of us, he read Greek—Homer, Aeschylus, and Sophocles. Giving Greek lessons was something he did in Genoa to supplement his income from the lichens, but, as with them, you had the feeling he would have done it quite apart from the money—for pleasure. The thing is, he was a poet. As a very young man, he had written a book of verse, "Thistle-down," which had been well received and was still remembered. Now he was about to bring out a new one, "Atiptoe." Brief poems, crisp as his lichens—indeed, so terse that at times it was hard to understand them at first sight.

He would often invite my parents out to dinner. "We are going to the notary public," he would say to us, trying to look serious but unable to look more than half serious. He was a friend of the whole family—of the cook and the maids, too, and of the curate who came to have dinner with us every Monday. But particularly of my mother.

They went for walks together, or, sitting on the garden brickwork, sipped coffee in the sun. Those, I think, were my mother's halcyon days. There was a joy in her conversation that was absent when she talked with my father. The reason was, in part, the subject matter. With my father, philosophy—perhaps some word he was looking for or some problem connected with the publication of a book—a letter he had received no reply to, his hopes for a huge peach orchard he had planted, the heavy financial situation in running the estate. And with Millo the lustre of a leaf, some comic scene in town that morning, how "inconceivably bad" an article was by a writer whom they knew.

My mother, really, did most of the talking. She had this extraordinary verve, which the wine helped, and which someone who listened as he did brought out. He listened with glee. He appreciated her sense of humor infinitely—as if he could listen forever and never have enough. He had the brightest eyes, and the glasses that he wore intensified not just his vision but his looks, added to him rather than detracted; one missed them if he took them off. He was chubby and not tall—shorter than my mother, who was spare and strong. His rounded face tended to the red, perhaps because of his fondness for wine. My father was slim and pale, with large, thoughtful eyes, and was considered very good-looking. As a boy, he had won a prize as the prettiest child in town. So at first I never thought of our friend as a rival to my father. He didn't seem the sort of person to rouse a passion. And then my mother, though she didn't seem as happy with my father as with Millo, had for my father such a strong attachment, such a deep affection, and respect and admiration. Perhaps these feelings—even put together and taken at their height—didn't amount to love, but at that time I was too young to make the distinction. Anyway, except during their tiffs, which I was quite prepared to disregard, I thought my mother loved my father thoroughly, loved him as much as he did her, though in a different way. My father paid a great many compliments to women and said silly things to them—even, and especially, in my mother's presence—but I don't think he was ever unfaithful to her. He had a puritanical streak, an austere control, and an intellectual nature that kept him above gossip or interest in petty things, and took him into a rather remote world crowded with hypotheses and theories.

Well, though I wasn't drawing any distinction between love and admiration, my brother was. Older than I by two years, he began to view the relationship between my mother and Millo with circumspection. He became morose, silent, and reluctant to read further Greek texts with him. He withdrew even more into his room and books. "They're always together," he said to me in a worried tone.

Poor boy, he loved my mother so much, had spent such a lot of time near her, had grown up amid her kisses and caresses, and now he felt the presence of someone else edging, intruding into his place, someone other than my father. My father's love, maybe because of its very nature, had never disturbed him, in the same way that my mother's affection for me, my younger brother, and my sister had never made him jealous. But this did. Perhaps it was that he felt protective toward my father, saw my father rather than himself as left out. At any rate, he began to resent the guest. Oh, not deeply or rudely—if anything, rather pitifully. My mother understood, of course, and I can see her kissing my brother on the forehead and stroking his curls, saying, "What is it, darling? Don't be sad." It wasn't easy to be sad in the house if she was happy, and, indeed, she could not really be happy if anyone in the house was sad. There was something in her of the nurse, the angel. Except, unlike angels, who are ever in a state of bliss, there was no paradise for her as long as anyone was in hell. And so, though my brother could hardly be described as being in hell, his state of mind disturbed her. "Come on, *cocchetto*, come with us to Florence. You need a change. You are always in your books. Let's go. We'll have fun. You and me, Papa, and Millo."

Millo would stand next to him and smile at him amiably. My brother would be persuaded to take the trip, and they would go to Florence, with my father driving his blue, open Chevrolet. And certainly the trip helped my brother's spirits. He would come back with a rare edition of Sophocles, perhaps, wrapped in tissue paper, and treat it as if he were handling a butterfly and barely let me touch it.

"I remember once they went to Rome together," my brother told me quite recently, by "they" meaning my mother and Millo, of course. *I* don't remember, or remember only vaguely. That *he* remembers shows how concerned he was.

Certainly I remember many trips, but most or all of them were with my father, in his car. We went to the sea, and Millo stayed with us there. And there were trips to the neighboring hill towns, and to Pisa, Lucca, and Pistoia, where my father bought fruit trees in the nurseries, and sometimes even to Genoa, Millo's home town. He always carried his old leather briefcase with him, for his lichens, and took more pleasure in strolling around the public parks than following us into the museums.

Often he would repair to a bar or coffee shop. These were like havens for him. He was a gourmet. In a restaurant he could become almost fierce with the chef if the cooking disappointed him. His usual mild, sweet countenance could turn an angry red. That was about the only aspect of him my mother had difficulty with. It was rare, though. He knew the best restaurants— especially in Genoa. There he would usually take you to the grottolike establishments near the harbor. The kitchen was near the entrance, so the fumes and steam could escape up through the open door. The cooks, usually women, greeted him by name. They would serve him well. They liked him—a real *intenditore* of their art.

He lived with his sister, who was unmarried. She worked in an office and looked after him. Recently, in an anthology, I've seen a poem of his in which she appears as a little girl. The poem is addressed to his father. "Father," it says, in rough translation, "even if you weren't my father I would have loved you, not only because one winter morning, glad, you gave us news of the first violet growing outside the window by the wall, and because you counted for us the lights of the houses as they went on up the mountain one by one, but also because once, as you were about to spank my little sister, you saw her cringing from you and, immediately stopping, you picked her up and kissed her and held her in your arms as if to protect her from the wicked fellow you'd been a moment before then."

My mother was forever writing to Millo, and often there was a letter from him in the mail. Both had the clearest writing, though there was nothing slow or childish about it. She wrote her letters on light, pale-blue stationery that she bought at Pineider, in Florence—one of the few luxuries she indulged in. She used not a fountain pen but a little wooden pen and nib that she dipped in a brass inkwell. Sometimes she would enclose a leaf, or a small drawing of it, or a sketch—perhaps the profile of one of us or of a guest—the thin line of her sharp pencil supplementing her description in quick, strong, black pen strokes. Sometimes I would watch her as she wrote, and in her face there was a reflection of the pleasure it showed when he was present; as she paused between one phrase and another, I could see that her eyes weren't on me or on the room but on whatever she was thinking of, and if I interrupted her she would say, "Be quiet a little now, love." One could see she put her best effort into her letters to him. All her letters were spirited and spontaneous, but those to him had something more—a certain brilliance.

After her death in 1963, Millo put together excerpts from them into a small book and published it. The letters spanned almost thirty years—from 1936 to 1963. "Reading them," one critic wrote, "it occurred to me that many of us ought to throw away the pen, which in our hands is a hoe and in hers a little April branch." They were full of quick flashes, impressions, vivid touches, thoughts about people, plants, places, books, her work, her mood, the war. Some of them were written to him from England, where we spent seven years as refugees during the war and where for a while he had even thought of coming to join us; a few from Africa, where she had gone after my sister had a baby there; most of them from the house in Siena; and one or two from the Rome clinic, a month before her death.

They were quite innocent, these letters, but my father, who in thirty years had never appeared jealous, now in his old age—he was in his late seventies— seemed to view the book with suspicion. Perhaps it was its form that troubled him—not whole letters but excerpts. The excerpts in themselves weren't compromising, but what about the rest? What had been left out? Why hadn't the opening and closing words or lines been included? No, he didn't altogether approve of the publication. He thanked Millo for the inscribed copy he received, but not with the cordiality of old times, and a word or two he used (which I never saw) upset Millo so much that he wrote assuring me that his relations with my mother had never been anything more than a strong friendship—that, in other words, they had not been lovers.

I thought of my mother's life, of how unreasonably and hatefully angry my father would get with her, of her silences, her patience, her impatience, and her gloom, of the many long winters in the lonely house, and I wrote to him that I was sorry to learn that they had not been lovers, that I wished they had been, for in that case my mother's life would have been richer, happier.

A few years later he died without answering that letter of mine. Now I think I know why: It didn't deserve an answer—if ever there was a relationship one didn't have to feel sorry about, it was theirs.

# Indian Summer of a Forsyte

## BY JOHN GALSWORTHY

### I

On the last day of May in the early nineties, about six o'clock of the evening, old Jolyon Forsyte sat under the oak tree below the terrace of his house at Robin Hill. He was waiting for the midges to bite him, before abandoning the glory of the afternoon. His thin brown hand, where blue veins stood out, held the end of a cigar in its tapering, long-nailed fingers—a pointed polished nail had survived with him from those earlier Victorian days when to touch nothing, even with the tips of the fingers, had been so distinguished. His domed forehead, great white mustache, lean cheeks, and long lean jaw were covered from the westering sunshine by an old brown Panama hat. His legs were crossed; in all his attitude was serenity and a kind of elegance, as of an old man who every morning put eau de Cologne upon his silk handkerchief. At his feet lay a woolly brown-and-white dog trying to be a Pomeranian—the dog Balthasar between whom and old Jolyon primal aversion had changed into attachment with the years. Close to his chair was a swing, and on the swing was seated one of Holly's dolls— called "Duffer Alice"—with her body fallen over her legs and her doleful nose buried in a black petticoat. She was never out of disgrace, so it did not matter to her how she sat. Below the oak tree the lawn dipped down a bank, stretched to the fernery, and, beyond that refinement, became fields, dropping to the pond, the coppice, and the prospect—"Fine, remarkable"—at which Swithin Forsyte, from under this very tree, had stared five years ago when he drove down with Irene to look at the house. Old Jolyon had heard of his brother's exploit—that drive which had become quite celebrated on Forsyte 'Change. Swithin! And the fellow had gone and died, last November, at the age of only seventy-nine, renewing the doubt whether Forsytes could live forever, which had first arisen when Aunt Ann passed away. Died! and left only Jolyon and James, Roger and Nicholas and Timothy, Julia, Hester, Susan! And old Jolyon thought: "Eighty-five! I don't feel it—except when I get that pain."

His memory went searching. He had not felt his age since he had bought his nephew Soames's ill-starred house and settled into it here at Robin Hill over three years ago. It was as if he had been getting younger every spring, living in the country with his son and his grandchildren—June, and the little ones of the second marriage, Jolly and Holly; living down here out of the racket of London and the cackle of Forsyte 'Change, free of his boards, in a delicious atmosphere of no

work and all play, with plenty of occupation in the per-
fecting and mellowing of the house and its twenty
acres, and in ministering to the whims of Holly and
Jolly. All the knots and crankiness, which had gathered
in his heart during that long and tragic business of
June, Soames, Irene his wife, and poor young Bosinney,
had been smoothed out. Even June had thrown off her
melancholy at last—witness this travel in Spain she
was taking now with her father and her stepmother.
Curiously perfect peace was left by their departure;
blissful, yet blank, because his son was not there. Jo
was never anything but a comfort and a pleasure to
him nowadays—an amiable chap; but women, somehow—even the best—got a little on one's nerves, unless
of course one admired them.

Far off a cuckoo called; a wood pigeon was cooing
from the first elm tree in the field, and how the daisies
and buttercups had sprung up after the last mowing!
The wind had got into the sou'west, too—a delicious
air, sappy! He pushed his hat back and let the sun fall
on his chin and cheek. Somehow, today, he wanted
company—wanted a pretty face to look at. People
treated the old as if they wanted nothing. And with the
un-Forsytean philosophy which ever intruded on his
soul, he thought: "One's never had enough! With a
foot in the grave one'll want something, I shouldn't be
surprised!" Down here—away from the exigencies of
affairs—his grandchildren, and the flowers, trees, birds
of his little domain, to say nothing of sun and moon
and stars above them, said, "Open, sesame," to him

day and night. And sesame had opened—how much, perhaps, he did not know. He had always been responsive to what they had begun to call "Nature," genuinely, almost religiously responsive, though he had never lost his habit of calling a sunset a sunset and a view a view, however deeply they might move him. But nowadays Nature actually made him ache, he appreciated it so. Every one of these calm, bright, lengthening days, with Holly's hand in his, and the dog Balthasar in front looking studiously for what he never found, he would stroll, watching the roses open, fruit budding on the walls, sunlight brightening the oak leaves and saplings in the coppice, watching the water-lily leaves unfold and glisten, and the silvery young corn of the one wheatfield; listening to the starlings and skylarks, and the Alderney cows chewing the cud, flicking slow their tufted tails; and every one of these fine days he ached a little from sheer love of it all, feeling perhaps, deep down, that he had not very much longer to enjoy it. The thought that some day—perhaps not ten years hence, perhaps not five—all this world would be taken away from him, before he had exhausted his powers of loving it, seemed to him in the nature of an injustice brooding over his horizon. If anything came after this life, it wouldn't be what he wanted; not Robin Hill, and flowers and birds and pretty faces—too few, even now, of those about him! With the years his dislike of humbug had increased; the orthodoxy he had worn in the sixties, as he had worn side whiskers out of sheer exuberance, had long dropped off, leaving him reverent before three things alone—beauty, upright conduct, and the sense of property; and the greatest of these now was beauty. He had always had wide interests, and, indeed, could still read *The Times*, but he was liable at any moment to put it down if he heard a blackbird sing. Upright conduct, property—somehow, they were tiring; the blackbirds and the sunsets never tired him, only gave him an uneasy feeling that he could not get enough of them. Staring into the stilly radiance of the early evening and at the little gold and white flowers on the lawn, a thought came to him: This weather was like the music of *Orfeo*, which he had recently heard at Covent Garden. A beautiful opera, not like Meyerbeer, nor even quite Mozart, but, in its way, perhaps even more lovely; something classical and of the Golden Age about it, chaste and mellow, and the Ravogli "almost worthy of the old days"—highest praise he could bestow. The yearning of Orpheus for the beauty he was losing, for his love going down to Hades, as in life love and beauty did go—the yearning which sang and throbbed through the golden music, stirred also in the lingering beauty of the world that evening. And with the tip of his cork-soled, elastic-sided boot he involuntarily stirred the ribs of the dog Balthasar, causing the animal to wake and attack his fleas; for though he was supposed to have none, nothing could persuade him of the fact. When he had finished, he rubbed the place he had been scratching against his master's calf, and settled down again with his chin over the instep of the disturbing boot. And into old Jolyon's mind came a sudden recollection—a face he had seen at that opera three weeks ago—Irene, the wife of his precious nephew Soames, that man of property! Though he had not met her since the day of the "At Home" in his old house at Stanhope Gate, which celebrated his granddaughter June's ill-starred engagement to young Bosinney, he had remembered her at once, for he had always admired her—a very pretty creature. After the death of young Bosinney, whose mistress she had so reprehensibly become, he had heard that she had left Soames at once. Goodness only knew what she had been doing since. That sight of her face—a side view—in the row in front, had been literally the only reminder these three years that she was still alive. No one ever spoke of her. And yet Jo had told him something once—something which had upset him completely. The boy had got it from George Forsyte, he believed, who had seen Bosinney in the fog the day he was run over—something which explained the young fellow's distress—an act of Soames towards his wife—a shocking act. Jo had seen her, too, that afternoon, after the news was out, seen her for a moment, and his description had always lingered in old Jolyon's mind—"wild and lost" he had called her. And next day June had gone there—bottled up her feelings and gone there, and the maid had cried and told her how her mistress had slipped out in the night and vanished. A tragic business altogether! One thing was certain—Soames had never been able to lay hands on her again. And he was living at Brighton, and journey-

ing up and down—a fitting fate, the man of property!
For when he once took a dislike to anyone—as he had
to his nephew—old Jolyon never got over it. He remembered still the sense of relief with which he had
heard the news of Irene's disappearance. It had been
shocking to think of her a prisoner in that house to
which she must have wandered back, when Jo saw her,
wandered back for a moment—like a wounded animal
to its hole after seeing that news, "Tragic death of an
Architect," in the street. Her face had struck him very
much the other night—more beautiful than he had remembered, but like a mask, with something going on
beneath it. A young woman still—twenty-eight perhaps. Ah, well! Very likely she had another lover by
now. But at this subversive thought—for married
women should never love: once, even, had been too
much—his instep rose, and with it the dog Balthasar's
head. The sagacious animal stood up and looked into
old Jolyon's face. "Walk?" he seemed to say; and old
Jolyon answered: "Come on, old chap!"

Slowly, as was their wont, they crossed among the
constellations of buttercups and daisies, and entered
the fernery. This feature, where very little grew as yet,
had been judiciously dropped below the level of the
lawn so that it might come up again on the level of the
other lawn and give the impression of irregularity, so
important in horticulture. Its rocks and earth were beloved of the dog Balthasar, who sometimes found a
mole there. Old Jolyon made a point of passing
through it because, though it was not beautiful, he in-

tended that it should be, some day, and he would think: "I must get Varr to come down and look at it; he's better than Beech." For plants, like houses and human complaints, required the best expert consideration. It was inhabited by snails, and if accompanied by his grandchildren, he would point to one and tell them the story of the little boy who said: "Have plummers got leggers, Mother?" "No, sonny." "Then darned if I haven't been and swallowed a snileybob." And when they skipped and clutched his hand, thinking of the snileybob going down the little boy's "red lane," his eyes would twinkle. Emerging from the fernery, he opened the wicket gate, which just there led into the first field, a large and parklike area, out of which, within brick walls, the vegetable garden had been carved. Old Jolyon avoided this, which did not suit his mood, and made down the hill towards the pond. Balthasar, who knew a water rat or two, gamboled in front, at the gait which marks an oldish dog who takes the same walk every day. Arrived at the edge, old Jolyon stood, noting another water lily opened since yesterday; he would show it to Holly tomorrow, when "his little sweet" had got over the upset which had followed on her eating a tomato at lunch—her little arrangements were very delicate. Now that Jolly had gone to school—his first term—Holly was with him nearly all day long, and he missed her badly. He felt that pain too, which often bothered him now, a little dragging at his left side. He looked back up the hill. Really, poor young Bosinney had made an uncommonly good job of the house; he would have done very well for himself if he had lived! And where was he now? Perhaps, still haunting this, the site of his last work, of his tragic love affair. Or was Philip Bosinney's spirit diffused in the general? Who could say? That dog was getting his legs muddy! And he moved towards the coppice. There had been the most delightful lot of bluebells, and he knew where some still lingered like little patches of sky fallen in between the trees, away out of the sun. He passed the cow houses and the hen-houses there installed, and pursued a path into the thick of the saplings, making for one of the bluebell plots. Balthasar, preceding him once more, uttered a low growl. Old Jolyon stirred him with his foot, but the dog remained motionless, just where there was no room to pass, and the hair rose slowly along the center of his woolly back. Whether from the growl and the look of the dog's stivered hair, or from the sensation which a man feels in a wood, old Jolyon also felt something move along his spine. And then the path turned, and there was an old mossy log, and on it a woman sitting. Her face was turned away, and he had just time to think: "She's trespassing—I must have a board put up!" before she turned. Powers above! The face he had seen at the opera—the very woman he had just been thinking of! In that confused moment he saw things blurred, as if a spirit—queer effect—the slant of sunlight perhaps on her violet-gray frock! And then she rose and stood smiling, her head a little to one side. Old Jolyon thought: "How pretty she is!" She did not speak, neither did he; and he realized why with a certain admiration. She was here no doubt because of some memory, and did not mean to try and get out of it by vulgar explanation.

"Don't let that dog touch your frock," he said; "he's got wet feet. Come here, you!"

But the dog Balthasar went on towards the visitor, who put her hand down and stroked his head. Old Jolyon said quickly:

"I saw you at the opera the other night; you didn't notice me."

"Oh, yes! I did."

He felt a subtle flattery in that, as though she had added: "Do you think one could miss seeing you?"

"They're all in Spain," he remarked abruptly. "I'm alone; I drove up for the opera. The Ravogli's good. Have you seen the cow houses?"

In a situation so charged with mystery and something very like emotion he moved instinctively towards that bit of property, and she moved beside him. Her figure swayed faintly, like the best kind of French figures; her dress, too, was a sort of French gray. He noticed two or three silver threads in her amber-colored hair, strange hair with those dark eyes of hers, and that creamy-pale face. A sudden sidelong look from the velvety brown eyes disturbed him. It seemed to come from deep and far, from another world almost, or at all events from someone not living very much in this. And he said mechanically:

"Where are you living now?"

"I have a little flat in Chelsea."

He did not want to hear what she was doing, did not want to hear anything; but the perverse word came out:

"Alone?"

She nodded. It was a relief to know that. And it came into his mind that, but for a twist of fate, she would have been mistress of this coppice, showing these cow houses to him, a visitor.

"All Alderneys," he muttered; "they give the best milk. This one's a pretty creature. Woa, Myrtle!"

The fawn-colored cow, with eyes as soft and brown as Irene's own, was standing absolutely still, not having long been milked. She looked round at them out of the corner of those lustrous, mild, cynical eyes, and from her gray lips a little dribble of saliva threaded its way towards the straw. The scent of hay and vanilla and ammonia rose in the dim light of the cool cow house; and old Jolyon said:

"You must come up and have some dinner with me. I'll send you home in the carriage."

He perceived a struggle going on within her; natural, no doubt, with her memories. But he wanted her company; a pretty face, a charming figure, beauty! He had been alone all the afternoon. Perhaps his eyes were wistful, for she answered: "Thank you, Uncle Jolyon. I should like to."

He rubbed his hands, and said:

"Capital! Let's go up, then!" And, preceded by the dog Balthasar, they ascended through the field. The sun was almost level in their faces now, and he could see, not only those silver threads, but little lines, just deep enough to stamp her beauty with a coinlike fineness— the special look of life unshared with others. "I'll take her in by the terrace," he thought: "I won't make a common visitor of her."

"What do you do all day?" he said.

"Teach music; I have another interest, too."

"Work!" said old Jolyon, picking up the doll from off the swing, and smoothing its black petticoat. "Nothing like it, is there? I don't do any now. I'm getting on. What interest is that?"

"Trying to help women who've come to grief." Old Jolyon did not quite understand. "To grief?" he repeated; then realized with a shock that she meant exactly what he would have meant himself if he had used that expression. Assisting the Magdalenes of London! What a weird and terrifying interest! And, curiosity overcoming his natural shrinking, he asked:

"Why? What do you do for them?"

"Not much. I've no money to spare. I can only give sympathy and food sometimes."

Involuntarily old Jolyon's hand sought his purse. He said hastily: "How d'you get hold of them?"

"I go to a hospital."

"A hospital! Phew!"

"What hurts me most is that once they nearly all had some sort of beauty."

Old Jolyon straightened the doll. "Beauty!" he ejaculated: "Ha! Yes! A sad business!" and he moved towards the house. Through a French window, under sun blinds not yet drawn up, he preceded her into the room where he was wont to study *The Times* and the sheets of an agricultural magazine, with huge illustrations of mangold wurzels, and the like, which provided Holly with material for her paintbrush.

"Dinner's in half an hour. You'd like to wash your hands! I'll take you to June's room."

He saw her looking round eagerly; what changes since she had last visited this house with her husband, or her lover, or both perhaps—he did not know, could not say! All that was dark, and he wished to leave it so. But what changes! And in the hall he said:

"My boy Jo's a painter, you know. He's got a lot of taste. It isn't mine, of course, but I've let him have his way."

She was standing very still, her eyes roaming through the hall and music room, as it now was—all thrown into one, under the great skylight. Old Jolyon had an odd impression of her. Was she trying to conjure somebody from the shades of that space where the coloring was all pearl-gray and silver? He would have had gold himself; more lively and solid. But Jo had French tastes, and it had come out shadowy like that, with an effect as of the fume of cigarettes the chap was always smoking, broken here and there by a little blaze of blue or crimson color. It was not *his* dream! Mentally he had hung this space with those gold-framed masterpieces of still and stiller life which he had bought in days when quantity was precious. And now where were they? Sold for a song! That something which made him, alone among Forsytes, move with the times had warned him against the struggle to retain them. But in his study he still had "Dutch Fishing Boats at Sunset."

He began to mount the stairs with her, slowly, for he felt his side.

"These are the bathrooms," he said, "and other arrangements. I've had them tiled. The nurseries are along there. And this is Jo's and his wife's. They all communicate. But you remember, I expect."

Irene nodded. They passed on, up the gallery and entered a large room with a small bed, and several windows.

"This is mine," he said. The walls were covered with the photographs of children and water-color sketches, and he added doubtfully:

"These are Jo's. The view's first-rate. You can see the Grand Stand at Epsom in clear weather."

The sun was down now, behind the house, and over the "prospect" a luminous haze had settled, emanation of the long and prosperous day. Few houses showed, but fields and trees faintly glistened, away to a loom of downs.

"The country's changing," he said abruptly, "but there it'll be when we're all gone. Look at those thrushes—the birds are sweet here in the mornings. I'm glad to have washed my hands of London."

Her face was close to the window pane, and he was struck by its mournful look. "Wish I could make her look happy!" he thought. "A pretty face, but sad!" And taking up his can of hot water he went out into the gallery.

"This is June's room," he said, opening the next door and putting the can down; "I think you'll find everything." And closing the door behind her he went back to his own room. Brushing his hair with his great ebony brushes, and dabbing his forehead with eau de Cologne, he mused. She had come so strangely—a sort of visitation, mysterious, even romantic, as if his desire for company, for beauty, had been fulfilled by—whatever it was which fulfilled that sort of thing. And before the mirror he straightened his still upright figure, passed the brushes over his great white mustache, touched up his eyebrows with eau de Cologne, and rang the bell.

"I forgot to let them know that I have a lady to dinner with me. Let cook do something extra, and tell Beacon to have the landau and pair at half-past ten to drive her back to Town tonight. Is Miss Holly asleep?"

The maid thought not. And old Jolyon, passing down the gallery, stole on tiptoe towards the nursery, and opened the door whose hinges he kept specially oiled that he might slip in and out in the evenings without being heard.

But Holly *was* asleep, and lay like a miniature Madonna, of that type which the old painters could not tell from Venus, when they had completed her. Her long dark lashes clung to her cheeks; on her face was perfect peace—her little arrangements were evidently all right again. And old Jolyon, in the twilight of the room, stood adoring her! It was so charming, solemn, and loving—that little face. He had more than his share of the blessed capacity of living again in the young. They were to him his future life—all of a future life—that his fundamental pagan sanity perhaps admitted. There she was with everything before her, and his blood—some of it—in her tiny veins. There she was, his little companion, to be made as happy as ever he could make her, so that she knew nothing but love. His heart swelled, and he went out, stifling the sound of his patent-leather boots. In the corridor an eccentric notion attacked him: To think that children should come to that which Irene had told him she was helping! Women who were all, once, little things like this one sleeping there! "I must give her a check!" he mused; "Can't bear to think of them!" They had never borne reflecting on, those poor outcasts; wounding too deeply the core of true refinement hidden under layers of conformity to the sense of property—wounding too grievously the deepest thing in him—a love of beauty which could give him, even now, a flutter of the heart, thinking of his evening in the society of a pretty woman. And he went downstairs, through the swinging doors, to the back regions. There, in the wine cellar, was a hock worth at least two pounds a bottle, a Steinberg Cabinet, better than any Johannisberg that ever went down throat; a wine of perfect bouquet, sweet as a nectarine—nectar indeed! He got a bottle out, handling it like a baby, and holding it level to the light, to look. Enshrined in its coat of dust, that mellow-colored, slender-necked bottle gave him deep pleasure. Three years to settle down again since the move from Town—ought to be in prime condition! Thirty-five years ago he had bought it—thank God he had kept his palate, and earned the right to drink it. She would appreciate this; not a spice of acidity in a dozen. He wiped the bottle, drew the cork with his own hands, put his nose down, inhaled its perfume, and went back to the music room.

Irene was standing by the piano; she had taken off her hat and a lace scarf she had been wearing, so that her gold-colored hair was visible, and the pallor of her neck. In her gray frock she made a pretty picture for old Jolyon, against the rosewood of the piano.

He gave her his arm, and solemnly they went. The room, which had been designed to enable twenty-four people to dine in comfort, held now but a little round table. In his present solitude the big dining table oppressed old Jolyon; he had caused it to be removed till his son came back. Here in the company of two really good copies of Raphael Madonnas he was wont to dine alone. It was the only disconsolate hour of his day, this summer weather. He had never been a large eater, like that great chap Swithin, or Sylvanus Heythorp, or Anthony Thornworthy, those cronies of past times; and to dine alone, overlooked by the Madonnas, was to him but a sorrowful occupation, which he got through quickly, that he might come to the more spiritual enjoyment of his coffee and cigar. But this eve-

ning was a different matter! His eyes twinkled at her
across the little table and he spoke of Italy and Swit-
zerland, telling her stories of his travels there, and
other experiences which he could no longer recount to
his son and granddaughter because they knew them.
This fresh audience was precious to him; he had never
become one of those old men who ramble round and
round the fields of reminiscence. Himself quickly fa-
tigued by the insensitive, he instinctively avoided fa-
tiguing others, and his natural flirtatiousness towards
beauty guarded him specially in his relations with a
woman. He would have liked to draw her out, but
though she murmured and smiled and seemed to be enjoying what he told her, he remained conscious of that
mysterious remoteness which constituted half her fascination. He could not bear women who threw their
shoulders and eyes at you, and chattered away; or
hard-mouthed women who laid down the law and
knew more than you did. There was only one quality
in a woman that appealed to him—charm; and the quieter it was, the more he liked it. And this one had
charm, shadowy as afternoon sunlight on those Italian
hills and valleys he had loved. The feeling, too, that she
was, as it were, apart, cloistered, made her seem nearer
to himself, a strangely desirable companion. When a
man is very old and quite out of the running, he loves
to feel secure from the rivalries of youth, for he would
still be first in the heart of beauty. And he drank his
hock, and watched her lips, and felt nearly young. But
the dog Balthasar lay watching her lips too, and despis-

ing in his heart the interruptions of their talk, and the tilting of those greenish glasses full of a golden fluid which was distasteful to him.

The light was just failing when they went back into the music room. And, cigar in mouth, old Jolyon said: "Play me some Chopin."

By the cigars they smoke, and the composers they love, ye shall know the texture of men's souls. Old Jolyon could not bear a strong cigar or Wagner's music. He loved Beethoven and Mozart, Handel and Gluck, and Schumann, and, for some occult reason, the operas of Meyerbeer; but of late years he had been seduced by Chopin, just as in painting he had succumbed to Botticelli. In yielding to these tastes he had been conscious of divergence from the standard of the Golden Age. Their poetry was not that of Milton and Byron and Tennyson; of Raphael and Titian; Mozart and Beethoven It was, as it were, behind a veil; their poetry hit no one in the face, but slipped its fingers under the ribs and turned and twisted, and melted up the heart. And, never certain that this was healthy, he did not care a rap so long as he could see the pictures of the one or hear the music of the other.

Irene sat down at the piano under the electric lamp festooned with pearl-gray, and old Jolyon, in an armchair, whence he could see her, crossed his legs and drew slowly at his cigar. She sat a few moments with her hands on the keys, evidently searching her mind for what to give him. Then she began and within old Jolyon there arose a sorrowful pleasure, not quite like anything else in the world. He fell slowly into a trance, interrupted only by the movements of taking the cigar out of his mouth at long intervals, and replacing it. She was there, and the hock within him, and the scent of tobacco; but there, too, was a world of sunshine lingering into moonlight, and pools with storks upon them, and bluish trees above, glowing with blurs of wine-red roses, and fields of lavender where milk-white cows were grazing, and a woman all shadowy, with dark eyes and a white neck, smiled, holding out her arms; and through air which was like music a star dropped and was caught on a cow's horn. He opened his eyes. Beautiful piece; she played well—the touch of an angel! And he closed them again. He felt miraculously sad and happy, as one does, standing under a lime tree in full honey flower. Not live one's own life again, but just stand there and bask in the smile of a woman's eyes, and enjoy the bouquet! And he jerked his hand; the dog Balthasar had reached up and licked it.

"Beautiful!" He said: "Go on—more Chopin!"

She began to play again. This time the resemblance between her and "Chopin" struck him. The swaying he had noticed in her walk was in her playing too, and the Nocturne she had chosen and the soft darkness of her eyes, the light on her hair, as of moonlight from a golden moon. Seductive, yes; but nothing of Delilah in her or in that music. A long blue spiral from his cigar ascended and dispersed. "So we go out!" he thought. "No more beauty! Nothing?"

Again Irene stopped.

"Would you like some Gluck? He used to write his music in a sunlit garden, with a bottle of Rhine wine beside him."

"Ah! yes. Let's have *Orfeo*." Round about him now were fields of gold and silver flowers, white forms swaying in the sunlight, bright birds flying to and fro. All was summer. Lingering waves of sweetness and regret flooded his soul. Some cigar ash dropped, and taking out a silk handkerchief to brush it off, he inhaled a mingled scent as of snuff and eau de Cologne. "Ah!" he thought, "Indian summer—that's all!" and he said: "You haven't played one *Che faro*."

She did not answer; did not move. He was conscious of something—some strange upset. Suddenly he saw her rise and turn away, and a pang of remorse shot through him. What a clumsy chap! Like Orpheus, she of course—she too was looking for her lost one in the hall of memory! And disturbed to the heart, he got up from his chair. She had gone to the great window at the far end. Gingerly he followed. Her hands were folded over her breast; he could just see her cheek, very white. And, quite emotionalized, he said: "There, there, my love!" The words had escaped him mechanically, for they were those he used to Holly when she had a pain, but their effect was instantaneously distressing. She raised her arms, covered her face with them, and wept.

Old Jolyon stood gazing at her with eyes very deep from age. The passionate shame she seemed feeling at her abandonment, so unlike the control and quietude of her whole presence was as if she had never before broken down in the presence of another being.

"There, there—there, there!" he murmured, and putting his hand out reverently, touched her. She turned, and leaned the arms which covered her face against him. Old Jolyon stood very still, keeping one thin hand on her shoulder. Let her cry her heart out—it would do her good! And the dog Balthasar, puzzled, sat down on his stern to examine them.

The window was still open, the curtains had not been drawn, the last of daylight from without mingled with faint intrusion from the lamp within; there was a scent of new-mown grass. With the wisdom of a long life old Jolyon did not speak. Even grief sobbed itself out in time; only Time was good for sorrow—Time who saw the passing of each mood, each emotion in turn; Time the layer-to-rest. There came into his mind the words: "As panteth the hart after cooling streams"—but they were of no use to him. Then, conscious of a scent of violets, he knew she was drying her eyes. He put his chin forward, pressed his mustache against her forehead, and felt her shake with a quivering of her whole body, as of a tree which shakes itself free of raindrops. She put his hand to her lips, as if saying: "All over now! Forgive me!"

The kiss filled him with a strange comfort; he led her back to where she had been so upset. And the dog Balthasar, following, laid the bone of one of the cutlets they had eaten at their feet.

Anxious to obliterate the memory of that emotion,

he could think of nothing better than china; and moving with her slowly from cabinet to cabinet, he kept taking up bits of Dresden and Lowestoft and Chelsea, turning them round and round with his thin, veined hands, whose skin, faintly freckled, had such an aged look.

"I bought this at Jobson's," he would say; "cost me thirty pounds. It's very old. That dog leaves his bones all over the place. This old 'ship bowl' I picked up at the sale when the precious rip, the Marquis, came to grief. But you don't remember. Here's a nice piece of Chelsea. Now, what would you say *this* was?" And he was comforted, feeling that, with her taste, she was taking a real interest in these things; for, after all, nothing better composes the nerves than a doubtful piece of china.

When the crunch of the carriage wheels was heard at last, he said:

"You must come again; you must come to lunch, then I can show you these by daylight, and my little sweet—she's a dear little thing. This dog seems to have taken a fancy to you."

For Balthasar, feeling that she was about to leave, was rubbing his side against her leg. Going out under the porch with her, he said:

"He'll get you up in an hour and a quarter. Take this for your protégées," and he slipped a check for fifty pounds into her hand. He saw her brightened eyes, and heard her murmur: "Oh! Uncle Jolyon!" and a real throb of pleasure went through him. That meant one or two poor creatures helped a little, and it meant that she would come again. He put his hand in at the window and grasped hers once more. The carriage rolled away. He stood looking at the moon and the shadows of the trees, and thought: "A sweet night! She—!"

## II

Two days of rain, and summer set in bland and sunny. Old Jolyon walked and talked with Holly. At first he felt taller and full of a new vigor; then he felt restless. Almost every afternoon they would enter the coppice, and walk as far as the log. "Well, she's not there!" he would think, "of course not!" And he would feel a little shorter, and drag his feet walking up the hill home, with his hand clapped to his left side. Now and then the thought would move in him: "Did she come—or did I dream it?" and he would stare at space, while the dog Balthasar stared at him. Of course she would not come again! He opened the letters from Spain with less excitement. They were not returning till July; he felt, oddly, that he could bear it. Every day at dinner he screwed up his eyes and looked at where she had sat. She was not there, so he unscrewed his eyes again.

On the seventh afternoon he thought: "I must go up and get some boots." He ordered Beacon and set out. Passing from Putney towards Hyde Park he reflected: "I might as well go to Chelsea and see her." And he called out: "Just drive me to where you took that lady the other night." The coachman turned his broad red face, and his juicy lips answered: "The lady in gray, sir?"

"Yes, the lady in gray." What other ladies were there! Stodgy chap!

The carriage stopped before a small three-storied block of flats, standing a little back from the river. With a practiced eye old Jolyon saw that they were cheap. "I should think about sixty pound a year," he mused; and entering, he looked at the name board. The name "Forsyte" was not on it, but against "First Floor, Flat C" were the words: "Mrs. Irene Heron." Ah! She had taken her maiden name again! And somehow this pleased him. He went upstairs slowly, feeling his side a little. He stood a moment, before ringing, to lose the feeling of drag and fluttering there. She would not be in! And then—Boots! The thought was black. What did he want with boots at his age? He could not wear out all those he had.

"Your mistress at home?"

"Yes, sir."

"Say Mr. Jolyon Forsyte."

"Yes, sir, will you come this way?"

Old Jolyon followed a very little maid—not more than sixteen one would say—into a very small drawing room where the sun blinds were drawn. It held a cottage piano and little else save a vague fragrance and good taste. He stood in the middle, with his top hat in his hand, and thought: "I expect she's very badly off!" There was a mirror above the fireplace, and he saw himself reflected. An old-looking chap! He heard a rustle, and turned round. She was so close that his mustache almost brushed her forehead, just under her hair.

"I was driving up," he said. "Thought I'd look in on you, and ask you how you got up the other night."

And, seeing her smile, he felt suddenly relieved. She was really glad to see him, perhaps.

"Would you like to put on your hat and come for a drive in the Park?"

But while she was gone to put her hat on, he frowned. The Park! James and Emily! Mrs. Nicholas, or some other member of his precious family would be there very likely, prancing up and down. And they would go and wag their tongues about having seen him with her, afterwards. Better not! He did not wish to revive the echoes of the past on Forsyte 'Change. He removed a white hair from the lapel of his closely buttoned-up frock coat, and passed his hand over his cheeks, mustache, and square chin. It felt very hollow there under the cheekbones. He had not been eating much lately—he had better get that little whippersnapper who attended Holly to give him a tonic. But she had come back and when they were in the carriage, he said:

"Suppose we go and sit in Kensington Gardens instead?" and added with a twinkle: "No prancing up and down there," as if she had been in the secret of his thoughts.

Leaving the carriage, they entered those select precincts, and strolled towards the water.

"You've gone back to your maiden name, I see," he said: "I'm not sorry."

She slipped her hand under his arm: "Has June forgiven me, Uncle Jolyon?"

He answered gently: "Yes—yes; of course, why not?"

"And have you?"

"I? I forgave you as soon as I saw how the land really lay." And perhaps he had; his instinct had always been to forgive the beautiful.

She drew a deep breath. "I never regretted—I couldn't. Did you ever love very deeply, Uncle Jolyon?"

At the strange question old Jolyon stared before him. Had he? He did not seem to remember that he ever had. But he did not like to say this to the young woman whose hand was touching his arm, whose life was suspended, as it were, by memory of a tragic love. And he thought: "If I had met *you* when I was young I—I might have made a fool of myself, perhaps." And a longing to escape in generalities beset him.

"Love's a queer thing," he said, "fatal thing often. It was the Greeks—wasn't it?—made love into a goddess; they were right, I dare say, but then they lived in the Golden Age."

"Phil adored them."

Phil! The word jarred him, for suddenly—with his power to see all round a thing, he perceived why she was putting up with him like this. She wanted to talk about her lover! Well! If it was any pleasure to her!

And he said: "Ah! There was a bit of the sculptor in him, I fancy."

"Yes. He loved balance and symmetry; he loved the wholehearted way the Greeks gave themselves to art."

Balance! The chap had no balance at all, if he remembered; as for symmetry—clean-built enough he was, no doubt; but those queer eyes of his, and high cheekbones—Symmetry?

"You're of the Golden Age, too, Uncle Jolyon."

Old Jolyon looked round at her. Was she chaffing him? No, her eyes were soft as velvet. Was she flattering him? But if so, why? There was nothing to be had out of an old chap like him.

"Phil thought so. He used to say: 'But I can never tell him that I admire him.' "

Ah! There it was again. Her dead lover; her desire to talk of him! And he pressed her arm, half resentful of those memories, half grateful, as if he recognized what a link they were between herself and him.

"He was a very talented young fellow," he murmured. "It's hot; I feel the heat nowadays. Let's sit down."

They took two chairs beneath a chestnut tree whose broad leaves covered them from the peaceful glory of the afternoon. A pleasure to sit there and watch her, and feel that she liked to be with him. And the wish to increase that liking, if he could, made him go on:

"I expect he showed you a side of him I never saw. He'd be at his best with you. His ideas of art were a little new—to me." He had stifled the word "fangled."

"Yes: but he used to say you had a real sense of beauty." Old Jolyon thought: "The devil he did!" but answered with a twinkle: "Well, I have, or I shouldn't be sitting here with you." She was fascinating when she smiled with her eyes like that!

"He thought you had one of those hearts that never grow old. Phil had real insight."

He was not taken in by this flattery spoken out of the past, out of a longing to talk of her dead lover—not a bit; and yet it was precious to hear, because she pleased his eyes and heart which—quite true!—had never grown old. Was that because—unlike her and her dead lover, he had never loved to desperation, had always kept his balance, his sense of symmetry. Well! It had left him power, at eighty-four, to admire beauty. And he thought, "If I were a painter or a sculptor! But I'm an old chap. Make hay while the sun shines."

A couple with arms entwined crossed on the grass before them, at the edge of the shadow from their tree. The sunlight fell cruelly on their pale, squashed, unkempt young faces. "We're an ugly lot!" said old Jolyon suddenly. "It amazes me to see how—love triumphs over that."

"Love triumphs over everything!"

"The young think so," he muttered.

"Love has no age, no limit, and no death."

With that glow in her pale face, her breast heaving, her eyes so large and dark and soft, she looked like Venus come to life! But this extravagance brought instant reaction, and, twinkling, he said: "Well, if it had limits, we shouldn't be born; for by George! it's got a lot to put up with."

Then, removing his top hat, he brushed it round with a cuff. The great clumsy thing heated his forehead; in these days he often got a rush of blood to the head—his circulation was not what it had been.

She still sat gazing straight before her, and suddenly she murmured:

"It's strange enough that *I'm* alive."

Those words of Jo's "wild and lost" came back to him.

"Ah!" he said; "my son saw you for a moment—that day."

"Was it your son? I heard a voice in the hall; I thought for a second it was—Phil."

Old Jolyon saw her lips tremble. She put her hand over them, took it away again, and went on calmly: "That night I went to the Embankment; a woman caught me by the dress. She told me about herself. When one knows that others suffer, one's ashamed."

"One of *those?*"

She nodded, and horror stirred within old Jolyon, the horror of one who has never known a struggle with desperation. Almost against his will he muttered: "Tell me, won't you?"

"I didn't care whether I lived or died. When you're like that, Fate ceases to want to kill you. She took care of me three days—she never left me. I had no money. That's why I do what I can for them, now."

But old Jolyon was thinking: "No money!" What

fate could compare with that? Every other was involved in it.

"I wish you had come to me," he said. "Why didn't you?" But Irene did not answer.

"Because my name was Forsyte, I suppose? Or was it June who kept you away? How are you getting on now?" His eyes involuntarily swept her body. Perhaps even now she was—! And yet she wasn't thin—not really!

"Oh! with my fifty pounds a year. I make just enough." The answer did not reassure him; he had lost confidence. And that fellow Soames! But his sense of justice stifled condemnation. No, she would certainly have died rather than take another penny from *him*. Soft as she looked, there must be strength in her somewhere—strength and fidelity. But what business had young Bosinney to have got run over and left her stranded like this!

"Well, you must come to me now," he said, "for anything you want, or I shall be quite cut up." And putting on his hat, he rose. "Let's go and get some tea. I told that lazy chap to put the horses up for an hour, and come for me at your place. We'll take a cab presently; I can't walk as I used to."

He enjoyed that stroll to the Kensington end of the gardens—the sound of her voice, the glancing of her eyes, the subtle beauty of a charming form moving beside him. He enjoyed their tea at Ruffel's in the High Street, and came out thence with a great box of chocolates swung on his little finger. He enjoyed the drive back to Chelsea in a hansom, smoking his cigar. She had promised to come down next Sunday and play to him again, and already in thought he was plucking carnations and early roses for her to carry back to town. It was a pleasure to give her a little pleasure, if it *were* pleasure from an old chap like him! The carriage was already there when they arrived. Just like that fellow, who was always late when he was wanted! Old Jolyon went in for a minute to say good-by. The little dark hall of the flat was impregnated with a disagreeable odor of patchouli, and on a bench against the wall—its only furniture—he saw a figure sitting. He heard Irene say softly: "Just one minute." In the little drawing room when the door was shut, he asked gravely: "One of your protégées?"

"Yes. Now thanks to you, I can do something for her."

He stood, staring, and stroking that chin whose strength had frightened so many in its time. The idea of her, thus actually in contact with this outcast, grieved and frightened him. What could she do for them? Nothing. Only soil and make trouble for herself, perhaps. And he said: "Take care, my dear! The world puts the worst construction on everything."

"I know that."

He was abashed by her quiet smile. "Well then—Sunday," he murmured: "Good-by."

She put her cheek forward for him to kiss.

"Good-by," he said again; "take care of yourself." And he went out, not looking towards the figure on the bench. He drove home by way of Hammersmith, that he might stop at a place he knew of and tell them to send her in two dozen of their best Burgundy. She must want picking up sometimes! Only in Richmond Park did he remember that he had gone up to order himself some boots, and was surprised that he could have had so paltry an idea.

III

The little spirits of the past which throng an old man's days had never pushed their faces up to his so seldom as in the seventy hours elapsing before Sunday came. The spirit of the future, with the charm of the unknown, put up her lips instead. Old Jolyon was not restless now, and paid no visits to the log, because she was *coming to lunch*. There is wonderful finality about a meal; it removes a world of doubts, for no one misses meals except for reasons beyond control. He played many games with Holly on the lawn, pitching them up to her who was batting so as to be ready to bowl to Jolly in the holidays. For she was not a Forsyte, but Jolly was—and Forsytes always bat, until they have resigned and reached the age of eighty-five. The dog Balthasar, in attendance, lay on the ball as often as he could, and the page boy fielded, till his face was like the harvest moon. And because the time was getting shorter, each day was longer and more golden than the last. On Friday night he took a liver pill, his side hurt him rather, and though it was not the liver side, there is no remedy like that. Anyone telling him that he had found a new excitement in life and that excitement was not good for him, would have been met by one of those steady and rather defiant looks of his deep-set iron-gray eyes, which seemed to say: "I know my own business best." He always had and always would.

On Sunday morning, when Holly had gone with her governess to church, he visited the strawberry beds. There, accompanied by the dog Balthasar, he examined the plants narrowly and succeeded in finding at least two dozen berries which were really ripe. Stooping was not good for him, and he became very dizzy and red in the forehead. Having placed the strawberries in a dish on the dining table, he washed his hands and bathed his forehead with eau de Cologne. There, before the mirror, it occurred to him that he was thinner. What a "threadpaper" he had been when he was young! It was nice to be slim—he could not bear a fat chap; and yet perhaps his cheeks were *too* thin! She was to arrive by train at half-past twelve and walk up, entering from the road past Drage's farm at the far end of the coppice. And, having looked into June's room to see that there was hot water ready, he set forth to meet her, leisurely, for his heart was beating. The air smelled sweet, larks sang, and the Grand Stand at Epsom was visible. A perfect day! On just such a one, no doubt, six years ago, Soames had brought young Bosinney down with him to look at the site before they began to build. It

was Bosinney who had pitched on the exact spot for
the house—as June had often told him. In these days
he was thinking much about that young fellow, as if
his spirit were really haunting the field of his last work,
on the chance of seeing—her. Bosinney—the one man
who had possessed her heart, to whom she had given
her whole self with rapture! At his age one could not,
of course, imagine such things, but there stirred in him
a queer vague aching—as it were the ghost of an impersonal jealousy; and a feeling, too, more generous, of
pity for that love so early lost. All over in a few poor
months! Well, well! He looked at his watch before entering the coppice—only a quarter past, twenty-five
minutes to wait! And then, turning the corner of the
path, he saw her exactly where he had seen her the first
time, on the log; and realized that she must have come
by the earlier train to sit there alone for a couple of
hours at least. Two hours of her society—missed! What
memory could make that log so dear to her? His face
showed what he was thinking, for she said at once:

"Forgive me, Uncle Jolyon; it was here that I first
knew."

"Yes, yes; there it is for you whenever you like.
You're looking a little Londony; you're giving too
many lessons."

That she should have to give lessons worried him.
Lessons to a parcel of young girls thumping out scales
with their thick fingers!

"Where do you go to give them?" he asked.

"They're mostly Jewish families, luckily."

Old Jolyon stared; to all Forsytes Jews seem strange and doubtful.

"They love music, and they're very kind."

"They had better be, by George!" He took her arm—his side always hurt him a little going uphill—and said:

"Did you ever see anything like those buttercups? They came like that in a night."

· Her eyes seemed really to fly over the field, like bees after the flowers and the honey. "I wanted you to see them—wouldn't let them turn the cows in yet." Then, remembering that she had come to talk about Bosinney, he pointed to the clock tower over the stables:

"I expect *he* wouldn't have let me put that there— had no notion of time, if I remember."

But, pressing his arm to her, she talked of flowers instead, and he knew it was done that he might not feel she came because of her dead lover.

"The best flower I can show you," he said, with a sort of triumph, "is my little sweet. She'll be back from church directly. There's something about her which reminds me a little of you," and it did not seem to him peculiar that he had put it thus, instead of saying: "There's something about you which reminds me a little of her." Ah! And here she was!

Holly, followed closely by her elderly French governess, whose digestion had been ruined twenty-two years ago in the siege of Strasbourg, came rushing towards them from under the oak tree. She stopped about a dozen yards away, to pat Balthasar and pretend that this was all she had in her mind. Old Jolyon who knew better, said:

"Well, my darling, here's the lady in gray I promised you."

Holly raised herself and looked up. He watched the two of them with a twinkle, Irene smiling, Holly beginning with grave inquiry, passing into a shy smile too, and then to something deeper. She had a sense of beauty, that child—knew what was what! He enjoyed the sight of the kiss between them.

"Mrs. Heron, Mam'zelle Beauce. Well, Mam'zelle—good sermon?"

For, now that he had not much more time before him, the only part of the service connected with this world absorbed what interest in church remained to him. Mam'zelle Beauce stretched out a spidery hand clad in a black kid glove—she had been in the best families—and the rather sad eyes of her lean yellowish face seemed to ask: "Are you well brrred?" Whenever Holly or Jolly did anything unpleasing to her—a not uncommon occurrence—she would say to them: "The little Tayleurs never did that—they were such well-brrred little children." Jolly hated the little Tayleurs; Holly wondered dreadfully how it was she fell so short of them. "A thin rum little soul," old Jolyon thought her—Mam'zelle Beauce.

Luncheon was a successful meal, the mushrooms which he himself had picked in the mushroom house, his chosen strawberries, and another bottle of the Steinberg Cabinet filled him with a certain aromatic spirituality, and a conviction that he would have a touch of eczema tomorrow. After lunch they sat under the oak tree drinking Turkish coffee. It was no matter of grief to him when Mademoiselle Beauce withdrew to write her Sunday letter to her sister, whose future had been endangered in the past by swallowing a pin—an event held up daily in warning to the children to eat slowly and digest what they had eaten. At the foot of the bank, on a carriage rug, Holly and the dog Balthasar teased and loved each other, and in the shade old Jolyon with his legs crossed and his cigar luxuriously savored, gazed at Irene sitting in the swing. A light, vaguely swaying, gray figure with a fleck of sunlight here and there upon it, lips just opened, eyes dark and soft under lids a little drooped. She looked content; surely it did her good to come and see him! The selfishness of age had not set its proper grip on him, for he could still feel pleasure in the pleasure of others, realizing that what he wanted, though much, was not quite all that mattered.

"It's quiet here," he said; "you mustn't come down if you find it dull. But it's a pleasure to see you. My little sweet's is the only face which gives me any pleasure, except yours."

From her smile he knew that she was not beyond liking to be appreciated, and this reassured him. "That's not humbug," he said. "I never told a woman I admired her when I didn't. In fact I don't know when I've told a woman I admired her, except my wife in the old days; and wives are funny." He was silent, but resumed abruptly:

"She used to expect me to say it more often than I felt it, and there we were." Her face looked mysteriously troubled, and, afraid that he had said something painful, he hurried on.

"When my little sweet marries, I hope she'll find someone who knows what women feel. I shan't be here to see it, but there's too much topsy-turvydom in marriage; I don't want her to pitch up against that." And, aware that he had made bad worse, he added: "That dog *will* scratch."

A silence followed. Of what was she thinking, this pretty creature whose life was spoiled; who had done with love, and yet was made for love? Some day when he was gone, perhaps, she would find another mate—not so disorderly as that young fellow who had got himself run over. Ah! but her husband?

"Does Soames never trouble you?" he asked.

She shook her head. Her face had closed up suddenly. For all her softness there was something irreconcilable about her. And a glimpse of light on the inexorable nature of sex antipathies strayed into a brain which, belonging to early Victorian civilization—so much older than this of his old age—had never thought about such primitive things.

"That's a comfort," he said. "You can see the Grand Stand today. Shall we take a turn round?"

Through the flower and fruit garden, against whose

high outer walls peach trees and nectarines were trained to the sun, through the stables, the vinery, the mushroom house, the asparagus beds, the rosery, the summerhouse, he conducted her—even into the kitchen garden to see the tiny green peas which Holly loved to scoop out of their pods with her finger, and lick up from the palm of her little brown hand. Many delightful things he showed her, while Holly and the dog Balthasar danced ahead, or came to them at intervals for attention. It was one of the happiest afternoons he had ever spent, but it tired him and he was glad to sit down in the music room and let her give him tea. A special little friend of Holly's had come in—a fair child with short hair like a boy's. And the two sported in the distance, under the stairs, on the stairs, and up in the gallery. Old Jolyon begged for Chopin. She played studies, mazurkas, waltzes, till the two children, creeping near, stood at the foot of the piano—their dark and golden heads bent forward listening. Old Jolyon watched.

"Let's see you dance, you two!"

Shyly, with a false start, they began. Bobbing and circling, earnest, not very adroit, they went past and past his chair to the strains of that waltz. He watched them and the face of her who was playing turned smiling towards those little dancers thinking: "Sweetest picture I've seen for ages." A voice said:

"Hollee! *Mais enfin—qu'est-ce que tu fais là— danser, le dimanche! Viens, donc!*"

But the children came close to old Jolyon, knowing that he would save them, and gazed into a face which was decidedly "caught out."

"Better the day, better the deed, Mam'zelle. It's all my doing. Trot along, chicks, and have your tea."

And, when they were gone, followed by the dog Balthasar, who took every meal, he looked at Irene with a twinkle and said:

"Well, there we are! Aren't they sweet? Have you any little ones among your pupils?"

"Yes, three—two of them darlings."

"Pretty?"

"Lovely!"

Old Jolyon sighed; he had an insatiable appetite for the very young. "My little sweet," he said, "is devoted to music; she'll be a musician some day. You wouldn't give me your opinion of her playing, I suppose?"

"Of course I will."

"You wouldn't like—" but he stifled the words "to give her lessons." The idea that she gave lessons was unpleasant to him; yet it would mean that he would see her regularly. She left the piano and came over to his chair.

"I would like, very much; but there is—June. When are they coming back?"

Old Jolyon frowned. "Not till the middle of next month. What does that matter?"

"You said June had forgiven me; but she could never forget, Uncle Jolyon."

Forget! She *must* forget, if he wanted her to.

But as if answering, Irene shook her head. "You know she couldn't; one doesn't forget."

Always that wretched past! And he said with a sort of vexed finality:

"Well, we shall see."

He talked to her an hour or more, of the children, and a hundred little things, till the carriage came round to take her home. And when she had gone he went back to his chair, and sat there smoothing his face and chin, dreaming over the day.

That evening after dinner he went to his study and took a sheet of paper. He stayed for some minutes without writing, then rose and stood under the master-piece "Dutch Fishing Boats at Sunset." He was not thinking of that picture, but of his life. He was going to leave her something in his Will; nothing could so have stirred the stilly deeps of thought and memory. He was going to leave her a portion of his wealth, of his aspirations, deeds, qualities, work—all that had made that wealth; going to leave her, too, a part of all he had missed in life, by his sane and steady pursuit of wealth. Ah! What had he missed? "Dutch Fishing Boats" responded blankly; he crossed to the French window, and drawing the curtain aside, opened it. A wind had got up, and one of last year's oak leaves, which had somehow survived the gardener's brooms, was dragging itself with a tiny clicking rustle along the stone terrace in the twilight. Except for that it was very quiet out there, and he could smell the heliotrope watered not long since. A bat went by. A bird uttered its last "cheep." And right above the oak tree the first star shone. Faust in the opera had bartered his soul for some fresh years of youth. Morbid notion! No such bargain was possible, that was *real* tragedy! No making oneself new again for love or life or anything. Nothing left to do but enjoy beauty from afar off while you could, and leave it something in your Will. But how much? And, as if he could not make the calculation looking out into the mild freedom of the country night, he turned back and went up to the chimney piece. There were his pet bronzes—a Cleopatra with the asp at her breast; a Socrates; a greyhound playing with her puppy; a strong man reining in some horses. "They last!" he thought, and a pang went through his heart. They had a thousand years of life before them!

"How much?" Well! enough at all events to save her getting old before her time, to keep the lines out of her face as long as possible, and gray from soiling that bright hair. He might live another five years. She would be well over thirty by then. "How much?" She had none of his blood in her! In loyalty to the tenor of his life for forty years and more, ever since he married and founded that mysterious thing, a family, came this warning thought—None of his blood, no right to anything! It was a luxury then, this notion. An extravagance, a petting of an old man's whim, one of those things done in dotage. His real future was vested in those who had his blood, in whom he would live on when he was gone. He turned away from the bronzes and stood looking at the old leather chair in which he had sat and smoked so many hundreds of cigars. And suddenly he seemed to see her sitting there in her gray dress, fragrant, soft, dark-eyed, graceful, looking up at him. Why! She cared nothing for him, really; all she cared for was that lost lover of hers. But she was there, whether she would or no, giving him pleasure with her beauty and grace. One had no right to inflict an old man's company, no right to ask her down to play to him and let him look at her—for no reward! Pleasure must be paid for in this world. "How much?" After all, there was plenty; his son and his three grandchildren would never miss that little lump. He had made it himself, nearly every penny; he could leave it where he liked, allow himself this little pleasure. He went back to the bureau. "Well, I'm going to," he thought, "let them think what they like. I'm going to!" And he sat down.

"How much?" Ten thousand, twenty thousand—how much? If only with his money he would buy one year, one month of youth. And startled by that thought, he wrote quickly:

DEAR HERRING—Draw me a codicil to this effect: "I leave to my niece Irene Forsyte, born Irene Heron, by which name she now goes, fifteen thousand pounds free of legacy duty."

Yours faithfully,
JOLYON FORSYTE

When he had sealed and stamped the envelope, he
went back to the window and drew in a long breath. It
was dark, but many stars shone now.

## IV

He woke at half-past two, an hour which long experience had taught him brings panic intensity to all awkward thoughts. Experience had also taught him that a
further waking at the proper hour of eight showed the
folly of such panic. On this particular morning the
thought which gathered rapid momentum was that if
he became ill, at his age not improbable, he would not
see her. From this it was but a step to realization that
he would be cut off, too, when his son and June returned from Spain. How could he justify desire for the
company of one who had stolen—early morning does
not mince words—June's lover? That lover was dead;
but June was a stubborn little thing; warmhearted, but
stubborn as wood, and—quite true—not one who forgot! By the middle of next month they would be back.
He had barely five weeks left to enjoy the new interest
which had come into what remained of his life. Darkness showed up to him absurdly clear the nature of his
feeling. Admiration for beauty—a craving to see that
which delighted his eyes. Preposterous, at his age! And
yet—what other reason was there for asking June to
undergo such painful reminder, and how prevent his
son and his son's wife from thinking him very queer?

He would be reduced to sneaking up to London, which tired him; and the least indisposition would cut him off even from that. He lay with eyes open, setting his jaw against the prospect, and calling himself an old fool, while his heart beat loudly, and then seemed to stop beating altogether. He had seen the dawn lighting the window chinks, heard the birds chirp and twitter, and the cocks crow, before he fell asleep again, and awoke tired but sane. Five weeks before he need bother, at his age an eternity! But that early morning panic had left its mark, had slightly fevered the will of one who had always had his own way. He would see her as often as he wished! Why not go up to town and make that codicil at his solicitor's instead of writing about it; she might like to go to the opera! But, by train, for he would not have that fat chap Beacon grinning behind his back. Servants were such fools; and, as likely as not, they had known all the past history of Irene and young Bosinney—servants knew everything, and suspected the rest. He wrote to her that morning:

MY DEAR IRENE—I have to be up in town tomorrow. If you would like to have a look in at the opera, come and dine with me quietly . . .

But where? It was decades since he had dined anywhere in London save at his Club or at a private house. Ah! that newfangled place close to Covent Garden . . .

Let me have a line tomorrow morning to the Piedmont
Hotel whether to expect you there at seven o'clock.
Yours affectionately,<br>
JOLYON FORSYTE

She would understand that he just wanted to give her
a little pleasure; for the idea that she should guess he
had this itch to see her was instinctively unpleasant to
him; it was not seemly that one so old should go out of
his way to see beauty, especially in a woman.

The journey next day, short though it was, and the
visit to his lawyer's, tired him. It was hot too, and after
dressing for dinner he lay down on the sofa in his bedroom to rest a little. He must have had a sort of fainting fit, for he came to himself feeling very queer; and
with some difficulty rose and rang the bell. Why! it
was past seven! And there he was and she would be
waiting. But suddenly the dizziness came on again, and
he was obliged to relapse on the sofa. He heard the
maid's voice say:

"Did you ring, sir?"

"Yes, come here"; he could not see her clearly, for
the cloud in front of his eyes. "I'm not well, I want
some sal volatile."

"Yes, sir." Her voice sounded frightened.

Old Jolyon made an effort.

"Don't go. Take this message to my niece—a lady
waiting in the hall—a lady in gray. Say Mr. Forsyte is
not well—the heat. He is very sorry; if he is not down
directly, she is not to wait dinner."

When she was gone, he thought feebly: "Why did I say a lady in gray—she may be in anything. Sal volatile!" He did not go off again, yet was not conscious of how Irene came to be standing beside him, holding smelling salts to his nose, and pushing a pillow up behind his head. He heard her say anxiously: "Dear Uncle Jolyon, what is it?" was dimly conscious of the soft pressure of her lips on his hand; then drew a long breath of smelling salts, suddenly discovered strength in them, and sneezed.

"Ha!" he said, "it's nothing. How did you get here? Go down and dine—the tickets are on the dressing table. I shall be all right in a minute."

He felt her cool hand on his forehead, smelled violets, and sat divided between a sort of pleasure and a determination to be all right.

"Why! You *are* in gray!" he said. "Help me up." Once on his feet he gave himself a shake.

"What business had I to go off like that!" And he moved very slowly to the glass. What a cadaverous chap! Her voice, behind him, murmured:

"You mustn't come down, Uncle; you must rest."

"Fiddlesticks! A glass of champagne'll soon set me to rights. I can't have you missing the opera."

But the journey down the corridor was troublesome. What carpets they had in these newfangled places, so thick that you tripped up in them at every step! In the lift he noticed how concerned she looked, and said with the ghost of a twinkle:

"I'm a pretty host."

When the lift stopped he had to hold firmly to the seat to prevent its slipping under him; but after soup and a glass of champagne he felt much better, and began to enjoy an infirmity which had brought such solicitude into her manner towards him.

"I should have liked you for a daughter," he said suddenly; and watching the smile in her eyes, went on:

"You mustn't get wrapped up in the past at your time of life; plenty of that when you get to my age. That's a nice dress—I like the style."

"I made it myself."

Ah! A woman who could make herself a pretty frock had not lost her interest in life.

"Make hay while the sun shines," he said; "and drink that up. I want to see some color in your cheeks. We mustn't waste life; it doesn't do. There's a new Marguerite tonight; let's hope she won't be fat. And Mephisto—anything more dreadful than a fat chap playing the Devil I can't imagine."

But they did not go to the opera after all, for in getting up from dinner the dizziness came over him again, and she insisted on his staying quiet and going to bed early. When he parted from her at the door of the hotel, having paid the cabman to drive her to Chelsea, he sat down again for a moment to enjoy the memory of her words: "You *are* such a darling to me, Uncle Jolyon!" Why! Who wouldn't be! He would have liked to stay up another day and take her to the Zoo, but two days running of him would bore her to death. No, he must wait till next Sunday; she had promised to come then. They would settle those lessons for Holly, if only for a month. It would be something. That little Mam'zelle Beauce wouldn't like it, but she would have to lump it. And crushing his old opera hat against his chest he sought the lift.

He drove to Waterloo next morning, struggling with a desire to say: "Drive me to Chelsea." But his sense of proportion was too strong. Besides, he still felt shaky, and did not want to risk another aberration like that of last night, away from home. Holly, too, was expecting him, and what he had in his bag for her. Not that there was any cupboard love in his little sweet—she was a bundle of affection. Then, with the rather bitter cynicism of the old, he wondered for a second whether it was not cupboard love which made Irene put up with him. No, she was not that sort either. She had, if anything, too little notion of how to butter her bread, no sense of property, poor thing! Besides, he had not breathed a word about that codicil, nor should he— sufficient unto the day was the good thereof.

In the victoria which met him at the station Holly was restraining the dog Balthasar, and their caresses made "jubey" his drive home. All the rest of that fine hot day and most of the next he was content and peaceful, reposing in the shade, while the long lingering sunshine showered gold on the lawns and the flowers. But on Thursday evening at his lonely dinner he began to count the hours; sixty-five till he would go down to meet her again in the little coppice, and walk up through the fields at her side. He had intended to consult the doctor about his fainting fit, but the fellow would be sure to insist on quiet, no excitement and all that; and he did not mean to be tied by the leg, did not want to be told of an infirmity—if there were one, could not afford to hear of it at this time of life, now that this new interest had come. And he carefully avoided making any mention of it in a letter to his son. It would only bring them back with a run! How far this silence was due to consideration for their pleasure, how far to regard for his own, he did not pause to consider.

That night in his study he had just finished his cigar and was dozing off, when he heard the rustle of a gown, and was conscious of a scent of violets. Opening his eyes he saw her, dressed in gray, standing by the fireplace, holding out her arms. The odd thing was that, though those arms seemed to hold nothing, they were curved as if round someone's neck, and her own neck was bent back, her lips open, her eyes closed. She vanished at once, and there were the mantelpiece and his bronzes. But those bronzes and the mantelpiece had not been there when she was, only the fireplace and the wall! Shaken and troubled he got up. "I must take medicine," he thought; "I can't be well." His heart beat too fast, he had an asthmatic feeling in the chest; and going to the window, he opened it to get some air. A dog was barking far away, one of the dogs at Gage's farm no doubt, beyond the coppice. A beautiful still night, but dark. "I dropped off," he mused, "that's it! And yet I'll swear my eyes were open!" A sound like a sigh seemed to answer.

"What's that?" he said sharply, "who's there?"

Putting his hand to his side to still the beating of his heart, he stepped out on the terrace. Something soft scurried by in the dark. "Shoo!" It was that great gray cat. "Young Bosinney was like a great cat!" he thought. "It was him in there, that she—that she was— He's got her still!" He walked to the edge of the terrace, and looked down into the darkness; he could just see the powdering of the daisies on the unmown lawn. Here today and gone tomorrow! And there came the moon, who saw all, young and old, alive and dead, and didn't care a dump! His own turn soon. For a single day of youth he would give what was left! And he turned again towards the house. He could see the windows of the night nursery up there. His little sweet would be asleep. "Hope that dog won't wake her!" he thought. "What is it makes us love, and makes us die! I must go to bed."

And across the terrace stones, growing gray in the moonlight, he passed back within.


V


How should an old man live his days if not in dreaming of his well-spent past? In that, at all events, there is no agitating warmth, only pale winter sunshine. The shell can withstand the gentle beating of the dynamos of memory. The present he should distrust; the future shun. From beneath thick shade he should watch the sunlight creeping at his toes. If there be sun of summer, let him not go out into it, mistaking it for the Indian summer sun! Thus peradventure he shall decline softly, slowly, imperceptibly, until impatient Nature clutches his windpipe and he gasps away to death some early morning before the world is aired, and they put on his tombstone: "In the fulness of years!" yea! If he preserve his principles in perfect order, a Forsyte may live on long after he is dead.

Old Jolyon was conscious of all this, and yet there was in him that which transcended Forsyteism. For it is written that a Forsyte shall not love beauty more than reason; nor his own way more than his own health. And something beat within him in these days that with each throb fretted at the thinning shell. His sagacity knew this, but it knew too that he could not stop that beating, nor would if he could. And yet, if you had told him he was living on his capital, he would have stared you down. No, no; a man did not live on his capital; it was not done! The shibboleths of the past are ever more real than the actualities of the present. And he, to whom living on one's capital had always been anathema, could not have borne to have applied so gross a phrase to his own case. Pleasure is healthful; beauty good to see; to live again in the youth of the young—and what else on earth was he doing!

Methodically, as had been the way of his whole life,

he now arranged his time. On Tuesdays he journeyed up to town by train; Irene came and dined with him. And they went to the opera. On Thursdays he drove to town, and, putting that fat chap and his horses up, met her in Kensington Gardens, picking up the carriage after he had left her, and driving home again in time for dinner. He threw out the casual formula that he had business in London on those two days. On Wednesdays and Saturdays she came down to give Holly music lessons. The greater the pleasure he took in her society, the more scrupulously fastidious he became, just a matter-of-fact and friendly uncle. Not even in feeling, really, was he more—for, after all, there was his age. And yet, if she were late he fidgeted himself to death. If she missed coming, which happened twice, his eyes grew sad as an old dog's, and he failed to sleep.

And so a month went by—a month of summer in the fields, and in his heart with summer's heat and the fatigue thereof. Who could have believed a few weeks back that he would have looked forward to his son's and his granddaughter's return with something like dread! There was such a delicious freedom, such recovery of that independence a man enjoys before he founds a family, about these weeks of lovely weather, and this new companionship with one who demanded nothing, and remained always a little unknown, retaining the fascination of mystery. It was like a draught of wine to him who has been drinking water for so long that he has almost forgotten the stir wine brings to his blood, the narcotic to his brain. The flowers were colored brighter, scents and music and the sunlight had a living value—were no longer mere reminders of past enjoyment. There was something now to live for which stirred him continually to anticipation. He lived in that, not in retrospection; the difference is considerable to any so old as he. The pleasures of the table, never of much consequence to one naturally abstemious, had lost all value. He ate little, without knowing what he ate; and every day grew thinner and more worn to look at. He was again a "threadpaper"; and to this thinned form his massive forehead, with hollows at the temples, gave more dignity than ever. He was very well aware that he ought to see the doctor, but liberty was too sweet. He could not afford to pet his frequent shortness of breath and the pain in his side at the expense of liberty. Return to the vegetable existence he had led among the agricultural journals with the life-size mangold wurzels, before his new attraction came into his life—no! He exceeded his allowance of cigars. Two a day had always been his rule. Now he smoked three and sometimes four—a man will when he is filled with the creative spirit. But very often he thought: "I must give up smoking and coffee; I must give up rattling up to town." But he did not; there was no one in any sort of authority to notice him, and this was a priceless boon. The servants perhaps wondered, but they were, naturally, dumb. Mam'zelle Beauce was too concerned with her own digestion, and too "well brrred" to make personal allusions. Holly had not as yet an eye for the relative appearance of him who was

her plaything and her god. It was left for Irene herself
to beg him to eat more, to rest in the hot part of the
day, to take a tonic, and so forth. But she did not tell
him that she was the cause of his thinness—for one
cannot see the havoc oneself is working. A man of
eighty-five has no passions, but the Beauty which produces passion works on in the old way, till death closes
the eyes which crave the sight of Her.

On the first day of the second week in July he received a letter from his son in Paris to say that they
would all be back on Friday. This had always been
more sure than Fate; but, with the pathetic improvi-
dence given to the old, that they may endure to the
end, he had never quite admitted it. Now he did, and
something would have to be done. He had ceased to be
able to imagine life without his new interest, but that
which is not imagined sometimes exists, as Forsytes are
perpetually finding to their cost. He sat in his old
leather chair, doubling up the letter, and mumbling
with his lips the end of an unlighted cigar. After tomorrow his Tuesday expeditions to town would have to be
abandoned. He could still drive up, perhaps, once a
week, on the pretext of seeing his man of business. But
even that would be dependent on his health, for now
they would begin to fuss about him. The lessons! The
lessons must go on! She must swallow down her scru-
ples, and June must put her feelings in her pocket. She
had done so once, on the day after the news of
Bosinney's death; what she had done then, she could
surely do again now. Four years since that injury was

inflicted on her—not Christian to keep the memory of old sores alive. June's will was strong, but his was stronger, for his sands were running out. Irene was soft, surely she would do this for him, subdue her natural shrinking, sooner than give him pain! The lessons must continue; for if they did, he was secure. And lighting his cigar at last, he began trying to shape out how to put it to them all, and explain this strange intimacy; how to veil and wrap it away from the naked truth—that he could not bear to be deprived of the sight of beauty. Ah! Holly! Holly was fond of her, Holly liked her lessons. She would save him—his little sweet! And with that happy thought he became serene, and wondered what he had been worrying about so fearfully. He must not worry, it left him always curiously weak, and as if but half present in his own body.

That evening after dinner he had a return of the dizziness, though he did not faint. He would not ring the bell, because he knew it would mean a fuss, and make his going up on the morrow more conspicuous. When one grew old, the whole world was in conspiracy to limit freedom, and for what reason?—just to keep the breath in him a little longer. He did not want it at such cost. Only the dog Balthasar saw his lonely recovery from that weakness; anxiously watched his master go to the sideboard and drink some brandy, instead of giving him a biscuit. When at last old Jolyon felt able to tackle the stairs he went up to bed. And, though still shaky next morning, the thought of the evening sustained and strengthened him. It was always such a pleasure to give her a good dinner—he suspected her of undereating when she was alone; and, at the opera to watch her eyes glow and brighten, the unconscious smiling of her lips. She hadn't much pleasure, and this was the last time he would be able to give her that treat. But when he was packing his bag he caught himself wishing that he had not the fatigue of dressing for dinner before him, and the exertion, too, of telling her about June's return.

The opera that evening was *Carmen*, and he chose the last *entr'-acte* to break the news, instinctively putting it off till the latest moment. She took it quietly, queerly; in fact, he did not know how she had taken it before the wayward music lifted up again and silence became necessary. The mask was down over her face, the mask behind which so much went on that he could not see. She wanted time to think it over, no doubt! He would not press her, for she would be coming to give her lesson tomorrow afternoon, and he should see her then when she had got used to the idea. In the cab he talked only of the Carmen; he had seen better in the old days, but this one was not bad at all. When he took her hand to say good night, she bent quickly forward and kissed his forehead.

"Good-by, dear Uncle Jolyon, you have been so sweet to me."

"Tomorrow then," he said. "Good night. Sleep well." She echoed softly: "Sleep well!" and from the cab window, already moving away, he saw her face screwed round towards him, and her hand put out in a gesture which seemed to linger.

He sought his room slowly. They never gave him the same, and he could not get used to these "spick-and-spandy" bedrooms with new furniture and gray-green carpets sprinkled all over with pink roses. He was wakeful and that wretched Habanera kept throbbing in his head. His French had never been equal to its words, but its sense he knew, if it had any sense, a gipsy thing—wild and unaccountable. Well, there *was* in life something which upset all your care and plans—something which made men and women dance to its pipes. And he lay staring from deep-sunk eyes into the darkness where the unaccountable held sway. You thought you had hold of life, but it slipped away behind you, took you by the scruff of the neck, forced you here and forced you there, and then, likely as not, squeezed life out of you! It took the very stars like that, he shouldn't wonder, rubbed their noses together and flung them apart; it had never done playing its pranks. Five million people in this great blunderbuss of a town, and all of them at the mercy of that Life Force, like a lot of little dried peas hopping about on a board when you struck your fist on it. Ah, well! Himself would not hop much longer—a good long sleep would do him good!

How hot it was up here!—how noisy! His forehead burned; she had kissed it just where he always worried; just there—as if she had known the very place and wanted to kiss it all away for him. But, instead, her lips left a patch of grievous uneasiness. She had never spoken in quite that voice, had never before made that lingering gesture or looked back at him as she drove away. He got out of bed and pulled the curtains aside; his room faced down over the river. There was little air, but the sight of that breadth of water flowing by, calm, eternal, soothed him. "The great thing," he thought, "is not to make myself a nuisance. I'll think of my little sweet, and go to sleep." But it was long before the heat and throbbing of the London night died out into the short slumber of the summer morning. And old Jolyon had but forty winks.

When he reached home next day he went out to the flower garden, and with the help of Holly, who was very delicate with flowers, gathered a great bunch of carnations. They were, he told her, for "the lady in gray"—a name still bandied between them; and he put them in a bowl in his study where he meant to tackle Irene the moment she came, on the subject of June and future lessons. Their fragrance and color would help. After lunch he lay down, for he felt very tired, and the carriage would not bring her from the station till four o'clock. But as the hour approached he grew restless, and sought the schoolroom, which overlooked the drive. The sun blinds were down and Holly was there with Mademoiselle Beauce, sheltered from the heat of a stifling July day, attending to their silkworms. Old Jolyon had a natural antipathy to these methodical creatures, whose heads and color reminded him of elephants; who nibbled such quantities of holes in nice green leaves; and smelled, as he thought, horrid. He sat down on a chintz-covered window seat whence he could see the drive, and get what air there was; and the dog Balthasar who appreciated chintz on hot days, jumped up beside him. Over the cottage piano a violet dust sheet, faded almost to gray, was spread, and on it the first lavender, whose scent filled the room. In spite of the coolness here, perhaps because of that coolness the beat of life vehemently impressed his ebbed-down senses. Each sunbeam which came through the chinks had annoying brilliance; that dog smelled very strong; the lavender perfume was overpowering; those silk-worms heaving up their gray-green backs seemed horribly alive; and Holly's dark head bent over them had a wonderfully silky sheen. A marvelous cruelly strong thing was life when you were old and weak; it seemed to mock you with its multitude of forms and its beating vitality. He had never, till those last few weeks, had this curious feeling of being with one half of him eagerly borne along in the stream of life, and with the other half left on the bank, watching that helpless progress. Only when Irene was with him did he lose this double consciousness.

Holly turned her head, pointed with her little brown fist to the piano—for to point with a finger was not "well brrred"—and said slyly:

"Look at the 'lady in gray,' Gran; isn't she pretty to-day?"

Old Jolyon's heart gave a flutter, and for a second

the room was clouded; then it cleared, and he said with a twinkle:

"Who's been dressing her up?"

"Mam'zelle."

"Hollee! Don't be foolish!"

That prim little Frenchwoman! She hadn't yet got over the music lessons being taken away from her. That wouldn't help. His little sweet was the only friend they had. Well, they were her lessons. And he shouldn't budge—shouldn't budge for anything. He stroked the warm wool on Balthasar's head, and heard Holly say: "When Mother's home, there won't be any changes, will there? She doesn't like strangers, you know."

The child's words seemed to bring the chilly atmosphere of opposition about old Jolyon, and disclose all the menace to his newfound freedom. Ah! He would have to resign himself to being an old man at the mercy of care and love, or fight to keep this new and prized companionship; and to fight tired him to death. But this thin, worn face hardened into resolution till it appeared all jaw. This was his house, and his affair; he should not budge! He looked at his watch, old and thin like himself; he had owned it fifty years. Past four already! And kissing the top of Holly's head in passing, he went down to the hall. He wanted to get hold of her before she went up to give her lesson. At the first sound of wheels he stepped out into the porch, and saw at once that the victoria was empty.

"The train's in, sir; but the lady 'asn't come."

Old Jolyon gave him a sharp upward look, his eyes seemed to push away that fat chap's curiosity, and defy him to see the bitter disappointment he was feeling.

"Very well," he said, and turned back into the house. He went to his study and sat down, quivering like a leaf. What did this mean? She might have lost her train, but he knew well enough she hadn't. "Good-by, dear Uncle Jolyon." Why "Good-by" and not "Good night"? And that hand of hers lingering in the air. And her kiss. What did it mean? Vehement alarm and irritation took possession of him. He got up and began to pace the Turkey carpet, between window and wall. She was going to give him up! He felt it for certain—and he defenseless. An old man wanting to look on beauty! It was ridiculous! Age closed his mouth, paralyzed his power to fight. He had no right to what was warm and living, no right to anything but memories and sorrow. He could not plead with her; even an old man has his dignity. Defenseless! For an hour, lost to bodily fatigue, he paced up and down, past the bowl of carnations he had plucked, which mocked him with its scent. Of all things hard to bear, the prostration of will power is hardest, for one who has always had his way. Nature had got him in its net, and like an unhappy fish he turned and swam at the meshes, here and there, found no hole, no breaking point. They brought him tea at five o'clock, and a letter. For a moment hope beat up in him. He cut the envelope with the butter knife and read:

DEAREST UNCLE JOLYON—I can't bear to write anything that may disappoint you, but I was too cowardly to tell you last night. I feel I can't come down and give Holly any more lessons, now that June is coming back. Some things go too deep to be forgotten. It has been such a joy to see you and Holly. Perhaps I shall still see you sometimes when you come up, though I'm sure it's not good for you; I can see you are tiring yourself too much. I believe you ought to rest quite quietly all this hot weather, and now you have your son and June coming back you will be so happy. Thank you a million times for all your sweetness to me.

Lovingly your IRENE

So, there it was! Not good for him to have pleasure and what he chiefly cared about; to try and put off feeling the inevitable end of all things, the approach of death with its stealthy, rustling footsteps. Not good for him! Not even she could see how she was his new lease of interest in life, the incarnation of all the beauty he felt slipping from him!

His tea grew cold, his cigar remained unlit; and up and down he paced, torn between his dignity and his hold on life. Intolerable to be squeezed out slowly, without a say of your own, to live on when your will was in the hands of others bent on weighing you to the ground with care and love. Intolerable! He would see what telling her the truth would do—the truth that he wanted the sight of her more than just a lingering on. He sat down at his old bureau and took a pen. But he could not write. There was something revolting in having to plead like this; plead that she should warm his eyes with her beauty. It was tantamount to confessing dotage. He simply could not. And instead, he wrote:

> I had hoped that the memory of old sores would not be allowed to stand in the way of what is a pleasure and a profit to me and my little granddaughter. That old men learn to forego their whims; they are obliged to, even the whim to live must be foregone sooner or later; and perhaps the sooner the better.
>
> My love to you,<br>JOLYON FORSYTE

"Bitter," he thought, "but I can't help it. I'm tired." He sealed and dropped it into the box for the evening post, and hearing it fall to the bottom, thought: "There goes all I've looked forward to!"

That evening after dinner which he scarcely touched, after his cigar which he left half-smoked for it made him feel faint, he went very slowly upstairs and stole into the night nursery. He sat down on the window seat. A night light was burning, and he could just see Holly's face, with one hand underneath the cheek. An early cockchafer buzzed in the Japanese paper with which they had filled the grate, and one of the horses in the stable stamped restlessly. To sleep like that child! He pressed apart two rungs of the venetian blind and looked out. The moon was rising, blood-red. He had never seen so red a moon. The woods and fields out there were dropping to sleep too, in the last glimmer of the summer light. And beauty, like a spirit, walked.

"I've had a long life," he thought, "the best of nearly everything. I'm an ungrateful chap; I've seen a lot of beauty in my time. Poor young Bosinney said I had a sense of beauty. There's a man in the moon tonight!" A moth went by, another, another. "Ladies in gray!" He closed his eyes. A feeling that he would never open them again beset him; he let it grow, let himself sink; then, with a shiver, dragged the lids up. There was something wrong with him, no doubt, deeply wrong; he would have to have the doctor after all. It didn't much matter now! Into that coppice the moonlight would have crept; there would be shadows, and those shadows would be the only things awake. No birds, beasts, flowers, insects; just the shadows— moving; "Ladies in gray!" Over that log they would climb; would whisper together. She and Bosinney! Funny thought! And the frogs and little things would whisper too! How the clock ticked, in here! It was all eerie—out there in the light of that red moon; in here with the little steady night light and the ticking clock and the nurse's dressing gown hanging from the edge of the screen, tall, like a woman's figure. "Lady in gray!" And a very odd thought beset him: Did she exist? Had she ever come at all? Or was she but the emanation of all the beauty he had loved and must leave so soon? The violet-gray spirit with the dark eyes and the crown of amber hair, who walks the dawn and the moonlight, and at bluebell time? What was she, who was she, did she exist? He rose and stood a moment clutching the window sill, to give him a sense of reality again; then began tiptoeing towards the door. He stopped at the foot of the bed; and Holly, as if conscious of his eyes fixed on her, stirred, sighed, and curled up closer in defense. He tiptoed on and passed out into the dark passage; reached his room, undressed at once, and stood before a mirror in his nightshirt. What a scarecrow—with temples fallen in, and thin legs! His eyes resisted his own image, and a look of pride came on his face. All was in league to pull him down, even his reflection in the glass, but he was not down—yet! He got into bed, and lay a long time without sleeping, trying to reach resignation, only too well aware that fretting and disappointment were very bad for him.

He woke in the morning so unrefreshed and strengthless that he sent for the doctor. After sounding him, the fellow pulled a face as long as your arm, and ordered him to stay in bed and give up smoking. That was no hardship; there was nothing to get up for, and when he felt ill, tobacco always lost its savor. He spent the morning languidly with the sun blinds down, turning and returning *The Times*, not reading much, the dog Balthasar lying beside his bed. With his lunch they brought him a telegram, running thus: "Your letter received coming down this afternoon will be with you at four-thirty. Irene."

Coming down! After all! Then she did exist—and he was not deserted. Coming down! A glow ran through his limbs; his cheeks and forehead felt hot. He drank his soup, and pushed the tray table away, lying very quiet until they had removed lunch and left him alone; but every now and then his eyes twinkled. Coming down! His heart beat fast, and then did not seem to beat at all. At three o'clock he got up and dressed deliberately, noiselessly. Holly and Mam'zelle would be in the schoolroom, and the servants asleep after their dinner, he shouldn't wonder. He opened his door cautiously, and went downstairs. In the hall the dog Balthasar lay solitary, and, followed by him, old Jolyon passed into his study and out into the burning afternoon. He meant to go down and meet her in the coppice, but felt at once he could not manage that in this heat. He sat down instead under the oak tree by the swing, and the dog Balthasar, who also felt the heat, lay down beside him. He sat there smiling. What a revel of bright minutes! What a hum of insects, and cooing of pigeons! It was the quintessence of a summer day. Lovely! And he was happy—happy as a sandboy, whatever that might be. She was coming; she had not given him up! He had everything in life he wanted— except a little more breath, and less weight—just here! He would see her when she emerged from the fernery, come swaying just a little, a violet-gray figure passing over the daisies and dandelions and "soldiers" on the lawn—the soldiers with their flowery crowns. He would not move, but she would come up to him and say: "Dear Uncle Jolyon, I am sorry!" and sit in the swing and let him look at her and tell her that he had not been very well but was all right now; and that dog would lick her hand. That dog knew his master was fond of her; that dog was a good dog.

It was quite shady under the tree; the sun could not get at him, only make the rest of the world bright so that he could see the Grand Stand at Epsom away out there, very far, and the cows cropping the clover in the field and swishing at the flies with their tails. He smelled the scent of limes, and lavender. Ah! that was why there was such a racket of bees. They were excited—busy, as his heart was busy and excited. Drowsy, too, drowsy and drugged on honey and happiness; as his heart was drugged and drowsy. Summer—summer—they seemed saying; great bees and little bees, and the flies too!

The stable clock struck four; in half an hour she would be here. He would have just one tiny nap, because he had had so little sleep of late; and then he would be fresh for her, fresh for youth and beauty, coming towards him across the sunlit lawn—lady in gray! And settling back in his chair he closed his eyes. Some thistledown came on what little air there was, and pitched on his mustache more white than itself. He did not know; but his breathing stirred it, caught there. A ray of sunlight struck through and lodged on his boot. A bumblebee alighted and strolled on the crown of his Panama hat. And the delicious surge of slumber reached the brain beneath that hat, and the head swayed forward and rested on his breast. Summer—summer! So went the hum.

The stable clock struck the quarter past. The dog Balthasar stretched and looked up at his master. The thistledown no longer moved. The dog placed his chin over the sunlit foot. It did not stir. The dog withdrew his chin quickly, rose, and leaped on old Jolyon's lap, looked in his face, whined; then, leaping down, sat on his haunches, gazing up. And suddenly he uttered a long, long howl.

But the thistledown was still as death, and the face of his old master.

Summer—summer—summer! The soundless footsteps on the grass!

1917.

# Part 2

# PASSION,

# HEARTACHE,

# AND

# RENEWAL

# The Man with the Dog

## BY RUTH PRAWER JHABVALA

I think of myself sometimes as I was in the early days, and I see myself moving around my husband's house the way I used to do: freshly bathed, flowers in my hair, I go from room to room and look in corners to see that everything is clean. I walk proudly. I know myself to be loved and respected as one who faithfully fulfils all her duties in life—towards God, parents, husband, children, servants, and the poor. When I pass the prayer-room, I join my hands and bow my head and sweet reverence flows in me from top to toe. I know my prayers to be pleasing and acceptable.

Perhaps it is because they remember me as I was in those days that my children get so angry with me every time they see me now. They are all grown up now and scattered in many parts of India. When they need me, or when my longing for them becomes too strong, I go and visit one or other of them. What happiness! They crowd round me, I kiss them and hug them and cry, I laugh with joy at everything my little grandchildren say and do, we talk all night there is so much to tell. As the days pass, however, we touch on other topics that are not so pleasant, or even if we don't touch on them, they are there and we think of them, and our happiness becomes clouded. I feel guilty and, worse, I begin to feel restless, and the more restless I am the more guilty I feel. I want to go home, though I dare not admit it to them. At the same time I want to stay, I don't ever ever want to leave them—my darling beloved children and grandchildren for whom what happiness it would be to lay down my life! But I have to go, the restlessness is burning me up, and I begin to tell them lies. I say that some urgent matter has come up and I have to consult my lawyer. Of course, they know it is lies, and they argue with me and quarrel and say things that children should not have to say to their mother; so that when at last I have my way and my bags are packed, our grief is more than only that of parting. All the way home, tears stream down my cheeks and my feelings are in turmoil, as the train carries me farther and farther away from them, although it is carrying me towards that which I have been hungering and burning for all the time I was with them.

Yes, I, an old woman, a grandmother many times over—I hunger and burn! And for whom? For an old man. And having said that, I feel like throwing my hands before my face and laughing out loud, although of course it may happen, as it often does to me nowadays, that my laughter will change into sobs and then back again as I think of him, of that old man whom I love so much. And how he would hate it, to be called an old man! Again I laugh when I think of his face if he could hear me call him that. The furthest he has got is to think of himself as middle-aged. Only the other day I heard him say to one of his lady-friends, 'Yes, now that we're all middle-aged, we have to take things a bit more slowly'; and he stroked his hand over his hair, which he combs very carefully so that the bald patches don't show, and looked sad because he was middle-aged.

I think of the first time I ever saw him. I remember everything exactly. I had been to Spitzer's to buy some little Swiss cakes, and Ram Lal, who was already my chauffeur in those days, had started the car and was just taking it out of its parking space when he drove straight into the rear bumper of a car that was backing into the adjacent space. This car was not very grand, but the Sahib who got out of it was. He wore a beautifully tailored suit with creases in the trousers and a silk tie and a hat on his head; under his arm he carried a very hairy little dog, which was barking furiously. The Sahib too was barking furiously, his face had gone red all over and he shouted abuses at Ram Lal in English. He didn't see me for a while, but when he did he suddenly stopped shouting, almost in the middle of a word. He looked at me as I sat in the back of the Packard in my turquoise sari and a cape made out of an embroidered Kashmiri shawl; even the dog stopped barking. I knew that look well. It was one that men had given me from the time I was fifteen right till—yes, even till I was over forty. It was a look that always filled me with annoyance but also (now that I am so

old I can admit it) pride and pleasure. Then, a few sec-
onds later, still looking at me in the same way but by
this time with a little smile as well, he raised his hat to
me; his hair was blond and thin. I inclined my head,
settled my cape around my shoulders, and told Ram
Lal to drive on.

In those days I was very pleasure-loving. The children were all quite big, three of them were already in
college and the two younger ones at their boarding-
schools. When they were small and my dear husband
was still with us, we lived mostly in the hills or on our
estate near X—(which now belongs to my eldest son,
Shammi); these were quiet, dull places where my dear
husband could do all his reading, invite his friends, and
listen to music. Our town house was let out in those
years, and when we came to see his lawyer or consult
some special doctor, we had to stay in a hotel. But after
I was left alone and the children were bigger, I kept the
town house for myself, because I liked living in town
best. I spent a lot of time shopping and bought many
costly saris that I did not need; at least twice a week I
visited a cinema and I even learned to play cards! I was
invited to many tea parties, dinners, and other func-
tions.

It was at one of these that I met him again. We recognized each other at once, and he looked at me in the
same way as before, and soon we were making conversation. Now that we are what we are to each other and
have been so for all these years, it is difficult for me to

look back and see him as I did at the beginning—as a stranger with a stranger's face and a stranger's name. What interested me in him the most at the beginning was, I think, that he was a foreigner; at the time I hadn't met many foreigners, and I was fascinated by so many things about him that seemed strange and wonderful to me. I liked the elegant way he dressed, and the lively way in which he spoke, and his thin fair hair, and the way his face would go red. I was also fascinated by the way he talked to me and to the other ladies: so different from our Indian men who are always a little shy with us and clumsy, and even if they like to talk with us, they don't want anyone to see that they like it. But he didn't care who saw—he would sit on a little stool by the side of the lady with whom he was talking, and he would look up at her and smile and make conversation in a very lively manner, and sometimes, in talking, he would lay his hand on her arm. He was also extra polite with us, he drew back the chair for us when we wanted to sit down or get up, and he would open the door for us, and he lit the cigarettes of those ladies who smoked, and all sorts of other little services which our Indian men would be ashamed of and think beneath their dignity. But the way he did it all, it was full of dignity. And one other thing, when he greeted a lady and wanted her to know that he thought highly of her, he would kiss her hand, and this too was beautiful, although the first time he did it to me I had a shock like electricity going down my spine and I wanted to snatch away my hand from him and wipe it clean on my sari. But afterwards I got used to it and I liked it.

His name is Boekelman, he is a Dutchman, and when I first met him he had already been in India for many years. He had come out to do business here, in ivory, and was caught by the war and couldn't get back; and when the war was over, he no longer wanted to go back. He did not earn a big fortune, but it was enough for him. He lived in a hotel suite which he had furnished with his own carpets and pictures, he ate well, he drank well, he had his circle of friends, and a little hairy dog called Susi. At home in Holland all he had left were two aunts and a wife, from whom he was divorced and whom he did not even like to think about (her name was Annemarie, but he always spoke of her as 'Once bitten, twice shy'). So India was home for him, although he had not learned any Hindi except 'achchha' which means all right and 'pani' which means water, and he did not know any Indians. All his friends were foreigners; his lady-friends also.

Many things have changed now from what they were when I first knew him. He no longer opens the door for me to go in or out, nor does he kiss my hand; he still does it for other ladies, but no longer for me. That's all right, I don't want it, it is not needed. We live in the same house now, for he has given up his hotel room and has moved into a suite of rooms in my house. He pays rent for this, which I don't want but can't refuse, because he insists; and anyway, perhaps it doesn't matter, because it isn't very much money (he has calculated the rent not on the basis of what would have to be paid today but on what it was worth when the house was first built, almost forty years ago). In return, he wishes to have those rooms kept quite separate and that everyone should knock before they go in; he also sometimes give parties in there for his European friends, to which he may or may not invite me. If he invites me, he will do it like this: 'One or two people are dropping in this evening, I wonder if you would care to join us?' Of course I have known long before this about the party, because he has told the cook to get something ready, and the cook has come to me to ask what should be made, and I have given full instructions; if something very special is needed, I make it myself. After he has invited me and I have accepted, the next thing he asks me, 'What will you wear?' and he looks at me very critically. He always says women must be elegant, and that was why he first liked me, because in those days I was very careful about my appearance, I bought many new saris and had blouses made to match them, and I went to a beauty parlour and had facial massage and other things. But now all that has vanished, I no longer care about what I look like.

It is strange how often in one lifetime one changes and changes again, even an ordinary person like myself. When I look back, I see myself first as the young girl in my father's house, impatient, waiting for things to happen; then as the calm wife and mother, fulfilling all my many duties; and then again, when children are bigger and my dear husband, many years older than myself, has moved far away from me and I am more his daughter than his wife—then again I am different. In those years we mostly lived in the hills, and I would go for long walks by myself, for hours and hours, sometimes with great happiness to be there among those great green mountains in sun and mist. But sometimes also I was full of misery and longed for something as great and beautiful as those mountains to fill my own life which seemed, in those years, very empty. But when my dear husband left us forever, I came down from the mountains and then began that fashionable town-life of which I have already spoken. But that too has finished. Now I get up in the mornings, I drink my tea, I walk round the garden with a peaceful heart; I pick a handful of blossoms and these I lay at the feet of Vishnu in my prayer-room. Without taking my bath or changing out of the old cotton sari in which I have spent the night, I sit for many hours on the veranda, doing nothing, only looking out at the flowers and the birds. My thoughts come and go.

At about twelve o'clock Boekelman is ready and comes out of his room. He always likes to sleep late, and after that it always takes him at least one or two hours to get ready. His face is pink and shaved, his clothes are freshly pressed, he smells of shaving lotion and eau-de-Cologne and all the other things he applies out of the rows of bottles on his bathroom shelf. In one hand he has his rolled English umbrella, with the other he holds Susi on a red leather lead. He is ready to go out. He looks at me, and I can see he is annoyed at the way I am sitting there, rumpled and unbathed. If he is not in a hurry to go, he may stop and talk with me for a while, usually to complain about something; he is never in a very good mood at this time of day. Sometimes he will say the washerman did not press his shirts well, another time that his coffee this morning was stone cold; or he could not sleep all night because of noise coming from the servant quarters; or that a telephone message was not delivered to him promptly enough, or that it looked as if someone had tampered with his mail. I answer him shortly, or sometimes not at all, only go on looking out into the garden; and this always makes him angry, his face becomes very red and his voice begins to shake a little though he tries to control it: 'Surely it is not too much to ask,' he says, 'to have such messages delivered to me clearly and at the right time?' As he speaks, he stabs tiny holes into the ground with his umbrella to emphasize what he is saying. I watch him doing this, and then I say, 'Don't ruin my garden'. He stares at me in surprise for a moment, after which he deliberately makes another hole with his umbrella and goes on talking: 'It so happened it was an extremely urgent message—' I don't let him get far. I'm out of my chair and I shout at him, 'You are ruining my garden,' and then I go on shouting about other things, and I advance towards him and he begins to retreat backwards. 'This is ridiculous,' he says, and some other things as well, but he can't be heard because I am shouting so loud and the dog too has begun to bark. He walks faster now in order to get out of the gate more quickly, pulling the dog along with him; I follow them, I'm very excited by this time and no longer know what I'm saying. The gardener, who is cutting the hedge, pretends not to hear or see anything but concentrates on his work. At last he is out in the street with the dog, and they walk down it very fast, with the dog turning round to bark and he pulling it along, while I stand at the gate and pursue them with my angry shouts till they have disappeared from sight.

That is the end of my peace and contemplation. Now I am very upset, I walk up and down the garden and through the house, talking to myself and sometimes striking my two fists together. I think bad things about him and talk to him in my thoughts, and likewise in my thoughts he is answering me and these answers make me even more angry. If some servant comes and speaks to me at this time, I get angry with him too and shout so loud that he runs away, and the whole house is very quiet and everyone keeps out of my way. But slowly my feelings begin to change. My anger burns itself out, and I am left with the ashes of remorse. I remember all my promises to myself, all my resolutions never to give way to my bad temper again; I remember my beautiful morning hours, when I felt so full of peace, so close to the birds and trees and sunlight and other innocent things. And with that memory tears spring into my eyes, and I lie down sorrowfully on my bed. Lakshmi, my old woman servant who has been with me nearly forty years, comes in with a cup of tea for me. I sit up and drink it, the tears still on my face and more tears rolling down into my cup. Lakshmi begins to smooth my hair, which has come undone in the excitement, and while she is doing this I talk to her in broken words about my own folly and bad character. She clicks her tongue, contradicts me, praises me, and that makes me suddenly angry again, so that I snatch the comb out of her hand, I throw it against the wall and drive her out of the room.

So the day passes, now in sorrow now in anger, and all the time I am waiting only for him to come home again. As the hour draws near, I begin to get ready. I have my bath, comb my hair, wear a new sari. I even apply a little scent. I begin to be very busy around the house, because I don't want it to be seen how much I am waiting for him. When I hear his footsteps, I am busier than ever and pretend not to hear them. He stands inside the door and raps his umbrella against it and calls out in a loud voice: 'Is it safe to come in? Has the fury abated?' I try not to smile, but in spite of myself my mouth corners twitch.

After we have had a quarrel and have forgiven each other, we are always very gay together. These are our best times. We walk round the garden, my arm in his, he smoking a cigar and I chewing a betel leaf; he tells me some funny stories and makes me laugh so much that sometimes I have to stand still and hold my sides and gasp for air, while begging him to stop. Nobody ever sees us like this, in this mood; if they did, they would not wonder, as they all do, why we are living together. Yes, everyone asks this question, I know it very well, not only my people but his too—all his foreign friends who think he is miserable with me and that we do nothing but quarrel and that I am too stupid to be good company for him. Let them see us like this only once, then they would know; or afterwards, when he allows me to come into his rooms and stay there with him the whole night.

It is quite different in his rooms from the rest of the house. The rest of the house doesn't have very much furniture in it, only some of our old things—some carved Kashmiri screens and little carved tables with mother-of-pearl tops. There are chairs and a few sofas, but I always feel most comfortable on the large mattress on the floor which is covered with an embroidered cloth and many bolsters and cushions; here I recline for hours, very comfortably, playing patience or cutting betel nuts with my little silver shears. But in his rooms there is a lot of furniture, and a radiogram and a cabinet for his records and another for his bottles of liquor. There are carpets and many pictures—some paintings of European countryside and one old oil-painting of a pink and white lady with a fan and in old-fashioned dress. There is also a framed pencil-sketch of Boekelman himself, which was made by a friend of his, a chemist from Vienna who was said to have been a very good artist but died from heatstroke one very bad Delhi summer. Hanging on the walls or standing on the mantelpiece or on little tables all over

the room are a number of photographs, and these I like
to look at even better than the paintings, because they
are all of him as a boy or as oh! such a handsome
young man, and of his parents and the hotel they
owned and all lived in, in a place called Zandvoort.
There are other photographs in a big album, which he
sometimes allows me to look at. In this album there
are also a few pictures of his wife ('Once bitten, twice
shy'), which I'm very interested in; but he never lets me
look at the album for long, because he is afraid I might
spoil it, and he takes it away from me and puts it back
in the drawer where it belongs. He is neat and careful
with all his things and gets very angry when they are
disarranged by the servants during dusting; yet he also
insists on very thorough dusting, and woe to the whole
household if he finds some corner has been forgotten.
So, although there are so many things, it is always tidy
in his rooms, and it would be a pleasure to go in there
if it were not for Susi.

He has always had a dog, and it has always been the
same very small, very hairy kind, and it has always
been called Susi. This is the second Susi I have known.
The first died of very old age and this Susi too is getting quite old now. Unfortunately dogs have a nasty
smell when they get old, and since Susi lives in
Boekelman's rooms all the time, the rooms also have
this smell although they are so thoroughly cleaned every day. When you enter the first thing you notice is
this smell, and it always fills me with a moment's disgust, because I don't like dogs and certainly would

never allow one inside a room. But for B. dogs are like his children. How he fondles this smelly Susi with her long hair, he bathes her with his own hands and brushes her and at night she sleeps on his bed. It is horrible. So when he lets me stay in his room in the night, Susi is always there with us, and she is the only thing that prevents me from being perfectly happy then. I think Susi also doesn't like it that I'm there. She looks at me from the end of the bed with her running eyes, and I can see that she doesn't like it. I feel like kicking her off the bed and out of the room and out of the house: but because that isn't possible I try and pretend she is not there. In any case, I don't have any time for her, because I am so busy looking at B. He is usually asleep before me, and then I sit up in bed beside him and look and look my eyes out at him. I can't describe how I feel. I have been a married woman, but I have never known such joy as I have in being there alone with him in bed and looking at him: at this old man who has taken his front teeth out so that his upper lip sags over his gums, his skin is grey and loose, he makes ugly sounds out of his mouth and nose as he sleeps. It is rapture for me to be there with him.

No one else ever sees him like this. All those friends he has, all his European lady-friends—they only see him dressed up and with his front teeth in. And although they have known him all these years, longer than I have, they don't really know anything about him. Only the outer part is theirs, the shell, but what is within, the essence, that is known only to me. But they wouldn't understand that, for what do they know of outer part and inner, of the shell and of the essence! It is all one to them. For them it is only life in this world and a good time and food and drink, even though they are old women like me and should not have their thoughts on these things.

I have tried hard to like these friends of his, but it is not possible for me. They are very different from any-one else I know. They have all of them been in India for many, many years—twenty-five, thirty—but I know they would much rather be somewhere else. They only stay here because they feel too old to go anywhere else and start a new life. They came here for different reasons—some because they were married to Indians, some to do business, others as refugees and because they couldn't get a visa for anywhere else. None of them has ever tried to learn any Hindi or to get to know anything about our India. They have some In-dian 'friends,' but these are all very rich and important people—like maharanis and cabinet ministers, they don't trouble with ordinary people at all. But really they are only friends with one another, and they always like each other's company best. That doesn't mean they don't quarrel together, they do it all the time, and sometimes some of them are not on speaking-terms for months or even years; and whenever two of them are together, they are sure to be saying something bad about a third. Perhaps they are really more like family than friends, the way they both love and hate each other and are closely tied together whether they like it or not; and none of them has any other family, so they are really dependent on each other. That's why they are always celebrating one another's birthday the way a family does, and they are always together on their big days like Christmas or New Year. If one of them is sick, the others are there at once with grapes and flowers, and sit all day and half the night round the sickbed, even if they have not been on speaking terms.

I know that Boekelman has been very close with some of the women, and there are a few of them who are still fond of him and would like to start all over again with him. But he has had enough of them—at least in that way, although of course he is still on very friendly terms with them and meets them every day almost. When he and I are alone together, he speaks of them very disrespectfully and makes fun of them and tells me things about them that no woman would like anyone to know. He makes me laugh, and I feel proud, triumphant, that he should be saying all this to me. But he never likes me to say anything about them, he gets very angry if I do and starts shouting that I have no right to talk, I don't know them and don't know all they have suffered; so I keep quiet, although often I feel very annoyed with them and would like to speak my mind.

The times I feel most annoyed is when there is a party in Boekelman's rooms and I'm invited there with them. They all have a good time, they eat and drink, tell jokes, sometimes they quarrel; they laugh a lot and kiss each other more than is necessary. No one takes

much notice of me, but I don't mind that, I'm used to
it with them; anyway, I'm busy most of the time running in and out of the kitchen to see to the prepara-
tions. I am glad I have something to do because
otherwise I would be very bored only sitting there.
What they say doesn't interest me, and their jokes
don't make me laugh. Most of the time I don't understand what they are talking about, even when they are
speaking in English—which is not always, for sometimes they speak in other languages such as French or
German. But I always know, in whatever language they
are speaking, when they start saying things about India. Sooner or later they always come to this subject,
and then their faces change, they look mean and bitter
like people who feel they have been cheated by some
shopkeeper and it is too late to return the goods. Now
it becomes very difficult for me to keep calm. How I
hate to hear them talking in this way, saying that India
is dirty and everyone is dishonest; but because they are
my guests, they are in my house, I have to keep hold
of myself and sit there with my arms folded. I must
keep my eyes lowered, so that no one should see how
they are blazing with fire. Once they have started on
this subject, it always takes them a long time to stop,
and the more they talk the more bitter they become,
the expression on their faces becomes more and more
unpleasant. I suffer, and yet I begin to see that they too
are suffering, all the terrible things they are saying are
not only against India but against themselves too—
because they are here and have nowhere else to go—

and against the fate which has brought them here and left them here, so far from where they belong and everything they hold dear.

Boekelman often talks about India in this way, but I have got used to it with him. I know very well that whenever something is not quite right—for instance, when a button is missing from his shirt, or it is a very hot day in summer—at once he will start saying how bad everything is in India. Well, with him I just laugh and take no notice. But once my eldest son, Shammi, overheard him and was so angry with him, as angry as I get with B.'s friends when I hear them talking in this way. It happened some years ago—it is painful for me to recall this occasion . . .

Shammi was staying with me for a few days. He was alone that time, though often he used to come with his whole family, his wife Monica and my three darling grandchildren. Shammi is in the army—he was still a major then, though now he is a lieutenant-colonel—which is a career he has wanted since he was a small boy and which he loves passionately. At the cadet school he was chosen as the best cadet of the year, for there was no one whose buttons shone so bright or who saluted so smartly as my Shammi. He is a very serious boy. He loves talking to me about his regiment and about tank warfare and 11•1 bore rifles and other such things, and I love listening to him. I don't really understand what he is saying, but I love his eager voice and the way he looks when he talks—just as he looked when he was a small boy and told me about his cricket. Anyway, this is what we were doing that morning, Shammi and I, sitting on the veranda, he talking and I looking sometimes at him and sometimes out into the garden, where everything was green and cool and birds bathed themselves in a pool of water that had oozed out of the hose-pipe and sunk into the lawn.

This peace was broken by Boekelman. It started off with his shouting at the servant, very loudly and rudely, as he always does; nobody minds this, I don't mind it, the servant doesn't mind it, we are so used to it and we know it never lasts very long; in any case, the servant doesn't understand what is said for it is always in English, or even some other language which none of us understands, and afterwards, if he has shouted very loudly, Boekelman always gives the servant a little tip or one of his old shirts or pair of old shoes. But Shammi was very surprised for he had never heard him shout and abuse in this way (B. was always very careful how he behaved when any of the children were there). Shammi tried to continue talking to me about his regiment, but B. was shouting so loud that it was difficult to pretend not to hear him.

But it might still have been all right and nothing would have been said and Shammi and I could have pretended to each other that nothing had been heard if Boekelman had not suddenly come rushing out on to the veranda. He held his shaving-brush in one hand, and half his face was covered in shaving lather and on the other half there was a spot of blood where he had cut himself; he was in his undervest and trousers, and the trousers had braces dangling behind like two tails. He had completely lost control of himself, I could see at once, and he didn't care what he said or before whom. He was so excited that he could hardly talk and he shook his shaving-brush in the direction of the servant, who had followed him and stood helplessly watching him from the doorway. 'These people!' he screamed. 'Monkeys! Animals!' I didn't know what had happened but could guess that it was something quite trivial, such as the servant removing a razor blade before it was worn out. 'Hundreds, thousands of times I tell them!' B. screamed, shaking his brush. 'The whole country is like that! Idiots! Fools! Not fit to govern themselves!'

Shammi jumped up. His fists were clenched, his eyes blazed. Quickly I put my hand on his arm; I could feel him holding himself back, his whole body shaking with the effort. Boekelman did not notice anything but went on shouting, 'Damn rotten backward country!' I kept my hand on Shammi's arm, though I could see he had himself under control now and was standing very straight and at attention, as if on parade, with his eyes fixed above Boekelman's head. 'Go in now,' I told B., trying to sound as if nothing very bad was happening; 'at least finish your shaving.' Boekelman opened his mouth to shout some more abuses, this time probably at me, but then he caught sight of Shammi's face and he remained with his mouth open. 'Go in,' I said to him again, but it was Shammi who went in and left us, turning suddenly on his heel and marching away with his strong footsteps. The fly-screen door banged hard behind him on its spring hinges. Boekelman stood and looked after him, his mouth still open and the soap caking on his cheek. I went up close to him and shook my fist under his nose. 'Fool!' I said to him, in Hindi and with such violence that he took a step backwards in fear. I didn't glance at him again but turned away and swiftly followed Shammi into the house.

Shammi was packing his bag. He wouldn't talk to me and kept his head averted from me while he took neat piles of clothes out of the drawer and packed them neatly into his bag. He has always been a very orderly boy. I sat on his bed and watched him. If he had said something, if he had been angry, it would have been easier; but he was quite silent, and I knew that under his shirt his heart was beating fast. When he was small and something had happened to him, he would never cry, but when I held him close to me and put my hand under his shirt I used to feel his heart beating wildly inside his child's body, like a bird in a frail cage. And now too I longed to do this, to lay my hand on his chest and soothe his suffering. Only now he was grown-up, a big major with a wife and children, who had no need of his foolish mother any more. And worse, much worse, now it was not something from outside that was the cause of his suffering, but I, I myself! When I thought of that, I could not restrain myself—a sob broke from me and I cried out 'Son!' and the next moment, before I knew myself what I was doing, I was down on the ground, holding his feet and bathing them with my tears to beg his forgiveness.

He tried to raise me, but I am a strong, heavy woman and I clung obstinately to his feet; so he too got down on the floor and in his effort to raise me took me in his arms. Then I broke into a storm of tears and hid my face against his chest, overcome with shame and remorse and yet also with happiness that he was so near to me and holding me so tenderly. We stayed like this for some time. At last I raised my head, and I saw tears on his lashes, like silver drops of dew. And these tender drops on his long lashes like a girl's, which always seem so strange in his soldier's face—these drops were such a burning reproach to me that at this moment I decided I must do what he wanted desperately, he and all my other children, and what I knew he had been silently asking of me since the day he came. I took the end of my sari and with it wiped the tears from his eyes and as I did this I said, 'It's all right, son. I will tell him to go.' And to reassure him, because he was silent and perhaps didn't believe me, I said, 'Don't worry at all, I will tell him myself,' in a firm, promising voice.

Shammi went home the next day. We did not mention the subject any more, but when he left he knew that I would not break my promise. And indeed that very day I went to Boekelman's room and told him that he must leave. It was a very quiet scene. I spoke calmly, looking not at B. but over his head, and he answered me calmly, saying very well, he would go. He asked only that I should give him time to find alternative accommodation, and of course to this I agreed readily, and we even had a quiet little discussion about what type of place he should look for. We spoke like two acquaintances, and everything seemed very nice till I noticed that, although his voice was quite firm and he was talking so reasonably, his hands were slightly trembling. Then my feelings changed, and I had quickly to leave the room in order not to give way to them.

From now on he got up earlier than usual in the mornings and went out to look for a place to rent. He would raise his hat to me as he passed me sitting on the veranda, and sometimes we would have a little talk together, mainly about the weather, before he passed on, raising his hat again and with Susi on the lead walking behind him, her tail in the air. The first few days he seemed very cheerful, but after about a week I could see he was tired of going out so early and never finding anything, and Susi too seemed tired and her tail was no longer so high. I hardened my heart against them. I could guess what was happening—how he went from place to place and found everywhere that rents were very high and the accommodation very small compared with the large rooms he had had in my house all these years for almost nothing. Let him learn, I thought to myself and said nothing except 'Good morning' and 'The weather is changing fast, soon it will be winter' as I watched him going with slower and slower footsteps day after day out of the gate.

At last one day he confessed to me that, in spite of all his efforts, he had not yet succeeded in finding anything suitable. He had some hard things to say about rapacious landlords. I listened patiently but did not offer to extend his stay. My silence prompted him to stand on his pride and say that I need not worry, that very shortly he would definitely be vacating the rooms. And indeed only two days later he informed me that although he had not yet found any suitable place, he did not want to inconvenience me any further and had therefore made an alternative arrangement, which would enable him to leave in a day or two. Of course I should have answered only 'Very well' and inclined my head in a stately manner, but like a fool instead I asked, 'What alternative arrangement?' This gave him the opportunity to be stately with me; he looked at me in silence for a moment and then gave a little bow and, raising his hat, proceeded towards the gate with Susi. I bit my lip in anger. I would have liked to run after him and shout as in the old days, but instead I had to sit there by myself and brood. All day I brooded what alternative arrangement he could have made. Perhaps he was going to a hotel, but I didn't think so, because hotels nowadays are very costly, and although he is not poor, the older he gets the less he likes to spend.

In the evening his friend Lina came to see him. There was a lot of noise from his rooms and also some thumping, as of suitcases being taken down; Lina shouted and laughed at the top of her voice, as she always does. I crept half-way down the stairs and tried to hear what they were saying. I was very agitated. As soon as she had gone, I walked into his room—without knocking, which was against his strict orders—and at once demanded, standing facing him with my hands at my waist, 'You are not moving in with *Lina?*' Some of his pictures had already been removed from the walls and his rugs rolled up; his suitcases stood open and ready.

Although I was very heated, he remained calm. 'Why not Lina?' he asked, and looked at me in a mocking way.

I made a sound of contempt. Words failed me. To think of him living with Lina, in her two furnished rooms that were already overcrowded with her own things and always untidy! And Lina herself, also always untidy, her hair blonde when she remembered to dye it, her swollen ankles, and her loud voice and laugh! She had first come to India in the nineteen-thirties to marry an Indian, a boy from a very good family, but he left her quite soon—of course, how could a boy like that put up with her ways? She is very free with men, even now though she is so old and ugly, and I know she has liked B. for a long time. I was quite determined on one thing; never would I allow him to move to her place, even if it meant keeping him here in the house with me for some time longer.

But when I told him that where was the hurry, he could wait till he found a good place of his own, then he said thank you, he had made his arrangements, and as I could see with my own eyes he had already begun to pack up his things; and after he had said that, he turned away and began to open and shut various drawers and take out clothes, just to show me how busy he was with packing. He had his back to me, and I stood looking at it and longed to thump it.

The next day too Lina came to the house and again I heard her talking and laughing very loudly, and there was some banging about as if they were moving the suitcases. She left very late at night, but even after she had gone I could not sleep and tossed this side and that on my bed. I no longer thought of Shammi but only of B. Hours passed, one o'clock, two o'clock, three, still I could not sleep. I walked up and down my bedroom, then I opened the door and walked up and down the landing. After a while it seemed to me I could hear sounds from downstairs, so I crept half-way down the stairs to listen. There was some movement in his room, and then he coughed also, a very weak cough, and he cleared his throat as if it were hurting him. I put my ear to the door of his room; I held my breath, but I could not hear anything further. Very slowly I opened the door. He was sitting in a chair with his head down and his arms hanging loose between his legs, like a sick person. The room was in disorder, with the rugs rolled up and the suitcases half packed, and there were glasses and an empty bottle, as if he and Lina had been having a party. There was also the stale smoke of her cigarettes; she never stops smoking and then throws the stubs, red with lipstick, anywhere she likes.

He looked up for a moment at the sound of the door opening, but when he saw it was I he looked down again without saying anything. I tiptoed over to his armchair and sat at his feet on the floor. My hand slowly and soothingly stroked his leg, and he allowed me to do this and did not stir. He stared in front of him with dull eyes; he had his teeth out and looked an old, old man. There was no need for us to say anything, to ask questions and give answers. I knew what he was thinking as he stared in front of him in this way, and I too thought of the same thing. I thought of him gone away from here and living with Lina, or alone with his dog in some rented room; no contact with India or Indians, no words to communicate with except 'achchha' (all right) and 'pani' (water); no one to care for him as he grew older and older, and perhaps sick, and his only companions people just like himself—as old, as lonely, as disappointed, and as far from home.

He sighed, and I said, 'Is your indigestion troubling you?' although I knew it was something worse than only indigestion. But he said yes, and added, 'It was the spinach you made them cook for my supper. How often do I have to tell you I can't digest spinach at night.' After a while he allowed me to help him into bed. When I had covered him and settled his pillows the way he liked them, I threw myself on the bed and begged, 'Please don't leave me.'

'I've made my arrangements,' he said in a firm voice. Susi, at the end of the bed, looked at me with her running eyes and wagged her tail as if she were asking for something.

'Stay,' I pleaded with him. 'Please stay.'

There was a pause. At last he said, as if he were doing me a big favour, 'Well, we'll see'; and added, 'Get off my bed now, you're crushing my legs—don't you know what a big heavy lump you are?'

None of my children ever comes to stay with me now. I know they are sad and disappointed with me. They want me to be what an old widowed mother should be, devoted entirely to prayer and self-sacrifice; I too know it is the only state fitting to this last stage of life which I have now reached. But that great all-devouring love that I should have for God, I have for B. Sometimes I think: perhaps this is the path for weak women like me? Perhaps B. is a substitute for God whom I should be loving, the way the little brass image of Vishnu in my prayer-room is a substitute for that great god himself? These are stupid thoughts that sometimes come to me when I am lying next to B. on his bed and looking at him and feeling so full of peace and joy that I wonder how I came to be so, when I am living against all right rules and the wishes of my children. How do I deserve the great happiness that I find in that old man? It is a riddle.

# The King Is Threatened

## BY MARGARETA EKSTROM

They recognized each other immediately across the pistachio-green lobby.

Recognizing each other couldn't really be taken entirely for granted: the majority of their colleagues here had trouble with both their eyesight and their memory, and it happened that the same old ladies or gentlemen introduced themselves anew around the breakfast table every day, not being at all aware of having breakfasted with more or less the same people for years.

More or less, that is, since departures as a result of natural causes were many. If one moved to a boarding house, or whatever one wanted to call the place, in one's eighties, one couldn't really expect to stay so very many years. Not even in this sort of a place. No, it wasn't a nursing home. If the boarders got too sick, they were transferred to other institutions, and dispersed, each to his own district.

Maud and Charles, however, had been friends on the outside. Through the years they had played bridge together in different places, eaten luxurious meals, talked about each other's children and grandchildren, yes, even sat around the same Christmas tree once in a while, and retired with a yawn to have drinks when they could no longer tolerate the children's and young people's rustling with the wrapping paper, followed by their spoiled comments.

Maud's father had been a cousin of Charles' mother's. But it wasn't just that distant relationship, it was also the fact that they had spent their summers near each other that had created special ties between them and between their families.

In Charles' case, it had been his wife who had persuaded him to take lodgings "for a while" as she put it, "at least two months," she had added, at Waybridge Manor. Maud, on the other hand, had made the decision herself, had moved in a few weeks before, and could now show Charles around. She had already become the habitué, she knew everyone and was so bright and capable that many wondered enviously why she was there at all, and there was actually a rumor that she was some sort of a spy from the world of the young and healthy, the world of the sexagenarians, or else, that she'd been smuggled in because she knew someone on the board of directors.

It was worse for poor Charles. He was a clear case for Waybridge. He sat mostly in his wheelchair. He could only manage to walk a few steps with the help of a supporting arm and a crutch. These steps were rationed for use between his bed and the bathroom, and between the wheelchair parking place outside the dining room and the table near the window. Exhausted and white in the face, he would collapse in a chair, and absentmindedly scatter thanks around—a sort of rigmarole that always ended with: "Imagine ending up like this!" And it was said with genuine astonishment.

If it was Maud who had helped him, which often was the case, she would pass her hand lightly over his sparse white hair, and in a motherly tone say: "We're old, all of us." Or else she'd say: "Lots of people are worse off, don't forget, Charles!"

That sort of expression flourished inside Waybridge. Situated as it was, on a hill near a bend in the river Way, it actually looked more like a sanitarium than a manor. This despite the fact that its exterior had not at all been altered since the time when Lord Southey, a destitute bachelor, had sold it to a foundation called "Care of the Aged" at the beginning of the 1930's. (After concluding the sale, the Lord went on a long dreamed about journey around the world, got stuck in Hong Kong when the war broke out, and disappeared among that city's tumultuous millions.)

It was as though the architect at the beginning of the nineteenth century had foreseen the future destiny of his building. There was something impersonal, pompous about its low broad crenelated tower, the bare, flat avenue leading to the entrance, with the harshly pruned poplars, and there was something decidedly unfriendly about its steep northern slope down to the river. A Russian boarder once had called it "the precipice" because it reminded him of a novel by Goncharov, and it has kept that name ever since.

Along the edge of the precipice, there were some do-
nated park benches that bore silent greetings from
former boarders on brass plates. "Mrs. Williamson's
bench, where she often used to enjoy the view," soon
became Maud and Charles' private bench. The nearby
little woods contained hundreds of song birds, and if
you managed to get away from your talkative neighbors, you could listen to redstarts, spotted flycatchers,
yellow buntings and blackbirds here. With "the place"
behind your back, you were spared its ugliness and
could for a short while feel like a free human being on
an excursion in nature.

Without thinking about the additional trouble,
Maud would on those occasions help Charles get out
of the wheelchair, and she would wheel it a bit out of
the way, so that he could be spared the sight of "that
dreadful contraption." He hadn't needed to ask her,
she had intuitively thought of these small gestures and
considerations which made him feel younger, healthier
and even more manly.

Not like with Christabel, Charles couldn't keep from
thinking. She would, instead, call attention to all that
was belittling and derogatory in his present situation.
Present, well, he was neither ignorant nor afraid, he realized that this "present" was permanent, sort of a ter-
minal station.

"At your age you don't have to worry about that,"
she had answered one time when he had in vain tried
to remember the origin of the word "scarlet."

"Woman," he had wanted to shout while thumping the floor with his cane spasmodically, "do you happen to know that you are speaking to an old etymologist?" But for some unknown reason, he had come out with entomologist—thus mixed up a linguistic scientist with an insect scientist, just as he had done as a schoolboy. It was incomprehensible because he had spent his whole adult life with etymology, and that mixup had already caused him so much embarrassment when he was twelve, when it had been especially mortifying, since it had happened in connection with his Eton entrance exam.

With an enormous effort he had later taken down the proper volume of the *Encyclopaedia Britannica* and greatly enjoyed refreshing his memory about the little scale insect which when dried produces such beautiful shades of red when mixed with stannous chloride. Comes from the Persian: saqirlat. And in his delight about the correctness in his unintentional mixing of linguistic scientist and insect scientist, of etymo and entomo, he muddled through an explanation, interrupted constantly by paroxysms of laughter, which made Christabel only shake her head like an idiot. Most likely she called the directress at Waybridge Manor for the first time on that particular evening.

He wondered quite a while whether he should tell Maud all about it, about Christabel, the scale insect and the encyclopedia (why, for God's sake, didn't the woman place his favorite books closer to the floor so that he could reach them from his wheelchair, instead of having to use the, to him now impossible, library ladder?), but he was overcome with so much disgust just thinking about Christabel's small meannesses that he decided to devote his attention to the singing of the birds, and, almost distractedly (as though he was looking for the handle of his crutch), he put his hand on Maud's knee, and she let it stay there.

The two old people had already spent more than a week at Waybridge before the relatives realized that the other one was there as well: that is, Christabel discovered during her Sunday visit that Aunt Maud was one of the boarders, and Maud's granddaughter Diana saw to her delight that it was Uncle Charles, who sat as close as possible to the sofa when afternoon tea was served in the lobby.

Later, when they strolled across the gravel court towards the parking area behind the gardener's place (where the ground was always soaked by hoses, which made all Waybridge visitors take along special boots or overshoes), they both loudly asserted their delight about the fact that the two old people could enjoy each other's company.

"It could become awfully boring otherwise," Diana said, and cast a glance over her shoulder at the pale gray walls with their pompous puffy stucco ornaments that looked as though made of whipped cream, and the obviously false mediaeval towers. "Grandmother asked me to bring along her chess set next time I come to visit."

"An excellent idea," said Christabel, but added: "However, I doubt whether Charles remembers the rules of the game. He can't manage so much nowadays."

Then, they talked a bit about boarding fees, and about prices of things in general, and when they took leave of each other Christabel said: "Perhaps, dear Diana, you think me heartless, but it feels so good to be able to rest a while. You can't imagine how good it feels." And, Diana, who lived alone, could very well imagine, but at the same time she thought that it would be inspiring to have an old Charles to talk with when the television got tiresome, and the dark of the night pressed against the window panes.

"Wasn't it sweet of Diana to send me the chess set?" Maud said gaily a couple of days later. Charles, who very well remembered that Maud explicitly had asked her granddaughter to send it, wondered over this unsought opportunity to make of this a special thing to be grateful for, when it really was a matter of course. Perhaps this was the way one "fixed up" one's existence as Christabel ill-humoredly used to say. "She's one of those people who fix up everything so that you won't be able to see how gray it actually is." But what is there actually? he wondered as he rolled himself closer to the table where Maud was already setting up the pieces. "I mean, what is there actually deep inside?" And he was glad that he hadn't tried to express himself aloud.

"Do you want us to throw dice for white or black?" she was wondering now, but he immediately said with a ready wit that amazed him: "You may be my white lady, dear Maud," and she smiled her quick smile and turned the board around so that he could play black.

"Such beautiful pieces," he said to gain a little time. It was a long time since he had played and he was searching inside his head for the layers and drawers in which chess knowledge had been packed away. If these archives were moth-eaten he would be lost. But there, as clear as small glass pearls in crystal-clear mineral water, words came to him like gambit, castle, stalemate and j'adoube.

"We bought them in Cairo. Edward and I," Maud said. "It was a long time after he retired from his post there. We were just on vacation."

Since they were sitting in the big lounge with its electric fire in the fireplace and all of the cozy groups of soft armchairs and little tables that were much too low, the word Cairo made another old lady look up. And she said, very loudly to her friend, because they were both deaf: "Cairo! Oh, do you remember? It's a sunken paradise now. It doesn't exist anymore!" "What did you say? Cairo doesn't exist?" the friend, who hadn't read the newspaper for many days, inquired. "Oh, it's gone, gone. Just like Rhodesia.

Rhodesia doesn't exist either. Only those—those bar-
barians!"

Maud was about to exchange an ironic smile of mutual understanding with her chess partner, but Charles
had obviously not heard a word of their neighbors'
conversation.

"Another time we can sit in my room and play,
Charles—," she said gently. "It is quieter there." But
she wasn't even sure that Charles had heard her nearby
voice. He was hesitatingly fingering his black horse,
and was thinking so hard that his forehead became
lined like music paper.


Maud's room was somewhat larger than Charles', as a
matter of fact it was larger than all the others on that
corridor. Neighbors, who at some time had come to
visit her, had found that fact just as suspicious as her
vigor and good health, and instead of having become a
center for social activities of her choice, as she had
hoped when she had seen that there was room enough
for a coffee table and easy chairs, the room had contributed to her being shut out.

God knows, there weren't so many you could associ-
ate with. There weren't many with an intact memory
and some sort of vitality in their legs or in their wits,
and she wasn't especially interested in some of those
arch-reactionary memories. She didn't belong to those
who considered "Rhodesia" or for that matter the rest

of Africa to be a sunken Atlantis. She read her *Observer* every week and telephoned Diana at least every other day and, sometimes, although remarkably seldom, she called Charles' wife, Christabel.

"Thank you," Christabel would say, somewhat on guard, "I am in contact with him myself, so you don't have to report on him, dear Maud."

But rather than feeling snubbed, Maud then became even more cordial and agreeable and she felt that it was only now, when she had Charles more or less in her care, that she really began to understand Christabel as well.

"Nothing wrong with my wife, really, you can't say other than good when it comes to women," Charles said, "but she is a cold woman. Really cold, Maud." They were sitting in easy chairs in Maud's room, and since the coffee table was so rickety and so little that it could only hold the chess board, Charles had to support himself with one hand on Maud's knee when he leaned forward over the game. "Please excuse me," he mumbled, but Maud pretended not to hear him. Nor did she take his hand away from her knee.

And when she went to bed that night, in the high resilient bed with the many thin blankets in layers to ward off the humidity which the night wind blew into the room, she passed her hand over that same knee, that still soft and rounded knee, and she felt that it was warmer than the other one.

———

"Diana," Christabel's voice said unexpectedly on the phone one early morning. "I'm sorry to bother you, but I have to ask you something about Waybridge. It seems to me that Charles isn't getting such good care there. What about Maud?"

"Well, Maud is so hearty and chipper," Diana said. "It really isn't a question of 'care' in her case . . . so, it's difficult to compare, I think. I thought Charles was getting diathermic treatments. And vitamin shots— have they stopped those?"

"Oh shots, shots, shots," Christabel chattered like an angry blackbird, "they think that helps! What he needs is massage. And help in walking with his crutches. The way things are now, I suppose he'll be sitting in his wheelchair until he won't be able to take a single step by himself, I mean, he just isn't getting the kind of care he gets at home."

"But I thought you needed a rest," Diana said unwittingly. "You did seem tired of waiting on him—but then, that's natural," she added, for the very silence seemed negatively charged.

"Tired of Charles . . ."

"I didn't say that, Christabel . . ."

"No, but tired of taking care of him then. Of course not! How can you possibly believe anything like that? Has Maud intimated anything of that sort?"

"Not at all. On the contrary, I think our two old people enjoy each other very much. They really take care of each other. Last time I called, Maud said she didn't have time to talk because Charles was sitting in her room having tea. She's got permission to have one of those instant tea makers in her room, you know, and what's more, she goes to the village to buy scones. She really sounded unusually bright!"

On that very same day Christabel called the directress at Waybridge and asked whether Charles could come home for a few days. She said that it was her birthday, as a pretext, but Charles, who suddenly seemed to remember almost everything, said that it certainly wasn't, and that he was well off where he was. And the directress thought that he sounded resentful.

At any rate, Christabel came to pick him up. She seemed very rested and managed to get him and the wheelchair into the car by herself. But when they got home, only the first evening had any trace of welcome celebration, and as a result Charles ate too much, got indigestion and had to spend the night in the bathroom in his wheelchair, in order to be near the necessary conveniences.

On the next day both he and Christabel were tired and washed out. Charles was yearning for the copy of *Broca's Brain* which he had left half finished in his room at Waybridge, and at teatime he complained that the tea was too strong, and asked where the chess set was.

Christabel took it down from the highest shelf in the library, and then he sat in the dusk, fingering the pieces that he had set up, knowing very well that Christabel didn't know how to play.

It was a gray wet day in March. The naked branches were shiny in the rain. A robin redbreast twittered hectically outside the window as though trying to hasten the arrival of spring. A blackbird raced back and forth between the arborvitae and the snowberry bush like a harassed black spirit. Nature outside was restless and contrasted strangely with the stuffy quiet inside where the hissing of the radiators was the only sound. When Christabel called that dinner was ready, there was no answer. She found Charles in his wheelchair which he had rolled to the telephone table in the hall, and she heard him say in an odd low voice: "Just leave the pieces as they were, Maud. Don't touch them. I'm coming back."

It was a very silent dinner and Charles blamed his lack of appetite on the events of the previous night. On the next day he insisted on being taken back to Waybridge, and Christabel granted his wish with mixed feelings of anxiety and relief. Already in the lobby, Maud came towards them with rouged cheeks and sparkling eyes. "There's our old darling," she shouted and hugged first Charles, then Christabel who chewed on that "our" all the way home in the car and understood that she, for the first time in her thirty-five-year-old marriage, shared her husband with another woman. Was that proper? she wondered and felt that she was blushing and almost drove through a red light.

"Diana?" said Christabel's voice early the next morning. "Diana, do you hear me? It's such a bad connection . . . well, listen, you'll have to excuse me but isn't it just a little too much, this business with Maud and Charles? Don't get me wrong, I'm not jealous, one doesn't get jealous at my age, and especially not with an old man like Charles who can't really do anything anymore, poor darling . . ." Here, she interrupted herself and giggled because she realized too late that "can't do anything anymore" was rather insinuating and, what's more, she had unconsciously called him "darling," just as Maud had.

While Diana was trying to help Christabel across these new and never-charted deep waters, Charles and Maud were sitting very close together with their chess board.

"I had such a strange dream last night," Charles said and cleared his throat. "I mean such a wonderful dream." Maud's gray eyes looked at him intently. Her white hair surrounded her forehead like a curly halo, but there wasn't any cool saintliness about her.

"I dreamed that I was standing on a black carpet that was completely square, and that I couldn't move. I remember that I was thinking that the wheelchair was far away, off the board. It was then that I realized that the black carpet was a chess square. And then, don't laugh now, dear Maud, after all, we are a couple of old and experienced people, and . . ." But he couldn't continue, and his eyes, which seemed least of all old and experienced, looked entreatingly at Maud.

In the corridor you could hear the sound of shuffling feet and high shrieking voices. A food wagon clattered by on its way to someone who had become bedridden and could not be part of the eating circle downstairs for a long time. Their eyes continued to look at each other with a timeless and mutual thirst.

"What happened then in your dream?" Maud urged him to continue.

"The white queen came towards me. And I was the black king. The pawns stepped aside, and the bishop ran away. A horse put out his hoof to trip her and laughed horribly, showing his big, yellow false teeth. I can't understand how I knew that they were false teeth, but you know what dreams are like, don't you! And the white queen just continued striding towards me. I have to get away from here, I thought, otherwise I'll be taken. And then, well, then I saw that the white queen was you, Maud. And I stood completely still. Completely still, I was only trembling, and then I took a step towards you." During the following month Christabel sent for her husband again and again. He must come home. Perhaps for good? He must be rested by now; she was, at any rate, she said in a tense and bitter voice.

He put up with these punitive command excursions, but sat silently at her beautifully set dinner table, and behaved generally like a stranger. One day in April she found him in his wheelchair out on the terrace. He was sitting there, and with unseeing eyes was facing the blooming forsythia, while tears ran down his cheeks.

Christabel sneaked back into the house and pretended not to have noticed, but his tears ran like drops of hydrochloric acid through her mind.

Charles' seeming so stimulated and happy whenever he returned to Waybridge counteracted his purposes constantly. "This isn't really the right place for you, young man," the doctor said jokingly when he made his weekly rounds among the boarders. "Blood pressure perfect. Heart and lungs the same. Nothing wrong with your memory. A slight weakness in your left knee, but that's not enough. We'll discharge you, and return you to your longing wife," he said and disappeared laughing into the corridor.

If he then, by mistake, had gone in to his patient again, he would have thought he saw an entirely different person: a broken old man, with an irregular heartbeat and higher blood pressure, who restlessly rubbed his veiny old hands, while his eyes wandered over the plaster decorations around the ceiling.

Finally it was summer. Summer, the season that was longed for and feared by all. Some of the old people would be able to "join their families in the country." Their well-intentioned children came and picked them up in clean shiny cars full of well-dressed grandchildren with white teeth and loud voices. Others were forgotten and suffered because of it. Still others felt forced to agree to a stay in the country which they secretly feared: the heat would be uncomfortable, they'd feel their age more, the children's happy good samaritan efforts would soon diminish and they would be left to boredom in someone else's garden, with only the cat as company.

Maud would of course go to her country place in Somerset, as usual. And Christabel, who had considered spitefully to let Charles stay at Waybridge all summer (now that Maud was out of the way), was forced by her conscience and by Diana's questioning eyes to take him out, which meant that he, and she, would be situated at only a ten-kilometer distance from Maud. And Maud who still rode her bicycle, and Diana who loved to drive a car!

Christabel postponed their departure as long as possible, but finally the heat and the quiet of the little suburb became too much for her as well, and she and Charles and the wheelchair drove out to their summer cottage.

Already on the second day Maud came over on her bicycle, and Christabel had to take the chess set out to the garden. From the kitchen window she could see them sitting very close to each other. Charles' almost bald head, and Maud's white hair halo, which, although very thin against the light, made quite a contrast against the bougainvillea that grew up the wall behind them.

For a moment she liked what she saw. They radiated a sort of peace that she did not share. A couple of pieces had found their places—but it wasn't her puzzle. She liked what she saw and at the same time she didn't. Something was tormenting her inside, and she refused to give it a name.

Then there were other days with more company. All mixed, children with grandchildren, relatives with relatives. And then both peace and tension were dispelled and Christabel said to Charles that it was a very nice summer, wasn't it? And sometimes Charles smiled at her and took her hand and said: "Yes, dear Christabel, I'm so well off!"

But when fall came, and he was silent and listless in his wheelchair and almost refused to eat, she returned him reluctantly to Waybridge, and when on the first Sunday in September she came for a visit, something happened. She opened the door to Charles' room, and, since he wasn't there, she immediately went across the corridor to Maud's room and opened that door as well, without knocking.

What she saw alarmed her at first from the point of view of Charles' health. She thought that he had had a stroke. Otherwise, why should he lie, as though unconscious, straight across Maud's easy chair, with such a stupidly open mouth, and showing mostly the whites of his eyes? The next moment her jealousy, quite rightly, got the upper hand, and she screamed a rather dirty word, went out and slammed the door with a bang.

It didn't take long for Maud to catch up with her on the wide staircase down to the lobby. "For God's sake Christabel, what is the matter?"

"There's nothing wrong with me. You're the one who's crazy, Maud. Man crazy! Can't you leave old Charles in peace? Don't you understand that you can kill him that way? If he gets worse he can't stay here, you know. I'll be the one to have to take care of him . . . I mean, of course I'll do it gladly, but not if it's a result of his . . . and your . . . and it's dirty! That's what it is: dirty! And dangerous, as a matter of fact!"

She sounded furious and bitter, like a schoolgirl who had seen a friend juggle with her favorite ornament: a cat made of thin gold-plated porcelain.

"But please," Maud said, and smoothed down her hair. Her cheeks were very flushed. "Please, Christabel. I am old. And Charles is old. And—" She didn't say: you are too, but she paused long enough for those words. "Do we really have to take it this way?"

They sat down in a couple of the deep easy chairs in the lobby, and were silent for a long time. Christabel whimpered now and then. Finally Maud began to speak. She spoke quietly and with a lot of tenderness. She put one hand on Christabel's arm, and Christabel let it stay there. After about an hour they got up, and Christabel said: "Well, the most important thing is that he doesn't find out that it was me. I feel so ridiculous."

And Maud lied: "No, of course not. He was sleeping, the old darling. I told him that one of the personnel had made a mistake." And: "You're careful with him, aren't you? He is all I have," Christabel whimpered. "Besides," and there was a spiteful schoolgirl tone in her voice, "besides, I'm going to take him home as soon as I get the wheelchair ramp built."

"When will that be?" Maud asked innocently.

"Hard to say," Christabel said nonchalantly. "It isn't easy to get workers nowadays." And the conversation turned into a general condemnation of workers, wages and labor unions.

One of the old ladies in another deep, flowery easy chair, picked up the word "socialist" and burst out: "And Rhodesia is gone! Gone for ever!"

When they said goodbye at the car, Christabel had almost started to believe that Charles had actually fallen forward in his sleep. But as soon as she had started the car and driven out towards the main road she hissed: "I did see what I saw!" and she stepped so hard on the accelerator that she only narrowly escaped hitting a young Arab at the crossing.

Maud walked across the lawn whistling to herself and dexterously avoided stepping on the "No Trespassing" sign. She walked as she did when she was a girl. She was thinking about an episode, a classic episode, in the lives of the Bloomsbury set when Lytton Strachey pointed at Vanessa Bell's skirt and said in his

squeaky voice: "What do I see there? Isn't that semen?"

Semen, she mumbled. The chestnuts were more yellow than the sunshine. The traffic hummed like the
summer's last bumblebee. A spot was congealing on
her skirt, it was as big as a halfpenny.

# The Girl Across the Room

## BY ALICE ADAMS

*Y*vonne Soulas, the art historian, is much more beautiful in her late sixties than she was when she was young, and this is strange, because she has had much trouble in her life, including pancreatic cancer, through which she lived when no one expected her to. Neither her doctor nor her husband, Matthew Vann, the musicologist-manufacturer, thought she would make it, such a small, thin woman. Make it she did, however, although she lost much of her hair in the process of treatment. Now, seated with Matthew on the porch of an inn on the northern-California coast, her fine, precise features framed in skillfully arranged false white waves, she is a lovely woman. In the cool spring night she is wearing soft pale woollen clothes, a shawl, and Italian boots, daintily stitched.

Matthew Vann is also a handsome person, with silky white hair and impressive dark eyes, and he, too, wears elegant clothes. His posture is distinguished. Yvonne has never taken his name, not for feminist reasons but because she thinks the combination is unaesthetic: Yvonne Vann? Matthew looks and is considerably more fragile than Yvonne, although they are about the same age: that is to say, among other things, of an age to wonder which of them will outlive the other. The question is impossible, inadmissible, and crucially important. Matthew *is* frailer, but then, Yvonne's illness could recur at any time.

They have been married for a little over thirty years, and they live, these days, in San Francisco, having decided that the rigors of New England winters and the overstimulation of Cambridge social life were, in combination, far too much for them. Trips to Europe, also, formerly a source of much pleasure, now seem, really, more strenuous than fun. And so Yvonne and Matthew have taken to exploring certain areas of California, beginning with the near at hand: Yosemite, Lake Tahoe, and now this extraordinarily beautiful stretch of coast at Mendocino, where rivers empty into the sea between sheer cliffs of rock.

They are sitting at the far end of the white-railed porch that runs the length of the building in which they are lodging. They have had an early dinner, hoping for quiet, and they are tired from a day of exploring the town and the meadows high above the vibrating sea. The other guests are almost all golfing people, since there is a course adjacent to the inn. They are people in late middle age, a little younger than Yvonne and Matthew, mostly overweight, tending to noise and heavy smoking and excessive drink. Not pleasant dinner companions. And Yvonne and Matthew were successful: they finished a quiet dinner of excellent abalone before the boisterous arrival of the golfing group. There was only one other couple in the dining room. That other couple had also been distinctly not a part of the golfing group, and they were as striking, in their way, as Yvonne and Matthew were in theirs. Yvonne had been unable not to stare at them—the girl so young and perfectly controlled in all her gestures, the man much older than the girl, so clearly and happily in love with her. It won't end well, Yvonne had thought.

Everything is fine, as they sit now on the porch. This place to which they have come is very beautiful. The walks through wild flowers and the views back to the river mouth, the beaches, the opposite banks of green are all marvellous. Everything is fine, except for a nagging area of trouble that has just lodged itself somewhere near Yvonne's heart. But the trouble is quite irrational, and she is an eminently sensible woman, and so she pushes it aside and begins a conversation with Matthew about something else.

"A thing that I like about being old," she observes to him, at the same time as she reflects that many of their conversations have had just this beginning, "is that you go on trips for their own sake, just to see something. Not expecting the trip to change your life." Not hoping that the man you are with will want to marry you, she is thinking to herself, or that Italy will cure your husband of a girl.

"Ye-e-es," drawls Matthew, in his vague New Hampshire way. But he is a good listener; he very much enjoys her conversation. "Yvonne is the least boring person in the world," he has often said—if not to her, to a great many other people.

"When you're young, you really don't see much beyond yourself," Yvonne muses.

Then, perhaps at having spoken the word "young," thinking of young people, of herself much younger, the trouble increases. It becomes an active heavy pressure on her heart, so that she closes her eyes for a moment. Then she opens them, facing it, admitting to herself: That girl in the dining room reminded me of Susanna, in Cambridge, almost thirty years ago. Not long after we were married, which of course made it worse.

What happened was this:

In the late forties, in Cambridge, Yvonne was viewed as a smart, attractive, but not really pretty Frenchwoman. A widow? Divorced? No one knew for sure. She had heavy dark hair, a husky voice, and a way of starting sentences with an "Ah!" that sounded like a tiny bark. Some people were surprised to find her married to Matthew Vann, a glamorous man, admired for having fought in Spain as well as for his great good looks, a man as distinguished as he was rich. Then a beautiful young Radcliffe girl who wanted to become a dancer, and for all anyone knew eventually became one—a golden California girl, Susanna—fell in love with Matthew, and he with her. But Yvonne wouldn't let him go, and so nothing came of it. That was all.

Thus went the story that circulated like a lively winter germ through the areas of Cambridge adjacent to Harvard Square, up and down Brattle Street, Linnaean, Garden Street, and Massachusetts Avenue, and finally over to Hillside Place, where Yvonne and Matthew then were living.

But that is not, exactly, how it was. It went more like this:

"You won't believe me, but I think a very young girl has fallen in love with me," Matthew said to Yvonne one night, near the end of their dinner of *lapin au moutarde*, a specialty of Yvonne's which she always thenceforward connected unpleasantly with that night, although she continued to make it from time to time. (Silly not to, really.) Then Matthew laughed, a little awkward, embarrassed. "It does seem unlikely."

"Not at all." Yvonne's tone was light, the words automatic. Her accent was still very French. "You are a most handsome man," she said.

"You might remember her. We met her at the Emorys'. Susanna something, from California. I've kept seeing her in Widener, and now she says she wants to help me with my research." He laughed, more embarrassed yet.

Yvonne experienced a wave of fury, which she quickly brought under control, breathing regularly and taking a small sip of wine. Of course she remembered the girl: long dark-gold hair and sunny, tawny skin; bad clothes, but not needing good clothes with that long lovely neck; a stiff, rather self-conscious dancer's walk; lovely long hands, beautifully controlled. Anyone would fall in love with her.

In those days, while Yvonne did her own work at the Fogg, Matthew was combining supervision of the factory he had inherited, in Waltham, with the musicologist's career that he had chosen. The research he had mentioned was for his book on Boccherini, for which they would later spend a year in Italy. They had married after a wildly passionate affair, during which Yvonne had managed to wrest Matthew away from poor Flossie, his alcoholic first wife, now long since dead in Tennessee.

And, thinking over the problem of Susanna, one thing that Yvonne said silently to her rival was: You can't have him, I've already been through too much for Matthew. Also, in her exceptionally clearheaded way, Yvonne *knew* Matthew, in a way that violent love can sometimes preclude. She knew that he would not take Susanna to bed unless he had decided to break with Yvonne—this out of a strong and somewhat aberrant New England sense of honor, and also out of sexual shyness, unusual in so handsome, so sensual a man. Yvonne herself had had to resort to a kind of seduction by force. But a young, proud girl could not know of such tactics.

Yvonne was right. Matthew did not have an affair with Susanna; he probably never saw her outside of Widener, except for an intense cup of coffee at Hayes-Bickford, where they were noticed together. However, Matthew suffered severely, and that was how Yvonne treated him—like someone with a serious disease. She was affectionate and solicitous, and very slightly distant, as though his illness were something that she didn't want to catch.

One March evening, after a bright, harsh day of intermittent sun, rain, and wind, Matthew came home for dinner a little late, with a look on his face of total and anguished exhaustion. Handing him his gin—they were in the kitchen; she had been tasting her good lamb stew, a *navarin*—Yvonne thought, Ah, the girl has broken it off, or has given him an ultimatum; such a mistake. She thought, I hope I won't have to hear about it.

All Matthew said during dinner was "The Boccherini project is sort of getting me down. My ideas don't come together."

"Poor darling," she said carefully, alertly watching his face.

"I should spend more time at the factory."

"Well, why don't you?"

As they settled in the living room for coffee, Yvonne saw that his face had relaxed a little. Perhaps now he would want to talk to her? She said, "There's a Fred Astaire revival at the U.T. tonight. I know you don't like them, but would you mind if I go? Ah, dear, it's almost time."

Not saying: You unspeakable fool, how dare you put me through all this? Are you really worth it?

Alone in the crowded balcony of the University Theatre, as on the screen Fred and Ginger sang to each other about how lovely a day it was to be caught in the rain, Yvonne thought, for a moment, that she would after all go home and tell Matthew to go to his girl, Susanna. She would release him, with as little guilt as possible, since she was indeed fond of Matthew. *Je tiens à Matthew.*

*Tenir à.* I hold to Matthew, Yvonne thought then. And she also thought, No, it would not work out well at all. Matthew is much too vulnerable for a girl like that. He is better off with me.

Of course she was right, as Matthew himself must have come to realize, and over the summer he seemed to recover from his affliction. Yvonne saw his recovery, but she also understood that she had been seriously wounded by that episode, coming as it did so early in their life together. Afterward she was able to think more sensibly, Well, much better early than later on, when he could have felt more free.

That fall they left for Italy, where, curiously, neither of them had been before—Yvonne because her Anglo-phile parents had always taken her to the Devon coast on holidays, or sometimes to Scotland, Matthew because with drunken Flossie any travel was impossible.

They settled in a small hotel in Rome, in a large romantically alcoved room that overlooked the Borghese Gardens. They went on trips: north to Orvieto, Todi, Spoleto, Gubbio; south to Salerno, Positano, Ravello. They were dazed, dizzy with pleasure at the landscape, the vistas of olive orchards, of pines and flowers and stones, the ancient buildings, the paintings and statuary. The food and wine. They shared a mania for pasta.

A perfect trip, except that from time to time Yvonne was jolted sharply by a thought of that girl, Susanna. And, looking at Matthew, she wondered if he, too, thought of her—with sadness, regret? The question hurt.

She would have to ask Matthew, and deliberately she chose a moment of pure happiness. They were seated on a vine-covered terrace, at Orvieto, across the square from the gorgeously striped cathedral, drinking cool white wine, having made love early that morning, when Yvonne asked, "Do you ever wonder what happened to that girl, Susanna?"

Genuine puzzlement appeared on Matthew's distinguished face, and then he said, "I almost never think of her. I don't have time."

Knowing Matthew, Yvonne was sure that he spoke the truth, and she wryly thought, I undoubtedly think more often of that girl, that episode, than Matthew does.

And so she, too, stopped thinking of Susanna—or almost, except for an occasional reminder.

Leaving Rome, they travelled up to Florence, then Venice, Innsbruck, and Vienna—where Boccherini did, or quite possibly did not, murder his rival, Mozart.

That was the first of a succession of great trips.

———

Yvonne and Matthew remained, for the most part, very happy with each other, and over the years their sexual life declined only slightly. Then, in her late fifties, Yvonne became terribly sick, at first undiagnosably so. Surgery was indicated. On being told the probable nature of her illness—she had insisted on that—Yvonne remarked to her doctor, one of the chief surgeons at Massachusetts General, "Well, my chances are not exactly marvellous, then, are they?"

He looked embarrassed, and gazed in the direction of the Charles, just visible from his high office window. "No, not marvellous," he admitted.

After surgery, oppressively drugged, Yvonne was mainly aware of pain, which surged in heavy waves toward her, almost overwhelming her, and very gradually receding. She was aware, too, of being handled a great deal, not always gently, of needles inserted, and tubes, of strong hands manipulating her small body.

Sometimes, half conscious, she would wonder if she was dreaming. But at least she knew that she was alive: dead people don't wonder about anything, she was sure of that.

The first face that she was aware of was her surgeon's: humorless, stern, seeming always to be saying, No, not marvellous. Then there was the face of a black nurse, kind and sad, a gentle, mourning face. At last she saw Matthew, so gaunt and stricken that she knew she had to live. It was that simple: dying was something she could not do to Matthew.

"She's got to be the strongest woman I've ever seen, basically," the dubious surgeon remarked later on to Matthew, who by then could beamingly agree.

Chemotherapy worked; it took most of her hair but fortunately did not make her sick. Yvonne very gradually regained strength, and some health, and with a great effort she put back on a few of the many lost pounds. Matthew learned to make a superior *fettuccine*, and he served it to her often.


After her illness and surgery, they did not make love anymore; they just did not. Yvonne missed it, in a dim sad way, but on the other hand she could sometimes smile at the very idea of such a ludicrous human activity, to which she herself had once devoted so much time. She was on the whole amused and a little skeptical of accounts of very sexually active seventy- and eighty-year-olds: why did they bother, really?

While she was recuperating, Yvonne finished a study of Marie Laurencin that she had been working on for years, and her book had considerable acclaim, even reasonably good sales. Matthew did not finish his Boccherini study, but from time to time he published articles in places like the *Yale Review*, the *Virginia Quarterly Review*.

A year ago, they left Cambridge and moved to the pleasant flat on Green Street, in San Francisco.

———

Now, on the porch in Mendocino, thinking of the girl across the room at dinner, and remembering Susanna, all that pain, Yvonne has a vivid insight as to how it would have been if she had abandoned Matthew to Susanna all those years ago. Matthew would, of course, have married the girl—that is how he is—and they would have been quite happy for a while. He would have gazed dotingly upon her in restaurants, like the man in the dining room, with his Susanna. And then somehow it would all have gone bad, with a sad old age for Matthew, the girl bored and irritable, Matthew worn out, not understanding anything.

But what of herself? What would have happened to her? The strange part is that Yvonne has never inquired into this before. Now, with perfect logic, she suddenly, jarringly sees just what would have happened: for a while, considerable unhappiness for her, a slow recovery. And then she would have been quite herself again, maybe a little improved. She would have remarried—amazing, she can almost see him! He is no one she knows, but a man much younger than herself, very dark. In fact, he is French; they have many intimate things in common. He might be a painter. He is very unlike Matthew. Would she still have had her great illness? She is not sure; her vision ends with that man, her marriage to him.

Something in her expression, probably, has made Matthew ask a question never asked between them, a question, in fact, for adolescent lovers: "What were you thinking about, just now?"

And he is given, by Yvonne, the requisite response: "I was thinking, my darling, of you. At least in part."

The air on the porch is perceptibly chillier than when they first came out from dinner. Time to go in, and yet they are both reluctant to move: it is so beautiful where they are. In the distance, gray-white lines of foam cross the sea, beneath a calm pale evening sky; closer to hand are the surrounding, sheltering pines and cypresses.

Then, from whatever uncharacteristic moment of strong emotion, Matthew says another thing that he has not said before. "I was thinking," he says, "that without you I would not have had much of a life at all."

Does he mean if they had never met? Or does he mean if he had left her for that girl, for fair Susanna? Or if she had died? It is impossible to ask, and so Yvonne frowns, unseen, in the gathering dusk—both at the ambiguity and at the surprise of it. And she, too, says something new: "Ah, Matthew, what an absolute fool you are." But she has said it lightly, and she adds, "You would have got along perfectly well without me." She knows that out of her true fondness for Matthew she has lied, and that it is still necessary for her to survive him.

# Mrs. Moonlight

## BY HELEN NORRIS

*D*uring the night she would forget about the treehouse. In the morning when she heard the hammering,
like a woodpecker gone just a little wild, she would
go outside and look at Mr. Snider halfway up the tree
and say to him, "What are you building?" And he
would stop and tell her gravely, "Ma'am, I'm making
you this treehouse like you ast me to do." And then
she would remember. To forget and then remember
made a wonderful surprise at the start of each day.
Sometimes she remembered without having to be told.
But whichever way it was, she was happy about the
treehouse.

She didn't tell him that she planned to live in it. She
knew better than that. She told him that she wanted it
for her granddaughter Mitzi. He didn't guess she
would live there to be out of her daughter's hair once
and for all so the question of the nursing home would
disappear.

Her daughter was to be away from home for two
weeks; she sold cosmetics on the road. And Mrs. Gideon figured she could get the treehouse ready in that

length of time and be all moved in when her daughter got back. So she asked Mr. Snider what his charge would be. He added up numbers in his little gray notebook with the stub of a pencil he kept hanging from it on a piece of string. He told her he could do it for four hundred if she wanted the best. If she wanted less than that, he could make it three-fifty. "I want the best," she said.

"What about plumbing?" she inquired.

"Plumbing? Oh, ma'am, they got restrictions."

"It's all right," she said. "I can come down for that."

"You planning on being up here some yourself?"

"I might," she said. "You can't tell."

He looked at her slantwise. "I wouldn't recommend it."

"What about a stove?"

"A stove?"

"For cooking."

"That ain't exactly possible. Unless . . ." He consulted the sky, the tree, and the ground. He turned and spat with care on the far side of her. "Unless a 'lectrician could run a line up the trunk. You might could have a little hot plate, something of that nature. I said might. They got restrictions."

"That's what I'll do," she said.

"I said he might could do it, ma'am."

"It's all right either way. I can fix sandwiches. And I'm very fond of junk food."

Sometimes the way he looked at her she thought he

might have guessed her plans, but she didn't care. He was being paid and that was that. She was sick to death of everybody dabbling in her business. Mattie the maid was always snooping. She had been told to do it. "Miss Fanny, you ain't et a bite a lunch." "Miss Fanny, I wouldn't walk that far if I was you." Her daughter was gone all day and Mitzi was in school till three o'clock. So Mattie trailed her. "Mattie, don't you have some cleaning you can do?"

Mrs. Gideon had a special treehouse in mind. She drew the plan for Mr. Snider on a paper napkin. "It has to look this way. I had a treehouse once and it was just like this. I want a window here, and just a little platform where I can sit and watch the moon."

He looked slantwise again. "I wouldn't recommend a person being up here after dark. A ladder ain't that safe."

"Make it safe," she said.

When the house was well along, she looked up one morning and was amazed to see that it was like the treehouse she had had when she was young. "Mr. Snider, this is wonderful! This is just the way my treehouse looked when I was young, the little porch and all."

"Ma'am, I'm building it the way you ast me to do."

"Did I?" she said in wonder. "Well, I'm glad." She had forgotten all about it.

But the treehouse of the past was very clear in her mind. It had been built when she was ten, and there the best years of her life had been spent. Sometimes she had slipped up to watch the sunrise. She had watched the moonrise too, heard the wind in the leaves and the treefrogs after rain and the chatter of the squirrels and birds going to sleep, all as if she had belonged to the world of the tree. Especially she remembered how clear her mind had been. Everything that happened seemed to fall into a crystal pool and she could look down and see it lying on the bottom whenever she chose. Not like it was today. Not like that at all.

Again she asked Mr. Snider what his charge would be. Then she wrote him out a check and pinned it to the leaf of the tree he was in. "I might forget it later on. Things slip my mind." She thought of telling him that she was seventy-eight. Or was she older than that? Or maybe she was younger. She would have to look it up, but it didn't matter.

She waited till one day when the house was almost finished. All it needed was the ladder and a second coat of fern green paint. Then she made a phone call. Just dialing made her happy.

He answered her at once, as if he had been waiting. He sounded just the same, but older of course.

"Robert, this is Fanny Gideon."

"Fanny Gideon!" he said, as if they shared something precious, which of course they did.

"I know it's a long way, but I got something to show you."

"Have you, now?"

"I know it's a long way."

"Not for me. Ten miles is not far. I got wheels." And he laughed. "That's what my grandson says."

"They let you drive?" she said. "That's wonderful, Robert. They took my wheels away."

"They wouldn't try it with me. I can outdrive 'em all."

"Can you come right away?"

"You bet I can." He sounded happy about it.

She made a little note for herself and put it on the door, just in case she forgot, which she didn't think she would. It said: "Robert is coming over to see the treehouse."

But she didn't need the note. She was waiting in the swing on the porch. And when he drove up and got out of his car, she knew again that they had made the big mistake of their lives when they hadn't gotten married when they were fifteen, hadn't run away again when they were caught and brought back, hadn't told the family just to go to hell.

She had seen him the last time, oh, she couldn't remember when. She would have to ask him. He came toward her, not as tall as then, not as steady on his feet, but just as straight. All his hair. All his teeth, as far as she could tell. A beautiful man.

She stood up to greet him. "I see you got both eyes and both hands and both feet."

He looked down at his feet and then he held up his hands. "So I have," he said, surprised. And with his hands he took hers.

"But we have to wear glasses," she said, gay and happy.

"No, we don't. But they tell us to do it, and we humor 'em."

She led him out to the treehouse. Mr. Snider was standing on his painting ladder. The ladder for the house he was going to build last. Only his paint-speckled shoes could be seen.

"What do you think?" she said.

His eyes misted over. He circled the tree. Leaves were winking in the sunlight.

"What do you think?"

"It's perfect," he said, moved. "It's just the way it was."

"I thought you would like it."

"Like it! It's the best thing been built in the last sixty years. Maybe sixty-five. How old are we, Fanny?"

"I can't remember. But I know how old we were. We were fifteen then. It was the best year of my life."

He gazed up at the treehouse, narrowing his eyes. He took off his glasses and sighted through one lens. "Mine too. The best."

"You see the little porch where we used to watch the moon?"

"I do," he said.

"You used to call me Mrs. Moonlight. You said it was because my hair was like moonlight."

"It still is," he said.

"Of course it's not. It never was . . . I wanted you to see what I was up to here."

"Why you doin' it, Fanny?"

"Well, because I have a little trouble remembering things. But I remember that, up there, things were clear as ice. I could look down on things and see the way they were. And I was closer to the sun and it warmed up my brain and made it work fine, and the moon cooled it off so it didn't overheat."

He laughed out loud. "You gonna climb up and heat up and cool off and recall things?"

She laughed along with him. "I aim to do just that."

"I might come and join you."

"Do you think your wife would mind?"

"She died," he said.

"Did I know that?" she said.

"You came to the funeral."

She was silent for a bit. "You see what I mean?" It must have been at the funeral that she had seen him last. She added, "I'm sorry . . . I'm sorry again."

He put his arm around her. "It was five years ago."

"Did you grieve a lot?"

He thought about it for a while. "She didn't like me very much."

She touched his hand lightly. "How could she not?"


Her daughter came back before the ladder was made. She stood and looked up at the treehouse in the early sun. She was smartly dressed. Her face was made up with some of the cosmetics she'd been selling on the road. A purplish shade of lipstick that was catching on.

Eye shadow to match. Nail polish to match. She wore white sandals, a white pleated skirt, a silk and linen sweater in a fuchsia shade, and a little white scarf to hide the lines in her throat. She left to talk with Mattie. She came out again and lay in wait for Mr. Snider. She told him she was sorry but it had to come down. He shook his head from side to side.

"Don't worry, you'll be paid."

"I done been paid," he said. "It's a shame to knock it down. I done my best work."

"Mr. Snider, I'm surprised at you. You should have known better."

"Better 'n what?" he said, indignant. "I work for hire."

Mrs. Gideon kept to her room. Through her door she heard the murmur of Mattie telling on her. When her daughter knocked, she stiffened every muscle in her body. "Come in," she said, although she didn't want to say it. She hardly knew her daughter with the purple lipstick on and her purple lids.

"Mama, I hope you know we can't leave it there."

"Why? Why?" said Mrs. Gideon. "I had it built to live in."

"To live in!" said her daughter. "When you have a nice room in a comfortable house?" She tore off her scarf as if she couldn't breathe.

"But I get in your way. You talk of putting me somewhere." She would not say the word. "I should think you'd be happy to have me out of the house."

Her daughter dropped to Mrs. Gideon's bed and

thrust her face into her purple-tipped fingers. "Mama, I want to keep you here, but you make it very hard when you do things like this. I have to work. I have to travel. I have to leave you alone. And Mattie can't keep up with you every minute of the day. How could you imagine you could live in a treehouse?"

"Well, I didn't," said Mrs. Gideon, seeing how the wind was blowing. "I thought it would be nice for Mitzi to play in."

"Mitzi is seventeen. She doesn't want a treehouse. She wants clothes and a car."

"I had a treehouse when I was fifteen, but maybe times have changed."

"It has to come down."

Mrs. Gideon was holding back the tears. "Why does it? Why does it? It looks lovely in the tree."

"Because, Mama, if I leave it you'll be climbing up some day."

"How could I when it doesn't have a ladder made?"

"You will find one somehow and you will fall and I will be to blame."

"No one would blame you if I fell."

"I would blame myself."

Mrs. Gideon thought tearfully that many of the wretched things that happen in the world grow out of people's saying that they don't want the blame for something that in the first place is totally not their business. She said with dignity, "I've never even seen what it is like inside, but if you like I'll promise you I won't go up."

"Mama, you'll forget. You always forget. You light the stove and forget. You plug in the iron and then you forget. You almost burn the house down once a week. You took the bus to town and forgot to come home."

"I didn't forget. I wasn't ready."

"Mama, you forgot. You've even forgotten now that you forgot."

"I can't win," said Mrs. Gideon. She blew her nose and looked through the window. "About the treehouse, I paid for it," she said at last, "entirely with my money. I remember that quite clearly. I wrote a check."

"Your money. Well, Mama, it's your money and it isn't. Because when you spend it up it's mine that keeps you going."

"I have enough to last me."

"Not at this rate you don't."

Afterward Mrs. Gideon lay on the bed and thought that she was tired of being treated as if she were too young to have sense and at the same time too old to have sense. She wouldn't let herself believe that they would tear the treehouse down . . .

But late in the morning she heard the sound of hammering and splintering wood. And she cried into her pillow as if her heart would break.

She would not come out for lunch, so Mattie left a tray on the floor outside her room. When her daughter had gone to work in the afternoon she ventured from the room, stepping over the tray of food, and looked out the back door. In the tree there was nothing. It was as if the treehouse had never been. It was just the way the other one had gone when she was young. Gone in an hour. Nothing left.

She turned away, tears blinding her eyes. Mattie was working in the bedroom upstairs. She passed the telephone and thought of calling Robert, for he would grieve too. But what could he do? The phone book was opened to the yellow pages, and there she saw marked the name of a nursing home, the number outlined.

She was cold all over. Her fingers were numb, but she found Robert's number. "I need you," she said.

He heard the cry in her voice. "I'm coming," he said.

When he came she was sitting in the swing on the porch. "Go look at the treehouse." She did not want to see its ruination again.

He returned in a moment. "What happened?" he asked.

"She had it torn down. That's what happened."

He saw her eyes red from weeping. After a while he said, "But we can remember it. She can't tear that down."

She swung for a little, while he stood below her in the grass. "I didn't tell you, Robert, but I was planning to live there. Be out of her way. Get all moved in by the time she got back . . . It's not crazy," she said. "I was going to have a little hot plate put in. Be out of her way . . ." The chain creaked as she swung. "But now you know what? I made the thing happen I didn't want to happen. The reason I did it was to keep it away. She called a nursing home. I saw the number by the phone. I'm so afraid, Robert. I'm so afraid."

He climbed the steps then and sat down beside her. They swung together. He held her hand.

"I'm so tired of being treated like I don't have sense enough to live here."

"I know," he said. "I get it too. But when he gets too out of line I tell my son off."

"You do? I wish I could."

"You gotta have guts, the older you get." He thought of it, swinging. "It takes more guts than it does when you're young."

"If we had got married when we tried then . . . If we had been faster so they couldn't have caught us . . ."

He squeezed her hand.

"I don't ever think about my husband," she said. "Isn't that strange? I never think about him. It was like when he died I had got that over with. I must have been sad, though. I can't recall."

They swung in silence.

"I wish I could start my life over again. I'd fix it so I wouldn't have to be afraid."

"I'm thinking," he said. "I'm thinking now. You wanta live in a treehouse? My kid brother has a little house in the woods. You remember Alfie. It's in the next county. Trees around it. You can't hardly see it for all the trees. Nothing fancy inside. He goes there to hunt in the wintertime."

She was suddenly so happy she began to cry. "You mean we could go?"

"Why not?" he said. "I slipped around and saw where he hides the key."

Her eyes were shining as she thought of it.

"You go in and leave a note for your daughter. Say you're with me and we've gone to the woods. I'll be in the car."

"I'll do it," she said. She went inside but didn't write the note. She grabbed her purse from the dresser and a sweater from the bed and slipped out when Mattie was running water in the sink. She climbed in beside him in the Pontiac.

Down the road a ways he said, "Did you leave her the note?"

"I think I forgot it."

"You didn't forget. You just didn't want to do it. I know you, Fanny Gideon, from way, way back."

"I was afraid she'd come and get me. Are you mad with me, Robert?"

"Hell, no, I'm not mad. She deserves what she gets."

"You didn't tell your son."

"I never tell him a thing. Once you start leaving notes it's like asking permission."

She couldn't remember when she had been so happy. "This is like when we were young and ran away to get married." She was smiling at him.

He was smiling too but looking hard at the road. Drivers everywhere were getting crazier all the time.

Just stay out of their way. If he lost his license now he wouldn't get it back.

"Robert," she said, "can you remember things?"

"Not as well as I did, but well enough I guess."

"Good," she said. "You take care of the past and I'll handle the present."

"Who's in charge of the future?"

"Oh, it's in charge of itself."

It seemed to him a very funny thing for her to say. "So should we finish what we started back then and get married?" He hadn't planned to say it, but it was said and he was glad.

"What about your wife?"

He tensed to make a turn. "She died."

". . . I'm truly very sorry."

"It's all right," he said. "It's over and done. So do you want to get married?"

"I sort of like the idea of living in sin. Don't you?"

"I do," he said.

At length he put it to her gravely, "If you married me I think they'd leave us alone. We could live somewhere."

"It's too late for that."

"Too late? Like you said, the future is in charge of itself."

A shade passed over her. "I'm too late."

They left the pavement. They drove into the country and now he relaxed. Beside them were fields of greening oats crosshatched with shadows from the passing clouds. Swarms of keening birds swept out of the sky. A whirl of wind whipped out of a tunnel beneath the road. It raked the pasture grasses and combed them all backward and followed the road. The willows in the ditches bridled and dipped.

She tied her sweater loosely in a knot about her throat. "It was raining before. We were driving through rain."

"The windshield misted up. I had to go slow."

"I remember everything about that day." They passed cattle standing knee deep in a lake. "We're running from them now like we did before."

"We're not running from them. Don't think about running. Don't think about them. Think about they're young, with the memories they're proud of crammed with junk, plain junk. There's not much about them we could recommend."

"They're faster," she said. "The people who come after you are always faster. Or they wouldn't win."

He turned into the trees and shifted gears. With a howl from the engine they drove up, up on a pine-needled road. And soon, very soon he pointed to the house tucked away in trees. She exclaimed with delight. There was a series of steps they must climb to reach it. Like a ladder, she laughed. He wanted to help her, but she waved him away. "I've still got my legs." "So you have," he observed her. "You're like a mountain goat. I've gotten slower."

Inside was a small and airless room with a hearth at

one end and a bed at the other. There was a smell of
ash. Against one wall was a rusting stove. "I told you
not fancy."

"I didn't come for fancy." It made her think of an
acorn, brown and secret, the way a room should be
that lives in trees. She could feel the swaying of her
childhood treehouse when the wind blew at dusk and
she pulled her long hair over her head to match the
birds snug in their rippling feathers.

"It's got a bathroom off that door by the bed."

"And a porch," she whispered, knowing it was there
on the other side of another door. She pulled it open
and walked out slowly. The sun was nesting in a giant
maple full of summer. The lowest branches swept the
weathered boards. The massive trunk fell out of sight
below. She dropped her purse and settled like a wren
among the leaves.

He watched her from the doorway. Then he joined
her, stepping through the branches to inspect what lay
beneath. The floor of the forest dropped sharply away.
The porch had the look of being blown into the hillside
and the house that followed it propped on piles. Fanny's own treehouse had been better made.

He returned to her and stood among the mammoth
branches, their leaf clusters hanging like fruit in the
motionless air. He smiled at her but he could not
speak. He had lost the power and the spell of a tree,
lost how it was to feel himself all gone into the green
. . . to desire it so much . . . to climb anything, to
swing from anything, a rope, a vine, daring death to

get it ... a craving so strong it was strange it wasn't called immoral or illegal. But then the moralists were all grown up. He had been young and full of the craving and Fanny Gideon had given him her tree. If she hadn't had a treehouse, would they have loved?

She looked up at him with happiness. "We have always been married."

He held out his hand. She pulled it down and kissed it and kept it in hers. "Your hand is just the way I need a hand to be. Not young and not old. Take care of it," she said.

"I will," he said, moved, and knowing he would have loved her without her tree. "Are you hungry?" he asked. "There might be something in there."

She shook her head. "I'm too happy to eat. This is the happiest I've ever been. I've forgotten the rest."

Her happiness began to make him afraid. Like the tree before them, it was larger than life. There was nothing to tell him if it was real, or if she had made it to hide her fear. Her fear was real, for he felt it stir in the deep of his throat, in the palm of his hand, the way he would know whatever was wrong when she was a girl. When they climbed the ladder it was always there for the tree to know. For him to know if he knew the tree. He had learned the tree. On the calmest day he could feel it wanting to circle and toss, have some fun, give them something to think about. On a windy day he would spin with it, going green inside, getting into its marrow, feeling within it the way she was, knowing he would marry the way she was, the way he felt the way she was . . . And now he was troubled with the empty years. They turned in his bones where they must have lain but he hadn't known. What he dreaded most at this time of his life was to live through anything over again. The flight they'd begun being ended again, the door they had opened being shut once more. Life had come to seem like a series of things that repeated themselves, until one day he had closed his heart. It was better perhaps to forget . . . like Fanny. He could feel something break like a bough in the woods.

Her eyes had never left the tree. The air was stirring. A shudder swept through the leaves and into her. "How long will we be here?"

"Till we want to leave."

"Till they find us, you mean?"

He did not reply. He was aware that the tree was growing dark within. Only the tips of branches were still green-gold. Somewhere deep within it was a whir of wings. He went inside and found some coffee to brew in a pan. There were crackers in a tin, but they seemed too stale. He came out with her coffee. "It's the best we have."

She took the cup absently and drank a little. "It's very good, Robert." She laid the cup on the floor. Her voice, it seemed to him, was just as it had been. In the failing light he saw her face again young and kindling the treehouse they had never let go. Her hair was the color it had been in the moonlight . . .

He found a weathered chair that had been tipped against the wall. He drew it across the floor and sat be-

side her in the dusk. It was dark in the tree. They could
hear the birds within settling into the night, and somewhere an owl. And a wind came from nowhere to sleep
in the woods, bedding down in the leaves but restless,
turning, sighing, troubled with dreams, sleepwalking in
leaf mold, crouching in the chimney, falling into the ravine . . . It was turning cooler. "Where is the moon?"
she asked with longing in her voice.

"It isn't time, Mrs. Moonlight. Give it time." He
stroked her hair while they sat between the tree dark
and the dark of their room, between two darks with an
equal claim, and neither would release them into the
other. But fireflies wove the darks into night . . . He
took her hand and led her, it seemed to her, into the
tree, but it must have been the room. For she lay on
the bed and he took off her glasses and then her shoes.
He covered her with a blanket that smelled of smoke.

"I want you near me," she said.

So he lay down beside her. "There isn't a light," he
whispered. "Do you mind the dark?"

"Not when you are with me."

He found her hands and kissed them. They were
trembling and cold. He drew the blanket closely about
her throat.

She said, "I won't think about anything but now. Or
remember . . . I won't remember anything but then. I
fight all the time to keep from losing myself. They try
to make me remember the things they want me to remember. Why do I have to remember *their* things?
Never mine. My things. Go to a nursing home because

I left my coat in the park? Such a fuss she made. I didn't care about the coat. I never liked it. I didn't try to remember it. I don't have room in my mind for all the things they want me to remember. I just have room for when you kissed me in the treehouse . . . and I was Mrs. Moonlight. It fills up my brain. There's no room for the rest."

"Don't think about the rest." He kissed her hair.

"I have to think of it. I have to," she said.

He could feel that she was losing all the joy of the tree, as if the wind they heard were blowing it away and blowing her with it away from him. "Don't think," he begged her.

"I have to think of it," she said. He could feel her pain. "When she tore down the treehouse it was like she tore me down. Like she tore down the things of mine I need to remember. I can't forgive her for that. And now I want to forget her . . . along with the rest. She will put me in that home so I might as well forget her . . . Help me do it," she said. She was weeping now. "Help me forget her and just remember you."

He held her face in his hands. "I would if I could but I don't know how. I have never known how." He took his hands away. His mind was heavy with the chirring of the crickets round their bed. Birds had flown in and were muttering in the gloom above the open door. After a time he said through her weeping, as if to himself. "Whiskey is a good thing but it doesn't last. I tried it for a while when my wife stopped loving me . . . It doesn't last."

"I need something to last."

"I know," he said. "I know. But it always comes back. I closed myself up for most of my life. Till today when you called . . ."

She turned to embrace him. "You will be always in my mind. All the rest will go but you. Do you believe it?" she said.

"I believe it, Mrs. Moonlight. I truly do."

She lay quietly beside him, sleeping a little, waking to find him sleeping, then waking again to find him waking too. A full moon had risen behind the tree. The churning leaves were frothing the light that struck the bed. "I'm trying to forget her. It's hard, so hard. It's like your own children get stuck in your mind. Maybe when they're born to you they aren't all born. Maybe a part of them is left inside . . . Hold me," she said.

He folded his arms about her.

"When you hold me I can almost . . . There's so much . . . so much. She would run and always open her little hands to fall. They were full of stone bruises and splinters and cuts . . . I would look at her hands and I'd kiss them and cry . . ."

"Try to sleep," he said.

"Red flowers made her smile . . ." It was a while before she asked, "Do you think they'll come?"

"My son is smart enough to figure this out."

"But not before morning?"

He felt the brush of a moth upon his lips. "Not before then."

"So we have tonight. We mustn't fall asleep."

But they did. When he woke she was gone. He sat up in panic. His fear was so strong his heart was beating in his throat. He could not hear a sound but the wind in the tree. Suppose she had forgotten where she was and fallen down the steps or walked into the woods and fallen into the ravine . . .

He stumbled to the porch, where he found her in the moonlight among the moving leaves. He did not trust his voice to speak. He drew her up to him and held her. She was as soft as a girl. As small as she had been. As yielding as then.

"Robert?" she said. "Robert?" Her voice was breaking with bewilderment. "Why are we here?" She pulled away from his arms. "This isn't our treehouse. Who does it belong to? My daughter tore it down . . . the one I had made. Why are we here?" she said again. "Are we running away?"

"There's no reason," he said. "Come inside," he begged.

"Don't let them take us back."

"No," he whispered. "No."

She caught her breath. "I forget . . . But the old things are there." She reached a hand to the tree. "New things that happen are so hard to keep. They fall through the leaves . . . Unless they break your heart. Unless they're what she did." She turned to search his face. "How did we get here? There's a room . . . and a bed."

"Yes, inside. Come inside."

"There's one way," she said.

"Tell me," he said, hardly hearing her words. She was trembling in his arms.

"Then I have to tell you this one thing you never knew. After they brought us back, they tore down our treehouse."

"I knew that," he said. "I went to see it one night and it was gone."

"But you didn't know that after that I tried to kill myself. I was crazy with grief. I didn't want to live. I cut my wrist. I wanted that much to die. When you're fifteen you're crazy like a fox, they said. I was ashamed of it later."

After a moment she pulled back her sleeve and showed him the scar. He found it in the moonlight and kissed it slowly.

"What if they hadn't found me and made me live?"

"What are you saying?"

"I want to go back and die to the rest of my life. I want to go back and die before my daughter came."

"But you went on living."

"What if I hadn't?"

"Then what are we now tonight?" he asked in despair.

"This is another life. Don't you feel it?" she said.

"You're saying it isn't real?"

"Oh, no, it's the realest thing that's ever been."

He was stroking her hair. "Your hair is like moonlight . . . Come back to bed."

He led her inside and they lay down together, side by side, hands touching, eyes closed against the dark. "I love you, Mrs. Moonlight." He heard her breath growing faint. "Please don't die," he pled. Her hair was like smoke. He drew the smoke of their blanket to cover them both.

"No, I'm only going backward. A part of me will die." She was weeping. They wept together. He held her in his arms."

"Don't go to sleep," she said. "I need you to help me."

"I don't know how," he wept. "I don't know what you're doing."

"I'm making it that she never happened to me."

"Are you sure it's what you want?"

"Yes, I am. I'm sure. You're the only one ever that belonged in my life . . . Think about the way we were. Think about the moon."

He could hear the owl. Beyond her hair, through the door he could see how the wind was slicing the moonlight, tossing it with leaves, thrusting it deep . . . and deeper into the tree. "You never let me kiss you but once a day, even though we said that we were going to be married. You were that shy."

"I'm not now," she said. "Kiss me now."

He kissed her long and gently, like an echo of the way it used to be. And the way it used to be reechoed till at last she was hearing nothing else, not the wind in the leaves, not the owl, not her daughter's voice . . . After a time she whispered, "It all slips away unless I hold on. It's like I am singing and the words blow away."

"Marry me," he said, "and I'll remember for you." Beneath his hand her head was tracing a refusal. "Everything you need to keep I'll keep for you."

"There's just a little bit and I can keep it myself and let go the rest."

He was losing his breath in the smoke of her hair. "If you do she'll put you in the home all the sooner."

"I know it," she said. "But this way it will be like a stranger has done it. Nothing a stranger does to you can make any difference."

It was morning when they woke to a thrasher's song. Beyond the door the tree was like another country in another season. It glistened. It unfolded. Light and shadow flew about in it like restless birds.

They heard the car outside. He rose and went to the window. "Well, they're here," he said. "It's my son's gray car."

Then her daughter entered, hair disheveled, eyes wild with reproach. "Mama, why have you done this? Why are you here?"

Fanny Gideon looked up at her serenely. "Do I know you?" she said.

The birdsong throbbed in the maple tree and circled the bed where Fanny Gideon lay with her hair on the pillow like a bridal veil. Her daughter turned upon him her shocked, accusing face. "How dare you take her?"

Long ago, when he was still a boy who swung from trees, before she was born, someone who was like her had asked him the same. It seemed to him that now he had grown into the answer. He summoned all his force to make a stand against her and against all the ones who ride you down to take you back and stash you in some corner, flush you down some snakehole, throw you away.

"Not this time," he said to her, calling up the memory of that ancient flight and capture. "This time we're married."

He saw her face give way . . . He found Fanny's glasses and put them on her.

She sat up in bed and looked past the strange woman standing beside her. The tree itself seemed to sing with the bird. She had only to rise to belong to the tree world, belong to its mystery, the mystery of greenness, her own sweet youth. She smiled at him, seeing him deep in the green, seeing him already shadowed with leaves. On this first morning of the rest of their life she remembered him. As she always would.

# Letter to the Lady of the House

## BY RICHARD BAUSCH

It's exactly twenty minutes to midnight, on this the eve of my seventieth birthday, and I've decided to address you, for a change, in writing—odd as that might seem. I'm perfectly aware of how many years we've been together, even if I haven't been very good about remembering to commemorate certain dates, certain days of the year. I'm also perfectly aware of how you're going to take the fact that I'm doing this at all, so late at night, with everybody due to arrive tomorrow, and the house still unready. I haven't spent almost five decades with you without learning a few things about you that I can predict and describe with some accuracy, though I admit that, as you put it, lately we've been more like strangers than husband and wife. Well, so if we are like strangers, perhaps there are some things I can tell you that you won't have already figured out about the way I feel.

Tonight, we had another one of those long, silent evenings after an argument (remember?) over pepper. We had been bickering all day, really, but at dinner I put pepper on my potatoes and you said that about how I shouldn't have pepper because it always upsets my stomach. I bothered to remark that I used to eat chili peppers for breakfast and if I wanted to put plain old ordinary black pepper on my potatoes, as I had been doing for more than sixty years, that was my privilege. Writing this now, it sounds far more testy than I meant it, but that isn't really the point.

In any case, you chose to overlook my tone. You simply said, "John, you were up all night the last time you had pepper with your dinner."

I said, "I was up all night because I ate green peppers. Not black pepper but green peppers."

"A pepper is a pepper, isn't it?" you said.

And then I started in on you. I got, as you call it, legal with you—pointing out that green peppers are not black pepper—and from there we moved on to an evening of mutual disregard for each other that ended with your decision to go to bed early. The grandchildren will make you tired, and there's still the house to do; you had every reason to want to get some rest, and yet I felt that you were also making a point of getting yourself out of proximity with me, leaving me to my displeasure, with another ridiculous argument settling between us like a fog.

So, after you went to bed, I got out the whiskey and started pouring drinks, and I had every intention of putting myself into a stupor. It was almost my birthday, after all, and—forgive this, it's the way I felt at the time—you had nagged me into an argument and then gone off to bed; the day had ended as so many of our days end now, and I felt, well, entitled. I had a few drinks, without any appreciable effect (though you might well see this letter as firm evidence to the contrary), and then I decided to do something to shake you up. I would leave. I'd make a lot of noise going out the door; I'd take a walk around the neighborhood and make you wonder where I could be. Perhaps I'd go check into a motel for the night. The thought even crossed my mind that I might leave you altogether. I admit that I entertained the thought, Marie. I saw our life together now as the day-to-day round of petty quarrelling and tension that it's mostly been over the past couple of years or so, and I wanted out as sincerely as I ever wanted anything.

My God, I wanted an end to it, and I got up from my seat in front of the television and walked back down the hall to the entrance of our room to look at you. I suppose I hoped you'd still be awake, so I could tell you of this momentous decision I felt I'd reached. And maybe you were awake: one of our oldest areas of contention being the feather-thin membrane of your sleep that I am always disturbing with my restlessness in the nights. All right. Assuming you were asleep, and don't know that I stood in the doorway of our room, I will say that I stood there for perhaps five minutes, just looking at you in the half-dark, the shape of your body under the blanket—you really did look like one of the girls when they were little and I used to stand in the doorway of their rooms; your illness last year made you so small again—and, as I said, I thought I had decided to leave you, for your peace as well as mine. I know you have gone to sleep crying, Marie. I know you've felt sorry about things, and wished we could find some way to stop irritating each other so much.

Well, of course, I didn't go anywhere. I came back to this room and drank more of the whiskey and watched television. It was like all the other nights. The shows came on and ended, and the whiskey began to wear off. There was a little rain shower. I had a moment of the shock of knowing I was seventy. After the rain ended, I did go outside for a few minutes. I stood on the sidewalk and looked at the house. The kids, with their kids, were on the road somewhere between their homes and here. I walked up to the end of the block and back, and a pleasant breeze blew and shook the drops out of the trees. My stomach was bothering me some, and maybe it was the pepper I'd put on my potatoes. It could just as well have been the whiskey. Anyway, as I came back to the house, I began to have the eerie feeling that I had reached the last night of my life. There was this small discomfort in my stomach, and no other physical pang or pain, and I am used to the small ills and side effects of my way of eating and drinking; yet I felt the sense of the end of things more strongly than I can describe. When I stood in the entrance of our room and looked at you again, wondering if I would make it through to the morning, I suddenly found myself trying to think what I would say to you if indeed this *was* the last time I would ever be able to speak to you. And I began to know I would write you this letter.

At least words in a letter aren't blurred by tone of voice, by the old aggravating sound of me talking to you. I began with this, and with the idea that, after months of thinking about it, I would at last try to say something to you that wasn't colored by our disaffections. What I have to tell you must be explained in a rather roundabout way.

I've been thinking about my cousin Louise and her husband. When he died, and she stayed with us last summer, something brought back to me what is really only the memory of a moment; yet it reached me, that moment, across more than fifty years. As you know, Louise is nine years older than I, and more like an older sister than a cousin. I must have told you at one time or another that I spent some weeks with her, back in 1933, when she was first married. The memory I'm talking about comes from that time, and what I have decided I have to tell you comes from that memory.

Father had been dead four years. We were all used to the fact that times were hard and that there was no man in the house, though I suppose I filled that role in some titular way. In any case, when Mother became ill there was the problem of us, her children. Though I was the oldest, I wasn't old enough to stay in the house alone, or to nurse her, either. My grandfather came up with the solution—and everybody went along with it— that I would go to Louise's for a time, and the two girls would go to stay with Grandfather. You'll remember that people did pretty much what that old man wanted them to do.


So we closed up the house, and I got on a train to Virginia. I was a few weeks shy of fourteen years old. I remember that I was not able to believe that anything truly bad would come of Mother's pleurisy, and was consequently glad of the opportunity it afforded me to travel the hundred miles south to Charlottesville, where Cousin Louise had moved with her new husband only a month earlier, after her wedding. Because *we* travelled so much at the beginning, you never got to really know Charles when he was young; in 1933, he was a very tall, imposing fellow, with bright-red hair and a graceful way of moving that always made me think of athletics, contests of skill. He had worked at the Navy yard in Washington, and had been laid off in the first months of Roosevelt's New Deal. Louise was teaching in a day school in Charlottesville, so they could make ends meet, and Charles was spending most of his time looking for work and fixing up the house. I had only met Charles once or twice before the wedding, but already I admired him, and wanted to emulate him. The prospect of spending time in his house, of perhaps going fishing with him in the small streams of central Virginia, was all I thought about on the way down. And I remember that we did go fishing one weekend, that I wound up spending a lot of time with

Charles, helping to paint the house, and to run water lines under it for indoor plumbing. Oh, I had time with Louise, too—listening to her read from the books she wanted me to be interested in, walking with her around Charlottesville in the evenings and looking at the city as it was then. Or sitting on her small porch and talking about the family, Mother's stubborn illness, the children Louise saw every day at school. But what I want to tell you has to do with the very first day I was there.

I know you think I use far too much energy thinking about and pining away for the past, and I therefore know that I'm taking a risk by talking about this ancient history, and by trying to make you see it. But this all has to do with you and me, my dear, and our late inability to find ourselves in the same room together without bitterness and pain.

That summer, 1933, was unusually warm in Virginia, and the heat, along with my impatience to arrive, made the train almost unbearable. I think it was just past noon when it pulled into the station at Charlottesville, with me hanging out one of the windows, looking for Louise or Charles. It was Charles who had come to meet me. He stood in a crisp-looking seersucker suit, with a straw boater cocked at just the angle you'd expect a young, newly married man to wear a straw boater, even in the middle of economic disaster. I waved at him and he waved back, and I might've jumped out the window if the train had slowed even a little more than it had before it stopped in the shade of the platform. I made my way out, carrying the cloth bag my grandfather had given me for the trip—Mother had said through her rheum that I looked like a carpetbagger—and when I stepped down to shake hands with Charles I noticed that what I thought was a new suit was tattered at the ends of the sleeves.

"Well," he said. "Young John."

I smiled at him. I was perceptive enough to see that his cheerfulness was not entirely effortless. He was a man out of work, after all, and so in spite of himself there was worry in his face, the slightest shadow in an otherwise glad and proud countenance. We walked through the station to the street, and on up the steep hill to the house, which was a small clapboard structure, a cottage, really, with a porch at the end of a short sidewalk lined with flowers—they were marigolds, I think—and here was Louise, coming out of the house, her arms already stretched wide to embrace me. "Lord," she said. "I swear you've grown since the wedding, John." Charles took my bag and went inside.

"Let me look at you, young man," Louise said.

I stood for inspection. And as she looked me over I saw that her hair was pulled back, that a few strands of it had come loose, that it was brilliantly auburn in the sun. I suppose I was a little in love with her. She was grown, and married now. She was a part of what seemed a great mystery to me, even as I was about to enter it, and of course you remember how that feels, Marie, when one is on the verge of things—nearly adult, nearly old enough to fall in love. I looked at Louise's happy, flushed face, and felt a deep ache as she ushered me into her house. I wanted so to be older.

Inside, Charles had poured lemonade for us, and was sitting in the easy chair by the fireplace, already sipping his. Louise wanted to show me the house, and the back yard—which she had tilled and turned into a small vegetable garden—but she must've sensed how thirsty I was, and so she asked me to sit down and have a cool drink before she showed me the upstairs. Now, of course, looking back on it, I remember that those rooms she was so anxious to show me were meagre indeed. They were not much bigger than closets, really, and the paint was faded and dull; the furniture she'd arranged so artfully was coming apart; the pictures she'd put on the walls were prints she'd cut out— magazine covers, mostly—and the curtains over the windows were the same ones that had hung in her childhood bedroom for twenty years. ("Recognize these?" she said with a deprecating smile.) Of course, the quality of her pride had nothing to do with the fineness—or lack of it—in these things but in the fact that they belonged to her, and that she was a married lady in her own house.

On this day in July, 1933, she and Charles were waiting for the delivery of a fan they had scrounged enough money to buy from Sears, through the catalogue. There were things they would rather have been doing, especially in this heat, and especially with me there. Monticello wasn't far away, the university was within walking distance, and without too much expense one could ride a taxi to one of the lakes nearby. They had hoped that the fan would arrive before I did, but since it hadn't, and since neither Louise nor Charles was willing to leave the other alone that day while traipsing off with me, there wasn't anything to do but wait around for it. Louise had opened the windows and drawn the shades, and we sat in her small living room and drank the lemonade, fanning ourselves with folded parts of Charles's newspaper. From time to time an anemic breath of air would move the shades slightly, but then everything grew still again. Louise sat on the arm of Charles's chair, and I sat on the sofa. We talked about pleurisy, and, I think, about the fact that Thomas Jefferson had invented the dumbwaiter, and how the plumbing at Monticello was at least a century ahead of its time. Charles remarked that it was the spirit of invention that would make a man's career in these days. "That's what I'm aiming for—to be inventive in a job. No matter what it winds up being."

When the lemonade ran out, Louise got up and went into the kitchen to make some more. Charles and I talked about taking a weekend to go fishing. He leaned back in his chair and put his hands behind his head, looking satisfied. In the kitchen, Louise was chipping ice for our glasses, and she began singing something low, for her own pleasure, a barely audible lilting, and Charles and I sat listening. It occurred to me that I was very happy. I had the sense that soon I would be embarked on my own life, as Charles was on his, and that an attractive woman like Louise would be there with me. Charles said, "God, listen to that. Doesn't Louise have the loveliest voice?"

And that's all I have from that day. I don't even know if the fan arrived later, and I have no clear memory of how we spent the rest of the afternoon and evening. I remember Louise singing a song, her husband leaning back in his chair, folding his hands behind his head, expressing his pleasure in his young wife's voice. I remember that I felt quite extraordinarily content just then. And that's all I remember.

But there are, of course, the things we both know: we know they moved to Colorado to be near Charles's parents; we know they never had any children; we know that Charles fell down a shaft at a construction site in the fall of 1957 and was hurt so badly that he never walked again. And I know that when she came to stay with us last summer she told me she'd learned to hate him, and not for what she'd had to help him do all those years. No, it started earlier and was deeper than that. She hadn't minded the care of him—the washing and feeding and all the numberless small tasks she had to perform each and every day, all day—she hadn't minded this. In fact, she thought there was something in her makeup that liked being needed so completely. The trouble was simply that whatever she had once loved in him she had stopped loving, and for many, many years before he died she'd felt only suffocation when he was near enough to touch her, only irritation and anxiety when he spoke. She said all this, and then looked at me, her cousin, who had been fortunate enough to have children, and to be in love over time, and said, "John, how have you and Marie managed it?"

And what I wanted to tell you has to do with this fact—that while you and I had had one of our whispering arguments only moments before, I felt quite certain of the simple truth of the matter, which is that, whatever our complications, we *have* managed to be in love over time.

"Louise," I said.

"People start out with such high hopes," she said, as if I wasn't there. She looked at me. "Don't they?"

"Yes," I said.

She seemed to consider this a moment. Then she said, "I wonder how it happens."

I said, "You ought to get some rest." Or something equally pointless and admonitory.

As she moved away from me, I had an image of Charles standing on the station platform in Charlottesville that summer, the straw boater set at its cocky angle. It was an image I would see most of the rest of that night, and on many another night since.

I can almost hear your voice as you point out that once again I've managed to dwell too long on the memory of something that's past and gone. The difference is

that I'm not grieving over the past now. I'm merely re-
porting a memory, so that you might understand what
I'm about to say to you.

The fact is, we aren't the people we were even then,
just a year ago. I know that. As I know things have
been slowly eroding between us for a very long time;
we are a little tired of each other, and there are annoy-
ances and old scars that won't be obliterated with a
letter—even a long one written in the middle of the
night in desperate sincerity, under the influence, admit-
tedly, of a considerable portion of bourbon whiskey,
but nevertheless with the best intention and hope: that
you may know how, over the course of this night, I
came to the end of needing an explanation for our difficulty. We have reached this—place. Everything we say
seems rather aggravatingly mindless and automatic,
like something one stranger might say to another in
any of the thousand circumstances where strangers are
thrown together for a time and the silence begins to
grow heavy on their minds and someone has to say
something. Darling, we go so long these days without
having anything at all to do with each other, and the
children are arriving tomorrow, and once more we'll be
in the position of making all the gestures that give
them back their parents as they think their parents are,
and what I wanted to say to you, what came to me as
I thought about Louise and Charles on that day so
long ago, when they were young and so obviously glad
of each other, and I looked at them and knew it and
was happy—what came to me was that even the harsh

things that happened to them, even the years of anger and silence, even the disappointment and the bitterness and the wanting not to be in the same room anymore, even all that must have been worth it for such loveliness. At least I am here, at seventy years old, hoping so. Tonight, I went back to our room again and stood gazing at you asleep, dreaming whatever you were dreaming, and I had a moment of thinking how we were always friends, too. And what I wanted finally to say was that I remember well our own sweet times, our own old loveliness. I would like to think that even if at the very beginning of our lives together I had somehow been shown that we would end up here, with this longing to be away from each other, this feeling of being trapped together, of being tied to each other in a way that makes us wish for other times, some other place, I would have known enough to accept it all freely for the chance at that love. And if I could, I would do it all again, Marie. All of it, even the sorrow. My sweet, my dear adversary. For everything that I remember.

# Tell Me a Riddle

## BY TILLIE OLSEN

### 1

For forty-seven years they had been married. How deep back the stubborn, gnarled roots of the quarrel reached, no one could say—but only now, when tending to the needs of others no longer shackled them together, the roots swelled up visible, split the earth between them, and the tearing shook even to the children, long since grown.

Why now, why now? wailed Hannah.

As if when we grew up weren't enough, said Paul.

Poor Ma. Poor Dad. It hurts so for both of them, said Vivi. They never had very much; at least in old age they should be happy.

Knock their heads together, insisted Sammy; tell 'em: you're too old for this kind of thing; no reason not to get along now.

Lennie wrote to Clara: They've lived over so much together; what could possibly tear them apart?

———

Something tangible enough.

Arthritic hands, and such work as he got, occasional. Poverty all his life, and there was little breath left for running. He could not, could not turn away from this desire: to have the troubling of responsibility, the fretting with money, over and done with; to be free, to be *care*free where success was not measured by accumulation, and there was use for the vitality still in him.

There was a way. They could sell the house, and with the money join his lodge's Haven, cooperative for the aged. Happy communal life, and was he not already an official; had he not helped organize it, raise funds, served as a trustee?

But she—would not consider it.

"What do we need all this for?" he would ask loudly, for her hearing aid was turned down and the vacuum was shrilling. "Five rooms" (pushing the sofa so she could get into the corner) "furniture" (smoothing down the rug) "floors and surfaces to make work. Tell me, why do we need it?" And he was glad he could ask in a scream.

"Because I'm use't."

"Because you're use't. This is a reason, Mrs. Word Miser? Used to can get unused!"

"Enough unused I have to get used to already. . . . Not enough words?" turning off the vacuum a moment to hear herself answer. "Because soon enough

we'll need only a little closet, no windows, no furniture, nothing to make work, but for worms. Because
now I want room. . . . Screech and blow like you're
doing, you'll need that closet even sooner. . . . Ha,
again!" for the vacuum bag wailed, puffed half
up, hung stubbornly limp. "This time fix it so it stays;
quick before the phone rings and you get too
important-busy."

But while he struggled with the motor, it seethed in
him. Why fix it? Why have to bother? And if it can't
be fixed, have to wring the mind with how to pay the
repair? At the Haven they come in with their own ma-
chines to clean your room or your cottage; you fish, or
play cards, or make jokes in the sun, not with knotty
fingers fight to mend vacuums.

Over the dishes, coaxingly: "For once in your life, to
be free, to have everything done for you, like a queen."

"I never liked queens."

"No dishes, no garbage, no towel to sop, no worry
what to buy, what to eat."

"And what else would I do with my empty hands?
Better to eat at my own table when I want, and to
cook and eat how I want."

"In the cottages they buy what you ask, and cook it
how you like. *You* are the one who always used to say:
better mankind born without mouths and stomachs
than always to worry for money to buy, to shop, to fix,
to cook, to wash, to clean."

"How cleverly you hid that you heard. I said it then
because eighteen hours a day I ran. And you never

scraped a carrot or knew a dish towel sops. Now—for you and me—who cares? A herring out of a jar is enough. But when *I* want, and nobody to bother." And she turned off her ear button, so she would not have to hear.

But as *he* had no peace, juggling and rejuggling the money to figure: how will I pay for this now?; prying out the storm windows (there they take care of this); jolting in the streetcar on errands (there I would not have to ride to take care of this or that); fending the patronizing relatives just back from Florida (at the Haven it matters what one is, not what one can afford), he gave *her* no peace.

"Look! In their bulletin. A reading circle. Twice a week it meets."

"Haumm," her answer of not listening.

"A reading circle. Chekhov they read that you like, and Peretz. Cultured people at the Haven that you would enjoy."

"Enjoy!" She tasted the word. "Now, when it pleases you, you find a reading circle for me. And forty years ago when the children were morsels and there was a Circle, did you stay home with them once so I could go? Even once? You trained me well. I do not need others to enjoy. Others!" Her voice trembled. "Because *you* want to be there with others. Already it makes me sick to think of you always around others. Clown, grimacer, floormat, yesman, entertainer, whatever they want of you."

And now it was he who turned on the television loud so he need not hear.

Old scar tissue ruptured and the wounds festered anew. Chekhov indeed. She thought without softness of that young wife, who in the deep night hours while she nursed the current baby, and perhaps held another in her lap, would try to stay awake for the only time there was to read. She would feel again the weather of the outside on his cheek when, coming late from a meeting, he would find her so, and stimulated and ardent, sniffing her skin, coax: "I'll put the baby to bed, and you—put the book away, don't read, don't read."

That had been the most beguiling of all the "don't read, put your book away" her life had been. Chekhov indeed!

"Money?" She shrugged him off. "Could we get poorer than once we were? And in America, who starves?"

But as still he pressed:

"Let me alone about money. Was there ever enough? Seven little ones—for every penny I had to ask—and sometimes, remember, there was nothing. But always *I* had to manage. Now *you* manage. Rub your nose in it good."

But from those years she had had to manage, old humiliations and terrors rose up, lived again, and forced her to relive them. The children's needings; that grocer's face or this merchant's wife she had had to beg credit from when credit was a disgrace; the scenery of the long blocks walked around when she could not pay; school coming, and the desperate going over the old to see what could yet be remade; the soups of meat bones begged "for-the-dog" one winter. . . .

Enough. Now they had no children. Let *him* wrack his head for how they would live. She would not exchange her solitude for anything. *Never again to be forced to move to the rhythms of others.*

For in this solitude she had won to a reconciled peace.

Tranquillity from having the empty house no longer an enemy, for it stayed clean—not as in the days when it was her family, the life in it, that had seemed the enemy: tracking, smudging, littering, dirtying, engaging her in endless defeating battle—and on whom her endless defeat had been spewed.

The few old books, memorized from rereading; the pictures to ponder (the magnifying glass superimposed on her heavy eyeglasses). Or if she wishes, when he is gone, the phonograph, that if she turns up very loud and strains, she can hear: the ordered sounds and the struggling.

Out in the garden, growing things to nurture. Birds to be kept out of the pear tree, and when the pears are heavy and ripe, the old fury of work, for all must be canned, nothing wasted.

And her one social duty (for she will not go to luncheons or meetings) the boxes of old clothes left with her, as with a life-practised eye for finding what is still wearable within the worn (again the magnifying glass superimposed on the heavy glasses) she scans and sorts—this for rag or rummage, that for mending and cleaning, and this for sending away.

*Being able at last to live within, and not move to the rhythms of others*, as life had helped her to: denying; removing; isolating; taking the children one by one; then deafening, half-blinding—and at last, presenting her solitude.

And in it she had won to a reconciled peace.

Now he was violating it with his constant campaigning: *Sell the house and move to the Haven.* (You sit, you sit—there too you could sit like a stone.) He was making of her a battleground where old grievances tore. (Turn on your ear button—I am talking.) And stubbornly she resisted—so that from wheedling, reasoning, manipulation, it was bitterness he now started with.

And it came to where every happening lashed up a quarrel.

"I will sell the house anyway," he flung at her one night. "I am putting it up for sale. There will be a way to make you sign."

The television blared, as always it did on the evenings he stayed home, and as always it reached her only as noise. She did not know if the tumult was in her or outside. Snap! she turned the sound off. "Shadows," she whispered to him, pointing to the screen, "look, it is only shadows." And in a scream: "Did you say that you will sell the house? Look at me, not at that. I am no shadow. You cannot sell without me."

"Leave on the television. I am watching."

"Like Paulie, like Jenny, a four-year-old. Staring at shadows. *You cannot sell the house.*"

"I will. We are going to the Haven. There you would not hear the television when you do not want it. I could sit in the social room and watch. You could lock yourself up to smell your unpleasantness in a room by yourself—for who would want to come near you?"

"No, no selling." A whisper now.

"The television is shadows. Mrs. Enlightened! Mrs. Cultured! A world comes into your house—and it is shadows. People you would never meet in a thousand lifetimes. Wonders. When you were four years old, yes, like Paulie, like Jenny, did you know of Indian dances, alligators, how they use bamboo in Malaya? No, you scratched in your dirt with the chickens and thought Olshana was the world. Yes, Mrs. Unpleasant, I will sell the house, for there better can we be rid of each other than here."

She did not know if the tumult was outside, or in her. Always a ravening inside, a pull to the bed, to lie down, to succumb.

"Have you thought maybe Ma should let a doctor have a look at her?" asked their son Paul after Sunday dinner, regarding his mother crumpled on the couch, instead of, as was her custom, busying herself in Nancy's kitchen.

"Why not the President too?"

"Seriously, Dad. This is the third Sunday she's lain down like that after dinner. Is she that way at home?"

"A regular love affair with the bed. Every time I start to talk to her."

Good protective reaction, observed Nancy to herself. The workings of hos-til-ity.

"Nancy could take her. I just don't like how she looks. Let's have Nancy arrange an appointment."

"You think she'll go?" regarding his wife gloomily. "All right, we have to have doctor bills, we have to have doctor bills." Loudly: "Something hurts you?"

She startled, looked to his lips. He repeated: "Mrs. Take It Easy, something hurts?"

"Nothing. . . . Only you."

"A woman of honey. That's why you're lying down?"

"Soon I'll get up to do the dishes, Nancy."

"Leave them, Mother, I like it better this way."

"Mrs. Take It Easy, Paul says you should start ballet. You should go to see a doctor and ask: how soon can you start ballet?"

"A doctor?" she begged. "Ballet?"

"We were talking, Ma," explained Paul, "you don't seem any too well. It would be a good idea for you to see a doctor for a checkup."

"I get up now to do the kitchen. Doctors are bills and foolishness, my son. I need no doctors."

"At the Haven," he could not resist pointing out, "a doctor is *not* bills. He lives beside you. You start to sneeze, he is there before you open up a Kleenex. You can be sick there for free, all you want."

"Diarrhea of the mouth, is there a doctor to make you dumb?"

"Ma. Promise me you'll go. Nancy will arrange it."

"It's all of a piece when you think of it," said Nancy, "the way she attacks my kitchen, scrubbing under every cup hook, doing the inside of the oven so I can't enjoy Sunday dinner, knowing that half-blind or not, she's going to find every speck of dirt. . . ."

"Don't, Nancy, I've told you—it's the only way she knows to be useful. What did the *doctor* say?"

"A real fatherly lecture. Sixty-nine is young these days. Go out, enjoy life, find interests. Get a new hearing aid, this one is antiquated. Old age is sickness only if one makes it so. Geriatrics, Inc."

"So there was nothing physical."

"Of course there was. How can you live to yourself like she does without there being? Evidence of a kidney disorder, and her blood count is low. He gave her a diet, and she's to come back for follow-up and lab work. . . . But he was clear enough: Number One prescription—start living like a human being. . . . When I think of your dad, who could really play the invalid with that arthritis of his, as active as a teenager, and twice as much fun. . . ."

"You didn't tell me the doctor says your sickness is in you, how you live." He pushed his advantage. "Life and enjoyments you need better than medicine. And this diet, how can you keep it? To weigh each morsel and scrape away each bit of fat, to make this soup, that pudding. There, at the Haven, they have a dietician, they would do it for you."

She is silent.

"You would feel better there, I know it," he says gently. "There there is life and enjoyments all around."

"What is the matter, Mr. Importantbusy, you have no card game or meeting you can go to?"—turning her face to the pillow.

For a while he cut his meetings and going out, fussed over her diet, tried to wheedle her into leaving the house, brought in visitors:

"I should come to a fashion tea. I should sit and look at pretty babies in clothes I cannot buy. This is pleasure?"

"Always you are better than everyone else. The doctor said you should go out. Mrs. Brem comes to you with goodness and you turn her away."

"Because *you* asked her to, she asked me."

———

"They won't come back. People you need, the doctor said. Your own cousins I asked; they were willing to come and make peace as if nothing had happened. . . ."

"No more crushers of people, pushers, hypocrites, around me. No more in *my* house. You go to them if you like."


"Kind he is to visit. And you, like ice."

"A babbler. All my life around babblers. Enough!"


"She's even worse, Dad? Then let her stew a while," advised Nancy. "You can't let it destroy you; it's a psychological thing, maybe too far gone for any of us to help."

So he let her stew. More and more she lay silent in bed, and sometimes did not even get up to make the meals. No longer was the tongue-lashing inevitable if he left the coffee cup where it did not belong, or forgot to take out the garbage or mislaid the broom. The birds grew bold that summer and for once pocked the pears, undisturbed.

A bellyful of bitterness and every day the same quarrel in a new way and a different old grievance the quarrel forced her to enter and relive. And the new torment:

I am not really sick, the doctor said it, then why do I feel so sick?

One night she asked him: "You have a meeting tonight? Do not go. Stay . . . with me."

He had planned to watch "This Is Your Life," but half sick himself from the heavy heat, and sickening therefore the more after the brooks and woods of the Haven, with satisfaction he grated:

"Hah, Mrs. Live Alone And Like It wants company all of a sudden. It doesn't seem so good the time of solitary when she was a girl exile in Siberia. 'Do not go. Stay with me.' A new song for Mrs. Free As A Bird. Yes, I am going out, and while I am gone chew this aloneness good, and think how you keep us both from where if you want people, you do not need to be alone."

"Go, go. All your life you have gone without me."

After him she sobbed curses he had not heard in years, old-country curses from their childhood: Grow, oh shall you grow like an onion, with your head in the ground. Like the hide of a drum shall you be, beaten in life, beaten in death. Oh shall you be like a chandelier, to hang, and to burn. . . .


She was not in their bed when he came back. She lay on the cot on the sun porch. All week she did not speak or come near him; nor did he try to make peace or care for her.

He slept badly, so used to her next to him. After all the years, old harmonies and dependencies deep in their bodies; she curled to him, or he coiled to her, each warmed, warming, turning as the other turned, the nights a long embrace.

It was not the empty bed or the storm that woke him, but a faint singing. *She* was singing. Shaking off the drops of rain, the lightning riving her lifted face, he saw her so; the cot covers on the floor.

"This is a private concert?" he asked. "Come in, you are wet."

"I can breathe now," she answered; "my lungs are rich." Though indeed the sound was hardly a breath.

"Come in, come in." Loosing the bamboo shades. "Look how wet you are." Half helping, half carrying her, still faint-breathing her song.

A Russian love song of fifty years ago.

He had found a buyer, but before he told her, he called together those children who were close enough to come. Paul, of course, Sammy from New Jersey, Hannah from Connecticut, Vivi from Ohio.

With a kindling of energy for her beloved visitors, she arrayed the house, cooked and baked. She was not prepared for the solemn after-dinner conclave, they too probing in and tearing. Her frightened eyes watched from mouth to mouth as each spoke.

His stories were eloquent and funny of her refusal to

go back to the doctor; of the scorned invitations; of her stubborn silence or the bile "like a Niagara"; of her contrariness: "If I clean it's no good how I cleaned; if I don't clean, I'm still a master who thinks he has a slave."

(Vinegar he poured on me all his life; I am well marinated; how can I be honey now?)

Deftly he marched in the rightness for moving to the Haven; their money from social security free for visiting the children, not sucked into daily needs and into the house; the activities in the Haven for him; but mostly the Haven for *her*: her health, her need of care, distraction, amusement, friends who shared her interests.

"This does offer an outlet for Dad," said Paul; "he's always been an active person. And economic peace of mind isn't to be sneezed at, either. I could use a little of that myself."

But when they asked: "And you, Ma, how do you feel about it?" could only whisper:

"For him it is good. It is not for me. I can no longer live between people."

"You lived all your life *for* people," Vivi cried.

"Not with." Suffering doubly for the unhappiness on her children's faces.

"You have to find some compromise," Sammy insisted. "Maybe sell the house and buy a trailer. After forty-seven years there's surely some way you can find to live in peace."

"There is no help, my children. Different things we need."

"Then live alone!" He could control himself no longer. "I have a buyer for the house. Half the money for you, half for me. Either alone or with me to the Haven. You think I can live any longer as we are doing now?"

"Ma doesn't have to make a decision this minute, however you feel, Dad," Paul said quickly, "and you wouldn't want her to. Let's let it lay a few months, and then talk some more."

"I think I can work it out to take Mother home with me for a while," Hannah said. "You both look terrible, but especially you, Mother. I'm going to ask Phil to have a look at you."

"Sure," cracked Sammy. "What's the use of a doctor husband if you can't get free service out of him once in a while for the family? And absence might make the heart . . . you know."


"There was something after all," Paul told Nancy in a colorless voice. "That was Hannah's Phil calling. Her gall bladder. . . . Surgery."

"Her *gall* bladder. If that isn't classic. 'Bitter as gall'—talk of psychosom——"

He stepped closer, put his hand over her mouth, and said in the same colorless, plodding voice. "We have to get Dad. They operated at once. The cancer was every-where, surrounding the liver, everywhere. They did what they could . . . at best she has a year. Dad . . . we have to tell him."

## 2

Honest in his weakness when they told him, and that she was not to know. "I'm not an actor. She'll know right away by how I am. Oh that poor woman. I am old too, it will break me into pieces. Oh that poor woman. She will spit on me: 'So my sickness was how I live.' Oh Paulie, how she will be, that poor woman. Only she should not suffer. . . . I can't stand sickness, Paulie, I can't go with you."

But went. And play-acted.

"A grand opening and you did not even wait for me. . . . A good thing Hannah took you with her."

"Fashion teas I needed. They cut out what tore in me; just in my throat something hurts yet. . . . Look! so many flowers, like a funeral. Vivi called, did Hannah tell you? And Lennie from San Francisco, and Clara; and Sammy is coming." Her gnome's face pressed happily into the flowers.

It is impossible to predict in these cases, but once over the immediate effects of the operation, she should have several months of comparative well-being.

*The money, where will come the money?*

Travel with her, Dad. Don't take her home to the

old associations. The other children will want to see her.

*The money, where will I wring the money?*

Whatever happens, she is not to know. No, you can't ask her to sign papers to sell the house; nothing to upset her. Borrow instead, then after. . . .

*I had wanted to leave you each a few dollars to make life easier, as other fathers do. There will be nothing left now. (Failure! you and your "business is exploitation." Why didn't you make it when it could be made?—Is that what you're thinking, Sammy?)*

Sure she's unreasonable, Dad—but you have to stay with her; if there's to be any happiness in what's left of her life, it depends on you.

*Prop me up, children, think of me, too. Shuffled, chained with her, bitter woman. No Haven, and the little money going. . . . How happy she looks, poor creature.*

The look of excitement. The straining to hear everything (the new hearing aid turned full). Why are you so happy, dying woman?

How the petals are, fold on fold, and the gladioli color. The autumn air.

Stranger grandsons, tall above the little gnome grandmother, the little spry grandfather. Paul in a frenzy of picture-taking before going.

She, wandering the great house. Feeling the books; laughing at the maple shoemaker's bench of a hundred years ago used as a table. The ear turned to music.

"Let us go home. See how good I walk now." "One step from the hospital," he answers, "and she wants to fly. Wait till Doctor Phil says."

"Look—the birds too are flying home. Very good Phil is and will not show it, but he is sick of sickness by the time he comes home."

"Mrs. Telepathy, to read minds," he answers; "read mine what it says: when the trunks of medicines become a suitcase, then we will go."

The grandboys, they do not know what to say to us. . . . Hannah, she runs around here, there, when is there time for herself?

Let us go home. Let us go home.

Musing; gentleness—*but for the incidents of the rabbi in the hospital, and of the candles of benediction.*

*Of the rabbi in the hospital:*

Now tell me what happened, Mother.

From the sleep I awoke, Hannah's Phil, and he stands there like a devil in a dream and calls me by name. I cannot hear. I think he prays. Go away, please, I tell him, I am not a believer. Still he stands, while my heart knocks with fright.

You scared *him*, Mother. He thought you were delirious.

Who sent him? Why did he come to me?

It is a custom. The men of God come to visit those

of their religion they might help. The hospital makes
up the list for them—race, religion—and you are on
the Jewish list.

Not for rabbis. At once go and make them change.
Tell them to write: Race, human; Religion, none.


*And of the candles of benediction:*

Look how you have upset yourself, Mrs. Excited
Over Nothing. Pleasant memories you should leave.

Go in, go back to Hannah and the lights. Two weeks
I saw candles and said nothing. But she asked me.

So what was so terrible? She forgets you never did,
she asks you to light the Friday candles and say the
benediction like Phil's mother when she visits. If the
candles give her pleasure, why shouldn't she have
the pleasure?

Not for pleasure she does it. For emptiness. Because
his family does. Because all around her do.

That is not a good reason too? But you did not hear
her. For heritage, she told you. For the boys, from the
past they should have tradition.

Superstition! From the savages, afraid of the dark, of
themselves: mumbo words and magic lights to scare
away ghosts.

She told you: how it started does not take away
the goodness. For centuries, peace in the house it
means.

Swindler! does she look back on the dark centuries?
Candles bought instead of bread and stuck into a po-

tato for a candlestick? Religions that stifled and said: in Paradise, woman, you will be the footstool of your husband, and in life—poor chosen Jew—ground under, despised, trembling in cellars. And cremated. And cremated.

This is religion's fault? You think you are still an orator of the 1905 revolution? Where are the pills for quieting? Which are they?

Heritage. How have we come from the savages, how no longer to be savages—this to teach. To look back and learn what humanizes man—this to teach. To smash all ghettos that divide us—not to go back, not to go back—this to teach. Learned books in the house, will humankind live or die, and she gives to her boys—superstition.

Hannah that is so good to you. Take your pill, Mrs. Excited For Nothing, swallow.

Heritage! But when did I have time to teach? Of Hannah I asked only hands to help.

Swallow.

Otherwise—musing; gentleness.


Not to travel. To go home.

The children want to see you. We have to show them you are as thorny a flower as ever.

Not to travel.

Vivi wants you should see her new baby. She sent the tickets—airplane tickets—a Mrs. Roosevelt she wants to make of you. To Vivi's we have to go.

A new baby. How many warm, seductive babies. She holds him stiffly, *away* from her, so that he wails. And a long shudder begins, and the sweat beads on her forehead.

"Hush, shush," croons the grandfather, lifting him back. "You should forgive your grandmamma, little prince, she has never held a baby before, only seen them in glass cases. Hush, shush."

"You're tired, Ma," says Vivi. "The travel and the noisy dinner. I'll take you to lie down."

*(A long travel from, to, what the feel of a baby evokes.)*

In the airplane, cunningly designed to encase from motion (no wind, no feel of flight), she had sat severely and still, her face turned to the sky through which they cleaved and left no scar.

So this was how it looked, the determining, the crucial sky, and this was how man moved through it, remote above the dwindled earth, the concealed human life. Vulnerable life, that could scar.

There was a steerage ship of memory that shook across a great, circular sea: clustered, ill human beings; and through the thick-stained air, tiny fretting waters in a window round like the airplane's—sun round, moon round. (The round thatched roofs of Olshana.) Eye round—like the smaller window that framed distance the solitary year of exile when only her eyes could travel, and no voice spoke. And the polar winds hurled themselves across snows trackless and endless and white—like the clouds which had closed together below and hidden the earth.

Now they put a baby in her lap. Do not ask me, she would have liked to beg. Enough the worn face of Vivi, the remembered grandchildren. I cannot, cannot. . . .

*Cannot what?* Unnatural grandmother, not able to make herself embrace a baby.

She lay there in the bed of the two little girls, her new hearing aid turned full, listening to the sound of the children going to sleep, the baby's fretful crying and hushing, the clatter of dishes being washed and put away. They thought she slept. Still she rode on.

It was not that she had not loved her babies, her children. The love—the passion of tending—had risen with the need like a torrent; and like a torrent drowned and immolated all else. But when the need was done—oh the power that was lost in the painful damming back and drying up of what still surged, but had nowhere to go. Only the thin pulsing left that could not quiet, suffering over lives one felt, but could no longer hold nor help.

On that torrent she had borne them to their own lives, and the riverbed was desert long years now. Not there would she dwell, a memoried wraith. Surely that was not all, surely there was more. Still the springs, the springs were in her seeking. Somewhere an older power that beat for life. Somewhere coherence, transport, meaning. If they would but leave her in the air now stilled of clamor, in the reconciled solitude, to journey to her self.

And they put a baby in her lap. Immediacy to embrace, and the breath of *that* past: warm flesh like this that had claims and nuzzled away all else and with lovely mouths devoured; hot-living like an animal—intensely and now; the turning maze; the long drunkenness; the drowning into needing and being needed. Severely she looked back—and the shudder seized her again, and the sweat. Not that way. Not there, not now could she, not yet. . . .

And all that visit, she could not touch the baby.

"Daddy, is it the . . . sickness she's like that?" asked Vivi. "I was so glad to be having the baby—for her. I told Tim, it'll give her more happiness than anything, being around a baby again. And she hasn't played with him once."

He was not listening, "Aahh little seed of life, little charmer," he crooned, "Hollywood should see you. A heart of ice you would melt. Kick, kick. The future you'll have for a ball. In 2050 still kick. Kick for your grandaddy then."

Attentive with the older children; sat through their performances (command performance; we command you to be the audience); helped Ann sort autumn leaves to find the best for a school program; listened gravely to Richard tell about his rock collection, while her lips mutely formed the words to remember: *igneous, sedimentary, metamorphic*; looked for missing socks, books, and bus tickets; watched the children whoop after their grandfather who knew how to tickle, chuck, lift, toss, do tricks, tell secrets, make jokes, match riddle for riddle. (Tell me a riddle, Grammy. I know no riddles, child.) Scrubbed sills and woodwork and furniture in every room; folded the laundry; straightened drawers; emptied the heaped baskets waiting for ironing (while he or Vivi or Tim nagged: You're supposed to rest here, you've been sick) but to none tended or gave food—and could not touch the baby.

After a week she said: "Let's us go home. Today call about the tickets."

"You have important business, Mrs. Inahurry? The President waits to consult with you?" He shouted, for the fear of the future raced in him. "The clothes are still warm from the suitcase, your children cannot show enough how glad they are to see you, and you want home. There is plenty of time for home. We cannot be with the children at home."

"Blind to around you as always: the little ones sleep four in a room because we take their bed. We are two more people in a house with a new baby, and no help."

"Vivi is happy so. The children should have their grandparents a while, she told to me. I should have my mommy and daddy. . . ."

"Babbler and blind. Do you look at her so tired?

How she starts to talk and she cries? I am not strong enough yet to help. Let us go home."

(To reconciled solitude.)

*For it seemed to her the crowded noisy house was listening to her, listening for her. She could feel it like a great ear pressed under her heart. And everything knocked: quick constant raps: let me in, let me in.*

*How was it that soft reaching tendrils also became blows that knocked?*

C'mon, Grandma, I want to show you. . . .

Tell me a riddle, Grandma. *(I know no riddles.)*

Look, Grammy, he's so dumb he can't even find his hands. (Dody and the baby on a blanket over the fermenting autumn mould.)

I made them—for you. (Ann) (Flat paper dolls with aprons that lifted on scalloped skirts that lifted on flowered pants; hair of yarn and great ringed questioning eyes.)

Watch me, Grandma. (Richard snaking up the tree, hanging exultant, free, with one hand at the top. Below Dody hunching over in pretend-cooking.) *(Climb too, Dody, climb and look.)*

Be my nap bed, Grammy. (The "No!" too late.) Morty's abandoned heaviness, while his fingers ladder up and down her hearing-aid cord to his drowsy chant: eentsiebeentsiespider. *(Children trust.)*

It's to start off your own rock collection, Grandma. That's a trilobite fossil, 200 million years old (millions of years on a boy's mouth) and that one's obsidian, black glass.

*Knocked and knocked.*

Mother, I *told* you the teacher said we had to bring it back all filled out this morning. Didn't you even ask Daddy? Then tell *me* which plan and I'll check it: evacuate or stay in the city or wait for you to come and take me away. (Seeing the look of straining to hear.) It's for Disaster, Grandma. *(Children trust.)*

Vivi in the maze of the long, the lovely drunkenness. The old old noises: baby sounds; screaming of a mother flayed to exasperation; children quarreling; children playing; singing; laughter.

*And Vivi's tears and memories*, spilling so fast, half the words not understood.

She had started remembering out loud deliberately, so her mother would know the past was cherished, still lived in her.

Nursing the baby: My friends marvel, and I tell them, oh it's easy to be such a cow. I remember how beautiful my mother seemed nursing my brother, and the milk just flows. . . . Was that Davy? It must have been Davy. . . .

Lowering a hem: How did you ever . . . when I think

how you made everything we wore . . . Tim, just think, seven kids and Mommy sewed everything . . . do I remember you sang while you sewed? That white dress with the red apples on the skirt you fixed over for me, was it Hannah's or Clara's before it was mine?

Washing sweaters: Ma, I'll never forget, one of those days so nice you washed clothes outside; one of the first spring days it must have been. The bubbles just danced while you scrubbed, and we chased after, and you stopped to show us how to blow our own bubbles with green onion stalks . . . you always. . . .

"Strong onion, to still make you cry after so many years," her father said, to turn the tears into laughter.

While Richard bent over his homework: Where is it now, do we still have it, the Book of the Martyrs? It always seemed so, well—exalted, when you'd put it on the round table and we'd all look at it together; there was even a halo from the lamp. The lamp with the beaded fringe you could move up and down; they're in style again, pulley lamps like that, but without the fringe. You know the book I'm talking about, Daddy, the Book of the Martyrs, the first picture was a bust of Socrates? I wish there was something like that for the children, Mommy, to give them what you. . . . (And the tears splashed again.)

(What I intended and did not? Stop it, daughter, stop it, leave that time. And he, the hypocrite, sitting there with tears in his eyes—it was nothing to you then, nothing.)

. . . The time you came to school and I almost died

of shame because of your accent and because I knew
you knew I was ashamed; how could I? . . . Sammy's
harmonica and you danced to it once, yes you did, you
and Davy squealing in your arms. . . . That time you
bundled us up and walked us down to the railway station to stay the night 'cause it was heated and we
didn't have any coal, that winter of the strike, you
didn't think I remembered that, did you, Mommy? . . .
How you'd call us out to see the sunsets. . . .

Day after day, the spilling memories. Worse now,
questions, too. Even the grandchildren: Grandma, in
the olden days, when you were little. . . .


It was the afternoons that saved.

While they thought she napped, she would leave the
mosaic on the wall (of children's drawings, maps, cal-
endars, pictures, Ann's cardboard dolls with their great
ringed questioning eyes) and hunch in the girls' closet
on the low shelf where the shoes stood, and the girls'
dresses covered.

For that while she would painfully sheathe against
the listening house, the tendrils and noises that
knocked, and Vivi's spilling memories. Sometimes it
helped to braid and unbraid the sashes that dangled, or
to trace the pattern on the hoop slips.

Today she had jacks and children under jet trails to
forget. Last night, Ann and Dody silhouetted in the
window against a sunset of flaming man-made clouds
of jet trail, their jacks ball accenting the peaceful noise

of dinner being made. Had she told them, yes she had told them of how they played jacks in her village though there was no ball, no jacks. Six stones, round and flat, toss them out, the seventh on the back of the hand, toss, catch and swoop up as many as possible, toss again. . . .

Of stones (repeating Richard) there are three kinds: earth's fire jetting; rock of layered centuries; crucibled new out of the old (*igneous, sedimentary, metamorphic*). But there was that other—frozen to black glass, never to transform or hold the fossil memory . . . (let not my seed fall on stone). There was an ancient man who fought to heights a great rock that crashed back down eternally—eternal labor, freedom, labor . . . (stone will perish, but the word remain). And you, David, who with a stone slew, screaming: Lord, take my heart of stone and give me flesh.

*Who* was screaming? Why was she back in the common room of the prison, the sun motes dancing in the shafts of light, and the informer being brought in, a prisoner now, like themselves. And Lisa leaping, yes, Lisa, the gentle and tender, biting at the betrayer's jugular. Screaming and screaming.

No, it is the children screaming. Another of Paul and Sammy's terrible fights?

In Vivi's house. Severely: you are in Vivi's house.

Blows, screams, a call: "Grandma!" For her? Oh please not for her. Hide, hunch behind the dresses deeper. But a trembling little body hurls itself beside her—surprised, smothered laughter, arms surround her neck, tears rub dry on her cheek, and words too soft to understand whisper into her ear (Is this where you hide too, Grammy? It's my secret place, we have a secret now).

And the sweat beads, and the long shudder seizes.


It seemed the great ear pressed inside now, and the knocking. "We have to go home," she told him, "I grow ill here."

"It's your own fault, Mrs. Bodybusy, you do not rest, you do too much." He raged, but the fear was in his eyes. "It was a serious operation, they told you to take care. . . . All right, we will go to where you can rest."

But where? Not home to death, not yet. He had thought to Lennie's, to Clara's; beautiful visits with each of the children. She would have to rest first, be stronger. If they could but go to Florida—it glittered before him, the never-realized promise of Florida. California: of course. (The money, the money, dwindling!) Los Angeles first for sun and rest, then to Lennie's in San Francisco.

He told her the next day. "You saw what Nancy wrote: snow and wind back home, a terrible winter. And look at you—all bones and a swollen belly. I called Phil: he said: 'A prescription, Los Angeles sun and rest.' "

She watched the words on his lips. "You have sold the house," she cried, "that is why we do not go home.

That is why you talk no more of the Haven, why there is money for travel. After the children you will drag me to the Haven."

"The Haven! Who thinks of the Haven any more? Tell her, Vivi, tell Mrs. Suspicious: a prescription, sun and rest, to make you healthy. . . . And how could I sell the house without *you*?"

At the place of farewells and greetings, of winds of coming and winds of going, they say their good-byes.

They look back at her with the eyes of others before them: Richard with her own blue blaze; Ann with the nordic eyes of Tim; Morty's dreaming brown of a great-grandmother he will never know; Dody with the laughing eyes of him who had been her springtide love (who stands beside her now); Vivi's, all tears.

The baby's eyes are closed in sleep.

*Good-bye, my children.*

3

It is to the back of the great city he brought her, to the dwelling places of the cast-off old. Bounded by two lines of amusement piers to the north and to the south, and between a long straight paving rimmed with black benches facing the sand—sands so wide the ocean is only a far fluting.

In the brief vacation season, some of the boarded

stores fronting the sands open, and families, young people and children, may be seen. A little tasselled tram shuttles between the piers, and the lights of roller coasters prink and tweak over those who come to have sensation made in them.

The rest of the year it is abandoned to the old, all else boarded up and still; seemingly empty, except the occasional days and hours when the sun, like a tide, sucks them out of the low rooming houses, casts them onto the benches and sandy rim of the walk—and sweeps them into decaying enclosures once again.

A few newer apartments glint among the low bleached squares. It is in one of these Lennie's Jeannie has arranged their rooms. "Only a few miles north and south people pay hundreds of dollars a month for just this gorgeous air, Grandaddy, just this ocean closeness."

She had been ill on the plane, lay ill for days in the unfamiliar room. Several times the doctor came by— left medicine she would not take. Several times Jeannie drove in the twenty miles from work, still in her Visiting Nurse uniform, the lightness and brightness of her like a healing.

"Who can believe it is winter?" he asked one morning. "Beautiful it is outside like an ad. Come, Mrs. Invalid, come to taste it. You are well enough to sit in here, you are well enough to sit outside. The doctor said it too."

But the benches were encrusted with people, and the sands at the sidewalk's edge. Besides, she had seen the far ruffle of the sea: "there take me," and though she leaned against him, it was she who led.

Plodding and plodding, sitting often to rest, he grumbling. Patting the sand so warm. Once she scooped up a handful, cradling it close to her better eye; peered, and flung it back. And as they came almost to the brink and she could see the glistening wet, she sat down, pulled off her shoes and stockings, left him and began to run. "You'll catch cold," he screamed, but the sand in his shoes weighed him down—he who had always been the agile one—and already the white spray creamed her feet.

He pulled her back, took a handkerchief to wipe off the wet and the sand. "Oh no," she said, "the sun will dry," seized the square and smoothed it flat, dropped on it a mound of sand, knotted the kerchief corners and tied it to a bag—"to look at with the strong glass" (for the first time in years explaining an action of hers)—and lay down with the little bag against her cheek, looking toward the shore that nurtured life as it first crawled toward consciousness the millions of years ago.

He took her one Sunday in the evil-smelling bus, past flat miles of blister houses, to the home of relatives. Oh what is this? she cried as the light began to smoke and the houses to dim and recede. Smog, he said, everyone knows but you. . . . Outside he kept his arms about her, but she walked with hands pushing the heavy air as if to open it, whispered: who has done this? sat down suddenly to vomit at the curb and for a long while refused to rise.

*One's age as seen on the altered face of those known in youth.* Is this they he has come to visit? This Max and Rose, smooth and pleasant, introducing them to polite children, disinterested grandchildren, "the whole family, once a month on Sundays. And why not? We have the room, the help, the food."

Talk of cars, of houses, of success: this son that, that daughter this. And *your* children? Hastily skimped over, the intermarriages, the obscure work—"my doctor son-in-law, Phil"—all he has to offer. She silent in a corner. (Car-sick like a baby, he explains.) Years since he has taken her to visit anyone but the children, and old apprehensions prickle: "no incidents," he silently begs, "no incidents." He itched to tell them. "A very sick woman," significantly, indicating her with his eyes, "a very sick woman." Their restricted faces did not react. "Have you thought maybe she'd do better at Palm Springs?" Rose asked. "Or at least a nicer section of the beach, nicer people, a pool." Not to have to say "money" he said instead: "would she have sand to look at through a magnifying glass?" and went on, detail after detail, the old habit betraying of parading the queerness of her for laughter.

After dinner—the others into the living room in men- or women-clusters, or into the den to watch TV—the four of them alone. She sat close to him, and did not speak. Jokes, stories, people they had known, beginning of reminiscence, Russia fifty-sixty years ago. Strange words across the Duncan Phyfe table: *hunger; secret meetings; human rights; spies; betrayals; prison; escape*—interrupted by one of the grandchildren: "Commercial's on; any Coke left? Gee, you're missing a real hair-raiser." And then a granddaughter (Max proudly: "look at her, an American queen") drove them home on her way back to U.C.L.A. No incident—except that there had been no incidents.

The first few mornings she had taken with her the magnifying glass, but he would sit only on the benches, so she rested at the foot, where slatted bench shadows fell, and unless she turned her hearing aid down, other voices invaded.

Now on the days when the sun shone and she felt well enough, he took her on the tram to where the benches ranged in oblongs, some with tables for checkers or cards. Again the blanket on the sand in the striped shadows, but she no longer brought the magnifying glass. He played cards, and she lay in the sun and looked towards the waters; or they walked—two blocks down to the scaling hotel, two blocks back—past chili-hamburger stands, open-doored bars, Next -to-New and Perpetual Rummage Sale stores.

Once, out of the aimless walkers, slow and shuffling like themselves, someone ran unevenly towards them, embraced, kissed, wept: "dear friends, old friends." A friend of *hers*, not his: Mrs. Mays who had lived next door to them in Denver when the children were small.

Thirty years are compressed into a dozen sentences; and the present, not even in three. All is told: the children scattered; the husband dead; she lives in a room two blocks up from the sing hall—and points to the domed auditorium jutting before the pier. The leg? phlebitis; the heavy breathing? that, one does not ask. She, too, comes to the benches each day to sit. And tomorrow, tomorrow, are they going to the community sing? Of course he would have heard of it, everybody goes—the big doings they wait for all week. They have never been? She will come to them for dinner tomorrow and they will all go together.


*So it is that she sits in the wind of the singing, among the thousand various faces of age.*

*She had turned off her hearing aid at once they came into the auditorium—as she would have wished to turn off sight.*

*One by one they streamed by and imprinted on her—and though the savage zest of their singing came voicelessly soft and distant, the faces still roared—the faces densened the air—chorded into children-chants, mother-croons, singing of the chained love serenades, Beethoven storms, mad Lucia's scream, drunken joy-songs, keens for the dead, work-singing while from floor to balcony to dome a bare-footed sore-covered little girl threaded the sound-thronged tumult, danced her ecstasy of grimace to flutes that scratched at a cross-roads village wedding*

*Yes, faces became sound, and the sound became faces; and faces and sound became weight—pushed, pressed*

"Air"—her hands claw his.

"Whenever I enjoy myself. . . ." Then he saw the gray sweat on her face. "Here. Up. Help me, Mrs. Mays," and they support her out to where she can gulp the air in sob after sob.

"A doctor, we should get for her a doctor."

"Tch, it's nothing," says Ellen Mays, "I get it all the time. You've missed the tram; come to my place. Fix your hearing aid, honey . . . close . . . tea. My view. See, she *wants* to come. Steady now, that's how." Adding mysteriously: "Remember your advice, easy to keep your head above water, empty things float. Float."

The singing a fading march for them, tall woman with a swollen leg, weaving little man, and the swollen thinness they help between.

The stench in the hall: mildew? decay? "We sit and rest then climb. My gorgeous view. We help each other and here we are."

The stench along into the slab of room. A washstand for a sink, a box with oilcloth tacked around for a cupboard, a three-burner gas plate. Artificial flowers, colorless with dust. Everywhere pictures foaming: wedding, baby, party, vacation, graduation, family pictures. From the narrow couch under a slit of window, sure enough the view: lurching rooftops and a scallop of ocean heaving, preening, twitching under the moon.

"While the water heats. Excuse me . . . down the hall." Ellen Mays has gone.

"You'll live?" he asks mechanically, sat down to feel his fright; tried to pull her alongside.

She pushed him away. "For air," she said; stood clinging to the dresser. Then, in a terrible voice:

After a lifetime of room. Of many rooms.

Shhh.

You remember how she lived. Eight children. And now one room   like a coffin.

She pays rent!

Shrinking the life of her   into one room   like a coffin   Rooms and rooms like this   I lie on the quilt and hear them talk

Please, Mrs. Orator-without-Breath.

Once you went for coffee   I walked   I saw   A Balzac   a Chekhov   to write it   Rummage   Alone   On scraps

Better old here than in the old country!

On scraps   Yet they sang like   like   Wondrous! *Humankind one has to believe*   So strong for what? To rot   not grow?

Your poor lungs beg you. They sob between each word.

Singing. Unused the life in them. She in this poor room with her pictures Max You The children Everywhere unused the life  And who has meaning? Century after century  still all in us not to grow?

Coffins, rummage, plants: sick woman. Oh lay down. We will get for you the doctor.

"And when will it end. Oh, *the end*." *That* nightmare thought, and this time she writhed, crumpled against him, seized his hand (for a moment again the weight, the soft distant roaring of humanity) and on the strangled-for breath, begged: "Man ... we'll destroy ourselves?"

And looking for answer—in the helpless pity and fear for her (for *her*) that distorted his face—she understood the last months, and knew that she was dying.

### 4

"Let us go home," she said after several days.

"You are in training for a cross-country trip? That is why you do not even walk across the room? Here, like a prescription Phil said, till you are stronger from the operation. You want to break doctor's orders?"

She saw the fiction was necessary to him, was silent; then: "At home I will get better. If the doctor here says?"

"And winter? And the visits to Lennie and to Clara? All right," for he saw the tears in her eyes, "I will write Phil, and talk to the doctor."

Days passed. He reported nothing. Jeannie came and took her out for air, past the boarded concessions, the hooded and tented amusement rides, to the end of the pier. They watched the spent waves feeding the new, the gulls in the clouded sky; even up where they sat, the wind-blown sand stung.

She did not ask to go down the crooked steps to the sea.

Back in her bed, while he was gone to the store, she said: "Jeannie, this doctor, he is not one I can ask questions. Ask him for me, can I go home?"

Jeannie looked at her, said quickly: "Of course, poor Granny. You want your own things around you, don't you? I'll call him tonight. . . . Look, I've something to show you," and from her purse unwrapped a large cookie, intricately shaped like a little girl. "Look at the curls—can you hear me well, Granny?—and the darling eyelashes. I just came from a house where they were baking them."

"The dimples, there in the knees," she marveled, holding it to the better light, turning, studying, "like art. Each singly they cut, or a mold?"

"Singly," said Jeannie, "and if it is a child only the mother can make them. Oh Granny, it's the likeness of a real little girl who died yesterday—Rosita. She was three years old. *Pan del Muerto*, the Bread of the Dead. It was the custom in the part of Mexico they came from."

Still she turned and inspected. "Look, the hollow in

the throat, the little cross necklace. . . . I think for the mother it is a good thing to be busy with such bread. You know the family?"

Jeannie nodded. "On my rounds. I nursed. . . . Oh Granny, it is like a party; they play songs she liked to dance to. The coffin is lined with pink velvet and she wears a white dress. There are candles. . . ."

"In the house?" Surprised, "They keep her in the house?"

"Yes," said Jeannie, "and it is against the health law. I think she is . . . prepared there. The father said it will be sad to bury her in this country; in Oaxaca they have a feast night with candles each year; everyone picnics on the graves of those they loved until dawn."

"Yes, Jeannie, the living must comfort themselves." And closed her eyes.

"You want to sleep, Granny?"

"Yes, tired from the pleasure of you. I may keep the Rosita? There stand it, on the dresser, where I can see; something of my own around me."


In the kitchenette, helping her grandfather unpack the groceries, Jeannie said in her light voice:

"I'm resigning my job, Grandaddy."

"Ah, the lucky young man. Which one is he?"

"Too late. You're spoken for." She made a pyramid of cans, unstacked, and built again.

"Something is wrong with the job?"

"With me. I can't be"—she searched for the word—

"What they call professional enough. I let myself feel things. And tomorrow I have to report a family. . . ." The cans clicked again. "It's not that, either. I just don't know what I want to do, maybe go back to school, maybe go to art school. I thought if you went to San Francisco I'd come along and talk it over with Momma and Daddy. But I don't see how you can go. She wants to go home. She asked me to ask the doctor."

The doctor told her himself. "Next week you may travel, when you are a little stronger." But next week there was the fever of an infection, and by the time that was over, she could not leave the bed—a rented hospital bed that stood beside the double bed he slept in alone now.

Outwardly the days repeated themselves. Every other afternoon and evening he went out to his newfound cronies, to talk and play cards. Twice a week, Mrs. Mays came. And the rest of the time, Jeannie was there.

By the sickbed stood Jeannie's FM radio. Often into the room the shapes of music came. She would lie curled on her side, her knees drawn up, intense in listening (Jeannie sketched her so, coiled, convoluted like an ear), then thresh her hand out and abruptly snap the radio mute—still to lie in her attitude of listening, concealing tears.

Once Jeannie brought in a young Marine to visit, a

friend from high-school days she had found wandering near the empty pier. Because Jeannie asked him to, gravely, without self-consciousness, he sat himself cross-legged on the floor and performed for them a dance of his native Samoa.

Long after they left, a tiny thrumming sound could be heard where, in her bed, she strove to repeat the beckon, flight, surrender of his hands, the fluttering footbeats, and his low plaintive calls.

Hannah and Phil sent flowers. To deepen her pleasure, he placed one in her hair. "Like a girl," he said, and brought the hand mirror so she could see. She looked at the pulsing red flower, the yellow skull face; a desolate, excited laugh shuddered from her, and she pushed the mirror away—but let the flower burn.

The week Lennie and Helen came, the fever returned. With it the excited laugh, and incessant words. She, who in her life had spoken but seldom and then only when necessary (never having learned the easy, social uses of words), now in dying, spoke incessantly.

In a half-whisper: "Like Lisa she is, your Jeannie. Have I told you of Lisa who taught me to read? Of the highborn she was, but noble in herself. I was sixteen; they beat me; my father beat me so I would not go to her. It was forbidden, she was a Tolstoyan. At night, past dogs that howled, terrible dogs, my son, in the snows of winter to the road, I to ride in her carriage like a lady, to books. To her, life was holy, knowledge was holy, and she taught me to read. They hung her. Everything that happens one must try to understand

why. She killed one who betrayed many. Because of betrayal, betrayed all she lived and believed. In one minute she killed, before my eyes (there is so much blood
in a human being, my son), in prison with me. All that
happens, one must try to understand.

"The name?" Her lips would work. "The name that
was their pole star; the doors of the death houses fixed
to open on it; I read of it my year of penal servitude.
Thuban!" very excited, "Thuban, in ancient Egypt the
pole star. Can you see, look out to see it, Jeannie, if it
swings around *our* pole star that seems to *us* not to
move.

"Yes, Jeannie, at your age my mother and grandmother had already buried children . . . yes, Jeannie, it
is more than oceans between Olshana and you . . . yes,
Jeannie, they danced, and for all the bodies they had
they might as well be chickens, and indeed, they
scratched and flapped their arms and hopped.

"And Andrei Yefimitch, who for twenty years had
never known of it and never wanted to know, said as
if he wanted to cry: but why my dear friend this mali-
cious laughter?" Telling to herself half-memorized
phrases from her few books. "Pain I answer with tears
and cries, baseness with indignation, meanness with re-
pulsion . . . for life may be hated or wearied of, but
never despised."

Delirious: "Tell me, my neighbor, Mrs. Mays, the
pictures never lived, but what of the flowers? Tell them
who ask: no rabbis, no ministers, no priests, no
speeches, no ceremonies: ah, false—let the living com-

fort themselves. Tell Sammy's boy, he who flies, tell him to go to Stuttgart and see where Davy has no grave. And what?" A conspirator's laugh. "And what? where millions have no graves—save air."

In delirium or not, wanting the radio on; not seeming to listen, the words still jetting, wanting the music on. Once, silencing it abruptly as of old, she began to cry, unconcealed tears this time. "You have pain, Granny?" Jeannie asked.

"The music," she said, "still it is there and we do not hear; knocks, and our poor human ears too weak. What else, what else we do not hear?"

Once she knocked his hand aside as he gave her a pill, swept the bottles from her bedside table: "no pills, let me feel what I feel," and laughed as on his hands and knees he groped to pick them up.

Nighttimes her hand reached across the bed to hold his.


A constant retching began. Her breath was too faint for sustained speech now, but still the lips moved:

*When no longer necessary   to injure others*
*Pick   pick pick   Blind chicken*
*As a human being   responsibility*

"David!" imperious, "Basin!" and she would vomit, rinse her mouth, the wasted throat working to swallow, and begin the chant again.

———

She will be better off in the hospital now, the doctor said.

He sent the telegrams to the children, was packing her suitcase, when her hoarse voice startled. She had roused, was pulling herself to sitting.

"Where now?" she asked. "Where now do you drag me?"

"You do not even have to have a baby to go this time," he soothed, looking for the brush to pack. "Remember, after Davy you told me—worthy to have a baby for the pleasure of the hospital?"

"Where now? Not home yet?" Her voice mourned. "Where *is* my home?"

He rose to ease her back. "The doctor, the hospital," he started to explain, but deftly, like a snake, she had slithered out of bed and stood swaying, propped behind the night table.

"Coward," she hissed, "runner."

"You stand," he said senselessly.

"To take me there and run. Afraid of a little vomit."

He reached her as she fell. She struggled against him, half slipped from his arms, pulled herself up again.

"Weakling," she taunted, "to leave me there and run. Betrayer. All your life you have run."

He sobbed, telling Jeannie. "A Marilyn Monroe to run for her virtue. Fifty-nine pounds she weighs, the doctor said, and she beats at me like a Dempsey. Betrayer, she cries, and I running like a dog when she calls; day and night, running to her, her vomit, the bedpan. . . ."

"She needs you, Grandaddy," said Jeannie. "Isn't that what they call love? I'll see if she sleeps, and if she does, poor worn-out darling, we'll have a party, you and I: I brought us rum babas."

They did not move her. By her bed now stood the tall hooked pillar that held the solutions—blood and dextrose—to feed her veins. Jeannie moved down the hall to take over the sickroom, her face so radiant, her grandfather asked her once: "you are in love?" (Shameful the joy, the pure overwhelming joy from being with her grandmother; the peace, the serenity that breathed.) "My darling escape," she answered incoherently, "my darling Granny"—as if that explained.

Now one by one the children came, those that were able. Hannah, Paul, Sammy. Too late to ask: and what did you learn with your living, Mother, and what do we need to know?

Clara, the eldest, clenched:

*Pay me back, Mother, pay me back for all you took from me. Those others you crowded into your heart. The hands I needed to be for you, the heaviness, the responsibility.*

*Is this she? Noises the dying make, the crablike hands crawling over the covers. The ethereal singing.*

*She hears that music, that singing from childhood; forgotten sound—not heard since, since. . . . And the hardness breaks like a cry: Where did we lose each other, first mother, singing mother?*

*Annulled; the quarrels, the gibing, the harshness between; the fall into silence and the withdrawal.*

*I do not know you, Mother. Mother, I never knew you.*

Lennie, suffering not alone for her who was dying, but for that in her which never lived (for that which in him might never live). From him too, unspoken words: *good-bye Mother who taught me to mother myself.*

Not Vivi, who must stay with her children; not Davy, but he is already here, having to die again with *her* this time, for the living take their dead with them when they die.

Light she grew, like a bird, and, like a bird, sound bubbled in her throat while the body fluttered in agony. Night and day, asleep or awake (though indeed there was no difference now) the songs and the phrases leaping.

And he, who had once dreaded a long dying (from fear of himself, from horror of the dwindling money) now desired her quick death profoundly, for *her* sake. He no longer went out, except when Jeannie forced him; no longer laughed, except when, in the bright kitchenette, Jeannie coaxed his laughter (and she, who seemed to hear nothing else, would laugh too, conspiratorial wisps of laughter).

Light, like a bird, the fluttering body, the little claw hands, the beaked shadow on her face; and the throat, bubbling, straining.

He tried not to listen, as he tried not to look on the face in which only the forehead remained familiar, but trapped with her the long nights in that little room, the sounds worked themselves into his consciousness, with their punctuation of death swallows, whimpers, gurglings.

*Even in reality* (swallow) *life's lack of it*
*Slaveships deathtrains clubs   eeenough*
*The bell   summons what enables*
78,000 *in one minute* (whisper of a scream) 78,000 *human beings   we'll destroy ourselves?*

"Aah, Mrs. Miserable," he said, as if she could hear, "all your life working, and now in bed you lie, servants to tend, you do not even need to call to be tended, and still you work. Such hard work it is to die? Such hard work?"

The body threshed, her hand clung in his. A melody, ghost-thin, hovered on her lips, and like a guilty ghost, the vision of her bent in listening to it, silencing the record instantly he was near. Now, heedless of his presence, she floated the melody on and on.

"Hid it from me," he complained, "how many times you listened to remember it so?" And tried to think when she had first played it, or first begun to silence her few records when he came near—but could reconstruct nothing. There was only this room with its tall hooked pillar and its swarm of sounds.

*No man one   except through others*
*Strong   with the not yet   in the now*
*Dogma dead   war dead   one country*

"It helps, Mrs. Philosopher, words from books? It helps?" And it seemed to him that for seventy years she had hidden a tape recorder, infinitely microscopic, within her, that it had coiled infinite mile on mile, trapping every song, every melody, every word read, heard, and spoken—and that maliciously she was playing back only what said nothing of him, of the children, of their intimate life together.

"Left us indeed, Mrs. Babbler," he reproached, "you who called others babbler and cunningly saved your words. A lifetime you tended and loved, and now not a word of us, for us. Left us indeed? Left me."

And he took out his solitaire deck, shuffled the cards loudly, slapped them down.

*Lift high banner of reason* (tatter of an orator's voice) *justice   freedom   light*
*Humankind   life worthy   capacities*
*Seeks* (blur of shudder) *belong   human being*

"Words, words," he accused, "and what human beings did *you* seek around you, Mrs. Live Alone, and what humankind think worthy?"

Though even as he spoke, he remembered she had not always been isolated, had not always wanted to be alone (as he knew there had been a voice before this gossamer one; before the hoarse voice that broke from silence to lash, make incidents, shame him—a girl's voice of eloquence that spoke their holiest dreams). But again he could reconstruct, image, nothing of what had been before, or when, or how, it had changed.

Ace, queen, jack. The pillar shadow fell, so, in two tracks; in the mirror depths glistened a moonlike blob, the empty solution bottle. And it worked in him: *of reason and justice and freedom ... Dogma dead:* he remembered the full quotation, laughed bitterly. "Hah, good you do not know what you say; good Victor Hugo died and did not see it, his twentieth century."

Deuce, ten, five. Dauntlessly she began a song of their youth of belief:

> *These things shall be, a loftier race*
> *Than e'er the world hath known shall rise*
> *with flame of freedom in their souls*
> *and light of knowledge in their eyes*

King, four, jack "In the twentieth century, hah!"

> *They shall be gentle, brave and strong*
> *to spill no drop of blood, but dare*
>
> *earth and fire and sea and air*

"To spill no drop of blood, hah! So, cadaver, and you too, cadaver Hugo, 'in the twentieth century ignorance will be dead, dogma will be dead, war will be dead,

and for all mankind one country—of fulfilment?'
Hah!"

*And every life* (long strangling cough) *shall be a song*

The cards fell from his fingers. Without warning,
the bereavement and betrayal he had sheltered—
compounded through the years—hidden even from
himself—revealed itself,
    uncoiled,
    released,
    *sprung*


and with it the monstrous shapes of what had actually
happened in the century.

A ravening hunger or thirst seized him. He groped
into the kitchenette, switched on all three lights, piled
a tray—"you have finished your night snack, Mrs. Cadaver, now I will have mine." And he was shocked at
the tears that splashed on the tray.

"Salt tears. For free. I forgot to shake on salt?"

Whispered: "Lost, how much I lost."

Escaped to the grandchildren whose childhoods were
childish, who had never hungered, who lived unrav-
aged by disease in warm houses of many rooms, had
all the school for which they cared, could walk on any
street, stood a head taller than their grandparents, tow-
ered above—beautiful skins, straight backs, clear
straightforward eyes. "Yes, you in Olshana," he said to

the town of sixty years ago, "they would be nobility to you."

And was this not the dream then, come true in ways undreamed? he asked.

*And are there no other children in the world?* he answered, as if in her harsh voice.

*And the flame of freedom, the light of knowledge?*

*And the drop, to spill no drop of blood?*

And he thought that at six Jeannie would get up and it would be his turn to go to her room and sleep, that he could press the buzzer and she would come now; that in the afternoon Ellen Mays was coming, and this time they would play cards and he could marvel at how rouge can stand half an inch on the cheek; that in the evening the doctor would come, and he could beg him to be merciful, to stop the feeding solutions, to let her die.

To let her die, and with her their youth of belief out of which her bright, betrayed words foamed; stained words, that on her working lips came stainless.

Hours yet before Jeannie's turn. He could press the buzzer and wake her to come now; he could take a pill, and with it sleep; he could pour more brandy into his milk glass, though what he had poured was not yet touched.

Instead he went back, checked her pulse, gently tended with his knotty fingers as Jeannie had taught.

She was whimpering; her hand crawled across the

covers for his. Compassionately he enfolded it, and with his free hand gathered up the cards again. Still was there thirst or hunger ravening in him.

That world of their youth—dark, ignorant, terrible with hate and disease—how was it that living in it, in the midst of corruption, filth, treachery, degradation, they had not mistrusted man nor themselves; had believed so beautifully, so . . . falsely?

"Aaah, children," he said out loud, "how we believed, how we belonged." And he yearned to package for each of the children, the grandchildren, for everyone, *that joyous certainty, that sense of mattering, of moving and being moved, of being one and indivisible with the great of the past, with all that freed, ennobled man.* Package it, stand on corners, in front of stadiums and on crowded beaches, knock on doors, give it as a fabled gift.

"And why not in cereal boxes, in soap packages?" he mocked himself. "Aah. You have taken my senses, cadaver."

Words foamed, died unsounded. Her body writhed; she made kissing motions with her mouth. (Her lips moving as she read, poring over the Book of the Martyrs, the magnifying glass superimposed over the heavy eyeglasses.) *Still she believed?* "Eva!" he whispered. "Still you believed? You lived by it? These Things Shall Be?"

"One pound soup meat," she answered distinctly, "one soup bone."

"My ears heard you. Ellen Mays was witness: 'Humankind . . . one has to believe.' " Imploringly: "Eva!"

"Bread, day-old." She was mumbling. "Please, in a wooden box . . . for kindling. The thread, hah, the thread breaks. Cheap thread"—and a gurgling, enormously loud, began in her throat.

"I ask for stone; she gives me bread—day-old." He pulled his hand away, shouted: "Who wanted questions? Everything you have to wake?" Then dully, "Ah, let me help you turn, poor creature."

Words jumbled, cleared. In a voice of crowded terror:

"Paul, Sammy, don't fight.

"Hannah, have I ten hands?

"How can I give it, Clara, how can I give it if I don't have?"

"You lie," he said sturdily, "there was joy too." Bitterly: "Ah how cheap you speak of us at the last."

As if to rebuke him, as if her voice had no relationship with her flailing body, she sang clearly, beautifully, a school song the children had taught her when they were little; begged:

"Not look   my hair   where they cut. . . ."

(The crown of braids shorn.) And instantly he left the mute old woman poring over the Book of the Martyrs; went past the mother treading at the sewing machine, singing with the children; past the girl in her wrinkled prison dress, hiding her hair with scarred hands, lifting to him her awkward, shamed, imploring eyes of love; and took her in his arms, dear, personal, fleshed, in all the heavy passion he had loved to rouse from her.

"Eva!"

Her little claw hand beat the covers. How much, how much can a man stand? He took up the cards, put them down, circled the beds, walked to the dresser, opened, shut drawers, brushed his hair, moved his hand bit by bit over the mirror to see what of the reflection he could blot out with each move, and felt that at any moment he would die of what was unendurable. Went to press the buzzer to wake Jeannie, looked down, saw on Jeannie's sketch pad the hospital bed, with *her*; the double bed alongside, with him; the tall pillar feeding into her veins, and their hands, his and hers, clasped, feeding each other. And as if he had been instructed he went to his bed, lay down, holding the sketch (as if it could shield against the monstrous shapes of loss, of betrayal, of death) and with his free hand took hers back into his.

So Jeannie found them in the morning.

That last day the agony was perpetual. Time after time it lifted her almost off the bed, so they had to fight to hold her down. He could not endure and left the room; wept as if there never would be tears enough.

Jeannie came to comfort him. In her light voice she said: Grandaddy, Grandaddy don't cry. She is not there, she promised me. On the last day, she said she would go back to when she first heard music, a little

girl on the road of the village where she was born. She
promised me. It is a wedding and they dance, while the
flutes so joyous and vibrant tremble in the air. Leave
her there, Grandaddy, it is all right. She promised me.
Come back, come back and help her poor body to die.

---

*For two of that generation*
*Seevya and Genya*

*Death deepens the wonder*

# We Are Nighttime Travelers

BY ETHAN CANIN

Where are we going? Where, I might write, is this path leading us? Francine is asleep and I am standing downstairs in the kitchen with the door closed and the light on and a stack of mostly blank paper on the counter in front of me. My dentures are in a glass by the sink. I clean them with a tablet that bubbles in the water, and although they were clean already I just cleaned them again because the bubbles are agreeable and I thought their effervescence might excite me to action. By action, I mean I thought they might excite me to write. But words fail me.

This is a love story. However, its roots are tangled and involve a good bit of my life, and when I recall my life my mood turns sour and I am reminded that no man makes truly proper use of his time. We are blind and small-minded. We are dumb as snails and as frightened, full of vanity and misinformed about the importance of things. I'm an average man, without great deeds except maybe one, and that has been to love my wife.

I have been more or less faithful to Francine since I

married her. There has been one transgression—leaning up against a closet wall with a red-haired purchasing agent at a sales meeting once in Minneapolis twenty years ago; but she was buying auto upholstery and I was selling it and in the eyes of judgment this may bear a key weight. Since then though, I have ambled on this narrow path of life bound to one woman. This is a triumph and a regret. In our current state of affairs it is a regret because in life a man is either on the uphill or on the downhill, and if he isn't procreating he is on the downhill. It is a steep downhill indeed. These days I am tumbling, falling headlong among the scrub oaks and boulders, tearing my knees and abrading all the bony parts of the body. I have given myself to gravity.

Francine and I are married now forty-six years, and I would be a bamboozler to say that I have loved her for any more than half of these. Let us say that for the last year I haven't; let us say this for the last ten, even. Time has made torments of our small differences and tolerance of our passions. This is our state of affairs. Now I stand by myself in our kitchen in the middle of the night; now I lead a secret life. We wake at different hours now, sleep in different corners of the bed. We like different foods and different music, keep our clothing in different drawers, and if it can be said that either of us has aspirations, I believe that they are to a different bliss. Also, she is healthy and I am ill. And as for conversation—that feast of reason, that flow of the soul—our house is silent as the bone yard.

Last week we did talk. "Frank," she said one evening at the table, "there is something I must tell you."

The New York game was on the radio, snow was
falling outside, and the pot of tea she had brewed was
steaming on the table between us. Her medicine and
my medicine were in little paper cups at our places.

"Frank," she said, jiggling her cup, "what I must tell
you is that someone was around the house last night."

I tilted my pills onto my hand. "Around the house?"

"Someone was at the window."

On my palm the pills were white, blue, beige, pink:
Lasix, Diabinese, Slow-K, Lopressor. "What do you
mean?"

She rolled her pills onto the tablecloth and fidgeted
with them, made them into a line, then into a circle,
then into a line again. I don't know her medicine so
well. She's healthy, except for little things. "I mean,"
she said, "there was someone in the yard last night."

"How do you know?"

"Frank, will you really, please?"

"I'm asking how you know."

"I heard him," she said. She looked down. "I was
sitting in the front room and I heard him outside the
window."

"You heard him?"

"Yes."

"The front window?"

She got up and went to the sink. This is a trick of
hers. At that distance I can't see her face.

"The front window is ten feet off the ground," I said.

"What I know is that there was a man out there last night, right outside the glass." She walked out of the kitchen.

"Let's check," I called after her. I walked into the living room, and when I got there she was looking out the window.

"What is it?"

She was peering out at an angle. All I could see was snow, blue-white.

"Footprints," she said.

I built the house we live in with my two hands. That was forty-nine years ago, when, in my foolishness and crude want of learning, everything I didn't know seemed like a promise. I learned to build a house and then I built one. There are copper fixtures on the pipes, sanded edges on the struts and queen posts. Now, a half-century later, the floors are flat as a billiard table but the man who laid them needs two hands to pick up a woodscrew. This is the diabetes. My feet are gone also. I look down at them and see two black shapes when I walk, things I can't feel. Black clubs. No connection with the ground. If I didn't look, I could go to sleep with my shoes on.

Life takes it's toll, and soon the body gives up completely. But it gives up the parts first. This sugar in the blood: God says to me: "Frank Manlius—codger, man of prevarication and half-truth—I shall take your life from you, as from all men. But first—" But first!

Clouds in the eyeball, a heart that makes noise, feet cold as uncooked roast. And Francine, beauty that she was—now I see not much more than the dark line of her brow and the intersections of her body: mouth and nose, neck and shoulders. Her smells have changed over the years so that I don't know what's her own anymore and what's powder.

We have two children, but they're gone now too, with children of their own. We have a house, some furniture, small savings to speak of. How Francine spends her day I don't know. This is the sad truth, my confession. I am gone past nightfall. She wakes early with me and is awake when I return, but beyond this I know almost nothing of her life.

I myself spend my days at the aquarium. I've told Francine something else, of course, that I'm part of a volunteer service of retired men, that we spend our days setting young businesses afoot: "Immigrants," I told her early on, "newcomers to the land." I said it was difficult work. In the evening I could invent stories, but I don't, and Francine doesn't ask.

I am home by nine or ten. Ticket stubs from the aquarium fill my coat pocket. Most of the day I watch the big sea animals—porpoises, sharks, a manatee—turn their saltwater loops. I come late morning and move a chair up close. They are waiting to eat then. Their bodies skim the cool glass, full of strange magnifications. I think, if it is possible, that they are beginning to know me: this man—hunched at the shoulders, cataractic of eye, breathing through water himself—

this man who sits and watches. I do not pity them. At lunchtime I buy coffee and sit in one of the hotel lobbies or in the cafeteria next door, and I read poems. Browning, Whitman, Eliot. This is my secret. It is night when I return home. Francine is at the table, four feet across from my seat, the width of two dropleaves. Our medicine is in cups. There have been three Presidents since I held her in my arms.

The cafeteria moves the men along, old or young, who come to get away from the cold. A half-hour for a cup, they let me sit. Then the manager is at my table. He is nothing but polite. I buy a pastry then, something small. He knows me—I have seen him nearly every day for months now—and by his slight limp I know he is a man of mercy. But business is business.

"What are you reading?" he asks me as he wipes the table with a wet cloth. He touches the salt shaker, nudges the napkins in their holder. I know what this means.

"I'll take a cranberry roll," I say. He flicks the cloth and turns back to the counter.

This is what:

*Shall I say, I have gone at dusk through narrow streets*
*And watched the smoke that rises from the pipes*
*Of lonely men in shirt-sleeves, leaning out of windows?*

Through the magnifier glass the words come forward, huge, two by two. With spectacles, everything is twice enlarged. Still, though, I am slow to read it. In a half-hour I am finished, could not read more, even if I bought another roll. The boy at the register greets me, smiles when I reach him. "What are you reading today?" he asks, counting out the change.

The books themselves are small and fit in the inside pocket of my coat. I put one in front of each breast, then walk back to see the fish some more. These are the fish I know: the gafftopsail pompano, sixgill shark, the starry flounder with its upturned eyes, queerly migrated. He rests half-submerged in sand. His scales are platey and flat-hued. Of everything upward he is wary, of the silvery seabass and the bluefin tuna that pass above him in the region of light and open water. For a life he lies on the bottom of the tank. I look at him. His eyes are dull. They are ugly and an aberration. Above us the bony fishes wheel at the tank's corners. I lean forward to the glass. *"Platichthys stellatus,"* I say to him. The caudal fin stirs. Sand moves and resettles, and I see the black and yellow stripes. "Flatfish," I whisper, "we are you, you and I, observers of this life."


"A man on our lawn," I say a few nights later in bed.

"Not just that."

I breathe in, breathe out, look up at the ceiling. "What else?"

"When you were out last night he came back."

"He came back."

"Yes."

"What did he do?"

"Looked in at me."

Later, in the early night, when the lights of cars are still passing and the walked dogs jingle their collar chains out front, I get up quickly from bed and step into the hall. I move fast because this is still possible in short bursts and with concentration. The bed sinks once, then rises. I am on the landing and then downstairs without Francine waking. I stay close to the staircase joists.

In the kitchen I take out my almost blank sheets and set them on the counter. I write standing up because I want to take more than an animal's pose. For me this is futile, but I stand anyway. The page will be blank when I finish. This I know. The dreams I compose are the dreams of others, remembered bits of verse. Songs of greater men than I. In months I have written few more than a hundred words. The pages are stacked, sheets of different sizes.

*If I could*

one says.

*It has never seemed*

says another. I stand and shift them in and out. They
are mostly blank, sheets from months of nights. But
this doesn't bother me. What I have is patience.


Francine knows nothing of the poetry. She's a simple
girl, toast and butter. I myself am hardly the man for it:
forty years selling (anything—steel piping, heater elements, dried bananas). Didn't read a book except one
on sales. Think victory, the book said. Think *sale*. It's
a young man's bag of apples, though; young men in
pants that nip at the waist. Ten years ago I left the
Buick in the company lot and walked home, dye in my
hair, cotton rectangles in the shoulders of my coat.
Francine was in the house that afternoon also, the way
she is now. When I retired we bought a camper and
went on a trip. A traveling salesman retires, so he goes
on a trip. Forty miles out of town the folly appeared to
me, big as a balloon. To Francine, too. "Frank," she
said in the middle of a bend, a prophet turning to me,
the camper pushing sixty and rocking in the wind,
trucks to our left and right big as trains—"Frank," she
said, "these roads must be familiar to you."

So we sold the camper at a loss and a man who'd
spent forty years at highway speed looked around for
something to do before he died. The first poem I read
was in a book on a table in a waiting room. My eyeglasses made half-sense of things.

———

*THESE*
  *are the desolate, dark weeks*

I read

  *when nature in its barrenness*
  *equals the stupidity of man.*

Gloom, I thought, and nothing more, but then I reread the words, and suddenly there I was, hunched and wheezing, bald as a trout, and tears were in my eye. I don't know where they came from.

In the morning an officer visits. He has muscles, mustache, skin red from the cold. He leans against the door frame.

"Can you describe him?" he says.

"It's always dark," says Francine.

"Anything about him?"

"I'm an old woman. I can see that he wears glasses."

"What kind of glasses?"

"Black."

"Dark glasses?"

"Black glasses."

"At a particular time?"

"Always when Frank is away."

"Your husband has never been here when he's come?"

"Never."

"I see." He looks at me. This look can mean several things, perhaps that he thinks Francine is imagining. "But never at a particular time?"

"No."

"Well," he says. Outside on the porch his partner is stamping his feet. "Well," he says again. "We'll have a look." He turns, replaces his cap, heads out to the snowy steps. The door closes. I hear him say something outside.

"Last night—" Francine says. She speaks in the dark. "Last night I heard him on the side of the house."

We are in bed. Outside, on the sill, snow has been building since morning.

"You heard the wind."

"Frank." She sits up, switches on the lamp, tilts her head toward the window. Through a ceiling and two walls I can hear the ticking of our kitchen clock.

"I heard him climbing," she says. She has wrapped her arms about her own waist. "He was on the house. I heard him. He went up the drainpipe." She shivers as she says this. "There was no wind. He went up the drainpipe and then I heard him on the porch roof."

"Houses make noise."

"I heard him. There's gravel there."

I imagine the sounds, amplified by hollow walls,

rubber heels on timber. I don't say anything. There is an arm's length between us, cold sheet, a space uncrossed since I can remember.

"I have made the mistake in my life of not being interested in enough people," she says then. "If I'd been interested in more people, I wouldn't be alone now."

"Nobody's alone," I say.

"I mean that if I'd made more of an effort with people I would have friends now. I would know the postman and the Giffords and the Kohlers, and we'd be together in this, all of us. We'd sit in each other's living rooms on rainy days and talk about the children. Instead we've kept to ourselves. Now I'm alone."

"You're not alone," I say.

"Yes, I am." She turns the light off and we are in the dark again. "You're alone, too."

My health has gotten worse. It's slow to set in at this age, not the violent shaking grip of death; instead—a slow leak, nothing more. A bicycle tire: rimless, thready, worn treadless already and now losing its fatness. A war of attrition. The tall camels of the spirit steering for the desert. One morning I realized I hadn't been warm in a year.

And there are other things that go, too. For instance, I recall with certainty that it was on the 23rd of April, 1945, that, despite German counteroffensives in the Ardennes, Eisenhower's men reached the Elbe; but I cannot remember whether I have visited the savings and loan this week. Also, I am unable to produce the name of my neighbor, though I greeted him yesterday in the street. And take, for example, this: I am at a loss to explain whole decades of my life. We have children and photographs, and there is an understanding between Francine and me that bears the weight of nothing less than half a century, but when I gather my memories they seem to fill no more than an hour. Where has my life gone?

It has gone partway to shoddy accumulations. In my wallet are credit cards, a license ten years expired, twenty-three dollars in cash. There is a photograph but it depresses me to look at it, and a poem, half-copied and folded into the billfold. The leather is pocked and has taken on the curve of my thigh. The poem is from Walt Whitman. I copy only what I need.

But of all things to do last, poetry is a barren choice. Deciphering other men's riddles while the world is full of procreation and war. A man should go out swinging an axe. Instead, I shall go out in a coffee shop.

But how can any man leave this world with honor? Despite anything he does, it grows corrupt around him. It fills with locks and sirens. A man walks into a store now and the microwaves announce his entry; when he leaves, they make electronic peeks into his coat pockets, his trousers. Who doesn't feel like a thief? I see a policeman now, any policeman, and I feel a fright. And the things I've done wrong in my life haven't been crimes. Crimes of the heart perhaps, but nothing against the state. My soul may turn black but

I can wear white trousers at any meeting of men. Have I loved my wife? At one time, yes—in rages and torrents. I've been covered by the pimples of ecstasy and have rooted in the mud of despair; and I've lived for months, for whole years now, as mindless of Francine as a tree of its mosses.

And this is what kills us, this mindlessness. We sit across the tablecloth now with our medicines between us, little balls and oblongs. We sit, sit. This has become our view of each other, a tableboard apart. We sit.

"Again?" I say.

"Last night."

We are at the table, Francine is making a twisting motion with her fingers. She coughs, brushes her cheek with her forearm, stands suddenly so that the table bumps and my medicines move in the cup.

"Francine," I say.

The half-light of dawn is showing me things outside the window: silhouettes, our maple, the eaves of our neighbor's garage. Francine moves and stands against the glass, hugging her shoulders.

"You're not telling me something," I say.

She sits and makes her pills into a circle again, then into a line. Then she is crying.

I come around the table, but she gets up before I reach her and leaves the kitchen. I stand there. In a moment I hear a drawer open in the living room. She

moves things around, then shuts it again. When she re-
turns she sits at the other side of the table. "Sit down,"
she says. She puts two folded sheets of paper onto the
table. "I wasn't hiding them," she says.

"What weren't you hiding?"

"These," she says. "He leaves them."

"He leaves them?"

"They say he loves me."

"Francine."

"They're inside the windows in the morning." She
picks one up, unfolds it. Then she reads:

*Ah, I remember well (and how can I
but evermore remember well) when first*

She pauses, squint-eyed, working her lips. It is a pause
of only faint understanding. Then she continues:

*Our flame began, when scarce we knew what was
The flame we felt.*

When she finishes she refolds the paper precisely.
"That's it," she says. "That's one of them."

————

At the aquarium I sit, circled by glass and, behind it, the senseless eyes of fish. I have never written a word of my own poetry but can recite the verse of others. This is the culmination of a life. *Coryphaena hippurus*, says the plaque on the dolphin's tank, words more beautiful than any of my own. The dolphin circles, circles, approaches with alarming speed, but takes no notice of, if he even sees, my hands. I wave them in front of this tank. What must he think has become of the sea? He turns and his slippery proboscis nudges the glass. I am every part sore from life.

*Ah, silver shrine, here will I take my rest*
*After so many hours of toil and quest*
*A famished pilgrim—saved by miracle.*

There is nothing noble for either of us here, nothing between us, and no miracles. I am better off drinking coffee. Any fluid refills the blood. The counter boy knows me and later at the cafe he pours the cup, most of a dollar's worth. Refills are free but my heart hurts if I drink more than one. It hurts no different from a bone, bruised or cracked. This amazes me.

Francine is amazed by other things. She is mystified, thrown beam ends by the romance. She reads me the poems now at breakfast, one by one. I sit. I roll my pills. "Another came last night," she says, and I see her eyebrows rise. "Another this morning." She reads them as if every word is a surprise. Her tongue touches teeth, shows between lips. These lips are dry. She reads:

*Kiss me as if you made believe*
*You were not sure, this eve,*
*How my face, your flower, had pursed*
*Its petals up*

That night she shows me the windowsill, second story, rimmed with snow, where she finds the poems. We open the glass. We lean into the air. There is ice below us, sheets of it on the trellis, needles hanging from the drainwork.

"Where do you find them?"

"Outside," she says. "Folded, on the lip."

"In the morning?"

"Always in the morning."

"The police should know about this."

"What will they be able to do?"

I step away from the sill. She leans out again, surveying her lands, which are the yard's-width spit of crusted ice along our neighbor's chain link and the three maples out front, now lost their leaves. She peers as if she expects this man to appear. An icy wind comes inside. "Think," she says. "Think. He could come from anywhere."

———

One night in February, a month after this began, she asks me to stay awake and stand guard until the morning. It is almost spring. The earth has reappeared in patches. During the day, at the borders of yards and driveways, I see glimpses of brown—though I know I could be mistaken. I come home early that night, before dusk, and when darkness falls I move a chair by the window downstairs. I draw apart the outer curtain and raise the shade. Francine brings me a pot of tea. She turns out the light and pauses next to me, and as she does, her hand on the chair's backbrace, I am so struck by the proximity of elements—of the night, of the teapot's heat, of the sounds of water outside—that I consider speaking. I want to ask her what has become of us, what has made our breathed air so sorry now, and loveless. But the timing is wrong and in a moment she turns and climbs the stairs. I look out into the night. Later, I hear the closet shut, then our bed creak.

There is nothing to see outside, nothing to hear. This I know. I let hours pass. Behind the window I imagine fish moving down to greet me: broomtail grouper, surfperch, sturgeon with their prehistoric rows of scutes. It is almost possible to see them. The night is full of shapes and bits of light. In it the moon rises, losing the colors of the horizon, so that by early morning it is high and pale. Frost has made a ring around it.

A ringed moon above, and I am thinking back on things. What have I regretted in my life? Plenty of things, mistakes enough to fill the car showroom, then a good deal of the back lot. I've been a man of gains and losses. What gains? My marriage, certainly, though it has been no knee-buckling windfall but more like a split decision in the end, a stock risen a few points since bought. I've certainly enjoyed certain things about the world, too. These are things gone over and over again by the writers and probably enjoyed by everybody who ever lived. Most of them involve air. Early morning air, air after a rainstorm, air through a car window. Sometimes I think the cerebrum is wasted and all we really need is the lower brain, which I've been told is what makes the lungs breathe and the heart beat and what lets us smell pleasant things. What about the poetry? That's another split decision, maybe going the other way if I really made a tally. It's made me melancholy in my old age, sad when if I'd stuck with motor homes and the national league standings I don't think I would have been rooting around in regret and doubt at this point. Nothing wrong with sadness, but this is not the real thing—not the death of a child but the feelings of a college student reading *Don Quixote* on a warm afternoon before going out to the lake.

Now, with Francine upstairs, I wait for a night prowler. He will not appear. This I know, but the window glass is ill-blown and makes moving shadows anyway, shapes that change in the wind's rattle. I look out and despite myself am afraid.

Before me, the night unrolls. Now the tree leaves turn yellow in moonshine. By two or three, Francine sleeps, but I get up anyway and change into my coat and hat. The books weigh against my chest. I don gloves, scarf, galoshes. Then I climb the stairs and go into our bedroom, where she is sleeping. On the far side of the bed I see her white hair and beneath the blankets the uneven heave of her chest. I watch the bedcovers rise. She is probably dreaming at this moment. Though we have shared this bed for most of a lifetime I cannot guess what her dreams are about. I step next to her and touch the sheets where they lie across her neck.

"Wake up," I whisper. I touch her cheek, and her eyes open. I know this though I cannot really see them, just the darkness of their sockets.

"Is he there?"

"No."

"Then what's the matter?"

"Nothing's the matter," I say. "But I'd like to go for a walk."

"You've been outside," she says. "You saw him, didn't you?"

"I've been at the window."

"Did you see him?"

"No. There's no one there."

"Then why do you want to walk?" In a moment she is sitting aside the bed, her feet in slippers. "We don't ever walk," she says.

I am warm in all my clothing. "I know we don't," I answer. I turn my arms out, open my hands toward her. "But I would like to. I would like to walk in air that is so new and cold."

She peers up at me. "I haven't been drinking," I say.

I bend at the waist, and though my head spins, I lean forward enough so that the effect is a bow. "Will you come with me?" I whisper. "Will you be queen of this crystal night?" I recover from my bow, and when I look up again she has risen from the bed, and in another moment she has dressed herself in her wool robe and is walking ahead of me to the stairs.

Outside, the ice is treacherous. Snow has begun to fall and our galoshes squeak and slide, but we stay on the plowed walkway long enough to leave our block and enter a part of the neighborhood where I have never been. Ice hangs from the lamps. We pass unfamiliar houses and unfamiliar trees, street signs I have never seen, and as we walk the night begins to change. It is becoming liquor. The snow is banked on either side of the walk, plowed into hillocks at the corners. My hands are warming from the exertion. They are the hands of a younger man now, someone else's fingers in my gloves. They tingle. We take ten minutes to cover a block but as we move through the neighborhood my ardor mounts. A car approaches and I wave, a boatman's salute, because here we are together on these rare and empty seas. We are nighttime travelers. He flashes his headlamps as he passes, and this fills me to the gullet with celebration and bravery. The night sings to us. I am Bluebeard now, Lindbergh, Genghis Khan.

No, I am not.

I am an old man. My blood is dark from hypoxia, my breaths singsong from disease. It is only the frozen night that is splendid. In it we walk, stepping slowly, bent forward. We take steps the length of table forks. Francine holds my elbow.

I have mean secrets and small dreams, no plans greater than where to buy groceries and what rhymes to read next, and by the time we reach our porch again my foolishness has subsided. My knees and elbows ache. They ache with a mortal ache, tired flesh, the cartilage gone sandy with time. I don't have the heart for dreams. We undress in the hallway, ice in the ends of our hair, our coats stiff from cold. Francine turns down the thermostat. Then we go upstairs and she gets into her side of the bed and I get into mine.

It is dark. We lie there for some time, and then, before dawn, I know she is asleep. It is cold in our bedroom. As I listen to her breathing I know my life is coming to an end. I cannot warm myself. What I would like to tell my wife is this:

> *What the*
> *imagination*
> *seizes*
> *as beauty must be truth. What holds you*
> *to what you see of me is*
> *that grasp alone.*

But I do not say anything. Instead I roll in the bed, reach across, and touch her, and because she is surprised she turns to me.

When I kiss her the lips are dry, cracking against mine, unfamiliar as the ocean floor. But then the lips give. They part. I am inside her mouth, and there, still hidden from the world, as if ruin had forgotten a part, it is wet—Lord! I have the feeling of a miracle. Her tongue comes forward. I do not know myself then, what man I am, who I lie with in embrace. I can barely remember her beauty. She touches my chest and I bite lightly on her lip, spread moisture to her cheek and then kiss there. She makes something like a sigh. "Frank," she says. "Frank." We are lost now in seas and deserts. My hand finds her fingers and grips them, bone and tendon, fragile things.

## ABOUT THE EDITORS

MARGARET FOWLER and PRISCILLA MCCUTCHEON are coeditors of the anthologies, *Songs of Experience*, published by Ballantine Books, and *Work and Life*, published by the National Council on the Aging (NCOA). Margaret Fowler holds an M.A. in Women's Studies with concentration in literature and aging. She has worked as an editor and served as a consultant to the NCOA. She has three children, seven grandchildren, and lives in Maryland. Priscilla McCutcheon, with an M.A. in American Studies and aging, is consultant to and past Director of the National Center on Arts and the Aging, a program of the NCOA. She has two grown children and lives with her husband in Colorado.